FIXATION

Also by Mark Schorr

NOVELS
Borderline
Red Diamond: Private Eye
Ace of Diamonds
Diamond Rock
Bully!
The Borzoi Control
Overkill
Seize the Dragon
Eye for an Eye
Gun Power

SHORT FICTION
The Volunteer
What Goes Around…
The Therapeutic Alliance

NONFICTION
On Becoming a Wounded Healer
A Three Layer Approach

Mark Schorr

FIXATION

Thomas Dunne Books

St. Martin's Minotaur   New York

THOMAS DUNNE BOOKS.
An imprint of St. Martin's Press.

www.minotaurbooks.com
www.thomasdunnebooks.com

ISBN-13: 978-0-312-35916-4
ISBN-10: 0-312-35916-0

First Edition: June 2008

10   9   8   7   6   5   4   3   2   1

To Vera and Bernie, with love

FIXATION

PROLOGUE

1898

PORTLAND WAS CHANGING AND Samuel didn't like it. It had become far too crowded, much too busy. Vancouver, Washington, the one-time fur trading center across the Columbia River, and Oregon City, once the booming town at the end of the Oregon Trail, were dominated by the big bully boy Portland.

A strapping twenty-six-year-old who seldom wore a hat over his bushy red hair, Samuel was a faller, a master tree-cutter. He was dandy enough to bathe at least twice a month. Most of his days were spent in a logging camp with other men who sweated and cussed and labored at chopping down Douglas firs, Sitka spruces, and western hemlocks. He was known for his cheery hello to the ten-year-old whistle punks who warned of steam train movements. The sawyers, skid greasers, and choker setters all admired the man who had risen to actually decide when the big trees would topple and give the final cry of "timber!"

Samuel was in town for his quarterly visit. Purchase supplies, visit a few bars, maybe get in a fight or two. Corseted women, as shapely as Lillian Russell but with faces that looked like they'd been battered by John L. Sullivan, leaned against storefronts and warbled hellos. Portland had a Sodom-like surplus of prostitutes. The more months away, and the more drinks Samuel had, the better they began to look. He missed his wife and four children, who he had left in Missouri. His youngest, the only boy, would be almost three now. Samuel had saved nearly enough money for them to join him.

He chose Connolly's, known as a tough bar with stiff drinks. The alcohol made a lot of things easier. The aches and pains from logging injuries, the distance from his family, the friends he had seen die when chains snapped or trees fell the wrong way.

Inside Connolly's were a few sailors, well into their liquor, barely holding heads aloft. The depressed whores were ugly even in the darkened bar. Loud music spewed from an off-key player piano. A comely woman in a feather boa and not too much else lounged in a gilt cage ten feet above the floor.

She had shapely legs and a generous bust. Samuel's attention was focused above him as the mutton-chopped bartender poured a generous Henry's Own in a chipped glass that was more clean than dirty.

"Haven't seen you here," the bartender said.

"I been away a few months."

"Been with your family?"

"Logging in the Tillamook forest. I have not seen the family in years." Samuel tried to say it as if he didn't care.

The bartender had the knack of easy conversation, like a barber or a preacher. Samuel finished another glass and told his life story:

Born in Dickensian poverty in Ireland, and his father, mother, and family of six emigrating to Hell's Kitchen in New York. Streets paved with dirty cobblestones, not gold. As a teen, he'd heard of cowboys and Indians, forty acres and a mule giveaways, fortunes to be made out west.

He had found the back-breaking, dangerous work of logging a rewarding trade. His hopes were beginning to shift, that his son someday might learn to read and write and get a fancy job in a store. And that his daughters would grow up to be as beautiful as their mom, and marry bankers or ranchers.

The bartender nodded along with Samuel's dreams. As the beer flowed, Samuel ogled the woman in the cage. She had long, auburn hair and the languid bedroom eyes of an opium addict. She drooped, looked like she would fall out of the cage but somehow never did. Samuel was not the only man who was disappointed and distracted.

The bartender had learned that he was alone in town, no one knew exactly where he was, and no one was expecting him anywhere that night.

Two beers later, Samuel started to feel woozy. Surprising, since he was proud of how he could hold his liquor. Like the hundreds of victims before him, Samuel didn't notice the difference in the floor beneath him, the hollow sound, the slightly larger gap around the planks in the four-by-four square.

None of the regulars cared as the smirking bartender pulled a thick lever and Samuel plunged into the pit.

From 1850 to the start of World War I, Portland was notorious for its Shanghai Tunnels. Originally developed for transporting goods to the waterfront during inclement weather, the miles of catacombs quickly became Portland's literal underworld. Semiconscious, unconscious, and in a few cases, dead men passed off as sedated, would be dragged down the tunnels and loaded on ships heading to the Willamette River, to the Columbia River, then out to the Pacific.

The conspiracy ranged from politicians, to street cops, to the "crimps" who made the deals and sold the unwary into slavery, sometimes for as little as fifty dollars a head. The unofficial boast was that "no ship ever left Portland needing a crew." The victims would wake up past Cape Disappointment and the Columbia River bar, at sea, with no choice but to cooperate, or be beaten and starved, or thrown overboard. During peak years around the turn of the twentieth century, several thousand were kidnapped and sold annually.

Two men grabbed Samuel as he hit the filthy mattress in the basement. He struggled as adrenaline overcame the Mickey Finn that clouded his head. The crimps called for help and two more goons joined in.

"A tough galoot he is," one of the bruised crimps said as his buddies held Samuel and he punched the logger in the gut.

It was dark in the cavernous basement room, dimly lit by a couple of flickering candles. Samuel could barely make out the faces of his attackers. A man with a waxed, handlebar moustache seemed to be the leader.

"We've got an order for two going out tomorrow," the mustachioed one said. "This one will be perfect. Plus that Swede."

They dragged Samuel down a long hall, broken glass crunching underfoot. Hundreds of bottles had been smashed on the floor, the shards catching glimmers of light from the candles every two dozen feet or so. Groans and moans echoed down the corridors from side rooms. Samuel was not a Bible-reading man, but it did sound like the hell he had heard about when his mother had brought him to church. He was terrified.

The man holding his right arm saw his expression. "Just some of our other guests, laddie," the man said with a Scottish burr.

The drug, the beating, and the fear enabled the crimps to transport him. When they reached a fifteen-by-twenty-foot room, and ordered him to hand over his boots, he understood the broken glass in the corridor.

He began to fight again but was quickly subdued.

"If we have to break anything, he isn't going to be as valuable," said the Scotsman.

"Put him in the brig," the mustachioed man said.

They hauled him into another large room, where a couple of unconscious men were manacled to a gray stone wall. In the flicker of the candlelight, it looked like drawings he had seen of castle dungeons. Off to one side was a closet-sized cell made of heavy wooden timbers. He was thrown inside. He stood quickly, to no avail, since they had already slammed home a bolt on the other side. The small space smelled of pee and crap and sweat. On the front were triangular-shaped metal bars, with barely a half inch between them, allowing a weak air flow.

"We will be back in a day or so," the mustachioed man said. "If you make a ruckus, no one will hear except us, and you'll catch a beating. It is not bad on board if you follow the rules."

The crimps moved off. Once he was assured they were away, Samuel hissed, "Hey, hey," trying to get the attention of the unconscious, manacled men. Neither one stirred. It was too dark for him to tell if either of them was breathing.

His thick fingers couldn't fit between the triangular shaped bars. He dug at them where they met the wood. They were solidly embedded, but with no other hope, he kept digging until his fingers were bloody. The framing was a dense hardwood, probably from a ship's timbers.

When the men returned, he had splinters and broken nails but only the bar on the far right side loosened. The bar needed a few more seconds' wiggling to be free, like a wobbly tooth hanging from the gums after a knockdown fight. If only he had a little more time he could use it as a pry bar or a weapon.

His head ached from the chloral hydrate and alcohol hangover, coupled with nothing to eat or drink for twenty-four hours. Still he struggled. They dragged him out, tied him up, and lugged him through passageways to the river. It was nighttime and the dock by the Willamette was relatively quiet. Bound heavily in rope and with a gag in his mouth, he was hustled on board the hundred-foot-long schooner *Cascadia*. The ship began its journey to Australia that night.

It took Samuel five years to make it back to the States. By the time he returned to Missouri, his wife and children had disappeared. Riding the railroad, too sickly to work, he drifted across the country, deciding he had no place better to go than Portland.

Connolly's had long since changed ownership, and no one knew the bartender he described. Samuel soon got a reputation as just another aging drunk who told tall tales of being kidnapped and spending years at sea. He died when he was forty-five, in a downtown hotel, from complications of alcoholism.

1

IRST DEVELOPED TO RIDE the hoopla of the 1905 Lewis and Clark Exposition, the Starlight Parade traditionally marked the start of Portland's Rose Festival. The early twentieth-century nighttime "electrical parade" was touted as "the most lavish spectacle of its kind on the continent," with twenty illuminated floats running along the new trolley route. Officials proudly noted Portland was among the first half dozen cities in the world to have such a line. Now the Starlight Parade was a two-mile-long procession with more than a hundred entries, convertibles full of local celebrities, high school marching bands, and spendy corporate sponsors.

"I remember this as a kid," Louise Parker said, watching as the Ambassadors of the Rose Court, the Royal Rosarians, waved white-gloved greetings.

Brian Hanson, standing next to her, silently scanned the crowd.

Louise asked, "Having fun?"

He rubbed her arm as a yes. They had known each other for six months but had been no more intimate than hugs and chaste kisses. At first, there had been only a professional relationship. He was a psychotherapist looking into a client's death. She was an FBI agent. As the case resolved, they'd gotten friendlier. He thought he wanted more, but wasn't sure enough to jeopardize the friendship.

For a counselor who considered himself perceptive, he felt awkward in his personal life. The scars from his divorce didn't seem to heal. He'd never liked dating as a teen—it had been when he'd first begun drinking seriously. As an adult in recovery, he found that dating had even less appeal. And Louise kept an emotional distance that reminded him of a high fashion model, though she was twice the age of a cover girl and far from anorexic. Often there was a hint of more—lingering eye contact, a throaty laugh when she threw her head back, a fingertip stroke of his arm when she made a point. Was it a playful tease, miscommunication, or was he too slow to join the mating dance?

She was wearing a loose-fitting silk blouse and tight slacks, dressed more formally than those around her, which was the way it usually was with her. He saw it as part of the appeal that marked her as unique, not a casual northwesterner.

The sidewalks were packed with Portlanders and many of the million or so visitors who swelled the city for the monthlong festival that began in early June. On Fourth Avenue, right by Saks and across from the multistory Smart Park lot, was a four-layer-deep, prime viewing spot. Young kids up front, seated on the floor or lying in sleeping bags, older kids and adults slouching in chairs behind them. Another row of chairs, or standing adults. And then a row of standing adults behind that. Hanson and Parker, each with their own reasons for being wary, preferred the last row, with more room to move.

Hanson spotted an opening by a lamppost and he put his hand on her hip and guided her toward the break in the crowd. She leaned into him, almost imperceptibly. It reminded him of times as a teen, when he'd made the classic fake stretch and bold move of laying his arm across the back of a new girlfriend's seat in the movie theater.

They stood with a clear view as the five-hundred-member One More Time Around Again Marching Band did their traditional "Louie, Louie." Brian and Louise, leaning against each other, joined the crowd and sang along with the simple, incoherent song. A big woman, only a few inches shorter than his six feet, Louise felt solid against him. He savored the warmth of her body, her faint, clean smell. No perfume, just a scented soap.

They were somewhere between friends and lovers, the low hum of sexual tension ever present.

Louise Parker allowed herself to relax against Brian. What if someone else from the bureau saw her? And why did she care? Brian created a warmth in her gut that traveled down lower, in a way she didn't usually think about. A warmth that made her feel goofy, giddy when he'd call and suggest they get together.

She had been married for six months in her midtwenties, trying to do the housewife routine and follow the teachings her parents had imprinted as part of the Church of Latter Day Saints. The marriage hadn't lasted, and when she'd found her way into the FBI, it had become her true love. She'd dated over the years but nothing had ignited her passion the way the job did. What others considered tedious paperwork, she savored. Seemingly endless hours on surveillance, she volunteered. Slapping the handcuffs on an offender was a rush that she imagined was similar to doing drugs.

Brian and Louise swayed ever so slightly as a float passed with two dozen befezzed and dark-sunglassed Al Kader Shriners playing "Dance of the Snake Charmer."

"You want to go dancing sometime?" he asked.

"I'd like that," she said, brushing her cheek against his shoulder.

He gave her hip a gentle squeeze, innocent, with a hint of naughty, like a shared milkshake at the malt shop in a fifties Frankie Avalon movie.

He suddenly took a deep breath, almost a gasp.

"What is it?" Louise asked, stepping back as she felt his body tense.

In Vietnam, his buddies had kidded him about his "spidey sense," named after the then-new superhero. Back in the World after the war, he was diagnosed with PTSD, his behavior labeled hypervigilance. He scanned the crowd, looking for a threatening face. No one around them moved closer, no dangerous gestures.

"A flashback?" she asked. Louise knew about the nightmares, the bouts of anger and depression, the commitment to his own recovery from alcohol and drugs.

His eyes swept back and forth, processing, analyzing. Nothing exceptional. It frustrated him that he couldn't figure out why. Knowing the cause was one way he kept control. Maybe he had seen someone who unconsciously reminded him of an enemy from back in the day? He shrugged. "Who knows?" he said, trying to sound casual. "Don't mean nothing. Want to go to the fun center?"

"If you'd like."

He put his arm around her and they moved slowly through the crowd.

From the third floor of the brick Smart Park lot, Terry fumed. That bitch! That bastard! Terry had been watching the Shriner's float and had coincidentally spotted the couple. And it was clear they were a couple. Bathed in the yellowish glow of the street light. The conniving bitch!

"Damn, damn, damn," Terry repeated, stepping back and kicking the ground.

"What a great view," said Duane. It was the same spot they had been coming to for the past fifteen years. Duane needed consistency. Although he wasn't attuned to social cues, he could tell Terry was upset. He ran his hand through his shoulder length brown hair, over and over.

"Shut the fuck up!" Terry snapped.

"You bit your lip. It's bleeding," Duane said.

"Just shut the fuck up. I don't need another mother. One was bad enough."

Duane looked hurt but said nothing. He peered down at the street, trying to figure out who Terry was fixated on. "What's the matter? What's the matter?" Duane asked, alternating left and right hands as he obsessively stroked his hair.

But Terry just glared.

"Is everything okay?" Louise persisted. They moved off Fourth, east on Taylor, and the crowd thinned.

"Am I that obvious?"

"It's not obvious," she said. "I'm also in the people-watching business."

"Though you look for different things than I do."

"You did a nice job of changing the subject."

He nodded. "Another similarity in our skills, asking persistent questions."

"Though you don't have to read Miranda warnings."

"Usually not," he said with a smile. "Okay, I had a momentary bad feeling."

"Something I said?"

He shook his head. "Quite the opposite. I was blissing out. That's what made it so jarring."

They walked a block in silence before he said, "Sometimes I think I have to screw things up to confirm my worldview."

"You've been through a lot, then sit and listen to more suffering every day. I couldn't do that," she said.

"I can't imagine doing anything else."

"I'm the same with my job. I've wanted to be an FBI agent for as long as I can remember, even when the idea of a female agent seemed out of the question. I would've settled for being an FBI secretary. I remember Uncle Louie buying me a Junior G-Man toy set when I was eight."

"And you still like what you do?"

"I love it. Sure, there's unfortunate incidents in the past. But for every civil rights violation there's been fifty civil rights cases where we helped minorities get equal rights. I've been involved in cases where we caught child pornographers, terrorists, dangerous armed robbers. Every day when I put my badge on, I know that I'm part of an organization that does good. Real good." She glanced at him, momentarily embarrassed. "Not that other organizations and people don't. Like you. I think what you do is great. But I could never only listen. If I heard about serious criminal activity, I'd want to go out and kick in a door."

"After getting a warrant," he said with a grin.

She smiled back, though it faded quickly. Mentioning a warrant had reminded her of what was coming up on Monday. She wanted to share it with him, to let him know how exciting it was, what a career booster it could be.

But just the way he had to keep his clients' secrets from her, this was something she couldn't tell him about. Until afterward.

2

Tom McCall Park, the wide strip of lawn next to the Willamette River, was named after the governor who welcomed tourists but told those interested in staying to "please go home." Cyclone fences ringed the area, which held a Mongol village's worth of white vinyl and canvas tents. The streetlights were supplemented by thousands of watts of halogen bulbs. Visitors eager for two-G force rides, eat every fried food imaginable, listen to thumping music, buy overpriced souvenirs, and lose money at the traditional carnie booths, strolled the crowded walkway. There were screams from the rides—The Spider, The Zipper, The Scrambler. A special absorbent sand covered the grass, the apparent answer after heavy rains turned past Fun Centers into Mud Centers. Hanson tossed a ring over a small bright blue teddy bear. He gave it to Louise, who cuddled the bear and gave Hanson a light kiss on the lips as a thank-you.

Brian was pleased he had been able to control his hand-to-eye coordination. He still felt the puddle of adrenaline in him from being inexplicably spooked at the parade a few minutes earlier. The Airborne logo, skull with wings, and the phrase "Death from Above" bubbled up from his subconscious. He hadn't looked upward, only at the faces right around him, the immediate threat. But had there been someone looking down, a hostile face he'd barely caught in his peripheral view? Who was it?

They were at the edge of the hubbub, in a darker area, when he collided with a sailor, spilling the navy man's beer on his white dress uniform.

"Fuck!" the sailor shouted. The smell, the sight of the uniform, and the youthfully belligerent face reminded Brian of Vietnam. Not that he had much interaction with swabbies. Just bar fights in Saigon and an occasional crossing with riverine forces at in-country bases.

"Sorry," Hanson said reflexively. Ironic, he'd been distracted trying to be more mindful.

"Fuck you. I want a new beer," the sailor said. He was at least six feet four inches and two hundred fifty pounds, with a strong jaw and bad teeth.

Hanson took out a five and gave it to him.

"That's it, you going to give it up like some pussy?" the sailor said.

"Five will pay for a beer and your inconvenience." Hanson tried to step around him but the sailor blocked his way.

Hanson raised his hands in what could be seen as a placating gesture. "Now, you don't want to be getting yourself in trouble with the Shore Patrol, do you?"

The sailor was too drunk to hear the low growl in the counselor's voice, but Louise did. She stepped back.

The sailor thought she was intimidated by him and reached toward her breast. "What would you do if I honked her hooters?"

His arm was fully extended when Hanson grabbed his wrist. Hanson twisted the hand to the outside in a painful *kotegaishi* grip. At the same time, the counselor's open right hand flashed out in a palm heel strike that caught the sailor hard on the chin. The sailor was falling to the ground before he fully realized what had happened.

Brian was drawing back his leg to kick the sailor in his stomach— assuring that the beer sloshing around his belly would be coming up— when Louise shouted, "Brian!" tugged his arm, and pulled him away.

"That wasn't necessary," Louise said when they were back on the streets with no one around.

"True. I tried to avoid it."

"Minimally. I haven't seen you smile like that. Like a crocodile."

"He pushed it." Brian knew he sounded like a defensive kid.

She faced him. "You might have killed him."

He shrugged. "Probably not."

"Don't you think I can take care of myself? Do you think I need you to defend my honor? Or is it your honor?'

He said nothing.

"Do you realize what the consequences could be for my career if you se- riously hurt him and authorities were called?"

"I guess I wasn't thinking about your career."

"I better go home now," she said.

"Sure."

"You scared me, Brian," she said, not wanting the evening to end badly.

"Sorry," he said, glad she didn't know how close to the edge he was.

. . .

Twenty men and four women sat in the chairs facing the dry erase board. Louise stood off to one side and at precisely nine A.M., hit the buttons on the remote control. A screen lowered from the ceiling, the lights went off, and her PowerPoint presentation started.

The first slide showed a slightly run-down, gray two-story clapboard house in the middle of a bucolic country setting. The second slide zoomed in to show a Nazi flag on a small pole in the front yard.

"This is the home to the White People's Freedom Party," Louise Parker began. "It's located about eighteen miles outside of Portland, about ten minutes from Hillsboro." A mug shot of a scowling man with fierce blue eyes and a low forehead filled the screen. "This is Jebediah Heaven. Jeb to his friends."

"And these are his friends." The next slide showed thirteen gun-carrying men lounging by beat-up cars. "This photo was taken last year, outside of Coeur d'Alene. The weapons you see are AK-47s, M16s, a few 12 gauges, and some Uzis. These fellows were not going deer hunting."

There was a general ripple of laughter. Parker felt more comfortable. After her night out with Hanson, unable to sleep, she had spent a couple hours going over her presentation. This was her first chance to be the On Scene Commander, the OSC in charge of the raid, probably the first female agent to direct an op of this magnitude in the region. Her boss, Jerry Sullivan, was either setting her up for a promotion or to take the blame if it failed. Knowing his political skill and connivance, she suspected that if all went well, he'd take credit. If it didn't, she'd be a staked goat. What did it mean that Sullivan was not at the briefing?

"Not all of them are White People's Freedom members." Mug shots flashed up on the screen. The men seemed to be either too fat or too thin. "Two are neo-Nazi party, three are KKK. Outside of the Deep South, Oregon has always had an unfortunately high Klan presence."

A photo of an African-American man with a child flashed on the screen. Louise had chosen it for emotional value. "This was Tyrell Washington. You may remember he was the cab driver who was beaten and killed by several skinheads in a robbery hate crime last year." Washington was gazing blissfully at his daughter.

A morgue shot of Washington came up next, his brutally battered face barely recognizable.

"White People's Freedom has made plans to disrupt the trial," she said, then changed the slide to an aerial view of the White People's Freedom property.

"Heaven's property is twenty-five point five acres, accessed by a quarter mile of unpaved country road with no other houses on it. This poses several tactical advantages and disadvantages. We don't have to worry about getting innocent bystanders out of the area. On the other hand, it will be difficult to ensure the element of surprise."

Louise clicked a button and a video shot during a surveillance flyby two days earlier began on the screen. She kept up a detailed narration of topographic and construction fixtures as the high definition video played. She froze the frame on a midlevel aerial shot. Animated lines appeared when she clicked the remote, detailing paths through the trees. "The CI says that Jebediah has a number of low-tech security devices. Strings stretched across pathways, a crude electric eye set up across the driveway near the mailbox." She took out her laser pointer and indicated where on the aerial photo. She pointed to another spot where there were a few fifty-five-gallon drums. "We believe he also has a large meth lab on the property.

"Our CI tells us to expect Heaven to be there with his nephews." A picture of two pimply boys, obviously brothers, came up on the screen. They were showing off meager biceps. One had an SS tattoo, the other a swastika.

"They were twelve and thirteen when these pictures were taken, three years ago. They're named Heinrich Himmler Jones and Adolf Hitler Jones. You can imagine the homes they grew up in and the hatred they've been taught.

"Questions?" she asked.

"What's our jurisdiction?" It was Ed, who was a few months from retirement and had minimal interest in anything other than keeping his paperwork up to date.

"The U.S. Attorney's office will have the warrant ready for us. Part of the planning was in Washington and Idaho. Telephone lines were used. The U.S. Attorney is considering a RICO charge, since there is evidence of a conspiracy. As well as civil rights violations. The planned disruption included physically assaulting the prosecutor and tossing a Molotov cocktail in the courtroom."

"Is it anything more than dirtbags mouthing off?" Ed asked.

"They had gone as far as scouting security at the courthouse, discussing ways to create a diversion at the metal detectors, plastic rods as weapons, if they could catch the prosecutor when she parked her car. I can provide additional details to anyone who needs them."

Ed nodded his assent.

Sensing that she had proven her authority to the group, Louise continued. "If we gather drug or firearms evidence, we will coordinate with the DEA and ATF. A courtesy call has also been placed to the Washington County Sheriff's office, who will have space available for juvenile detention. But we're the lead agency and will handle the personnel and logistics for the raid."

"Which are?" one of the women asked. Marge had ten years on the job and a chronic case of the Jane Wayne syndrome. Her father had been a Chicago cop and it seemed like she had to prove she was as tough as any of the men.

"I'm going to let Paul take over the specifics as the tactical lead," she said, gesturing for Paul Sanchez to come forward. Sanchez was the lead on the FBI's Portland field office Hostage Rescue Team (HRT). The FBI formed its own SWAT-type teams ostensibly as a reaction to the terrorist Munich massacre, in preparation for the Los Angeles 1984 Olympics. Actually it was driven by Department of Justice legal concerns over use of military units on American soil, a violation of the U.S. Posse Comitatus Act. Now there was a ninety-member national team, as well as smaller groups at field offices.

"Alpha Team does a break and rake at the rear of the main structure," Sanchez said as he indicated the back of the house with the laser pointer. "Drop in the flash bangs to say good morning. Bravo is second entry. They hit the front door simultaneously," he said. "The Tactical Command Post is here, with the remaining agents assigned to the operation maintaining the perimeter."

He moved to the dry erase board and made a few drawings that looked like a coach plotting a sophisticated football play.

"When do we do it?" Marge asked.

"Tomorrow, six A.M."

"We'll go in the two FAVs, plus TOC," he said, abbreviating the Fully Armored Vehicles and the Tactical Operations Center. "Total of twenty personnel. Two six-man entry squads, three sniper/observer teams for the perimeter, plus Agents Parker and Williams in the command post. Assembly point a mile from the house, in this area here." He flashed another map on the screen that showed a small road going off to the side. "Leads from the tac teams make your own specific assignments. Pick up flash bangs, vests, and any other gear you'll need. This should be pretty straightforward, if there ever is such a thing. I have specific assignment sheets. Remember, everyone is important. We're only as strong as our weakest link. Any other questions?"

"Why not use the APC?" an agent asked, referring to the Armored Personnel Carrier that looked like the offspring of an armored car and a Hummer. It offered a little better protection against gunfire than the Suburban and was handy for ripping bars off windows and doors off hinges.

"The APC is being used on a major op in Seattle. The FAVs should be good enough and they're more discreet."

There were more questions about details, but Sanchez handled them with crisp efficiency. Rumor was he had been with Delta Force before coming to the FBI. He certainly had the military lingo and bearing down pat. Sanchez was greyhound thin and an alpha male, even among alphas.

Parker stood off to the side, watching, and knowing that ultimately the raid would really be Sanchez's show once they became operational. About all she could do was call it off. And she wondered if she could truly stop the momentum.

"You did a great job," said Trent Gorman as he sidled up to her, speaking softly. He was a Rob Lowe–handsome agent, with dark hair and eyes, and a smooth manner. Although he'd never said anything inappropriate, he stood a little too close and was a little too complimentary. He had a reputation as a skilled street agent and a womanizer.

"Thanks. It'll all be up to the team."

Duane sat in his nondescript Ford van, parked in the six-story, white Crown Plaza parking structure one block from the FBI's Portland office. The powerful Dell Inspiron M600 laptop glowed next to him, the digital scanning equipment feeding in its signal. He had an ic-r7100 antenna, modified so it could rove between 800 and 1800 megahertz. The scanner was picking up major cell phone frequencies for a two-block radius. More than a hundred calls per minute were being placed in that sector of downtown, with several low office buildings and hundreds of cars moving through. The calls were monitored by voice interpretative gear for key words, flagged and filed for him to review personally. And though Duane had trouble communicating face to face, when he could study the sounds of speech in an isolated format, he was masterful.

He knew he had some sort of brain disease. One of the teachers had said he was retarded. But when they tested him he did poorly in verbal, but genius level in spatial intelligence. He could hear people's words, but they expected him to act in ways that he couldn't understand. Sometimes their words appeared as letters in his head. Which was fine when he was immersed in technology. ASP. CDMA. D-AMPS. DECT, GPRS, HDML, HSCSDPAN, SMS, SSL, W3C, WAE. WCDMA, WTP. People weren't that interesting and made him feel clumsy. But not electronic gear. He could work a soldering iron before he could tie his shoes.

Terry had explained, "Lots of people don't relate to electronics and gadgets. They get confused, even scared. You relate to electronics and gadgets, but not people so well."

He was happy, sitting in the van, watching the lights on the small scanner console blink on as they captured calls, and off as calls ended. Plus he was doing a favor for Terry.

It didn't get any better than this.

3

H E'S HERE," THE RECEPTIONIST said into the phone, a slight quiver in her voice.

"I'll be right up."

Hanson set down the papers he'd been working on and hurried from his cluttered ten-by-ten-foot office to the waiting area. Morris "Moose" Brown, his first appointment of the afternoon, was twenty-five, six feet four inches, about three hundred pounds. A layer of flab covered his muscle but he still had the ferocity that once made him one of the city's most promising high school football players. No physical punishment a linebacker could inflict on him hadn't been done already by an abusive stepfather and three vicious older stepbrothers.

When he didn't make the pros, Moose enlisted in the marines, winding up in Iraq in 2003. He had served there for six months, involved in firefights in Fallujah in April and November 2004. He had seen a half dozen buddies wounded and several die. The combat experience, coupled with past abuse, led him to the same path of drugs and acting out that Hanson had followed thirty years earlier.

Alone in his Northeast apartment one night, Moose had taken a shotgun and tried to blow his head off. A last-minute flinch led to his surviving, with half of his face a mass of grisly scar tissue. The receptionist was not the only one who openly recoiled on seeing him.

"That bitch don't like me," Moose said, as he was buzzed through the door. The hall seemed even narrower and smaller as he followed Hanson down the corridor. "Some asshole in the waiting room was looking at me. One more minute, I would've ripped his fuckin' head off." It didn't take a skilled therapist to recognize Moose had an anger management problem.

Their sessions always began the same way. In a loud diatribe laced with obscenities, Moose recounted all the people he thought about assaulting over the past week. Usually because someone had looked at him funny. Or not looked at him. Or seemed to be doing one or the other. The first few times, the receptionist had buzzed into Hanson's office, asking in code if she needed to call police. Hanson had reassured her, and returned his attention to Moose.

After about fifteen minutes of fury, Moose would begin to calm and they could actually have a conversation about his current situation.

The session followed the usual pattern, then Moose was quiet.

"What's going on for you right now?' Hanson asked.

"You're about the only one that looks me in the face. I fucked up bad when I tried to kill myself."

"You regret injuring yourself?"

"Damn straight. I wish my hand had been steady, and I wouldn't be around looking like a monster." He tapped the right side of his face, where the eye drooped and pulp masses of light pink scar tissue were slapped on like a Play-Doh pile.

"Nothing worth living for since then?"

There was a long pause while Brown thought. "Maybe."

"Care to share?"

"I heard enough about you that when you came from Nam, you were eating that shit sandwich yourself. Ever try to kill yourself?" Moose asked.

Hanson hesitated. Disclosure was a high risk intervention. It increased intimacy but weakened boundaries. And it had to be in the client's interest, not boastful or working through the counselor's issues. Plus Hanson noted how Moose had changed the subject. "Not directly. But I put myself in situations where I could've died and was disappointed when I didn't."

"I can see that. A couple of times I got in a fight with the cops. I was hoping they would draw down on me."

"Police assisted suicide."

"They kicked my butt real bad after I broke one cop's arm." Moose smiled, looking like the Batman villain Two-Face. "You ever miss that excitement?"

Hanson nodded. "Takes your mind off everything else. Firing on all four cylinders."

"Fuck four cylinders, it's a goddamn V8."

Hanson nodded.

"Ever feel like you've fucked up your life and there's no hope?" Moose's voice was usually either belligerent or bantering. This was like a child's curious inquiry.

"I went through a few years of doing my best to screw up my life. Then quite a few years trying to straighten it up. It took a while."

"But you never wound up looking like Freddy Krueger." He ran a thick finger along his pulpy cheek.

"You think about plastic surgery?"

"More than Michael Jackson."

It was the first time Moose had showed signs of a sense of humor and Hanson smiled.

"I can't afford it," Moose said. "Can barely afford my antidepressants and blood pressure pills."

"How about through the VA?"

"Tried that. Ain't a war-connected injury, they said. I got a little bit of sympathy and a lot of no." Moose kept stroking his face. "I remember looking in the mirror when I was in high school, thinking what a damn good-looking dude I was. Babes all over me. Now flies would rather land on a turd."

"You sound hurt."

"Wouldn't you be?"

"Probably. What do you say to yourself when you start getting down?"

"The Lord must've had a reason for putting you in this mess. He don't give folks nothing they weren't meant to handle." He smiled again, less threatening, but sadder. "My grandma told me that. I haven't thought of her in a while. She was the only thing decent in the fucked up world that was my growing up."

"Let's talk about her some more next time."

They set another appointment. As he left, Moose shook Hanson's hand. Another first.

Hanson jotted a quick progress note, returned a call from a defense attorney wanting information on one of Hanson's clients, then hurried down the hall to the clinical director, Betty Pearlman. Betty was only a couple of years older than Hanson, but she had been in the system longer and was better than him at schmoozing.

"Got a second?" Hanson asked her, leaning against the doorway to her cluttered office.

"About fifteen of them. Then I've got to run to PSU. We want to refine the internship program. Are you interested in being involved?"

Hanson was notorious at avoiding meetings and denouncing them as contributing to the demise of civilization. "I'll take a student but if I have to sit in one meeting and hear about theories of education, I'm going to tell students how they're going to pay big bucks for a degree and get a job that pays less than a shift manager at Burgerville."

"I'll keep you caged unless the academics annoy me. What do you need?"

"You know anyone at the VA who can cut through the b.s.?"

"The VA is to bureaucracy as Tiger Woods is to golf."

"I've got a client who's starting to work hard at getting better. If there's any way he could get reparative plastic surgery . . ."

"Morris Brown?"

"Your memory continuously impresses me."

"You need to practice your flattery. He's not an easy character to forget." She tapped a pencil on her desk. "Let's see, best bet is probably Kathy Wozniak. She's an RN in their community relocation program. She's been there since the Spanish-American War. Knows everyone." She dug into Outlook on her computer and read off the phone number.

"Thanks." Hanson turned to go, then turned back. "You really do have a good memory."

She nodded. "Next time, compliment my hair."

"Is it a new style?"

"I spent a hundred bucks on it," she said with mock indignation. "No one has noticed. You better get going before I put you in charge of the college liaison committee."

Back at his desk, Hanson called Wozniak. As expected, he got a recording and left a message. He had just hung up his phone when the receptionist beeped.

"Mariah Finn's here." The receptionist liked Mariah, saying that although she thought Finn was "snooty," she was more polite than many of the clients.

Finn was a fine-featured redhead in her midthirties. She had a slow, measured way of walking and talking that made it clear she expected to be noticed. She had come into services after a suicide attempt sparked by the end of a two-year romance. The majority of clients on Hanson's caseload had a suicide attempt in their recent past—getting service without a near death experience had gotten progressively tougher as the Oregon Health Plan paid for less and less. Too often the stories sounded the same, childhood abuse, drugs, domestic violence, mental illness, homelessness, criminal activity. Hanson knew that after all the cognitive behavioral techniques, it often came down to being with someone who was suffering and bearing witness.

"And how are you today, Brian?" Mariah asked as she eased into a chair and he shut the door. She leaned forward, chin resting on her hand, extremely engaged. But she looked posed, like a new counselor struggling hard at playing therapist.

"I'm fine, Mariah. And you?"

"Better since I see you. Have you read all of those?" she asked, gesturing to the pressed wood, oak veneer bookshelves.

"Most of them."

She got up languidly and moved the few short steps to the bookcase with what seemed like an extra bounce to her hips. She was wearing a short, tight red skirt and a blouse cut low in the front. Hanson wondered if she always dressed so provocatively or whether it was to get his attention.

She took a copy of *Cognitive Behavioral Treatment of Borderline Personality Disorder* off the shelves. "Dialectical Behavioral Therapy. What do you think?"

"Very effective for those who struggle with their emotions."

"Who doesn't?"

"True. Every DBT therapist I know has incorporated it in their lives."

"At the hospital, they said I needed it. Told me I was a borderline."

"You may have borderline personality disorder traits but you're more than a diagnostic label."

She smiled, apparently pleased. Hanson actually thought she had characteristics from several distinct personality disorders, a Cluster B mix of borderline, narcissistic, antisocial, and histrionic. After so many years as a psychotherapist, being in a room with someone with a personality disorder, he could feel the energy crackling.

Mariah was the daughter of a prominent Portland banker, a man whose family came to the Northwest on the Oregon Trail. She spoke proudly of her parents, whose photos attending charitable functions had frequently turned up on the social page of *The Oregonian*. She spoke more vaguely about a couple of brothers and a sister. To hear Mariah tell it, she'd had an ideal childhood of privilege. A bright girl, she had graduated from the posh, private, prestigious Oregon Episcopal School. No skiing at Mount Hood for her, it was Aspen or Jackson Hole. Dropped out after two years at Stanford, a major disappointment to her parents. Lived in Silicon Valley for a while, rode the dot.com bubble and bust, then returned to Portland to take care of her aging mother when her father died. After her mother died, Mariah had inherited their spacious old house in a once rundown Northeast Portland neighborhood that was now being gentrified.

She had tried to tantalize Brian with tales of decadent parties where she cavorted with men and women. Hanson consistently redirected her to talk about her thoughts when it happened, rather than supply prurient details. A couple of times she'd gotten angry.

"What's the matter, afraid you're going to get too turned on? Your wife not keeping you satisfied?"

With Finn it was vital to keep firm boundaries. Any disclosure, such as that he was divorced, would be misinterpreted. "My professional opinion is that it isn't helpful to go into specifics," he would say calmly.

Today, she stroked the book's spine and said, "I've studied psychology. What about Carl Rogers's call for genuineness? How can you have unconditional positive regard and empathy for me if you don't know how my very hot roommate used to bring me off after we did Ecstasy?"

"What comes to mind as you disagree with me?"

"My father, smug at the dining room table, grilling us on the Bible and insisting we follow his interpretation." She put on a stern frown. "Young lady, you're going to hell," she said, mimicking her father's voice. She switched back to her own voice. "You should have seen the guests we had at our dinners. Governors, mayors, lumber barons. The people with power. Some of them were complete pervs."

An unstated question—why was Mariah Finn relegated to the public mental health system when her family could easily afford the priciest psychiatrists in town? Was Mariah so independent, or alienated from them, that she wouldn't take their help? Was it necessary for her to be in overcrowded clinics when she could have been sitting in a West Hills office with pricey antiques and a psychiatrist who could see her weekly? Or maybe they knew that for those with severe mental illness, community clinics could provide the best care, like sending a gunshot victim to an inner city ER?

He had tried open-ended questions but inevitably she'd digress. They were early on in the engagement process and Hanson didn't want to probe too deeply or ask anything that could be perceived as a rejection.

She took Irv Yalom's book, *Every Day Gets a Little Closer: A Twice-Told Therapy*, off the shelf. "I remember this one. Sessions as seen from a client and her therapist." She cocked her head. "So what would I say about you? Handsome, intelligent, perceptive, caring." When he didn't respond, she said, "And what would you say about me?"

"I'm getting to know you."

"Do you think I'm attractive?"

"What do you think?"

"I wish I had bigger boobs."

"How does that affect your life?"

"My last boyfriend left me for a girl with thirty-eight D cups. Do you think I should get a boob job?"

"You have to decide what you need."

The talk of plastic surgery reminded him of Moose. The counselor tried not to make value judgments about Finn's cosmetic desires versus Moose's real need.

"You think I'm vain?" Finn asked, her playful tone replaced by an angry edge. Clients with personality disorders had an unsettling habit of shifting quickly from emotion to volatile emotion.

"I can tell it is important to you," Hanson said. "If you decided to set plastic surgery as a goal, we'd have to discuss how realistic it is. From what you've said, your finances are limited."

"But my family has lots of money. They might pay for it." She cupped her hands under her breasts and looked at him expectantly.

Hanson maintained a neutral expression. "What leads you to think that?"

"You don't believe me?"

"I don't know one way or the other, Mariah," Hanson said.

She got pouty quiet, then sighed. "Maybe not. I don't think they love me."

"What leads you to say that?"

"Things they've said and done. I don't really have much contact with any of them. A mutual decision." She leaned forward and her shirt gapped away from her body. "Do you think I'm lovable?"

"Do *you* think you're lovable?"

"I asked first," she responded mischievously.

And so the session went. Hanson was tired when they were done. Clients with personality disorders demanded the wariness of a chess master. Any statement could be a misstep in the relationship, an excuse for the client to blow out of treatment, a grievance, or violence against self or others. At the same time, a therapist couldn't be too invested in the outcome, balancing compassion with professional objectivity.

His next session went smoother. Charlene King was twenty-four and had two young kids. Both had been taken away by child protective services. She carried a diagnosis of bipolar disorder and had ninety days clean and sober from a meth and alcohol addiction. Part of her staying straight could be credited to her being in a domestic violence shelter, where she had fled after her latest boyfriend knocked her out. A healthier diet at the shelter, and being off meth, had helped her put a half dozen pounds on her gaunt frame. Her skin had regained some of its color, her dark black hair more lustrous.

"Well, Charlene, what should we talk about today?" Brian asked after she settled in.

She looked down.

"Is something the matter?" he asked.

She shook her head.

"You can tell me, Charlene."

He waited quietly as several minutes passed. Most people would begin to talk after a couple minutes of the bludgeon of therapeutic silence. The technique had to be used cautiously, particularly with more fragile clients. The battery-operated wall clock, a drug company promotional trinket, ticked loudly. It was Hanson who spoke first. "Do you want me to guess?"

She nodded.

"Relapse?"

"Sort of." So faint he had to strain to hear.

"Meth, alcohol, or Ron?"

"Ron."

Ronald Harkins was her ex-boyfriend. He was ten years older than her, six inches taller, fifty pounds heavier, and a one-time biker. He had numerous arrests for drugs, aggravated assault, and various petty crimes. He had come to a session once, his greasy hair pulled back in a ponytail, his thick arms covered with dark, ape-like hair, a cliché of a petty criminal and bully. Hanson tried to feel concern for him as a troubled fellow human but would have preferred to whack him with a baseball bat.

"What happened?"

She burst into tears. Brian handed her a box of tissues and she wiped her eyes. Her makeup had run, creating garish black streaks on her face.

"We had a group at the shelter. All the women, they were talking about their men. I was so lonely I gave him a call, even though they tell us not to. If they find out, I get thrown out. You're not gonna tell them, are you?"

"No. But I have to agree, it isn't a safe thing to do. Did you tell him where you were?"

"No. He wanted to get together. Said he was sorry for hitting me. He said it hurt him more than it hurt me. He spent two weeks in jail because of me."

"Actually he spent two weeks in jail because of himself. Hitting people is against the law."

"It was my fault. He had had a hard day. I shouldn't have bothered him."

She was looking up now. Dark brown eyes with slightly pixie-ish features and an IQ in the eighties. Even factoring in the poor education she'd been given, he still suspected she had fetal alcohol symptoms.

"Charlene, even if he had a truly terrible day, that doesn't give him the right to hit you."

She sniffled. "I guess."

"I know you love him. He may even love you. First it was just yelling. Then pushing. Then a slap. This time he gave you a concussion. Do you see where it's heading?"

"He's not a bad man."

Hanson allowed himself a slow inhalation and exhalation. "Ron does the best he can, I'm sure. But the law doesn't allow him to hit people and he hasn't learned that yet. How many arrests did you say he had?"

"The cops pick on him."

"What about your kids? They've seen him smack you around. How do you think it affects them?"

"He don't mean to."

"Do you want your daughter to grow up thinking it's okay to be beat up?" In her first session, Charlene had offered pictures of her four-year-old daughter and six-year-old son. She had brought in photos every few months, showing birthdays, family get-togethers, and miscellaneous cute moments. "What happens if your son tries to protect you? Do you think Ron would let him? Or would Ron hurt your son, too?"

Charlene stiffened, sat up straighter. "I wouldn't let him."

"I honestly don't think you could stop Ron. It took how many cops to arrest him last time? And they have training, plus guns."

"I'd kill him if he hurt my little Travis."

"Don't let it come to that. For the kids' sake. For your sake. Even for Ron's sake."

They sat quietly, the only sound King's occasional sniffling.

"Charlene, you know it takes most people about eight times to give up something, even when they want to? That goes for abusive relationships, cigarettes, whatever."

"Really?"

"Really."

"He can be so kind. You wouldn't know it to look at him."

Hanson fought the urge to say, "Damn straight." Instead, he nodded supportively. "I'm sure you see lots of good in him. But you've got to see that it's not working." The delicate balance of not blaming the victim, but getting her to take responsibility.

King continued to praise Ron. Hanson worked cautiously to undermine it, stressing the need to protect the children. The session ended with her vowing not to call Harkins again.

The last client of the day was a no-show. Hanson had missed a call from Kathy Wozniak. He continued the game of phone tag when he got her voice mail. He wrote a one week overdue behavioral health assessment, a three month overdue annual review, and made a few check-in calls to clients who were doing well and getting by with once a month contacts.

It was 4:55 P.M. and he was shutting down his computer when the phone rang.

"One of your clients is threatening to jump from the Broadway Bridge," Robin Shallcross, head of the crisis team, said without any greeting. She was a fast talking, fast thinking ex–New Jerseyite who was an ideal fit for a crisis counselor. She could deftly switch to slow and sympathetic, fielding a cell phone call, retrieving a number from her Palm Pilot, and juggling three balls. Literally. She had done several trainings on juggling for stress reduction.

"Who?"

"Fred Robbins."

"What do you need?"

"Cops are trying to talk him down. I read them your crisis alert sheet."

Robbins was a forty-year-old Caucasian male with chronic health problems including diabetes, high blood pressure, hepatitis B and C, and chronic back pain. He was a former male prostitute who had settled into his longest relationship—six months—and seemed to be stabilized. Hanson had filled out the crisis alert two weeks ago, when Fred had said he was going to kill himself because the relationship was ending. As an intervention, Hanson had suggested reminding him of his two Siamese cats, who had been with him longer than any partner.

"He's asking for you," Robin said.

"I'll head over."

"It's screwing up rush hour traffic. The police are ready to shoot him off the bridge and call it a day."

4

THE BROADWAY BRIDGE WAS less than a mile from Brian's Old Town office. At rush hour, particularly with the congestion the incident would be causing, it was easiest to walk. Hanson moved briskly past the brick buildings that bore the wear and tear of the poor immigrants who had made them home, market, or workplace for more than a hundred years. At the missions, the evening meal lines had already formed. Several people standing in line greeted Hanson. Normally he would've stopped to chat, but he kept going, long strides, and was at the foot of the bridge less than ten minutes after hanging up the phone.

The Broadway Bridge, built in 1912 and one of ten that spanned the Willamette River, carried close to 30,000 vehicles every business day. Traffic was being diverted from the bridge, causing a level of horn honking that was a breach of Oregon civility.

A woman cop with a bristly hair cut and a demeanor to match stopped him with a raised hand. "Where you going?"

"I'm the therapist for the guy on the bridge."

She got on her radio and alerted the lieutenant.

Walking slowly up the bridge on-ramp, police and ambulance lights flashing, news helicopter overhead, crowds on the street looking up, photographers with tripod mounted telephoto lenses on neighboring rooftops, fire rescue boat in the river below, Hanson missed his days as a full-time crisis clinician. Since he'd been a crisis clinician for several years, he knew most of the senior officers. Marv Rosen had more than twenty-five years on the job. Hanson remembered him when his neatly trimmed goatee wasn't gray. They exchanged brief greetings.

"You'll work your therapeutic magic on him so we can let these impatient assholes get home?" he asked, gesturing to the car clog below them.

"I'll do my best."

"Okay. He doesn't have a weapon. Been out there about a half hour. His arms are pretty tired, I'm guessing. Don't go any closer than six feet."

Hanson nodded, and continued out onto the bridge.

"Not too close!" Rosen shouted.

Even though it was another warm evening, the breeze off the Willamette seventy feet below was strong.

"Hi, Freddy. What's going on?" Hanson slowed at about a dozen feet away, but continued to edge forward. There was no one else on the broad sidewalk. The bridge, painted Golden Gate red, looked postcard pretty in the evening light.

Robbins was usually quite dapper, deceptively well dressed on a thrift store budget. Now he was stubbly, wearing a stained tie-dyed T-shirt. His pants were too tight, his shoes scuffed. He rocked back and forth, standing on the narrow lip on the river side of the railing.

"Tony is going to leave me this time," Robbins said, his voice quivery. "The vicissitudes of fate have not been kind. He is weary of my being subject to the thousands of shocks flesh is heir to. His love for me has withered on the vine." Freddy had tried to make it as an actor in Los Angeles, and his speech often sounded like a high school Shakespeare performance.

"C'mon Freddy, you've been through relationship ups and downs before."

"Ups and downs. A touch ironic in this situation, don't you think?" Freddy gazed off into the distance. "I dreamt a dream of darkness wherein I was going to die alone. My family has cast me aside like yesterday's newspaper. This relationship is doomed, like the others have been. The ones who know me best are my physicians. Is that a sign of a sick life? Is that a life worth living?"

"What about Mr. Biggles and Mini Me?"

"Mr. Biggles is dead," he said.

"I'm truly sorry to hear that. What happened?"

"My so-called boyfriend accidentally released him into the cold, hard world. Or so he claims. Mr. Biggles was the victim of a hit and run."

"That's very sad. How is Mini Me taking it?"

"He mourns. We both do."

"What happens to Mini Me if you go?"

Freddy looked perplexed. In his depressed state, he hadn't thought that far ahead. "Will you take care of him?"

"I couldn't be the loving owner to him that you'd be."

"That is one of the kindest things anyone has ever said to me, Brian."

"Thanks. Now how about you come back over the railing?"

Freddy swayed. "Is a feline companion worth living for?"

"Yes," Hanson said, trying not to sound too eager. "Come back over the railing and we can talk about it."

"Maybe you and I could have a gentlemanly discussion, but I'm afraid the constabulary would be tackling me with gusto."

Another breeze blew and Hanson felt a chill. Freddy's words had a determined tone, like he was milking his time in the spotlight but had planned how the performance would end. With no possibility for an encore. Hanson took a step forward.

"Even if your relationship with Tony ends, how do you know that Mr. Right is not just around the corner?" Hanson took another step.

The swaying stopped as Freddy considered. "I've been in this game for too long. Too many loves come and gone. Can I trust you to find a warm home for Mini Me?"

Their eyes locked and Hanson knew. The counselor dove forward as Freddy pushed off. Hanson managed to grab his shoulder. The shirt tore and Freddy fell backward, dangling by an arm. Hanson was pulled to the railing. He bent his knees slightly, bracing himself. Freddy thrashed, and Hanson struggled to avoid going over with him. Then Rosen was grabbing him and Freddy and the three were in a writhing mass on the floor.

Then more cops, and paramedics. Freddy was hustled off in handcuffs. Lt. Rosen was standing with his face inches from Hanson, shouting, "Idiot! You know how close you came to going over?"

The adrenaline didn't set in until Hanson was back in his apartment. His hands shook so much he could barely sip a glass of water. And he craved a glass of scotch. Or vodka. Or Southern Comfort. Or rum. In Vietnam, it had been pot or hash, sometimes laced with heroin. Booze was for lifers. Back in the World, he'd quickly kicked the illegal drugs, but substituted liquor. Anything to burn his insides and make the feelings go away.

Now, instead he did a hundred situps, seventy-five pushups, and a couple of long *qi gong* sets to focus his attention. The adrenaline aftermath passed. No more thoughts about what could have happened. The simple joy in having done some good, taken a risk, and survived.

His phone rang a few minutes after eleven P.M.

"Are you okay?" Louise Parker asked.

"Huh?"

"Did you see the news? Or are you just content to make it?"

"The jumper?"

"Yes. It was the top story. They got a nice shot of you pulling that nut in and wobbling like you were going to go over yourself."

"I couldn't let him fall."

"What were you thinking?"

"I wasn't really thinking."

"Well, I'm glad you're okay." She hesitated. "Sometimes, I, I worry about you."

"I'm not usually pulling people off bridges."

"Or getting in street fights."

"That, too."

"I've known men who are like that. The first to kick in a door when serving a warrant or go down an alley after an armed robber." She hesitated again. "Forget it. I don't have any right to tell you how to live your life."

"No, no. I appreciate it. Really." His words sounded condescending to him. He longed to be more eloquent but couldn't figure out what to say. "I'd like to continue this conversation sometime. Face to face."

"Deal."

He got a few more calls from friends and acquaintances, a mix of curious and congratulatory. After eleven-thirty, he took his phone off the hook and tried to sleep.

As he lay in bed, he thought of Louise's concern. And Moose's questions about his own suicidal ideation. He thought about Dante's *Inferno* and the tortures inflicted on those who died by their own hand. And samurai who considered it noble to slit their guts.

The old saying about there being no atheists in foxholes was true. But what happened to those lucky enough to survive the foxholes? Where was God as they staggered through the world, bearing the burden of past physical scars, traumatic memories, survivor guilt? He had tried his father's Catholicism, his mother's Judaism, and his ex-wife's Lutheranism. He had dabbled in Unitarianism, Buddhism, and Native American traditions. No faith could answer his question, why?

He got up and dug out his *Seven Samurai* DVD. The Kurosawa classic was one of many works of art that portrayed the dilemma of the warrior, loved in battle, despised in peace. The conflict between love and death for the warrior Katsushiro. The insanity of Toshiro Mifune's character as he tried to be the samurai he imagined he was. The sadness and the wisdom in actor Takashi Shimura's eyes as he stroked his head and contemplated the warriors' fate.

Brian dozed on the sofa, watching the more than three-hour-long movie. He drifted off to the words of a Vietnam marching song in his head, something they'd chanted during those few times they didn't have to keep noise discipline:

> *If I die in the combat zone, box me up and ship me home,*
> *Pin my medals on my chest, tell my mom I done my best.*

5

JEBEDIAH HEAVEN WAS DEEP into his favorite dream—where his troops were invading a synagogue full of scantily clad, buxom Jewish cheerleaders—when the phone rang. The sound echoed in his head. Jeb had matched his young visitors the night before, drinking a case of Hamm's.

It was dark outside and he glanced at the window while fumbling for his phone. Five-thirty. Was that day or night? he pondered, scrunching up his face. What goddamned *scheisskopf* would be calling him at five-thirty in the morning?

"Yeah?" he snapped into his phone.

"The forces of the Zionist Occupational Government are nearly upon you."

"What?"

"You're about to be raided by ZOG," the heavily muffled voice said before the connection was broken.

A prank call? Would anyone dare mess with the supreme chairman-in-chief of the White People's Freedom party? He sat up and looked at his fourteen-year-old cousin, Mary Ann, naked and still asleep. She had a fresh prettiness but he knew she'd be just another skanked out hag in a few years. She'd run away from her own abusive family and hid at his place, partying with the guys. She was a wild one with a little meth in her. And it was great for the cause. Kept those teenage boys coming to hear the message like a pack of mutts after a bitch in heat.

Wearing only boxers, he moved to the window. A light fog gave the landscape an eerie cast, the sun beginning as a faint glow to the east. Nothing suspicious, but the sneaky bastards wouldn't come walking up with a warrant.

Banging Mary Ann or getting security in place? A tough call. What if it was a prank? Well, then they'd have had a safety drill.

He padded quickly to the living room where the two brothers were in sleeping bags on the floor. One wall was dominated by a large red Nazi flag with a white center ring and a black swastika.

"Prepare for a raid," Heaven snapped. "Get ready to teach them Jew lovers what happens when they tangle with real men."

The brothers awoke instantly and though they reeked of beer, showed no signs of impairment. They hustled to the corner where two AK-47s leaned. Adolf, the older one, grabbed a few spare clips and handed some to his brother. They put the clips in the oversized pockets of the camo pants they had been wearing as pajamas.

"White pride," Heaven said, giving a "heil Hitler" salute.

"White pride," the teens echoed, and responded with the same stiff-armed gesture.

It was time to wake their unexpected guest. Arnold Beil had snuck in last night. Jeb was honored that his house was a favored fugitive stop for those oppressed by the Zionist Occupational Government. Beil had been on the run for more than five years, after killing an ATF agent in Tennessee, and rumored to have been involved in the death of a couple of other feds, as well as beatings of several Jews and queers. Beil had served in the marines and learned the oppressor's tactics before being dishonorably discharged for fighting with a nigger sergeant.

Jeb knew better than to startle Beil. Heaven knocked gently at the door to the guest bedroom. Beil opened the door, as if he'd been awake and waiting, holding a .32 Colt loosely at his side. "What?"

Sprawled on the bed was a dark-skinned woman with questionable features. Beil had brought her with him. Heaven had wondered about her racial background but hadn't dared ask. Women had always been the spoils of war, and the babe had an ass that could make a grown man sigh.

"I got a call, we may be getting attacked by the ZOG."

Beil nodded, seemingly unsurprised. He slipped on pants, a shoulder holster, and grabbed a sawed-off shotgun that had been next to the bed. He was a squat, muscled man with a neck like a tank turret, a nose that had been broken at least once, and piercing eyes under a scarred brow. His hair was a little longer than a marine buzz cut. He radiated a lethal power, his physique shaped by daily five-mile runs, along with two hundred fingertip pushups and five hundred crunches.

"What's going on?" the woman in the bed asked sleepily.

"Nothing to worry about," Beil whispered. "Go back to sleep and dream about what I'm gonna do when I get back."

The four males assembled in the kitchen.

"They'll hit us from multiple directions," Beil said. "Probably use flash bangs. Stuff tissues in your ears. If you hear a crash, don't look in that direction. Shut at least one eye. You got gas masks?"

"No," Heaven said, embarrassed.

"Get towels wet and be ready to cover your faces," Beil barked. "Who's the best shot?"

"You, I suspect," Adolf said.

Beil had assumed leadership and though Jeb felt a twinge of jealousy, he knew his guest had far more real combat experience. Beil had already lived through two raids by federal agents. Aside from throwing a few bricks through windows, and hitting a rabbi from behind with a two by four, Heaven's contribution to the cause was limited to aggressive rhetoric.

"Sure, but I'm gonna be taking the war to them," Beil said. "For inside here?"

"Heinrich is a crack shot," Adolf said, beaming at his brother. "Killed his first raccoon when he was ten."

His baby brother bobbed his head awkwardly.

"It's different killing a raccoon and a real coon, but remember, these aren't men. They're vermin who have chosen to ally themselves with Mud People, Jews, and those who would take away our rights and murder us. Understand?"

"Jawohl! Sieg heil!" the teens shouted.

"Heinrich, there's a vent in the attic at the front of the house. Grab that scoped deer rifle I saw in the closet. Stay back so you can't be seen. Shoot anyone you can get a bead on. Go for a head shot—they'll be wearing flak vests. If they're wearing helmets, shoot for over here." He tapped a spot at the base of the neck." He turned to Adolf. "Guard the back." He handed him the sawed-off 12 gauge Remington pump action shotgun. "Point this in the general direction and pull. Across a room this size, it'll have a three-foot spread." To Jeb, he said, "Stay in the hallway. They may hit the front or more likely, one of the sides."

"Where you going?" Jeb asked.

"Like I said, to take the war to them," Beil said, checking his weapons. He put a half dozen Teflon-coated copkiller loads in the M16 clip. "Don't fire until my signal."

"How will you signal?" Heaven asked.

"I'm gonna blow up the lab."

"Do you have to?" Heaven asked. "What if it's only a false alarm?"

Beil regarded him contemptuously. "You better hope it's not a false alarm."

"It'll be a great distraction," Heinrich said, looking forward to the explosion.

"And it'll destroy lots of evidence," Adolf added.

"These kids got more brains than you." Beil grabbed a Baggie of crystal meth, a .32 Beretta, and the M16 and hustled out the back door. He dropped to the ground and began crawling away from the house faster than a cockroach when the lights went on.

It had been twenty minutes since the phone had rung. Jeb's heart was pounding and he couldn't stand still. He didn't know whether he was more scared of a raid or Beil's wrath if the call was a prank.

"Alpha in position," said Alpha team leader. One of the team had disconnected the wires to the electric eye near the mailbox.

"Bravo, too," Bravo team leader responded from inside the lead dark green Chevy Suburban.

While there was always risk on serving a warrant, the truth was there was less danger than most traffic stops. The bureau had the advantage of surprise and Heaven and his teen followers were recognized as hateful goofballs more than truly dangerous. Louise Parker had heard the agents joking how they should drop Heaven in any ghetto in the middle of the night, and he wouldn't last long enough to mouth, "White power!"

Louise sat in the mobile command post van, with a Plantronics Voyager 510 Bluetooth headset clipped to her ear, and a pencil eraser–sized microphone on a boom barely an inch from her mouth. It was three minutes before six A.M. Sanchez had advanced his teams silently through the eerie fog. The vicious but untrained dogs had been silently neutralized with tranquilizer darts. The teams were in place, about fifty feet from the house, waiting for her to give the go-ahead. She was dependent on the confidential informant, the agent who had been running him, her boss, the agents in the field, the two agents in the van with her. But ultimately, it was her call.

Was there anything she had missed? Lives depended on it.

"Do you copy?" Sanchez asked.

"Roger," Louise said, wishing she felt more confident.

"Request permission to engage?"

Before she could answer, an explosion shook the van. Then the shooting began. Marge Williams, who had been disappointed she'd been assigned to being the command post driver, suddenly gasped. A red hole in her head widened and began pouring blood. Her eyes rolled and she sagged over dead in awkward slow motion. Louise grabbed her Glock, opened the side door, and dove out. There was a loud explosion a few feet away, and large chunks of shrapnel flew through the air like demonic bats.

A sniper in the house killed one of the advancing agents and wounded another. It was a full twenty minutes before the shooting stopped. The forensic techs would later put together the probable scenario:

Beil, initially described as unknown subject, or Unsub, had crawled several hundred feet from the house before blasting an ether drum by the meth lab. Concealed by one of Heaven's cannibalized Ford pickups, the raiders had swept past him. He had recognized that the command post van was lightly armored and placed his shots well.

At the same time Heinrich had fired at the Tac Team Two leader, the bullet hitting the agent's helmet. The agent was knocked out, and suffered a concussion and whiplash but no permanent injuries. More than 250 shots were fired in the subsequent gun battle. Sanchez was hit by a bullet that nicked his carotid artery. Prompt emergency medical care saved his life, but he had suffered anoxia and subsequent brain damage.

One adult female had tried shooting a raider with the .32 she'd had by the bedside. A teenage female was injured by glass shattering as she tried to sneak out a window. When it was done Jeb Heaven was dead, as were Adolf, Heinrich, and the adult female. Two agents were killed, three injured.

Bureau headquarters was notified by Special Agent in Charge Sullivan about fifteen minutes after the battle was over. The media began showing up about fifteen minutes after that.

Louise supervised the cordoning off of the area, trying not to think about Marge Williams's death or the gut-wrenching fear as she'd dived from the vehicle. She slipped away to a grove of trees and doubled over with the dry heaves. She realized she hadn't had anything other than two cups of black coffee all morning. She leaned against a small birch for support and wished Brian was there.

Hanson had just finished his session with a nineteen-year-old who was trying to make sense out of his first psychotic break when he got the message to stop by Betty's office as soon as he could. With a few minutes between appointments, the counselor hurried down the hall.

"I promise to get those overdue treatment plans done," Hanson said by way of greeting.

Betty pointed at the small, nine-inch TV she kept on the bookshelf. Hanson glanced over—the last time Betty had called him in to watch TV had been 9/11.

"This is Tiffany Chang reporting first, live from five miles west of Hillsboro. There's been a tragic shootout here involving FBI agents and suspected white supremacists. At least three people are dead, including a female FBI agent whose identity is being withheld pending notification of her next of kin."

Hanson fell into a seat, grabbed his cell phone, and called Louise's number. He got voice mail. "Louise, hope you're all right. Please call me as soon as you get this message." He stood up and paced.

"I didn't know whether to tell you. I know you've been seeing her."

"Sort of. Hard to explain. Have they said anything more?"

"Not much. The landowner is a white supremacist who goes by the name Jebediah Heaven. The FBI raided early this morning. Neighbor said there was an explosion, a few hundred shots. Ambulances."

Hanson hurried to his desk and dug out Louie Parker's phone number. Her uncle was a client of Hanson's and had first referred him to Louise on an old case. Calling him was an ethical violation, not purely in the client's interest. He could justify it as checking on Louie to see how he was handling the stress facing his niece. He got through to Louie, who said, "I was just about to call."

"How is she?"

"Shook up but okay," Louie said. "The raid was her baby. Scumbums got killed, including teens. Louise wanted me to let you know she hadn't been shot."

"How'd she sound?"

"Numb. She feels responsible for the agent who died. Right next to her. And she didn't say it, but she's going to catch the sack of crap that comes out of this snafu. It was her operation."

"Have her give me a call when you hear from her," Hanson said.

"Now the brass come in and shoot the wounded. My Louise-y won't go down easy."

"Have her call me, please," Hanson repeated.

"I've got my appointment with you next week. Maybe I'll bring her."

"That's okay, Louie. Our session is meant to be your time."

"Seeing you two together is therapeutic for me. Are you two serious?"

"I've got to get off. Please have her call."

Hanson walked back to his supervisor's office.

"She's okay?" Betty asked.

"Yeah. I guess I didn't realize how strong my feelings were, until I thought . . ." He stopped, not wanting to state the painful possibility.

The receptionist stuck her head through the doorway. "Here you are," she said to Hanson. "I've been looking all over. There's an angry man in the lobby wants to talk with you."

"Who is he?"

"Won't say. Should I call the police?"

"Not yet." He knew the receptionist had a tendency to overreact. "I'll handle it."

"After what you just went through, Brian, maybe I better take this one," Betty said.

"He's demanding to speak to Brian," the receptionist insisted.

"I can do it," Brian said. Walking down the hall, he unclenched his fists, taking deep, slow breaths.

Waiting was a small, balding man in paint-spattered clothes with an expression that was more petulant than intimidating. He didn't appear to have any weapons.

"Why'd you take him off the bridge?" the man asked loudly as soon as he spotted Hanson.

"Let's go back and talk," the counselor said, gesturing for the man to come through the door.

He moved forward, continuing to shout. "Who do you think you are, playing God like that?" The belligerent man stomped down the corridor and into Brian's office.

"What's your name?" Hanson asked.

"Tony. I'm Freddy's partner. He wanted to die."

"Well, Tony, I can't say anything about Freddy, even whether he's a client here or not."

"What do you mean you can't say anything?" Tony shouted. "Your picture grabbing him was in the newspaper and on every channel!"

"It seems strange, but any interaction about a possible client is still covered by confidentiality laws."

Tony slammed his fist down on Hanson's desk. "I don't want a lecture on the law. He has the right to die. You shouldn't have interfered."

"I'm happy to listen to your concerns," Hanson said. "I need you to lower your voice so it doesn't disturb other people. And I can understand you better."

"I don't care about other people." He slammed his fist down again. "You don't know what it's been like with him. He's constantly suffering, making me suffer. He should've been allowed to end it. That would've been better for everyone."

"You sound very frustrated with him," Hanson said. "You want him to get better but it seems like there's nothing you can do."

Tony sighed, disarmed by the active listening. "I feel guilty when I want him to die. But I can't go on like this. Do you know how miserable he is?"

"I can't talk about anything I might have discussed with any client," Hanson said, as gently as he could. "Respecting confidentiality is at the heart of counseling."

"Do you know he's HIV positive?"

Hanson worked hard to hide his surprise. Freddy had mentioned numerous health concerns, but had specifically said he didn't have the AIDS virus. "That would be confidential, if we discussed it. If he's a client."

Tony folded his arms across his chest. "I try to be there for him, but it's never enough. One of these days, it's going to be me on top of the bridge."

"If it would be helpful to talk to someone, I'd be happy to arrange it. I know caregivers can be under an enormous strain. There's special programs for those helping people with HIV."

Tony stood. "Talking, that's all you people do. There's a time for action." He marched out of the office, slamming the door.

Even though Tony was not a client, Hanson wrote a progress note. Tony's nonspecific threat didn't seem to bear followup. But Hanson knew that having his clinical rationale documented would keep Betty, the licensing board, and the agency's lawyers appeased.

6

THE FBI SCHEDULED THE press conference for eight-thirty P.M. Pacific time, saying that they needed to organize information. The real reason was to make the broadcast too late for the East Coast eleven P.M. news. Headquarters couldn't hold the story over later or control the cable networks. The event was already being touted as "Waco Northwest," with liberal pundits decrying excessive use of force and conservatives blasting it as an intrusion on civil rights. Some bemoaned that teenagers were killed. The incident gave the networks a chance to show footage of Waco and Ruby Ridge, and recapitulate the FBI's foulups in the past three decades.

What infuriated Portland Special Agent in Charge Jerry Sullivan was the Unsub, who, after fingerprints were collected, was identified as Arnold Beil. One of the ten most wanted. The forty-two-year-old was a suspect in six assaults on federal officers.

What a coup it would have been if Beil had been captured or killed. Sullivan was a known "blue flamer," bureau slang for a supervisor desperate for advancement who had blue flames coming out of his ass as he tried to launch himself to a larger field office. Now, instead of New York, San Francisco, Los Angeles, or Chicago, he'd probably be chasing bank robbers in Lincoln, Nebraska. His wife, from a Boston banking family and barely tolerating what she considered the hick town of Portland, would make their marriage even more unpleasant.

Bad intelligence. The white supremacists had been too ready. There were no indications that Heaven's primitive security had alerted him. Someone must have tipped them off. According to information from Heaven's cousin, they had gotten a phone call. Dumping the phone records for incoming calls had led to a payphone downtown. Agents would be checking every outgoing call for the past month.

The media and headquarters would demand a scapegoat. Swift and decisive action was the only hope for salvaging his career.

The press conference was held in a meeting room unadorned with FBI logos. The only sign it was a federal facility was the American flag in the corner. He was coached by the Washington D.C. FBI public information officer (PIO) and then told he would be doing it alone. Headquarters wanted to distance themselves—he wished he could do the same.

Standing behind two rows of mikes, and under the glare of a battery of lights, he realized the deodorant he'd wiped across his face barely controlled his sweating. As he stepped behind the podium he tried to remember all the tricks the PIO had told him. Don't get pulled into the question's framing, give the answer you want. Don't worry about repeating yourself. Keep it brief, unless you don't want it to be used. Or say, "As I stated previously . . ." so it seems like information had been cut out. Use phrases like "That's a good question and we are looking into it" to buy time to think. Use TV reporters' first names if you know them—it lets the airheads feel important. Most of all, look sincere, it's more important than whatever you say for the TV audience. He took a deep breath, and began:

"Thank you for coming. I'm going to read a brief statement, then answer a few questions. I will not be able to comment on some things due to this being a pending investigation. But I will tell you all I can of what we know at this time."

Louise curled up on the red microfiber-covered couch in front of her TV, sipping from a warm bottle of Arrowhead Water. Jerry Sullivan looked composed as the camera zoomed in tight. She knew him well enough to recognize the furrow lines around his eyes that meant he was barely containing his anger.

The water soothed her throat, parched from the gagging and sobbing. She had managed to remain composed for the rest of the day, but as soon as she locked the door at home, tears overflowed her dam of stoicism. Visions of Marge's death haunted her.

Aside from investigators she'd had to talk to, she hadn't spoken with anyone except for her uncle. Louie was the only one who might be able to really understand, having been through his own political scandal. Brian, and a few other friends, had left messages asking to come over, if she needed anything, expressing their support. Then there were the pseudo friends who wanted morbid details or to be able to tell everyone, "I spoke with her and she didn't sound like a pariah." She knew not to make statements to anyone and took the phone off the hook.

She had moved to the cozy eleven-hundred-square-foot, bungalow-style house in Ladd's Addition three months earlier. Portland's oldest planned community, the neighborhood dated back to 1891, when the landowner decided to develop it using Washington, D.C., as the model.

With her long work hours, she was not yet unpacked. She hadn't even bothered to put up curtains, and now feared reporters gathering on her lawn and spying in. There were no pictures on the walls, no decorative bric-a-brac artfully placed. The depressing starkness fit her mood perfectly.

"At approximately zero-six-hundred hours, federal agents armed with an arrest warrant went to the headquarters of the White People's Freedom Party to arrest Jebediah Heaven, on suspicion of conspiracy," Sullivan was saying on the screen. "Agents were fired upon, and let me stress this, the occupants of the house fired first, killing one agent. We have identified this man"—Arnold Beil's mug shot flashed on the screen—"as one of those who was present and escaped. He is armed and extremely dangerous, and a fifty-thousand-dollar reward is available for any information leading to his arrest. We have wanted posters available in print or electronic form and they will be distributed when we finish today. Mr. Beil has used a number of disguises and aliases to evade capture.

"Apparently a methamphetamine lab on the site was detonated either deliberately or accidentally by the suspects. The property is contaminated and will be sealed off until hazmat teams pronounce it clear.

"Mr. Beil is the suspect in a number of vicious assaults on federal officers, people of color, Jews, and gay men or lesbians."

He continued to talk but Parker flashed back to the shots, the explosion, the screams. Louise only returned attention to the screen when her boss's voice stopped and reporters began hurling accusatory questions at him. He looked sincerely at the cameras as he responded:

"No, children were not killed at the raid. A couple of armed teenagers, with known affiliations to hate groups, fired on federal officers and agents returned fire. Both assailants were neutralized."

"Yes, there was a teenage girl present who was injured, and apparently had no direct ties to hate groups. She is in stable condition and being questioned.

"Agent Louise Parker was in charge of the raid and is on paid administrative leave, as is normal in such circumstances.

"Apparent gaps in intelligence are being investigated and a full briefing will take place when information is available."

After five minutes of Q & A, he said thank you and hurried from the podium. Reporters kept hurling questions until the door had closed behind him.

Then the station began running segments they'd been airing for most of the day:

Mary Ann's parents, with their attorney, talking about their poor daughter and how only the multimillion-dollar lawsuit they were filing against the federal government could help her heal.

Professor Carolyn Mounts, a hate group expert from the University of Oregon, explaining how Jeb Heaven was more of a wannabe hate monger, and how significant it would have been if Arnold Beil had been caught. "In the extremist community, he's a mythic figure on par with Timothy McVeigh."

The pixilated face and distorted voice of a man who said he was an associate of Jeb Heaven, and that Heaven only wanted to help children become aware of their racial heritage and develop a sense of self-esteem.

Louise shut the TV. She had no idea how long she'd be off of work or what the penalty would be for the botched raid. What could she have done differently? Insisted on more confirmation from the CI? Had the trucks farther back? More agents? The agent working the CI was generally reliable, in fact he was Sullivan's nephew. And Sanchez certainly knew how to set up a tactical operation. No one could have anticipated that Beil would be there, but someone had to be blamed.

She glanced at the phone and debated whether to call Brian. But it was near midnight and she didn't want to wake him. And if she talked, and started crying, she'd be embarrassed. She prided herself on her independence, and had vowed after her divorce that she would never again rely on a man for emotional support.

She found the curtains and began putting them up.

Brian finally got through to her late the next morning. "How're you doing?"

"About as well as can be expected, considering I'm on forced leave and being investigated for incompetence." She paused, then said, "Sorry to be snappy. I'm trying to keep busy. I unpacked a few boxes, put up curtains, did a food shop."

"I hope you get cleared soon. It must be tough."

"It was weird going to the store. I kept a hat pulled down, sunglasses on.

I thought there might be news people around and didn't want anyone to recognize me. They ran an old photo of me on some of the newscasts."

"If you're willing to go out again, how about I take you to dinner tonight? I found a great Thai place not far from you."

"Uh, no thanks. I'm more comfortable at home."

"I like the idea of going out with a woman in disguise," he said, trying to cheer her up.

"I'm not in the mood."

"How about I bring over Pizzacato? Your choice of toppings," Brian said. "As part of my full service package, I not only deliver, but I can help you settle in. You don't know it, but I can put up shelves, hang pictures, change light fixtures. Light bulbs, too."

"Maybe sometime soon."

"I can take time off, we can go cheer the dragon boat racers." Ninety-six teams share eight boats, racing a course between the Marquam and Hawthorne Bridges. Both Brian and Louise had participated on past teams in the Portland-Kaohsiung Sister City Association race. "We can heckle if the Nike team that beat us is there."

"Right now I need quiet time by myself."

"That's fair. But if I don't hear from you soon, I'm going to bother you again."

"That would be nice."

Hanson got off the phone as he was beeped for his next client.

Sandy was a sickly-looking forty-year-old with a long history of physical hospitalizations. Inevitably, she got worse while being treated. A suspicious doctor had arranged for a webcam in her room, and it had recorded her putting feces in her IV line. She had denied it, even after they cultured the horrendous infection at the IV site and found *E. coli.*

Sandy suffered from Munchausen syndrome. Theorists hypothesized it was a warped way of getting love, based on unhealthy patterns established in childhood. Others saw it as a way to make mental pain manifest physically. Some believed it was a watered down death wish. Medical professionals hated Munchausen patients for demanding resources and driving up hospital iatrogenic infections statistics. They had been nicknamed "hospital hoboes" for jumping from institution to institution as their reputations became known. A few doctors had seriously proposed tattooing their diagnosis on them to save medical costs.

She seemed to be coping better—with only one hospitalization in the past year—using the Dialectical Behavioral Therapy techniques Hanson had taught her. Hanson often utilized the approach, which stressed mindfulness, acceptance balanced with change, relaxation breathing, and other coping skills. He wanted to get her into a DBT group but she was reluctant.

"Maybe there's a group at the hospital?" she asked hopefully.

"Remember our goal, to have you have as little contact with the medical system as possible?"

"But would going to a group there really be so terrible?"

"Don't you think you'd be tempted, seeing the nurses and doctors, hearing those codes being paged?"

He could tell she was reminiscing and she recognized it. "I guess."

"That's the spirit. Let's review distract and self-soothe. Keep you out of the hospital and find a better place to go."

"It's hard to believe that there's someplace better than a hospital."

"There's a heckuva lot of folks that would disagree."

With the session done, Hanson fortunately was at his desk when VA nurse Kathy Wozniak called.

"I don't have a release so I can't go into names, but I have a client who seriously self-injured during a suicide attempt," Hanson said after greetings. "Many of his symptoms come from PTSD that is directly attributable to his time as a marine."

"Sure, sure, I understand, the goddess of HIPAA will smite you if you break confidentiality." She had a blunt, confident tone, not the sort to waste time or be intimidated by societal conventions. "Combat veteran?"

"Yes."

"Still, they're not generous about suicide attempts. We've got less and less, with more and more boys coming home injured. Thirty percent of World War Two casualties died, down to twenty percent by Vietnam War. Now it's hovering around twelve percent. We do better at saving lives in combat but not much when they get back here. Bureaucrats have insisted on reclassifying some who were diagnosed with PTSD to personality disorders. Less money to pay out."

"That sucks."

"You're lucky I've mellowed or I'd tell you how I feel about it in a lot stronger language than that. What are you looking for?"

"Plastic surgery. Extensive facial work."

"Is this for Moose Brown?"

"I can't say, but what makes you guess?"

"He's famous here. Maybe I'd be more accurate saying infamous. He's got that scary face. And he got physical with a few security guards one time. He's *persona non grata* to many folks."

"How about you?"

"I'm just a harmless old lady. Never got into any testosterone power plays with him. We got along fine. Now I've got a question for you. You serve your country?"

"Vietnam. Army. Saw six different shades of ugly all down the Ho Chi Minh Trail. From Khe Sanh, to Dakto, Pleiku, and Tay Ninh, near Saigon."

"Your client is lucky he's got someone who can understand what it does to a person." She sighed. "I'm not optimistic, but let me make a few calls."

"Thank you."

"Don't thank me unless I actually can get something done."

Louise moped around on the couch for a while, then forced herself to clean and unpack a couple more boxes. As she found places for her belongings, the feeling of accomplishment added to her momentum. It was a beautiful June day and she decided to do yard work. Having lived in a downtown Portland apartment for four years, the idea of her own home garden pleased her. She thought of her parent's house—her father putting in tomato plants, corn, cucumbers, and carrots, while her mother was responsible for the brightly colored flower beds.

Portland Nursery, covering several acres at two sites in Southeast, had a hundred-year history of supplying virtually any plant a gardener could want. The parking lot was dominated by a full-sized red caboose. She relaxed as she passed the small booths that looked like they should be for amusement park ticket takers. The nursery was a place to get lost, where there was as much space for clay pots as most landscaping businesses had devoted to plants. Staff was excessively knowledgeable, and as Louise asked questions, she got more information than she needed. Around the huge site, workers used walkie-talkies to communicate with each other about esoterica of flora and the stock on hand. Louise had to make two trips to her car, using the nursery's telltale kid's red wagons, to load everything in.

She spent the next few hours turning over the moist, heavy soil in front of her house, mulching, and setting up flower beds with an explosive rainbow of impatiens, begonias, and pansies. In her backyard she put in cherry and plum tomatoes, cucumbers, and carrots.

By day's end, she was exhausted, but content. She didn't bother to watch the news, choosing instead to reduce her pile of reading. She went through two *New Yorker*s, a *Discover*, and a *National Geographic*.

She received a few calls from colleagues, and was touched by the words of support. She had to cut a couple of conversations short when she teetered on the verge of tears.

Lying in bed at night was hardest. She replayed the scenes in her mind, wondering if there was anything she could have done differently.

7

E VERY SUNDAY MORNING, AND whenever he could spare the time, in a slightly sloping field in the foothills overlooking the Mount Tabor Park reservoir, Brian would practice martial arts. The reservoir, ringed by dark brick crenellated towers, had a gothic charm. And on a clear day, much of the city could be seen stretched out below.

He wasn't alone—Saturday and Sunday mornings the idyllic spot, densely matted with grass, drew dozens of practitioners from throughout the city. In the months after his divorce, when he felt tempted to find a bar and make it his new home, he had sublimated his energy into martial arts. Four nights a week, and much of the weekend, he'd work out. Advancing into middle age, with injured joints and battle scars, slower-paced *tai chi chuan* and the weapons of Filipino stick fighting had a greater appeal for him. Mondays and Wednesdays he'd do *tai chi* with Jamie Tan, Tuesdays and Thursdays Filipino stick arts with Mike Morrell. Fridays he'd sit and soak in his tub, musing on how much ibuprofen he was taking, and why he kept pushing himself.

During his obsessive period, he'd heard about the great, eclectic open-air *dojo*. It also attracted musicians, who, on varying days, provided background bagpipes, guitar, trumpet, flute, and/or drums. Though he'd dropped his night classes, whenever possible on weekends and sometimes on difficult weekdays, he'd visit the park.

The martial artists primarily followed Chinese traditions—*tai chi chuan, ba gua, qi gong, kung fu, hsing i*. But on a crowded day, there'd be people doing Brazilian *jiu jitsu,* rolling on the grass with legs locked around each other. Joint-locking *hapkido* and *aikido* practitioners, hard kicking *tae kwon do* and *karatekas* going through their *katas*. The clacking sticks of *escrima* and *arnis,* occasionally those doing sword or staff sets. It was by the reservoir, in the anxiety-filled days right after 9/11, that an overzealous security guard drew down on a Chinese sword set student who had been practicing harmlessly there for years.

Most of the time practitioners stuck with their own kind, near each other but not blending. Occasionally people would pair up, agree on rules of engagement, and practice their respective disciplines. A Chinese *chin na* practitioner locking an elbow could see that she had more in common with a Japanese *jiu jitsuka* than not. A Russian *sambo* student found his throws only slightly different from a *judoka*.

Bruises, scratches, and occasional sprains were common. Sometimes someone with a bullying or sadistic streak would attempt to crash the party. He would be shunned. If he insisted on playing rough, Bonnie Tidd would usually convince him to not come back.

Hanson waved to Bonnie at the far end of the small field. She was with her latest girlfriend, Cookie, an African American woman with skin so dark it seemed to absorb light. Bonnie was a tall and sinewy blonde, her weather-worn, high-cheek-boned face looking like she should be welcoming home her sweaty man from a job on an oil rig while county and western music twanged in the background.

After stretching a couple minutes, Tidd and Hanson bowed to each other, nesting right fist in open left hand. As they engaged, he kept his right hand on her left elbow, his left hand on her right forearm. He had a much longer reach and outweighed her by fifty pounds. Hanson hoped to control her about one out of three times.

"Haven't seen you in a couple weeks," Hanson said. "I was concerned you got hurt."

"You can call or stop by my office any time, Brian Hanson." She lowered her voice, even though there was no one within fifteen feet of them. "I did a piece of work for a good ole boy in the cattle business. A hostile competitor sent a couple of tough characters to rough him up. I was corn bread and marmalade sweet with them and they decided to be peaceable."

"Really?"

She chuckled and Brian knew not to ask any more. Bonnie was an executive protection specialist. She disliked the term bodyguard. When an exec wanted someone who could mingle at a party without looking like hired muscle, or who could hang out unobtrusively shopping with his wife, Tidd's Protective Services was one of the first names to come up.

Few people liked to work out with her. The practitioners were predominantly male and most were sensitive to being bested by a woman. She had been studying *muay thai* kickboxing since she was a little girl in Thailand. Her father had been a career military man; disappointed at only having a daughter, he encouraged her to be tough. She'd added skills from *wing chun*—the Chinese martial art invented by a Buddhist nun, and *capoeira*, the Brazilian martial art developed by slaves. It was more than internationalism that led to the choices—*wing chun* emphasized upper body, *capoeira* lower body, and *muay thai* close-in work.

Bonnie and Brian's Push Hands movements were a mix of gentleness and suppressed energy. Advancing, retreating, diverting, confronting. Tidd came at it from a *wing chun* Sticky Hands approach, while Hanson's energy was more *tai chi* Push Hands style.

Hanson sensed an opening and pushed, but it was a feint by Bonnie. He recovered his balance but before he could get fully grounded, she shoved hard and he fell on the grass.

"A pushover," she said, offering a hand and pulling him up.

"I'm just warming up," he said with a grin.

"Good. I would hate to think you'd gotten soft in my absence."

And so it went, with a bit of bantering and a lot of intensity, they pushed for more than an hour. When they were done, Brian's forehead gleamed with perspiration. Bonnie had one bead of sweat on her upper lip that she licked away.

Hanson, Tidd, and Cookie headed toward the parking lot, with Bonnie and Cookie holding hands. They passed by a group of five men wearing matching soccer jerseys. Having lost their match, seeing a biracial lesbian couple was the final affront to their universe.

"Hey, you know what you lezbos need?" said the apparent leader, who had a Fu Manchu mustache and a nose that had been broken and badly set. He grabbed his crotch and made a thrusting motion.

Hanson and the women continued walking, but Fu Manchu blocked them. "D'you hear what I said?" he demanded.

Bonnie released her partner's hand. She calmly stepped in until she was a foot away from the leader. She was a few inches shorter and had to look up.

Since they were so close together, it was hard to see what was going on. But Fu Manchu's startled expression and Bonnie's soft-spoken words made it clear.

"This move is called 'monkey steals a peach,'" she said, as her right hand grabbed his testicles. "The next part, I drop my weight down and hang on for dear life. You wind up singing two octaves higher. Or, we part now as friends. Your choice, honeychile."

"Sorry," he whispered.

"Apology accepted," she said, and they walked away.

Louise had gone to the Mormon temple twice in all her years in Portland. It would have been a good career move—there were many LDS members within the bureau. But part of her reason for leaving the family in Utah had been a flight from the church. Not that there weren't things about it that she didn't love, that resonated in her soul. The idea of getting back to the true teachings of Christ, after so many centuries of interpretation and misinterpretation. The strong sense of structure, of family, of community. The fact that it was American-born and shaped, that holy sites were right in this country and could be seen.

But there was the patriarchy's sometimes choking rigidity. She was not the sort to deliberately ask provocative questions but she also didn't like being slapped down hard when she had.

As she struggled with trying to make sense out of what happened on the Jebediah Heaven raid, the answer seemed beyond her. She prayed for wisdom, but nothing came. Maybe she had been away for too long. The church called to her.

For nonbelievers, the beautiful six-spired building just off the I-205 freeway was where they thought Mormons worshiped. The white marble building, with the angel Moroni looking down from on high, was so bright it seemed to glow with a divine energy. But on any given Sunday, that wasn't where LDS members would be. Weekly services were held in ward buildings, far more mundane. Clean brick one-story structures that fit into most neighborhoods. A spire on top, but no cross. She wondered whether it was because of early persecution. This building had a parking lot that could hold the couple hundred followers, a grass lawn, and a modest sign announcing it was the place of worship for the Church of Jesus Christ of Latter Day Saints.

Parker moved through the wooden doors, nodding to those she knew, welcomed back into the community. She thought of wards she had visited over the years. It was always so soothing. She thought of Brian, and his lack of faith, and was sad for him.

She recalled the compelling stories she had learned growing up, of a teenage Joseph Smith in Palmyra, New York, praying for heavenly advice over which Christian faith to follow, his facing an evil presence, and the arrival of the light that drove off the evil.

Louise found a seat, and noticed a couple of special agents with their families. They exchanged smiles.

The bishop took the pulpit. A dapper man with a deep voice, he paused dramatically, and began, "O God our Eternal Father, we come unto thee as thy thankful sons and daughters. We approach thee in the name of thy Beloved Son, the Lord Jesus Christ, our Savior and Redeemer, the great Messiah."

She could feel herself sinking into the comfortable warmth of the church. Even the hard pew felt good against her, a solid support. She felt guilt over her own self-pity, compared to the persecution and eventual martyrdom of the Prophet Joseph Smith, victim with his brother of an angry Illinois mob.

How many hundreds of times had she heard the familiar words? "We believe in God, the Eternal Father, and in His Son, Jesus Christ, and in the Holy Ghost. We believe that the first principles and ordinances of the Gospel are: first, Faith in the Lord Jesus Christ; second, Repentance; third, Baptism by immersion for the remission of sins; fourth, laying on of hands for the gift of the Holy Ghost. We believe the Bible to be the word of God as far as it is translated correctly and that the Book of Mormon is the word of God."

Louise felt her troubles being carried away with the bishop's familiar words.

"We believe all that God has revealed, and will yet reveal many great and important things pertaining to the Kingdom of God. We believe in the literal gathering of Israel and in the restoration of the Ten Tribes; that the New Jerusalem will be built upon the American continent; that Christ will reign upon the earth; and, that the earth will be renewed and receive its paradisiacal glory. We believe in being honest, chaste, benevolent, virtuous, and in doing good to all men."

She was vaguely aware of those around her and felt herself blending in. There were a couple of big boned, dark-skinned Hawaiians, a nervous-looking man who had courteously taken off his AC/DC baseball cap and set it carefully on his lap, a gaunt Latino woman with a face scarred by suffering, and lots of the conservatively dressed white families like those she had grown up with. All were welcome.

After the service, there was socializing in the room that could be converted into a gym or meeting hall. The agents she had seen in the crowd came up to her and shook her hand. Their wives offered hugs. She was invited to an after-service barbecue. One wife mentioned that she had a brother "about her age, a righteous man, widowed" and hinted at arranging a date. Louise hesitated but promised to consider it. She thought about Brian and wished there were some way she could share the experience with him. She wondered how much he could mask his cynicism.

Parker said her goodbyes and headed back to her car. She reached into her pocketbook for the keys, and saw that her wallet was missing. Could she have forgotten it at home? No, she had a clear recollection of putting it in the pocketbook. The realization it was stolen hit her like a wintry blast in the Columbia Gorge. She had been too trusting, setting the bag next to her on the pew.

She got inside her Camry and put the key in the ignition, her hands shaking so much she was unable to turn the car on. She sat in the lot, watching the other parishioners head home. It wasn't until the lot was nearly empty that she felt calm enough to drive home.

Hanson's apartment was not that far from Portland State University and sometimes the students' partying would keep him up at night. Many of the more wealthy ones, often Arabs or Asian exchange students, felt the thrill of being halfway around the world, away from the repressions of home.

But this Sunday night was quiet, so his insomnia couldn't be blamed on their inconsideration. Ever since Vietnam he'd been a poor sleeper. Difficulty falling asleep, difficulty staying asleep, and waking up earlier than he wanted. Punctuated by occasional nightmares. He knew all the tricks, he'd taught groups on "sleep hygiene," but his mind refused to cooperate. During the day he'd kept busy, keeping disturbing thoughts away.

The confrontation at Mount Tabor, coming so soon after the incident at the waterfront park, had been triggers. What was it about men and violence? The incidents sparked pathways to the amygdala, where emotional memory was stored. The messages transmitted to the hormonal system, the squirting of adrenaline, the sympathetic nervous system activated. He imagined himself cut away, like a cheesy old TV commercial showing the anatomical benefits of a particular stomach medicine.

He stared out the window at the lights of the city glowing against the night sky. Every now and then, one would blink off, and he'd feel more alone. He'd been offered sleeping pills by doctors but being in recovery, he feared his addict thinking. If one was good, two would be better. And six would be great. He didn't want to ever again be dependent on any mind-altering drugs.

He thought about Louise and what it would be like to be more intimate. Could she tolerate his quirks and imperfections? What would it be like to share a space with her? What would it be like to make love?

Hanson considered calling his son, freshly graduated from UCLA, struggling in his first job as a freelance writer. Brian had visited him a few times in Los Angeles, and they exchanged phone calls at least once a week. Jeff had pulled away from both parents during their unpleasant divorce. Hanson was beginning to reconnect with him, though there were often long awkward silences. With the mood the counselor was in, it was no time to jeopardize their fragile relationship.

He put on a dark sweatshirt and running pants. It was nearly midnight when he rode the elevator down. PSU kids were still out strolling, less and less people as he neared the Willamette. He started his slow jog parallel to Tom McCall Park and the river. The Fun Center was closed now, silhouetted with that eerie shuttered amusement park atmosphere. The lights on the rides were dark, the noises muted, the food smells blown away. He brooded on his scuffle with the sailor.

He ran north, toward Old Town, and the scruffiest part of downtown. He passed a few homeless people camped out on benches.

He wondered if he was like Moose, deliberately seeking violence? Was he looking for a discharge of his anger or to be punished for the wartime harm he had done? Was it to prove his manhood, or to die?

8

I T'S THE FBI, YOUR Honor, they keep wanting to use the anal probe on me," interrupted David Palermo. It was not the strangest allegation that had been made in Multnomah County Courthouse room 220 and everyone kept a straight face. Around the huge boat-shaped table was the judge, a clerk, Palermo and his attorney, an attorney for the state, and two county-appointed mental health examiners. Two dark-green-uniformed deputies sat back from the table, a few feet away from Palermo.

The room showed signs of the county's constant lack of funding—to muffle the slam of the worn wooden door, there was a cut piece of carpet on the knob. A bear-sized soot stain marred one wall. The chairs were only slightly more comfortable than what could be found in a bus terminal. Brian Hanson sat in the front row, along with three other witnesses. The therapist had been under oath and testifying when Palermo began his tirade.

Judge Jay Margulies was known for his patience. He treated every client with more dignity than most had encountered throughout their lives. He coaxed and coached the fledgling attorneys who were often assigned to his division of family court. He avoided the trappings of power—no black robe, gavel, or large judicial bench to hide behind.

"Mr. Palermo, you'll get your chance to speak. Your attorney was questioning Mr. Hanson," Margulies said. "I need to listen to the evidence being presented."

"You can't believe them." Palermo was a forty-five-year-old with deep-set eyes and a booming voice. "Ask them about Roswell. Ask them about Area Fifty-one. Ask them about the anal probes they've put in everyone! It may have happened to you while you slept."

Hanson suspected Palermo had not been taking his medicine. Cheeking it so hospital staff couldn't tell. Palermo had been first diagnosed with schizophrenia when he was twenty, and had been in and out of the hospital a dozen times since then. As he grew more paranoid, he would accuse passersby of being FBI agents who were following him. When they denied it or tried to move away, he would assault them.

He'd be put on medication and get stabilized in supported housing. Then he'd stop taking his medication, based on the belief that he was being poisoned, or because of very real side effects. After a few months he'd be back on the street screaming at strangers, and then back into the hospital.

Hanson was there to testify as to Palermo's diagnosis and how well he could do when he was taking his medication. The judge would decide whether there was a clear and convincing imminent danger, and if so, whether Palermo should be held for up to six months.

"Your concerns have been duly noted, Mr. Palermo. Now I must ask you to be quiet so we can move on."

Often, the hearings were perfunctory, like a meeting between world leaders where diplomats had worked out details beforehand and everyone just had to go through the motions. Both sides knew what was best for the client and there was a tacit agreement. Palermo's attorney, Eric Jacoby, was more aggressive than most. He was slender, with thinning hair and fierce brown eyes. His long fingers gestured and produced papers with a magician's ease.

"Please continue," the judge said.

"Let me remind you, Mr. Hanson, you're still under oath," Jacoby said. "From your previous testimony, we've established that you are aware of the abuses that have gone on in the state hospitalization system."

"I've read the articles. But I have no personal knowledge of it."

"Of course," he said, in an accusatory tone. "Have you heard accounts of what has gone on from other clients?"

"Yes." Hanson glanced over at the deputy district attorney, wondering if a hearsay objection was in order. But the overworked prosecutor was leafing through his file, distracted and seemingly ill prepared for the case.

Hanson had testified more than twenty times over the course of his career but this appearance was more draining than most. Jacoby had an intensity like he was arguing a capital case in front of the supreme court. The defense attorney was skillful at leading in one direction, then making a sharp, somewhat confusing turn in the questioning to keep Hanson off balance.

"The medications you're recommending are Risperdal and Zoloft. An antipsychotic and an antidepressant. I don't understand why my client must be imprisoned for so long, why these drugs take so long to work?"

"That's outside my scope of expertise, Mr. Jacoby. I don't prescribe drugs."

"So you're not familiar with antidepressants and antipsychotics? How long have you been in the field?"

"Long enough not to get pulled into answering medical questions." Hanson noticed that the judge chuckled. "I would be happy to arrange to have one of our medical providers testify, if the court wishes."

Judge Margulies cleared his throat and turned to the deputy district attorney. "This questioning is starting to border on badgering the witness. You might want to raise an objection."

"Uh, yes, Your Honor," the deputy district attorney said.

Before the hearing could progress, Palermo jumped up. "I cannot be silenced. I will protect myself and the humanoid species from this dangerous violation of our rights. I will kill every last federal agent that invades my space."

"Your Honor, I'd like to talk to my client," said Jacoby. "Can we have a fifteen minute recess?"

Judge Margulies nodded. "I think that would be wise. We'll resume in fifteen minutes."

But court resumed in ten minutes, since Palermo had taken a swing at one of the deputies, and been led away. The judge continued Palermo's stay in the hospital.

Brian walked out next to Jacoby.

"You handled yourself well," the attorney said. "I'm sure you understand why I had to try and rough you up."

"It's part of the process," Hanson said.

"I've got to make sure his rights are protected," Jacoby said. "I like to litigate, that's why I take this indigent panel work." As they reached the door and turned in different directions, Jacoby winked and said, "Besides, this anal probe is killing me."

Palermo's ranting about the FBI had increased Hanson's concerns about Louise. He was glad when he got back to his office and there was a voice mail from her:

"Hi, Brian. Thanks for the *What About Bob?* DVD. I'm not really in the mood for a comedy right now, but when I am, maybe we can watch it together. I'll call soon."

The counselor liked the comedy about a pompous, tightly wound psychiatrist played by Richard Dreyfus being stalked by a persistently annoying, anxious client, played by Bill Murray. But why would Parker thank him for a DVD he had never sent? He was going to call her back but it was time for his next appointment.

Svetlana was a forty-one-year-old Serbian woman who had survived the ethnic cleansing and horrors of the breakup of Yugoslavia. A strikingly attractive brunette, she showed no signs of the unforgiving circumstances she had lived through. Hanson was amused by the fact that during the Cold War, Slavic women were portrayed as potato ugly and built like tractors. Now it seemed like whenever he read the lifestyle section of the paper, the women being marketed as desirable had names like Porizkova, Kournikova, Jovovich.

Svetlana's father, husband, and two of their children had been murdered in front of her. She was vague, but implied she had been repeatedly gang raped. She worked sixty hours a week at two nurse's aide jobs, while studying for her citizenship test and learning English. Her surviving child, a fourteen-year-old boy, was intoxicated with American culture. Many of their sessions were spent discussing her son and trying to understand adolescent rebellion.

"My son play music all the time. Loud men cursing. They say bad things. My son likes it but I tell him it is junk. We yell at each other and he go out. He comes back late."

"You're worried about him."

"He's all I have left."

Hanson was face to face with Svetlana and her brutally existential sorrow. He could only be a witness to her determination to make a better life for herself and her surviving son.

"It's hard," Hanson said. They sat, silent. There was a powerful sensation Hanson sometimes got, like tears forming behind his eyeballs, connecting to another's misery. Feeling both his own pain and doing a bit to relieve theirs.

After a few minutes, she looked up, her eyes moist. "There is no point crying. They like it more when you cry."

"Who is they?" he asked, handing her the box of tissues he kept handy.

She shook her head, not wanting to answer.

"You're in a safe place now," Hanson said. He noted that she had used "bad" to describe the rappers and the soldiers in Serbia. Was the violent rap music a trigger for her? It was something to explore later. For now all he said was, "It's okay to cry."

"I must be strong."

"Strong people cry."

She sniffled once, "I think about it."

9

N OTIFYING THE FBI IN person about the loss of her identification was humiliating. Although she knew the clerk who took the information, there seemed to be a smirk barely hiding behind the woman's thin lips. Louise appreciated the impersonality of filing the police report about her stolen wallet by phone.

Her cat, Clyde, jumped into her lap, demanding to be petted. It was his way of helping her calm down. The British shorthair, who looked like Winston Churchill with yellow eyes, settled in as she rubbed his plush, gray fur. He gave a little yip when she was distracted, a little too rough.

"Sorry Mr. C," she said, and resumed with the desired amount of friction. He soon returned to his deep purring. Some thought she had named him after J. Edgar Hoover's longtime companion, Clyde Tolson. Others thought maybe Clyde Barrow from Bonnie and Clyde. Bonnie's real last name was after all Parker. But the name came from Clyde "the Glide" Drexler, the last classy Portland Trailblazer.

After a few minutes Louise got restless and set him down on the floor. He made a spitting, hissing sound of discontent, and marched off to sulk under her bed.

She had canceled her credit cards, but whoever had stolen them had managed to use them in the couple hours she had taken before reporting the theft. The thief had ordered several DVDs from Movie Maven, an online video and DVD merchant.

"I'm confused," the investigator from MasterCard said when he read the shipping address and it was hers.

"What?"

"Can you explain why this order is being sent to your house if the card was stolen?"

"That's crazy."

"You said it."

But the next day more DVDs arrived: *Cape Fear*, with Robert Mitchum as a revenge-seeking ex-con terrorizing lawyer Gregory Peck's family; *The Phantom of the Opera; The Collector,* where Samantha Eggar meets a man obsessed with more than butterfly collecting.

She grilled the Federal Express delivery man. "Where are these from? Who sent them?"

The well-groomed, muscular man in the freshly starched uniform tried his best customer service skills. "I don't know, ma'am. I just handle the packages. What does the return address label say?"

"Movie Maven." She knew her voice was shrill but couldn't control it. "Who sent them? How were they paid for?"

"You'll have to open the packages. I really have no way of knowing." He backed up a few steps. "I have to be going." He hurried off as she tore open the package and found three DVDs, along with a note that read, "Sorry to hear about the death."

The name printed below the words was Brian Hanson.

She watched the FedEx truck speed away.

She was inside, staring at the movies like they were rattlesnakes that had crawled into her house. The phone rang, startling her. She let it ring until the machine kicked over.

"Hi, this is Louise, we're not in right now." She used the plural, like many single women, to deter creeps. "Please leave your name, number, and a brief message and I'll get back to you."

"Hi, Louise, this is Brian. I'm calling because I wonder . . ."

She picked up the phone. "Hi. How you doing?'

"Fine. Screening your calls?"

"Yes."

"Well, I'm glad you took mine." She told him about the movies. "It's the same place you got *What About Bob?* from. What was the comment about, " 'Sorry about the death'?"

"That's why I'm calling. I didn't send *What About Bob?* or anything else. I've tried calling you but got a busy signal."

After a long silence, she said, "There's definitely a theme to the movies."

"Women being victimized," he said. "Any idea who's doing this?"

Her doorbell rang.

"Are you expecting anyone?" Brian asked.

"No."

"I'll wait on the line while you answer," he volunteered.

"It's not necessary. I can take care of myself."

"I know."

The bell rang again.

"Okay. Not a very subtle assassin if they're leaning on my doorbell," she muttered as she set the phone down. She hustled to her closet, grabbed her 40 caliber Glock 23, and moved cautiously to the door to the street. With the gun held behind her back, standing slightly off to one side, she peered through the peephole that was set into the solid wooden door.

A pimply pizza delivery kid, in a Pizza House hat and T-shirt with company logo, was turning to walk away.

"I thought you weren't home," he said by way of apology. "I got your order. One large with sardines and anchovies."

"I didn't order it," she said.

She transferred her weapon to her left hand and opened the door with her right. "How much?"

"Fifteen. But you gave credit card information when you called. And here's the callback number." He read off Louise's home phone number.

"A woman's voice called this in?"

"I didn't take the order. I can find out."

"Please."

She closed the door, leaving him waiting on the small porch, and went back to the phone. "It's fine, Brian. No need to worry."

"I could hear faintly what was going on. A prank pizza?"

"Probably some teenage boy has a crush on me and thinks this is the way to get my attention."

"How'd he get your home address?"

She told him briefly about the theft of her wallet. "I was careless. Stupidity is its own reward."

"It's natural to let your guard down in a house of worship," he said. "I'll come by tonight with dinner."

"Not necessary," she said.

"Unless you forbid me, I'm coming by. Around six-thirty."

After a moment's hesitation, she said, "Okay," then they said quick goodbyes.

Back on the front porch, the pizza delivery guy was annoyed at being kept waiting. "Becky took the call. She thinks it was a man, but isn't sure. A bad connection and we're real busy." He said it like a rebuke for Louise's delaying him, but smiled when she gave him a five-dollar tip and took the cooling pizza off his hands.

She picked the anchovies and sardines off and gave most of them to Clyde. He accepted the offering graciously.

Brian's concern was not something she could accept. Could he really be trusted? Obviously he hadn't stolen her wallet—she would have recognized him at the services. Could he have had an accomplice? Was it a coincidence that he called right when she got the prank pizza? Or that he had mentioned pizza the last time they talked? No, that was too juvenile a stunt. The DVDs had his name on it. Ridiculous to put your name on it, then deny it. But his actions at the Fun Center were irrational. No, that couldn't be the Brian she knew.

Feeling lost, Louise did what she had done for much of her life. She called her oldest sister. Diane lived in Salt Lake City, and boasted that she had been within the same zip code for her entire life. Diane was seven years older than Louise, and was Norman Rockwell perfect. "A" student, captain of the cheerleaders, cum laude from Brigham Young, five children with a Babbitt-like husband, head of the PTA, active in the church, and several times regional award winner for her pastries.

Diane answered on the second ring, as crisp as a high-priced law office receptionist, which is what she had been until her husband made enough for her to be a stay-at-home mom.

"I saw the television about that raid," Diane said. "So sorry."

Louise was about to ask, "Why didn't you call me?" but she held her words. Diane's role was to be the brilliant, efficient sister, not the nurturer.

"Yeah, and I've been having troubles ever since." Louise recounted the theft and unwanted gifts.

"Who do you suspect?"

"I don't know. I've got a guy I've been friendly with. He's somewhat troubled. I can't believe he'd do such a thing."

"What would his motive be?"

"I don't know. Maybe he could pretend to protect me."

"Is he the one you mentioned the last time we spoke? The Vietnam drug addict?"

"He was in Vietnam and he did have problems with drugs. But he's been straight for years."

"You know that for a fact?'

"He works as a psychotherapist."

Diane snorted. "As if those people were any more stable. You should get pastoral counseling."

"There's no one I trust."

"Have you been reading the Bible?"

"Not recently."

Another snort. "I won't ask what that means. In the Book of Judges there's a story you might take to heart." She paused, and Louise knew she was reciting it from memory. "Jephthah the Gileadite was the son of a prostitute, driven out by Gilead's others sons. He was an outcast, a bandit, until the Ammonites attacked the Israelites. Then the Israelites asked him back, to lead them. Jephthah did, vowing to the Lord that if he won, he would sacrifice whatever came out of his house when he first returned. You might not know that in those days, people kept their livestock within their homes. Well, the first one to come out of his house was his only child, a daughter. He killed her to keep his vow."

"I remember the story vaguely. It's right around the part where they test people by asking them to say "shibboleth," and if they can't they're from the other tribe, so they kill them."

"Very good," Diane said, and Louise inwardly glowed from the praise. "And what do you think the relevancy is?"

"I've thought it meant don't make a promise you can't keep. Particularly to God."

"There's other wisdom in there. Jephthah is an example of a great warrior who is dangerous to have around during peacetime. For whatever reason, killing as a skill comes easily to him. Being in a loving relationship is much harder."

"You think I shouldn't trust Brian?"

"I can't say. Your calling me means you have questions. Remember what President Reagan said?"

"Is he one of the apostles?"

"Sarcasm doesn't become you, Louise," said Diane, who was never known for her sense of humor.

Louise said, "Trust, but verify."

"Very good. You should come and stay with us until this blows over. It's been a while."

"I'd like to visit but not until I clear this up. Parkers don't run, Dad always told us." They talked for a few more minutes, mainly with Diane pressuring Louise to come see her nieces and nephews.

She went outside and gardened for an hour, then returned inside and unpacked a couple more boxes, trying to distract herself from painful rumination. She debated whether she should call the office for an update and decided not to.

Who was behind the petty harassment? A white supremacist sympathizer? But whoever had targeted her had been able to get personal information quickly. Was it someone in her life? An agent upset over her handling of the raid? A neighbor or false friend? Brian?

What about the raid? What could she have done differently? Was there another way of confirming who was at the hideout? Could she have challenged Sanchez on the tactical placement of the tactical operations van? Had she been guilty of being prideful, and should she have encouraged SAC Sullivan to choose someone with more experience?

Idle hands do the devil's work, her mother had said. Louise went back out to the garden and continued mulching. After laying down fabric weed block, she cut open bags of bark dust and began spreading them. The physical work felt good, even though she still ruminated on the raid. She watered her fresh plantings and studied the yard work she had done.

Whenever she slowed her pace, she was aware that whoever was harassing her had not gone away.

Hanson's afternoon went quickly, with one client who was stable and transitioning out of services, and another client who insisted he had been clean and sober for weeks, but his UA was positive for opiates. After initially claiming he had had two loaves of poppy seed bread, he reluctantly admitted he had relapsed on Vicodin. Hanson balanced confrontation with support and they agreed that the client would be coming to more groups, and providing random UAs a couple times a week. During the session they focused on identifying his relapse triggers, and what he could do to avoid them.

Hanson's session with Mariah Finn began with her breathlessly excited. "I saw you on TV the other night. You're a hero."

"Thanks. What has been going on for you?'

"What was it like up there, with all eyes on you? Were you scared?'

"Sure."

"So you were scared but you did it anyway. That's even more brave."

"Is there something that scares you, Mariah? Something you'd like to tackle talking about?"

"You don't want to talk about what you did?"

"Not really. This is your time, not mine."

"You're always so caring about me."

"Mariah, it's my job." Hanson spoke gently to cushion the harsh words. "I'm here to support you in making the changes you want to make."

"Do you care about me?"

"Yes. Professionally, not like a friend."

"Or a lover?" She tilted her head and smiled seductively.

"Right."

"You're so cute when you're determined to be professional. Okay. Maybe I will talk about my family. That's what you'd like to hear about, right?"

"If that would be helpful for you."

She talked about the older brother she was jealous of, and the younger brother she was sorry for. But she felt her younger brother had gotten an unfair amount of attention from her parents and repressed anger colored her descriptions. Hanson decided to confront her feelings in a future appointment.

The day ended with Brian getting a disturbing tip. One of the other counselors heard from a friend who worked at a domestic violence shelter that Charlene King had disappeared. She had taken her belongings, with no indications of foul play or force. Hanson was pretty sure he knew who she was with.

10

AFTER PICKING UP A few dishes at a Hunan restaurant on Hawthorne Boulevard, he stopped at a florist and got a small bouquet of roses. He forced thoughts of Charlene King from his mind. Louise would need him to be upbeat.

She greeted him at the door with a hug and a "thanks for coming." She gave him a peck on the cheek, took the flowers, then set them in a crystal vase. Clyde peered from his perch on the window ledge with his usual disdainful greeting, his tail flicking nervously from side to side. He would occasionally deign to have Hanson rub his back, which Louise said was more than he allowed most visitors.

The table was set and they moved to her small dining room, just off the entrance. She had brightly colored aquamarine Fiesta plates and a tablecloth with a Southwest theme. "Freshly unpacked," she said, gesturing at the setting.

"Very nice."

She set the vase of roses down in the middle of the table. "The perfect finishing touch."

"I haven't eaten all day," she said, after they finished the hot and sour soup, ma po bean curd, and four flavor scallops. "Uhhhhh, that was delicious."

"I guess I should be heading home."

"I'd like it if you'd stay. Coffee? Tea?"

"Peppermint tea would be great."

He followed her into the modest kitchen as she put up a kettle of water. He leaned against the tiled counters. The kitchen hadn't been updated in twenty years and looked unused. He suspected most of her meals were take-out.

When the tea was ready, she poured him a cup, and herself a mug of Taster's Choice coffee.

"You know, you can get run out of the Northwest for drinking that stuff," he said, indicating the instant coffee.

"This actually violates my church's rules. The body as a sacred temple."

"I suppose being a forbidden fruit makes even instant palatable," he said with a smile. "Anything else exciting going on?"

She shrugged. "I've had better times."

"Care to talk?"

"I wish I could. One of the questions I'll be asked under oath is if I've discussed the incident with anyone. If I name you, that means you get subpoenaed. Appearing before a federal grand jury isn't fun."

"I'll take the risk."

She reached over and held his hand. "Not now."

"Whenever you're ready," he said.

"Soon." She leaned over and kissed him chastely. They sat at the table and sipped their drinks. "Let's get back to talking about the existence of evil."

They had discussed good versus evil, the meaning of life, was there a soul, what happened after death. Their intense conversations sometimes went late into the night, as animated as a college dorm discussion. They debated the rivalry between religion and therapy and which could truly transform lives for the better. He was averse to trappings and traditions, relishing Unitarianism and Zen Buddhism. She preferred the more structured and straightforward beliefs of the Church of Latter Day Saints.

"I believe in evil," he said. "I've seen its aftermath countless times."

"But as a therapist don't you believe everyone is redeemable? Can a truly evil person be redeemed?"

"Redemption is a religious term. Rehabilitation is sometimes possible. Usually not with psychopaths."

"I've read Hare's work," she responded. "They're a mix of narcissism and antisocial. Charming and dangerous."

"Without empathy. People exist solely to be used."

"So empathy is what makes us human?"

"Part of what makes us more than animals. Now, what about you? What about redemption in your view?"

"Prayer. Faith in Our Lord, Jesus Christ."

"Our Lord or your Lord? Can non-Mormons be redeemed?"

"If they recognize the teachings of Joseph Smith and follow the faith. It's more complicated. There's actually six different possibilities. Outer darkness, for Satan and the truly wicked. Then the telestial, the terrestrial, and the celestial. There are subdivisions within celestial, which is most like other Christian ideas of heaven. I'd be happy to get you some literature explaining it in detail."

"Ultimately, there's no redemption without conversion."

"You make it sound wrong. But if you knew the right way, and offered it willingly to people, and they chose not to follow it, what would you say?"

"That whatever force runs the universe has blessed us with free will."

"So that we may make the right choice."

"I prefer the Buddhist idea that people seeking wisdom, or looking for the moon, sometimes mistake the finger pointing at the moon for the moon itself."

And so their conversation went until he glanced at his watch and said, "I better be going."

"I'm talked out," she said.

"I never thought that could happen."

She slapped him playfully on the shoulder.

He said, "And the federal agent doth smite the unbeliever, and so it shall be written."

"No more talk. You know what I could really use?"

"A copy of the Kabalah?"

"You're looking to get smited again. My neck is so tense. Could I get a rub?"

He stepped behind her chair, then gently began kneading. He could feel the knotted muscles, from under her jaw down to her shoulders. After a couple of minutes, she gave a contented groan. It was close enough to a sexual sound that he felt a throbbing in his groin.

"Sooooo nice," she purred.

He was debating whether he should lean over and try a kiss when she suddenly said, "Darn!"

"What's the matter?"

"I just realized that of course the videos and my purse being stolen were connected. He used my credit card to pay for the videos." She stood up. "I mean, I thought the perp could've gotten my credit card number by going through garbage or an Internet scam. But I never buy anything over the Internet. Never give out my social security number. Never give confidential info over the telephone." She sat back down and he resumed rubbing but her muscles were tighter than ever.

Brian asked, "Would you like to stay at my place for a while? You can have the bedroom. I've got a comfortable couch I can use."

"Thanks, but I'm not running due to some creep's sense of humor. I've had threats before."

"Like this?"

"No. Usually just a suspect showing off."

"This person was willing to get close enough to swipe your wallet. And he knows where you live," he said. "Do you think the harassment is connected with the raid?"

"It's too subtle for these white supremacists. They're much more brick-through-the-window types. And I think they would have included something like *Mississippi Burning* or *The Klansman* if they were trying to send a message."

"Stalkers have a weird dynamic, gifts meant to ingratiate and intimidate. It starts with this harassment type stuff and frequently escalates."

"You've worked with many stalkers?"

"A few."

"Jail time is the best treatment."

"Depends on the type. You've got ones motivated by rejection, or seeking intimacy, or completely socially inept, jealous of someone else's success, and the real ugly types, the predators."

"Like the serial killer who follows his victim for a while, getting off on the power of knowing what is coming."

"Right. Fortunately, they're the smallest group," Hanson said. "Can you get a photo of this Beil guy?"

"That shouldn't be hard."

"I'd feel better if you got copies and really memorized it. I assume he's going to disguise himself. Maybe give copies to your neighbors."

"That's a nice way to get welcomed into the neighborhood," she said with a snort. "I'm okay. And if this person wanted to hurt me, like you said, they were close enough to take my wallet, they could've done it then."

"Not in a crowded church," Hanson said.

"It could be anyone," she said. "A fixated loser I don't even know. I've been going through mental checklists, wondering about the clerk at the 7-Eleven who seemed to linger over my ID. Or the pump jockey at the gas station who was looking into my car too long. Or defendants I had who seemed to take it personally and made threats. Or other people in my life." She was silent, like she'd said too much.

"Do you mean me?"

"I don't think it's you, Brian."

"But the thought has to have crossed your mind. My beating up the sailor, my past problems, I could understand you wondering."

"I trust you."

He leaned over, tenderly holding her face in his hands, and stared into her eyes. "I am not involved in any of the harassment." He kissed her. "I would never do that."

"I believe you."

They sat on the couch. Clyde jumped on her lap and she stroked him. He looked at Hanson through hooded eyes.

"He looks smug," the counselor said.

"He lives well. Probably not enough tuna to suit him, but nothing to contact the humane society about." She petted Clyde without saying anything for a couple of moments. "There's something we need to talk about."

"The incident at the Fun Center?"

She nodded. "It scared me. And I don't mean that drunken sailor. What would have happened if I hadn't yelled?"

"I don't know what it was about the parade that set me off." He reached out and took her hand. "I'm not using PTSD as an excuse. There is no excuse. It bothers me, too."

"I care about you. And if I feel that I'm with someone who's going to blow up, well, I don't want to go there."

"I understand."

"Is something else going on for you?" she asked.

He shrugged, debated how much to tell her, then said, "A domestic violence client checked out of the shelter and I suspect went back to her abusive boyfriend."

"Doesn't that happen a lot?"

"All the time. It's a major cause of burnout for people who work exclusively with DV clients."

She reached over and squeezed his hand. "I know that's not who you really are when you're so violent."

"I'm supposed to be here reassuring you."

"I'm okay. I appreciate your coming over. And I appreciate that you've never put the moves on me."

"I can't say I haven't thought about it. If I was in my twenties, I would've been humping your leg on our first night out." He consciously avoided the word "date."

"There's an attractive image."

"With age has come wisdom. Restraint. And less hormones."

"Whatever the cause. I'm glad. For now."

"I better get going before I lose my restraint."

She walked him to the door. As he stepped out on the porch, she said, "I find you attractive, too." She leaned in and they kissed, her lips opening just enough for him to sense the possibilities. Then she stepped back and shut the door.

Walking to his car, Hanson felt like he had when he was fifteen and had gone out on his first real date. He'd kissed Jenny Miller and been high on life for hours afterward. His chaste relationship with Louise was hard to understand. He'd had numerous one-night stands when he was active in his addiction. Most of them didn't even last a night. Wham, bam, thank you, ma'am. Or pass out. And even right after his divorce, he'd had a few quick relationships that were an unsuccessful attempt to paint over his hurt. The kind of relationships therapists and AA warned against. At least he hadn't relapsed.

This was different, like enjoying the meal slowly with anticipation of a great dessert. Even though he felt like a dorky teen.

By the time he reached his black Subaru Forester, the pleasure faded. He peered around at other parked cars, at the hedges, in the darkened driveways. No one was in sight, but he was not reassured.

Someone hateful was after Louise.

11

A T WORK THE NEXT day, Hanson had to force himself not to call her multiple times. He knew his support was appreciated, but if he wasn't careful, it could be intrusive.

Moose was his first client and the session followed the usual pattern with Brown loudly complaining about some outside encounter. This time, he had gotten in an argument with a TriMet bus driver who had insisted he hadn't paid full fare. The driver was about to call police when Moose slammed the extra coins into the box.

"I shoulda popped that motherfucker right when he was driving. Treating me like shit just because he's got a job."

"You're a smart man, Moose."

"What d'you mean?"

"How much did he beat you for?"

"Like a buck-fifty."

"And if the cops had come?"

"I would've taught those fuckers a lesson."

"Can we agree that eventually they would've won even if they had to mobilize half the Police Bureau?"

"Yeah. So?"

"This shows how smart you've gotten. In the old days you would've fought to the death over what? A buck-fifty? Is that how much your freedom is worth?"

"It ain't that. It's about respect. You let people dis you, you ain't nothing but a bitch."

"Sitting here right now, without any of the injuries you would've gotten in a fight, without the time in a jail cell, without another arrest on your record, do you think you made the right decision?"

After a long silence, Moose nodded.

"That's why I say keep up the good work."

The rest of the session was spent discussing time-outs, relaxation techniques, and getting Moose to see that a lot of what he perceived as a threat or a deliberate slight was lack of awareness by others.

His next client was Louie Parker, Louise's uncle and namesake. He was well into his seventies, but still had the bouncy bantamweight energy of the boxer he had once been. He had been a political fixer in Portland, snared in a conspiracy to rig construction bids. The people he had been protecting had sworn to take care of him. They hadn't. He had been too proud to take help from his family and resistant to any social services. By the time he'd come into treatment with Hanson's agency, he was close to requiring hospitalization. Initially diagnosed with severe chronic major depression, he had gotten better over time. Hanson kept him on his caseload for monitoring and, though he'd never admit it to the hardnosed Utilization Management auditors, he enjoyed Louie's war stories.

But Louie was in a somber mood. "I'm worried about Louise-y."

"Louie, I'm in a funny spot here. You know I'm friendly with Louise. I'm not sure what I can say. I'm your counselor and Louise's friend, which makes it complicated."

"I wish you were more than her friend. What's with you two anyway?"

"Tell me what's bothering you about Louise?"

"I don't like what's happened to her. She's getting a bum rap from the FBI. I know how the feds work, it's find a scapegoat and don't care who it is." Parker hesitated. "I'm worried. You know depression runs in the family."

"I can understand your concern, but I think she's doing okay. I can tell you that, since she's not my client. But it still feels a little funny."

"You'll keep an eye on her. Take care of her."

"Yes."

"Good. I'm not going to be around forever. The idea of death don't scare me much anymore. There's lots of days when I feel like saying, 'Let's get this over with.' "

"Are you feeling philosophical or suicidal?"

"Just fed up with aches and pains. And I miss the guys who've passed on. And I'm curious about what the next stage is all about. But I worry about Louise-y. I'd like to know that there was someone taking care of her."

Hanson nodded.

Louie could tell the counselor wasn't going to respond further, so he said, "You know, I actually know that creep Arnie Beil?"

"What?"

"Haven't seen him in like thirty years. He was a kid then. His father was a small-time gangster here who got snagged when Bobby Kennedy had hearings on organized crime."

"What was Beil like as a kid?'

"A mean little cuss. The kind of kid you'd never trust around a younger kid. I remember little Arnie staring at me one time. He couldn't have been more than ten, but there was something missing. You ever go to an aquarium with sharks and see them looking at you through the glass? That's what it was like."

Hanson questioned him, knowing that it was investigating more than counseling but there was nothing Parker knew that could help track Beil.

He finished the session, did a quick chart note that made the session sound more therapeutic than it had been, then checked voice mail.

"This is Judy Orem, I'm the charge nurse at Three-G at Providence Portland medical center." Hanson thought for a moment—he was used to calls from hospital psych wards—Three-G wasn't a psych floor. "I'm faxing over a release. One of your clients is here and wants me to talk with you," she said, giving a phone number.

Hanson retrieved the signed release, called back, and got Orem. "Charlene has asked that you be notified and see if you can get her safe housing."

"Is she okay?"

"She's in stable condition. She told us it was a car accident, but I used to be a trauma nurse. This was no car accident. Someone beat her up."

"Her kids?"

"Apparently she has an aunt took them before it happened."

"Can I talk with her?"

"She's sedated right now. I'll let her know we spoke. We'll keep her here a day or so."

"Thanks."

"I've been trying to talk with her," Orem said. "I had an abusive boyfriend once, too. I know how hard it is to leave."

"Anything you can do for her is appreciated."

"Well, maybe by you. She's not interested in hearing it."

Four miles in from the trailhead, and a few hundred yards off the trail in the Gifford Pinchot National Forest, the couple was enjoying their time alone in the woods. Their bright green Gore-Tex tent was set up in a clearing, surrounded by towering Douglas firs and red alders. A small creek babbled and burbled a stone's throw from the clearing. Deer and elk had come by to drink. It was getting dark and the couple had already eaten dinner. They rinsed their utensils in the creek and stowed the remaining food in a bag. The man took the bag and walked fifty feet from the site. He tied it up in a tree, aware of the danger of attracting bears. He returned to his girlfriend and they began making out. When it was dark, they would make love again under a sky boldly speckled with stars.

They had no idea they were being watched. Arnold Beil was fifty feet away, crouched down by a tree, a few small fallen branches on top of him. Unless someone looked carefully, he was invisible. He had been watching the couple since early afternoon.

He guessed it would be another half hour until it was dark enough for him to move. He stretched and settled into a comfortable position. He had trained to be a sniper in the Marine Corps, the M40A1 his best friend. Nearly fifteen pounds of stark beautiful death. With a $10 \times$ scope, accurate at a thousand yards in the right hands. The 7.62 mm slug leaving the barrel at 2,550 feet per second. So sweet, that little kick it gave. Then the sudden red mist of a clean head shot. Body dropping as if he were God throwing a thunderbolt. He had ten confirmed kills in Lebanon.

He had enlisted as a marine even though he hated the U.S. government. He had seen what they did to his father and other upstanding men. His father had been beaten down and quick to take his anger out on young Arnie. By the time he was fifteen, he had decided he wanted to go into the military. Where else could he get the education he needed? Even at that young age, he could plan ahead. Think strategy as much as tactics. His father had already died of a heart attack and his mother was overwhelmed by his misdeeds in high school and eager for him to see "healthy male role models."

If only she knew.

After five years, he got tired of doing the dirty work for the Jews, tired of having to share living space with niggers, wetbacks, gooks. Not that there weren't good white men in the marines. Some of them taught him about true white pride and helped him out in recent years when he'd been underground.

Out of the service, with a dishonorable discharge because he'd refused to put up with an order from a colored sergeant, he held a few low-paying jobs. Then he got in with three cranksters who robbed banks. But they weren't just bank robbers—they were following the noble outlaw tradition of Jesse James, John Dillinger, Robin Hood. Even George Washington and the patriots who rebelled against the British tyrants. The Founding Fathers stated it was the moral duty of citizens to fight oppression.

And Beil was willing to pay the price. He'd done hard time at Leavenworth and Marion. He'd been beaten, tear gassed, and shot by federal goons. He'd seen friends die. The only things that kept him alive were luck, the stupidity of the federal thugs, and God, who wanted him to act as an agent of purification.

He watched the couple, starting to make out, and thought about Roxie, the woman killed in the FBI raid on Heaven's place. Beil resented that something he liked was taken away from him. Roxie was a wild girl, not too bright, but willing to do anything for him. She'd help him steal credit cards and drivers' licenses by turning tricks, even though she wasn't a prostitute. She'd distracted a guard while he stole two thousand dollars from a small bank. And she never said no to partying. He missed her and added his feeling of loss to the long list of grievances against the feds.

During the raid, he had swiftly dug a trench a few inches deep and hunkered down. The feds had walked within inches of him and he'd debated whether he should kill more. He who fights and runs away, ultimately was his decision.

But he memorized the face of that cunt who had been leading the assault. Louise Parker, they'd said on TV. He'd seen her dive out of the van, looking like her ass was on fire. He'd make sure she would never betray the white people again and commit crimes against freedom fighters. A message to FBI agents who had become protectors of the mud people, race traitors who had been fooled by Satan and his Jewish minions.

He knew he was doing the right thing. If what he was doing was wrong, God would have stopped him anytime He wanted to. Instead, the Good Lord provided for him.

Like the couple who had taken their air mattress out of the tent, and were going at it under the open sky. He would take what he wanted.

Beil had been living on berries and the meat of a rabbit he had snared the day before. Now that it was dark, he moved to where the man had stashed the food bag. Using his pocket knife, he made rough slashes so it looked like an animal had clawed the food bag open. He took energy bars, beef jerky, and apples. The couple would be angry, and excited, that some large and powerful animal had attacked their bag. A cougar? A bear? A great story to tell their friends.

They had no idea how dangerous an animal had really been sniffing around.

12

THE LOUD KNOCK AT her door made Louise jump. It wasn't Brian, he'd always call.

Another prank pizza? She took the time to grab her Glock from the closet before going to the front door and peering through the peephole.

Two men in suits—one Caucasian, the other Asian—were waiting on her front porch. The Caucasian male was short and stout, the Asian tall and thin.

"Yes?" she asked, standing slightly off to one side, so if one of them suddenly fired, they'd have less of a chance of hitting her.

The tall Asian produced an FBI badge and ID. "Special Agent Wong, Ms. Parker. This is Special Agent Wilson. We're here from the Office of Professional Responsibility."

She opened the door, holding the gun casually at her side, out of their view. OPR was the FBI equivalent of police internal affairs, investigating allegations of serious misconduct or criminal behavior by FBI agents. The division's size and power had grown significantly when then director Louis Freeh had instituted the "bright line policy," increasing penalties for lying under oath, falsifying documents to make a case, theft of government property, and even padding expense reports.

"You're here about my stolen badge?" she asked.

"No. Though that's serious enough," Wilson said. "May we come in?"

She waved for them to enter.

"Please put the firearm away," Wong said.

She retrieved her black leather Bianchi holster from the closet, tucked the gun in, and then put the holster on. More for symbolic value than protection. She was one of them and they shouldn't forget it.

The agents walked into her small living room. One sat on the couch, the other in a wingback chair a half dozen feet away. An interrogation strategy—the subject would be swiveling her head back and forth as questions were fired at her, like a spectator at a vigorous game of tennis. The problem with questioning someone from law enforcement was she knew the same strategies. The advantage was that most law enforcement agents caught in criminal activity felt guilty and were relieved to be caught.

Her mind racing, she stood so she could be looking down on them. "Yes?" Was there anything else she had done that was improper? Maybe a suspect had alleged she had violated his rights? That kind of thing happened all the time. The vast majority of the allegations were a nuisance maneuver by smart criminals and their attorneys.

"Would you like to sit down?" Wong asked.

"No, thank you."

"We've received word about your account in the Grand Cayman Islands," Wilson snapped at her.

"What?"

"We have the specific account number and a copy of your e-mail making inquiries about it," Wilson continued.

"That's ridiculous."

"I'm sure there's some explanation," Wong said.

Their clumsy good cop–bad cop roles were painfully evident.

"There's no explanation because I don't have an offshore account," she responded. "Who said I do?"

"The source of our information is confidential," Wilson said. "It came with a tip to look at your work on the DeFiore case."

"I was peripherally involved in that one. It was mainly a DEA case."

"Let's go through it slowly," Wong suggested.

"I was assigned to the joint task force. They needed assistance with electronic surveillance warrants. And I participated in the raid on his girlfriend's apartment." Why that case? Why the allegation? Louise's mind had the peculiar feeling of being both sluggish—hard to concentrate—and speeding—with facts and details stumbling over each other.

Wilson stared at her dispassionately, like a scientist studying an interesting bug. Wong was trying to look compassionately concerned.

"There was money in her apartment?" Wong prompted.

"Roughly one point one million dollars. That was a high publicity case. And I was mentioned in the media as being involved." She tried not to sound too defensive.

"Funny you should know the exact amount." Wilson said accusingly.

"I helped voucher it."

"Are you sure it wasn't two million?" Wong asked.

"Positive."

"What about your allegedly missing badge?" Wilson asked.

"I filed the report. I left my bag next to me on the pew. I'm pretty sure that's where it happened. I'm usually very aware of my ID case and my credit cards, of course." Her anger and uncertainty over the false allegation of stealing money was replaced by guilt. It was her fault that her identification was stolen. "I don't know how it happened. I guess I lowered my guard and left it on the pew. It was church. There were other agents there."

"Are you saying one of them took your ID?" Wilson asked snidely.

"No. That I felt safe there."

"That's understandable," Wong said. "Now about the raid on Jebediah Heaven's property, at what point did you decide it was permissible to use lethal force?"

"I followed the MAOP," she said, referring to the FBI's Manual of Administrative and Operational Procedures. "I never gave the order to make contact. We were fired upon and agents made the field decision to respond accordingly."

"I see," Wilson said. "You bought this house about two months after the money disappeared from DeFiore's girlfriend's apartment. How do you explain that?"

And so it went, with the agents snapping questions at her about the money, the badge, and the raid. Every now and then they tried a new tack, bringing up an anonymous brutality claim that had been filed against her, or money donated in her name to a known Islamic terrorist group. She was off balance and sputtering several times. They asked many questions where she had to respond, "I don't know," making her feel more defensive. Several times, she wondered if she should lawyer up and refuse to answer any more questions. She knew it was naïve to expect to convince them of her innocence, but the idealistic part of her believed that by telling the truth, she could make her case.

She told them about the pizza and DVD deliveries.

"You're claiming a conspiracy?" Wilson asked.

"Not a conspiracy, but certainly harassment."

"Pizza delivery and free DVDs. Sounds like the work of Al Qaida," Wilson said.

"Have you filed a report on it?" Wong asked.

"Not yet."

Wilson snorted. "Let's not get side-tracked from the main issue here." And he resumed his accusatory questioning.

Two hours after they arrived, Wilson said, "That's all. For now."

Wong nodded. "Thanks for your cooperation."

"Do I have a choice?' Louise asked.

"We all have choices, Ms. Parker," Wilson said. "Some people just make bad ones. You are officially on paid administrative leave pending the outcome of the investigation."

"I can't do some sort of restricted duty?"

Wong shook his head. "It's the official policy."

"At least you've got a bunch of DVDs you can watch," Wilson said with a smirk as they walked out.

"Charlene King is going to be discharged today," Hanson told Betty Pearlman.

The clinical director nodded. "Let me guess, you want to go to the hospital and make sure she gets to the shelter safely?"

Hanson nodded. He was more of a counselor than a case manager but the roles often blurred when dealing with people in extreme situations. It was hard to do therapy when someone was worrying about their safety, or where they were going to live, or if there would be food for the next meal.

"You know it's outside usual policies and procedures," Betty said.

"That's why I'm talking with you about it."

"Cover your ass if it goes wrong?'

"I thought of it more as seeking out your wisdom."

"Nice save. Okay, what's your clinical rationale?"

"She's at a vulnerable point. I think there's a chance she can make the separation from her batterer this time. I had a brief conversation with her this morning by phone. She's got more insight than I've ever heard."

Pearlman sat behind her desk, twiddling with a pen that said "Zoloft" on it. "What about your desire to play the knight in shining armor?"

"Are you saying that's a bad thing? Tell you what, I'll do an extra intake if you let me put on my armor."

She made a gesture toward his shoulder with her pen, as if she was a queen knighting him. "Watch out for dragons."

Hanson drove to the hospital, mulling over the best way to help King. He favored a motivational interviewing approach, which theorized people moved through five stages of change. Precontemplation, or clueless that there was a problem. "It's not his fault, I left the silverware dirty and he had a hard day at work. It's okay he hit me." Contemplation, where there was acknowledgement of a problem, but the belief it was not important or not changeable. "He didn't really hurt me, it was just a slap. It's who he is, and I love him." Plan, when the client actually begins to think about what they can do. "I could go to a shelter." Action, where the client actually does it. And Maintenance, where the gains made are continued. Relapse, unfortunately, is a natural part of the process. Whether the problem was addiction, mental illness, or domestic violence.

He was confident Charlene King was past precontemplation. But was she ready for action?

Hanson identified himself at the nurse's station, noticing a hospital security guard hovering in the background. After he showed ID, a gray-haired nurse with bright blue eyes explained, "Charlene indicated that the guy who did this to her knows she's here. He's made a few attempts to contact her. Apparently he's trying to convince her not to press charges."

"Has he threatened her?"

"You're hoping to add additional charges," she said.

He nodded.

"So far, he's still relying on his charm. I don't expect that will last very long."

The counselor nodded again.

"I'm not used to seeing men as escorts. Usually it's a couple of tough women."

"I'm really a very ugly woman."

"I don't think so," the nurse said. "Anyway, she's ready to go."

Brian had to mask his reaction when he saw how badly Charlene had been battered. He helped her to the elevator and they rode down to the lobby.

"Are you going to say 'I told you so'?" she asked.

"Nope. Like we discussed, it's part of the process. I hope you make a better decision now."

"I learned my lesson. Ron and I are done."

As they walked toward Hanson's car, his hypervigilance kicked over. He wanted to walk quickly but King was post-hospital slow.

They were fifteen feet from his car when swaggering, greasy-ponytailed Ron Harkins stepped in front of them. "Honey, how are you?" he asked King.

"I don't want to talk," Charlene said. "Leave me alone."

"C'mon, sugar. I lost my temper. I'm sorry. I promise it won't happen again."

Hanson's senses hummed, higher order thinking shutting down. Charlene's battered face and all she had told him about her past abuse flooded Hanson's brain. Adrenaline-saturated blood pumped into his arms and legs. "The lady doesn't want to talk."

"Listen, asshole, mind your own business," Harkins said.

"I'm asking you nicely to leave," Hanson said through gritted teeth. "You'll have your day in court."

"This ain't going to court. I've got too many other beefs. They're going to nail me." He turned back to Charlene. "You got to drop the charges."

"Let's go, Charlene," Brian said, putting his arm gently across her shoulder and guiding her forward.

Harkins stepped directly in front of Brian. "Get your hands off my girl."

The counselor did as ordered. Harkins didn't notice how Brian shifted his feet into a more defensive stance. The counselor's hands were up in front, palms gesturing downward, as if he was making a placating gesture.

Ron was clearly a better bully than a street fighter. He threw a messily telegraphed left jab that Hanson caught on his right shoulder. The follow up right cross Hanson evaded, though the first grazed the counselor's cheek. The blows had hurt, but Hanson guessed they were Ron's hope for a quick and easy knockout.

Pivoting from his hips, Brian rocked Harkins backward with a left-handed palm heel strike square on his bearded chin. Hanson followed up with a solid punch in Ron's ample belly, folding him forward. Hanson grabbed him, pulling his head downward and simultaneously raising his knee. There was a squishy sound as Ron's nose shattered against Hanson's leg. Brian continued to pull on Harkins's head, and threw him face down to the floor. He kicked him hard in the ribs.

Hanson was drawing back his foot to kick again when King screamed, "You're hurting him."

She dropped to her knees, and used her fingers to wipe blood from Ron's face. "Are you okay?"

"This is your fault," Harkins said. "See what you did to me?"

Brian was breathing deeply, chest heaving as he struggled to regain control. "The only one responsible for this is him. Let's go."

He took Charlene's shoulder, almost too roughly, and led her to the car. He fumbled with the keys, hands shaking, and let her in.

They said nothing on the ride to the shelter.

Beil awoke in the middle of the night. The stars were wondrous as he stretched and rose from beneath the branches. He felt like a powerful forest beast and he wanted to give a wolfish howl. But he resisted the urge and crept up to the campsite where the happy couple slept.

Lit by the dim starlight filtering through the thin tent material, the woman didn't look half bad. But he was disciplined enough to know that while he could get away with petty crimes, a rape or assault would call attention to the area. He had a more important mission than getting his rocks off on a couple of granola-eating dimwits.

He contented himself with stealing the man's wallet, the fifty dollars the woman had in her backpack, and the car keys. He moved quickly to the trailhead, where he found their Kia Sportage.

It was time to head to Portland.

13

L OUISE PARKER HAD GOTTEN a fitful night's sleep, awakened twice by phone calls. No voice on the other end, just a funeral dirge. She'd tried star 69 but the calls had been blocked. After the second time she'd taken the phone off the hook.

In the quiet of the night, she ruminated on who it could be. She had never realized how quickly her life could be so disrupted, the fragility of her achievements: her career; her relationships; her identity. The idea that the bureau was so quick to turn on her was most painful. She could understand it from a bureaucratic, cover your rear approach, which was what she expected of her boss. But the calls from her colleagues had begun to dwindle. And several had hinted at "where there's smoke there's fire" thinking, the excessively suspicious nature of anyone in law enforcement. The world divided up between insiders and outsiders. And she was becoming an outsider.

Starting early in the morning, she tried to distract herself by working in the garden. The gate to her backyard was open, though she was pretty sure she had latched it. She moved cautiously, holding a cultivator like a weapon, but saw nothing more out of the ordinary. Maybe the meter reader had left it unlatched? Or perhaps Wilson and Wong had decided to inspect the rear of her house? She'd have to buy a hasp and lock.

Clyde, who was not generally an outdoor cat, joined her. He perched on her picnic table and watched like a sheriff keeping an eye on a county jail work crew.

She had three small Japanese maple trees still bagged in burlap. She dug two-foot-deep holes, packed in several inches of compost, and soaked them down. Then she cut the burlap bags that covered the root balls and lowered them into their respective holes. She put in more compost, then earth, then wet it down again, staying focused on her task. By the time she was done she had a light sheen of sweat and a satisfied glow. Putting in a tree was an event, knowing that most likely it would be above ground living when she was below the earth.

The FedEx truck pulled up, with a different delivery man. He seemed wary, as if the other driver had warned him about the volatile woman.

She said nothing, but began tearing the Movie Maven package open before the delivery man had made it back to his truck. *Fear,* where sociopath Mark Wahlberg stalks Reese Witherspoon; *Fatal Attraction,* where Michael Douglas's fling with Glenn Close leads her to torment him; and *Play Misty for Me,* where DJ Clint Eastwood is stalked by psychotic fan Jessica Walter. The message inside said, "Enjoy your time off, Jerry Sullivan." The Special Agent in Charge of the office. Did her harasser think she was so stupid that she'd call her boss and seem even more incompetent? Could it be Wilson's idea of a joke, or to put more stress on her to see what happened?

She called Movie Maven and after twenty minutes bouncing around voice mail purgatory, found out the videos had been paid for through an untraceable PayPal account.

Near tears, she called Brian and got his voice mail.

Arnold Beil knew how to survive as a fugitive. Assume every phone was bugged, every friendly stranger, and even those who weren't strangers, were snitches. The price of carelessness was death or prison. It wasn't fair that the authorities could blunder along, making mistake after mistake, and they'd do fine. He only had to make one error and the chase would be over.

While the Marine Corps had taught him world-class combat skills, it was his comrades in the white supremacy movement who had taught him how to live as an outlaw. From Mojo, a meth cook and identity master thief in Flagstaff, he'd learned how to establish a new identity with a fake driver's license. From Peewee, an ex-con and grifter in Pittsburg, Kansas, he'd learned basic door jimmying and car theft. From Debbie in Las Vegas, he'd learned how to put on makeup and a wig. He might've still been with her if the ZOG pigs hadn't swooped down. She was doing time now for tax evasion, based on unreported prostitution income. Government harassment for someone known to assist freedom fighters.

He had a little over the fifty dollars he had taken from the camping couple and figured he had at least a day before the credit cards were reported stolen. He stopped at a thrift shop and bought a Seattle Seahawks baseball cap, four cheap shirts, a wig, and a loose-fitting dungaree jacket. Later, he'd get to Coeur d'Alene, retrieve his stash with fake passport and five thousand dollars in cash from a long-ago bank robbery. Then up to the Idaho panhandle, into Canada, maybe Australia, where he heard they didn't even let coloreds in.

He still had the .32 Beretta Tomcat he had taken right before the raid. There were only two rounds left in it. He was carrying the gun in the small of his back. Several times it had slipped and nearly fallen out. He also had had to ditch the M16. Not exactly something he could carry down Main Street. Besides, it was a shot from that gun that had killed the FBI agent. No point in making it easier for prosecutors.

Mojo had taught him about going to a graveyard, finding the tombstone of a baby that had died around the time he was born, then going to the local Bureau of Records and getting a duplicate birth certificate. It was more difficult in the age of computers and cross checking post 9/11. Then there was the easy way.

He stopped at the Fred Meyer supermarket in North Portland and bought a large screwdriver, disposable dust masks, a three-inch pocket knife, black Glad trash bags, road flares, black electrical tape, wire, and eight-by-eleven-inch sheets of clear plastic laminate. He stocked up on food that didn't need refrigeration or cooking. Bread, peanut butter, jelly, pretzels, energy bars, energy drinks. A case of Heineken. Sleeping bag and a small battery-operated fluorescent lantern, a pocket-sized Maglite, and a garden trowel. Two cans of charcoal fire starter and several boxes of wooden matches. He kept his cap pulled down low on his head, keeping his face largely hidden from the ubiquitous video cameras, one of the basic rules of living off the grid. The video cameras all over Oklahoma City, frozen by the shock wave of the explosion, had helped nail Timothy McVeigh. Despite their resources, the feds had never gotten John Doe Number Two. Just the way they'd never caught the anthrax mailer.

At an amusement arcade in Northeast, he took four pictures in a photo booth. He drove to Peninsula Park, found a deserted picnic bench, and took out the Washington State license he had stolen from the camper. The guy's name was Paul Rankin. Unfortunately, he was five years younger, an inch taller, and fifteen pounds lighter than Beil. But few people ever read the physical description. Beil used the blade to carefully slice the picture and replace it with his photo from the arcade. He repeated the name Paul Rankin a few dozen times, as well as the address in Camas.

He found a deserted part of the park where few cars were parked. He parked his own car on the end, and crawled over to a Honda Civic. He stole the front license plate only. He'd change plates again that night. It was too risky during the day—but it was riskier to drive around a car with hot plates. Of course, with any luck, the happy campers were still deep in the woods, not even noticing that they'd lost their wallet and car keys.

Sitting at her desk at home, wearing the clothes she'd slept in, Louise began assembling a list of people who might be harassing her. People from her personal life, like Brian; people from her career, mainly criminals, especially white supremacist sympathizers but possibly even fellow agents; people peripherally in her life who seemed odd, like the cashier at the grocery store who studied every item she bought. She had stopped shopping there, but maybe he didn't want to end their "relationship."

She started with a list of three dozen names of people she had arrested within the past five years. On some cases, she was not the arresting agent but was significant enough in the investigation that a malevolent defendant might single her out. She'd called friends at various task forces and agencies, tracking down the whereabouts of those she'd arrested and their associates. FBI, ATF, Secret Service, U.S. Marshals Service, Bureau of Prisons, federal probation, local police in six different jurisdictions. Although she was officially suspended, not everyone knew it, and some who did didn't care. The officers and investigators she contacted were helpful but had no real leads. Several of the defendants were dead, casualties of drug deals or armed robberies gone bad, driving recklessly, health problems, and domestic violence. The majority were still in prison and didn't have significant networks to arrange the harassment.

Vic, Louise's cube mate from one pod away, had already done research. He was his usual cautious, cryptic self on the phone, but his message was clear—there were no obvious suspects among her FBI caseload. She momentarily suspected that perhaps Vic could be behind it, but ruled him out. As much as she could rule out anyone.

She had not taken countersurveillance measures on leaving the office. No varying routes, doubling back, checking mirrors, speeding through yellow lights. She had allowed herself to settle into a routine. Anyone could have followed her.

Several times, when friends called to reassure her and offer to stop by, she felt herself about to cry. She insisted she was doing fine, though she doubted anyone believed her. No one pushed too hard to visit and deep down she felt she was an outcast.

A few women from a cyber terrorism task force insisted that she join them that evening for drinks. They were at a bar just off SE Division, only a half mile from her house. They vowed to drag her out of the house in handcuffs if she didn't voluntarily come for at least one drink. They had dubbed themselves the Dirty Half Dozen, and met a couple times a month, to gossip, discuss which movie star they'd most like to arrest, and which one they'd like most on a long stakeout. Maybe she could brainstorm and get additional leads for her investigation.

Could one of them be behind her troubles? Sometimes they'd seemed jealous of her success. And who would know better how to get away with a crime than a law enforcer? She convinced herself that she had to face them, had to stop questioning everyone in her life. And even if one of them was the perpetrator, the best way to find out would be to watch her. Keep your friends close and your enemies closer.

Louise put on a little makeup and brushed her hair. She found an outfit that she had worn a couple days earlier that wasn't too wrinkled. As she walked to her car, she noticed it was tilting slightly. Three flat tires. Obvious punctures in the sidewalls. She kicked the tires a few times and went back in the house. She sat in her living room, lights out, with her Glock on her lap, watching the front. Hoping whoever was bothering her would return.

14

THE RECEPTIONIST BUZZED HANSON at his desk. "Brian, there's two officers here who need to see you."

It happened occasionally that police found out a suspect was a client and asked for assistance in getting them to surrender peaceably. Usually it was detectives, but this time there were uniformed cops waiting in the lobby. One was a sergeant, the other seemed so awkward Hanson assumed he was a rookie. The nine clients in the waiting room looked even more uncomfortable. Hanson suspected there were more than a few outstanding warrants among them. Even the innocent ones had fearful fantasies about the authorities.

Hanson led the police back to his office, closed the door, and gestured for them to have a seat.

"It's not that simple," the sergeant said. "Brian Hanson, you're under arrest for assault two. That's a felony. You have the right to remain silent, if you choose to give up that right, everything you say can and will be used against you in a court of law."

Hanson stood, slack jawed.

"Please sit down and keep your hands in view until I finish," the cop continued. Hanson noticed the sergeant's hand rested on the nightstick in the ring on his belt. The rookie had his hand on his holstered gun. "Do you understand your rights so far?"

"I do."

"You have the right to an attorney. If you choose to give up that right, one will be appointed by the court. Any questions?"

"What the hell is going on?"

"Did you assault a Ron Harkins yesterday?"

"That scumbag pressed charges?"

"Mr. Hanson, I'm aware of who you are and what a dirtbag he is. Ever hear the saying never wrestle with a pig, you both get dirty, and he likes it?"

"What about Charlene?"

"My understanding is she will be testifying for the state."

"That I attacked him?" the counselor asked incredulously.

"If you wish to make a statement, you can give one downtown," the rookie said. "We need to transport you to the jail for booking."

"I've got clients coming in who are very vulnerable." Hanson knew that Morris Brown was due. If he saw Hanson being led away by police, the counselor suspected Moose would try to rescue him. "Can I at least tell my supervisor?"

The rookie looked at the sergeant.

"Make it quick," the sergeant said.

Hanson picked up the phone and called Betty. "Uh, I had a little run-in yesterday with Charlene King's boyfriend."

"Is that why there were cops in the waiting room?"

"Well, yes. I need to go with them downtown."

"You don't have to go anywhere with them," said Betty, a former sixties radical who continued to demonstrate for social justice. "Unless they arrest you."

"Wellll . . ."

"Goddammit, Brian, did you let some macho crap get you in trouble again?"

"I'm not sure when I'll be back," he responded, avoiding her question. "Maybe just a few hours."

"I'll arrange bail and an attorney."

"Thanks."

"You really disappoint me, Brian."

Hanson hung up and turned to the sergeant. "Do I have to be handcuffed?"

"It's required," the rookie said.

Hanson stuck his hands out in front.

"No, behind your back," the rookie said.

"I'll take responsibility for him," the sergeant said. "Cuff him in front. You got a sweater or something you can drape over your hands?"

Hanson took a sweater off a hook on the wall, and draped it over the cuffs after they were clicked on his wrists.

"If there's a back way out, you don't have to do the perp walk through the waiting room," the sergeant said.

"Appreciate that."

They went down the hall and out through the back door. Even with the cuffs covered, it was clear what being escorted by a cop on either side meant. And it was too warm to be sweater weather.

They were on the sidewalk, nearly in the squad car, when a deep voice bellowed, "Hey, what's going on?"

Moose lumbered up.

"Nothing. I'll catch you later," Hanson said. "Check in with the front desk."

"Move it along, fella, there's nothing to see," the rookie said. He tried to sound confident, but was staring up at Moose's mangled face. He had his hand on his gun again.

"This is a free sidewalk, motherfucker," Moose said.

The sergeant had stepped back off to the side and had slipped a Taser into his hand.

Hanson turned to face his client. "Moose, listen. Please don't make a scene. It'll only make it worse for both of us. I'm asking you a favor, stand down."

"He knows what stand down means?" the sergeant asked.

"Served in the Iraq war. Combat vet."

The sergeant nodded. "If he walks away now, we don't charge him with obstructing."

Betty, who must've seen the confrontation through the window, came hurrying out. "Mr. Morris, please come into the clinic." She moved quickly up to the big man and forcefully took his sleeve. Hanson noticed that she had positioned herself between the rookie, who had drawn his gun, and Moose. The rookie was saying something into the walkie-talkie mouthpiece clipped to his shoulder.

"They shouldn't be messing with Mr. Hanson," Moose said. Betty's tugging had as little effect as a breeze on a slab of concrete.

"I'm sure it's a mistake," Hanson said. "Moose, I'll call you later today."

"Motherfuckers ain't taking you nowhere without going through me."

Hanson heard the sound of sirens getting louder. "I'm getting in the car willingly. You go inside with Betty. She's arranging bail and an attorney. Please stand down," Hanson repeated.

Moose folded his mammoth arms across his chest.

"Betty, get him inside, please," Hanson said. "The cavalry's coming and they're going to be looking for some ass to kick."

The sergeant shot Hanson a dirty look and a not much friendlier look at his rookie. Hanson got in the patrol car and they drove off as Moose lumbered behind Betty into the clinic.

"Cancel the policeman needs assistance call," the sergeant said to his rookie. "That guy should be arrested," the rookie said.

"He served his country—I'm cutting him slack." The sergeant turned and spoke to Hanson through the grill separating front and back seats. "He get that face in the war?"

"You could say that," Hanson said.

Terry sat at the computer, working with Photoshop software. Using an 800mm telephoto lens, Duane had taken several pictures of Louise Parker. The clearest were of her coming out of the house. Others showed her working in the backyard.

"How'd you get these?" Terry asked.

"I climbed up a telephone pole by the neighbor," Duane said proudly. Duane still had ID from his nine months as a phone company employee. His skill with gadgets ultimately was outweighed by his difficulty at getting along with people. "But none of the neighbors even noticed."

"Nice shots," Terry said, and Duane glowed from the praise.

"Terry, I've got a question."

"Yes?'

"Some of what we're doing seems funny, like sending her those videos. But stealing her wallet in church, well, that's kinda mean. It's church, like don't you think God will be mad at us?"

"God understands that she's an evil person pretending to be a good person. We're doing God's will, punishing her like this."

"If you say so," Duane said without conviction. "What're you doing?"

"Come take a look."

Duane glanced at the screen and giggled. "Wow, she's hot."

"I'd do her," Terry said.

Duane giggled some more.

Hanson was released three hours later. Back at the clinic, he ran his dual diagnosis support group, and then checked the fourteen voice mail messages. The only one he returned was the call from Louise.

"I thought you'd call me sooner," she said tensely.

"Long story," he said, not eager to explain. "I'll tell you when I see you. What's up?"

She told him about the interrogation, the additional DVDs, and the slashed tires. Her voice quivered as she fought to maintain control.

"I can't take much more of this," she said.

"You've had some truly rotten things happen. When I hear people talk the way you are, I've got to ask, are you feeling suicidal?"

"Never! That's a sin. Disgusting. How could you accuse me of that?"

"An occupational hazard."

"Is that the way you see me, like one of your lunatic patients?"

"No, not at all. Anyone would be overwhelmed with what you've gone through recently."

"Well, thank you for nothing. For all I know, you're behind this."

"You can't seriously think that?"

"You don't know what I think," she said, and hung up.

Hanson set the phone down and leaned back in his chair. He'd had worse days, but none in recent memory. He considered calling Louise back or showing up at her door. Would that inadvertently convince her that he was behind her harassment? And on another level, he was hurt that she would even think of him being behind her misery.

When the phone rang an hour later, Louise hoped it was Brian. She knew she had dumped her anger on him. She had thought about apologizing but didn't want to speak to anyone.

"Hello?" she asked hopefully.

"Is it true you like men with monster dicks?"

"What?" She didn't recognize the voice.

"I've got a ten-incher. I'd like to show it to you."

She slammed down the phone.

Over the next hour, she got seventeen calls. Different voices, different graphic sexual offers. Taking the phone off the hook would be giving in to the freaks. On the seventh call, she asked, "Why are you calling me?"

"You said you like it." The voice sounded nasally, adolescent. "I'm willing to pay."

"What?"

"Do you accept credit cards?"

"What are you talking about?"

"Your Web site."

"What?"

"www.hotFed.com."

She slammed the phone down, went to the computer, and logged on. The home page for the site was a photo of her badge and ID. Another click and there were pictures of her she had never posed for. Someone had grafted Parker's head on another woman's body. A woman who was entertaining one, two, and sometimes three men in ways that Louise hadn't even imagined. Women as well.

"THIS FBI AGENT WANTS YOU TO INVESTIGATE HER," the text read. "GIVE ME A CALL AND TELL ME WHAT YOU LIKE." It had her home phone number.

She slumped onto her couch like a heavy wave had crashed into her and the weight of the ocean dragged her down.

15

I^T WAS AFTER WORK hours, but Hanson called Moose Brown's apartment.

Brown answered the phone, "Who's this?"

"It's Brian."

"You okay?"

"Fine. I wanted to say what a great job you did."

"If I had done a great job, I would've torn them a fucking new one," Moose said.

"No, that maybe would've felt good in the short run. It would've been the worst thing in the long run."

There was silence on the line.

"You hear what happened after they took you away?" Moose asked.

"No."

"About half the damn Police Bureau showed up, that's what. Some of them fuckers were carrying shotguns. You shoulda seen your boss lady. She stood at the door, wouldn't let them in the clinic. Said she had called your company's lawyer. Then the TV crews showed up and the cops faded."

"Oh, great."

"That's one ballsy lady."

"Tell me about it."

"Hey, when am I gonna see you next?"

Hanson checked his book. "I've got a cancellation on my Thursday ten A.M."

"Early, but I can do it."

"You take care."

"You, too. And better stay on your boss's good side."

"I wish."

Brian tried calling Louise's number. Busy. He called a couple of other clients who had been canceled while he was in police custody, and rescheduled. He tried Louise again. Busy.

The craving hit him stronger than it had in years. Just one drink. A shot of scotch, straight up, with George Thorogood. Or Southern Comfort, Janis Joplin wailing in the background. Waste away in Margaritaville with Jimmy Buffet. There was no law against it. He had been cautious for so long, maybe he needed a test. He knew the arguments for controlled drinking. He also knew that wouldn't work for him. The first would lead to the second to the third, and on and on.

He dug out his AA meetings schedule and found a downtown one he had attended before. A mix of business and street people, all with one thing in common.

Arnold Beil parked the stolen car in a lot near the Portland airport. He had trimmed the cheap wig, making it look a lot less phony, and stuffed a pillow under his loose-fitting shirt to appear twenty pounds heavier. He loaded most of his purchases into a double-wrapped trash bag and rode the Max light rail to Skidmore Fountain. A baseball cap obscured his face from overhead video surveillance.

In Old Town he shifted his way of carrying himself, trying to look more shuffling, more decrepit, but not intoxicated. He didn't want to get stopped on some nonsense charge since the driver's license wouldn't fool a suspicious cop. After making sure no one was watching, he set the trash bag down near a pile of similar bags waiting for morning pickup.

He had the small flashlight tucked into his pocket, along with the big screwdriver. No one paid attention to him as he entered Garelick's. Loud rock music and cheap drinks attracted a mixed crowd, the ideal entry point.

Arnold Beil's grandfather had worked as a laborer in a brewery. With the passage of the Volstead Act in 1919, Beil's grandfather became an entrepreneur. Arnold had grown up with stories from his father about his grandfather's success during Prohibition. When Arnold was ten, his father took him into Portland's Underground to show where bootleg liquor had been stored. Arnold's father, who made most of his money off gambling but dabbled in marijuana, also used the space for storage. Arnold roamed the tunnels during his teen years, unfazed by the mildewy smell, the skitter of rats, the thump and boom of noises above.

In the back of a seldom used storeroom in Garelick's, a shabby wooden door was held in place with a rusted lock on a hasp. Beil removed four screws, prying off the hardware rather than struggling with the remaining stripped and rusted ones. The familiar dank air washed over his face. He took a deep breath, stepped in, and closed the door behind him.

Beil was home. Narrow, rickety stairs led down to a dusty floor. Beil played his flashlight around, finding a few passageways had been sealed and others retrofitted for earthquakes. He had to twist and wiggle around some new plumbing, but still could scramble quickly through vaguely familiar tunnels.

The darkness pressed around the edge of the flashlight beam. Shadows rose and fell on cobwebbed walls. Breathing the dank air put him on edge. He felt a jumpiness he didn't remember from his youth. Beil preferred the tunnels to checking into one of the seedy hotels above ground. Their cost was nominal, but so were his funds. And the places were usually infested with as many snitches as rats and roaches.

He found a large underground room stuffed with pieces of wooden bar chairs and a broken wicker couch. He took the torn seat cushion inside one of the barred window four-by-six-foot holding cells. He felt safer than he had in a while. He'd retrieve his trash bag full of goodies a half hour after the bars closed, when the streets of Old Town were deserted.

Louise had taken the phone cord out of the wall after leaving the headset off the hook for hours. Clyde sat on her lap and she stroked his head without being aware of what she was doing.

She turned on the TV and tried to distract herself, but nothing held her attention. She kept flashing back to the disgusting images of herself posted on the Internet for everyone to see. Even though it wasn't her, who would know that? What would the bureau think? The members of her church? Uncle Louie? Brian?

Arnold Beil explored the Shanghai Tunnels slowly. The two-battery flashlight didn't have much of a spread. In a few chambers, light leaked from gaps in floorboards above. Some of the areas he passed through had been cleaned up. A couple of times, he came to dead-ends where there used to be thoroughfares. He found the wooden bunks that had once been an opium den and the scattered areas with bricks and bars that had been holding pens for shanghaied sailors while the crimps sought for eager captains.

He guessed the location nearest where he had stowed the trash bags, and found a stairway up. There was a mound of rubble to climb and the door took a solid slam of his shoulder to open, but then he was in a stairwell and able to get to the deserted street, a half block from the garbage bags that held his gear.

He retrieved his gear and returned to the tunnels. With the brighter lantern he could move quicker. He found a defensible position in one of the old holding cells. No one could sneak up on him and he knew of at least four exits within a few hundred yards. He took the road flares and cut them with the knife, then attached black tape and wires. He strung wires in a couple of spots across passageways and attached them to the mock bombs. He had learned the "hoax device" strategy from the Aryan Republican Army, who used it to create chaos during bank robberies. If police tracked him to the tunnels, they would back off and call for the bomb squad.

Warm in his sleeping bag, in the musty tunnels of his youth, munching on an energy bar and sipping a Heineken, he was quite content.

16

A HARSH KNOCKING AT her door startled Louise awake from where she had dozed on the sofa. Clyde jumped from her sudden move and hid under the couch. His yellow eyes glared out menacingly, like a saber tooth tiger in a cave.

It was Wilson and Wong again. She unlocked the door and they marched in.

"Did you post pornographic pictures of yourself on the Internet?" Wilson asked without saying hello.

"No. Those pictures are composites. I can't believe our lab can't prove that."

"They're at the FBI lab right now," Wilson said, his emphasis on "FBI" making it clear it was no longer "our" lab for Louise. "Do you have Photoshop on your computer?"

"I believe it came as part of the bundled software package."

"But of course you never use it," Wilson said sarcastically.

"I've used it a few times. But I didn't put those pictures up. Surely that can be proven."

"And your badge and ID?"

"I told you before they were stolen."

"Very convenient. Like the criminal who reports the car stolen right before it's used in a robbery," Wilson said. "Maybe you like to see yourself naked and don't want to pose with the Full Monty."

"You're disgusting. If you're accusing me of anything, arrest me now. If not, get out."

"We're here to confiscate your service firearm," Wilson said.

"On what grounds?"

"Possible mental instability," Wong said.

"Too many law enforcement types eat their gun when they get stressed," Wilson said brusquely. "I'll need your on duty weapon and any off-duty gun you might have."

"The Glock is bureau property. The other is my personal weapon. I'll check with my lawyer if legally I have to surrender custody."

"It's recommended," Wilson insisted. "A sign of your cooperation."

Wong said, "We've seen agents under investigation make impulsive mistakes."

"My mistake would be giving up all my resources. Someone is out to get me."

"Maybe so, or maybe self-sabotage," Wilson responded.

Louise ultimately gave them the Glock. Wilson took the thirteen-shot clip out while Wong handed her a receipt for the weapon. They told her they would be coming back with a warrant for her computer.

"Don't go erasing anything," Wilson warned. "Everything leaves traces. It looks worse to the court and can add to the charges you face."

"I won't touch it."

"We'll keep you posted," Wong said as they headed out.

Louise was surprised when Hanson showed up at her house wearing a jogging outfit.

"Our usual jog?" he prompted as she looked at him blankly.

"Oh, yeah, I forgot."

They had been doing the leisurely two-mile run every week for the past four months, rain or shine.

"Sorry. I'm not in the mood."

"C'mon, fake it till you make it," he said, stepping inside. "Sorry, sometimes that AA speak just comes out."

Reluctantly, and mainly because she felt guilty that Hanson had come all the way to her house, Louise agreed to a brisk walk in the scenic neighborhood. The eighty-block-square Ladd's Addition had streets set diagonally from the rest of Portland, as well as connecting alleyways, roundabouts with roses, streets lined with Dutch elms, and a historic collection of old Victorians, Arts and Crafts, and rejuvenated bungalows.

After a few minutes small talk about Dutch elm blight and yard sales, Hanson asked, "Louise, what's going on?"

She recited what had happened in a monotone, shoulders slumped, feeling even more exhausted when she was done.

"That's terrible. What can we do to keep you safe?"

"There's nothing 'we' can do," she said. "I have to take care of myself."

"I want to help."

"That's nice, Brian. But you can't be there always."

"You're being stalked and I've got a friend who does bodyguard work. I'd like to have her help us out."

"I don't need anyone's help. I'm a federal agent." She sighed and it sounded like she was fighting back a sob. "At least I was."

"You're going through a crappy time," he said. "I'm worried you're getting depressed."

"I'm sad. That's normal."

"There is a difference. If sadness is a cold, depression is pneumonia. Sadness lessens or passes. Depression gets deeper. It affects your eating, sleeping, concentrating."

"I don't want to talk about it. I'll pull myself out of it."

He turned to face her. He rested his hands on her shoulders and gazed intently into her eyes. "You're a bright, strong, competent person. Lots of people who battle depression are."

"I don't want to talk about it."

"I'm just saying at some point you might want to consider talking to a counselor. Or try an antidepressant. I'm not a fan of drug company hype, but I have seen major turnarounds."

"Will you come in to my next performance review and explain that to my supervisor? 'Louise is taking happy pills, but don't worry about it.' "

"I care about you too much to stay silent."

"Fine, are you done?"

"Yes."

They returned without saying much. He fought the desire to push more. Louise gave him a terse goodbye at her doorstep and didn't invite him in.

Brian dialed Bonnie's cell. "Tidd's Protective Services."

"It's Brian."

"Hi, sugar, I can't come out and play," Bonnie said.

"I wish that was why I was calling. I've got a friend being harassed." The counselor gave Tidd a quick history.

"I'm not a cheap date, Brian. I can give you my sliding fee scale rate. I only go down to a thousand for a ten-hour day job, plus expenses."

"Whew, am I in the wrong field."

"I'm always looking for dependable field associates. Sometimes a principal wants more coverage than I can provide. With a little coaching, you would be an asset. You'd get seven hundred dollars a day."

"I'll think about it. Is there anyone more affordable in town?"

"Lots of bargain muscle but I wouldn't trust most of them to walk my dog. For the price of a lunch, I'll give you a free consult. I can teach you to harden the target but figuring out who the bad guy is isn't my forte. Are the police involved?"

"My friend's an FBI agent. Skeptical about local authorities and she's alienated from her agency. She's getting paranoid and depressed. Of course that's just my opinion. And confidential."

"You really like her, don't you?"

"What makes you say that?"

"Woman's intuition. And the way you talk about her. It's sweet," Bonnie said, surprisingly tenderly. "It's going to be tough to help if she's not cooperative."

"I'll work on that."

"You know Ogelsby at Lewis & Clark?"

"Damn, I hadn't thought of him. Professor Nicholas Ogelsby. I'll follow up."

"See you Sunday."

"Can't wait."

Louise regretted how snappy she had been with Brian even as she'd been talking. She'd wanted to stop but the angry words just spilled out. She curled up in her bed. Clyde, who usually preferred to sleep in his safe den under the bed, hopped in with her. He lay next to her and she knew he sensed her mood. She was so touched by his gesture that she began to cry. And once she started, she couldn't control her tears. Clyde seemed to understand. After several minutes of sobbing, she fell asleep.

Louise awoke abruptly, thinking it was a bad dream. As she came fully back to consciousness and realized her travails were reality, the pain of depression pierced her. She looked for Clyde, who was no longer in bed. Panicked, she hurried around the house, calling his name. Finally she heard a meow and returned to the bedroom. She lifted the bed ruffle and saw his eyes staring at her from the darkness. He was safe in his den, and she was envious.

There were a couple more plants in pots that she had to put in. And the freshly planted ones needed watering. The thought of going out and working was daunting. Just deciding to put on her gardening jeans was difficult.

Stepping into the sunlight, she lifted her face, enjoying warm, soothing rays. She glanced around and froze. It looked like a tornado had rampaged through her garden. The plants were trampled flat, the trees were uprooted and smashed, the ceramic pots were kicked over and cracked.

She bit her lip to keep from moaning, then ran to her next door neighbor and rang the bell. No answer. She ran to her neighbor on the other side, an elderly English woman who reminded her of a character from a "cozy" novel. Their few conversations had centered on the joy of cats.

"Did you see anything?" Parker demanded.

"And what are you inquiring about, dearie?" her neighbor asked, not seeming to notice Louise's shrill tone.

"My yard. Did you see anyone in my yard?"

"No. Has someone been there?"

Louise hurried away without answering. She checked the nearby houses and found few people home. One person thought they had noticed a light-colored van parked on the block. But it was gone now, there had been no writing on it, and he hadn't seen the driver.

Louise raced into her home and shut the door. She was breathing hard, and realized she had been running from house to house. She double-checked her locks and drew her backup gun, holding the weapon at her side as she paced.

Louie Parker sat down in the chair like it was his office. "So doc, beat up anyone today?" He chuckled.

"What do you mean?"

"I got big ears," he said, tugging at his Lyndon Johnson–like lobes. "I heard about that Harkins guy trying to break your knee with his nose. You need a sharp shyster, I can make recommendations and be sure they cut you a decent rate."

"Thanks."

"I know who you got through the agency. Hunky-dory for mental health law, but not the criminal stuff. Go with Eric Jacoby. Believe me, you go with the wrong attorney, you'll have years to regret it."

"I'll keep that in mind," Hanson said. "This time is not supposed to be wasted on my legal issues. How are you doing?"

"Aches and pains but I get by."

Hanson listened as Louie reviewed his week. "So, what's up with Louise?"

"What do you mean?" Hanson asked.

"She's taking this raid thing worse than I'd have figured. Of course she always wanted to be an FBI agent. I hope those bastards don't make her lose her dream." Apparently Louie didn't know about the harassment.

"It's a difficult situation," the counselor said evasively.

"Is that the best you can do?" Louie asked. "I think she's getting depressed."

Hanson bobbed his head slightly, feeling himself on the tricky terrain of a dual relationship. "I can understand your concern. Maybe you could give her some information."

"She'd be a lot better off with a man in her life. Like you. When you going to get serious about her?"

"Louie, let's talk about your concerns."

"My concern is that I'm gonna die one of these days and I'd like to know she's got someone to take care of her."

"She strikes me as very independent," Hanson said, feeling himself getting defensive and out of his therapeutic role.

"The toughest person in the world needs someone to lean on every now and then. You two would make a great couple, and you know it."

Louie called Louise but there was no answer. Knowing when he'd been depressed and not answered the phone, he called in a favor and had one of his neighbors give him a lift to her house. Louie knocked on the door.

"Go away!" she shouted, without checking who it was. Louie waved for his friend with the car to leave.

"Is that any way to talk to your beloved uncle?"

"Louie?"

"Certainly not that successful weasel on your father's side with the bad toupee."

She opened the door. "I don't feel like socializing."

"Neither do I." He took a bottle of 7 Up and a container of Tropicana orange juice out of the shopping bag he'd been carrying. "I brought you a present. You remember I used to make an OJ Up for you when you were a kid?"

"I'm not really hungry."

"Then put them in your fridge."

"You've never dropped in on me like this before," she said, as they moved to the living room. There was a stuffy smell in the house and Louie went to open a window.

"No. I need to keep it closed."

"For what?"

"Security."

Louise sat on the sofa and he settled into a chair with an old man's weariness. "Louise-y, I know what's happened. I talked with Brian. There's an expert he wants us to see."

"You think I need mental health treatment?" she asked angrily.

"I'm going to talk to you the way no one else could because there's no one in this world who loves you as much as I do," Louie said, leaning forward. "Depression runs in our family. I've got it, a couple of your cousins got it, I even think your mother has it. And you've been through enough with that stupid raid to send anyone into a spiral."

"I'm sad. It's normal."

"I'm worried and Brian's worried." Parker took out a card Hanson had given him. "Just listen and don't get on your high horse. Here's some of the symptoms. Tearfulness, either eating too much or not eating, either sleeping too much or not sleeping, either having sluggish movements or agitated twitches, suicidal thoughts, difficulty concentrating, lack of a sense of pleasure, irritability. Do I have to go on?"

"That's ridiculous. What is this either too much or too little nonsense?"

"Brian gave me this information out of a book on depression. Gave me some handouts if you'd like to see them."

"He sent you here?" she demanded.

"I could see he was uncomfortable to talk about you with me," he said. "But he wants you to know this, figured you wouldn't listen to him. I can tell you're not eating, which he said makes it harder to concentrate. Isolating. Like why aren't you answering the phone?"

As if in response to his question, the phone began ringing. She picked it up, listened for a moment, then hung up.

"What's going on?" Louie asked.

"Nothing. Some teenager playing phone pranks."

"Call the phone company," Louie said. "Or you want me to talk to the little jerk?"

"I've already contacted Telco security. It'll take twenty-four hours to get a tracer on my line. And I do take the phone off the hook periodically. I hate that someone can force me to do that. I hate being helpless."

"You're not helpless. You need to keep fighting back."

"What do you want me to do?"

"Trust me," Louie said. "Trust Brian."

"Did he ever seem weird to you?"

"What do you mean?"

"I don't know."

Louie gave her a disbelieving look. "I do most of the talking when we meet. Which is the way it's supposed to be. But he's been straight with me and I checked him out. He was wild when he was a kid, well into his twenties. But he's had his act together ever since then."

"After what you went through, how long did it take before you could trust people again?"

"Who said I trust people?" he asked with a wink. "Except you. Seriously, it wouldn't hurt for you to try an antidepressant. It's done me a lot of good."

"I'll think about it." Louise hugged him.

"Now have some OJ Up," he said. "You're getting too skinny."

17

HANSON HAD GRADUATED FROM Lewis & Clark College in 1987, about eight years before Nicholas Ogelsby's arrival. Gratitude over how the school had helped him had motivated Hanson to make a few-hundred-dollar donation each year to the alumni fund. Not much compared to the major donors but it improved access when he called wanting an urgent appointment with Ogelsby.

When Hanson attended, counseling psych classes had been housed in an uninspired one-story brick building. Now it was in a new locale, across the tree-lined road from the expanded 137-acre undergrad campus, in a converted nunnery.

Ogelsby headed the two-year-old forensics program. His importance was indicated by the size of his office and the commanding view of a grove of Douglas firs from his large window. The office had two walls solid with floor-to-ceiling packed bookshelves. His cherrywood desk was the size of a nontenured professor's office. He had a brass-buttoned high-backed black leather chair, and a pipe in an ashtray on the desk. The heavily chewed meerschaum was unlit and there was no smell of smoke in the office.

The professor looked like Santa Claus, with a thick white beard and bright red cheeks. His eyes were more skeptical and piercing than jolly. Ogelsby got up from behind his desk, extended a meaty hand, and gave Hanson a handshake that could've dislocated his shoulder. Ogelsby returned to his chair, took out a yellow legal pad, set it on his desk, and put the unlit pipe between his lips.

"Well, I'm a professor with a captive audience, and you called asking about my area of special interest." The professor had a well-modulated baritone that could hold the attention of a jury or an auditorium full of freshmen. In his office, however, the effect was nearly overpowering. "The first known prosecution for stalking behavior occurred in 1704 in England, when a Dr. Lane became enamored of a Miss Dennis. She was an heiress, and Dr. Lane went so far as to assault a man accompanying her and later a barrister. Neither the first nor the last doctor to want to beat up an attorney." He paused like a standup comic waiting for a laugh. Brian responded with a polite smile.

"I'm interested in . . ."

"Of course, not ancient history. The watershed case for American jurisprudence was the 1989 stalking-murder of the actress, and former Portlander, Rebecca Schaeffer, by a deranged fan in Los Angeles. That was coupled with four stalking-related domestic violence deaths in Orange County. The California law set the national precedent and now every state has some sort of regulation. Stalking, like drunk driving, for many years had been dismissed as a mild offense. The lovesick swain syndrome. Despite the change in attitude and increased enforcement, there's an estimated one million people stalked annually. Roughly three-quarters are women." He detailed more recent events: Madonna's bodyguard shooting a repeat offender who had climbed the fence to her estate and talked of slitting her throat, Sandra Bullock's husband nearly being run over by a stalker obsessed with the actress, various investigations by the Secret Service into nonpolitical potential assassins. Ogelsby, who had been involved in several dozen trials as an expert witness, continued his celebrity list: The Lennon Sisters, Clint Eastwood, Michael Landon, Elle MacPherson, Toni Braxton, Sonny Bono, Princess Caroline of Monaco; Monica Seles, Jerry Lewis, Colin Farrell, Lindsay Lohan. He reviewed significant cases, noting federal legislation from 1996 that was sparked by the stalking of Senator Kay Bailey Hutchinson of Texas.

Hanson glanced at his watch, and Ogelsby said, "Ahhh, a college professor can put a filibustering senator to shame. But much as I love the sound of my own voice, I suspect you'd like to tell me the specifics."

Hanson reviewed what had been going on for Louise, starting with the raid on Heaven's property, to the receipt of the *What About Bob?* DVD, to the escalating pattern of harassment.

"Well, as you may know, we break stalkers down into five categories. Let's work through them in order of frequency," Ogelsby said. "Rejected, they're about thirty-six percent. Was there any sort of relationship breakup in the six months prior to your first identified incident?"

"Not that I know of."

"This could be a romantic partner, a business partner, someone she did a sport with?"

Hanson shook his head. "She hasn't mentioned any significant relationship change."

"Next are intimacy seekers, about thirty-four percent. They can be someone you don't know. Sometimes called erotomania. They may have seen her picture in the paper or heard an interview. They see her as their soul mate."

"I can't think of anyone."

"The incompetent? Fifteen percent. They usually have limited social skills. It's their way of courting. They frequently have prior histories of stalking."

"No one comes to mind. I wish that she could be here. I had asked and she refused."

"Stalking victims often become isolative and distrustful. Take no offense," Ogelsby said. "Though vicarious investigation is even more difficult than the usual sort. How about the resentful? A real or imagined grudge. They make up eleven percent."

"I'd say that was most likely. She's been responsible for at least a few hundred people winding up behind bars. The timing points to the raid gone sour at Heaven's place."

"I'd agree that's the most probable. The final four percent is predatory. They're sadistic, and get aroused, often sexually, from their power and control, and suffering they inflict. The serial killer type, not that I mean to be an alarmist."

"I haven't seen signs of anyone like that."

"Well, of course you haven't seen anything to indicate who it is. There definitely are unusual factors in your situation. We use similar predictive models to the FBI's Behavioral Sciences Unit. For example, although there are same sex stalkers, such as the bodybuilder who tracked Steven Spielberg, and females who pursue men, like the woman who fixated on David Letterman, the majority of stalkers are males pursuing females. For age and intelligence, they're pretty much across the full range. Though the incompetent often are lower IQ." He played with his pipe. "You're in the field. What are your hypotheses?"

"Well, the individual is at least average IQ. Fairly organized. This isn't just a matter of stalking or harassing by simply showing up. The person knows his movies and certainly has better than average computer skills to do the Photoshop and create a Web site."

"Very astute. Any other observations?"

"He used the stolen credit card and delivery people to harass by giving unwanted gifts. With a not so subtle message."

Ogelsby nodded and took the pipe he was nibbling out of his mouth.

"We call it stalking by proxy. The giving of gifts we often see with intimacy seekers, sometimes the incompetent. It's their way of connecting, however inappropriate, like when a cat leaves a dead bird for their owner's approval. Even the posting on the Internet can be seen as a perverse compliment. Showing Louise off to the world," Ogelsby said, gesturing with the pipe. "Perhaps fulfilling his own fantasies."

"He was able to blend in at the Mormon temple, so he can present as normal," Hanson said and Ogelsby bobbed his head. "Dress appropriately, no obvious talking to himself, gross failures of personal hygiene. Physically, Louise didn't notice anyone exceptionally tall, or short, or heavy, or thin. He's probably not psychotic."

Hanson felt like there was a factor Ogelsby wanted him to recognize.

"There's a pattern of escalation," Hanson said, and Ogelsby gave an enthusiastic nod. "From anonymous gift-giving to the concealed interpersonal contact of the theft, to the vandalism of the garden."

"A fascinating case." Ogelsby looked embarrassed. "Sorry, I view these as an intellectual exercise. Your lady friend is probably in substantial psychological distress."

"Any specific suggestions or observations?'

"I'll have to go over my notes. It often takes a bit of cogitating for me to develop a profile. One thing, which I think you already know, it's going to get worse."

18

ARNOLD BEIL COMBAT-PARKED THE stolen Ford Taurus outside an Internet café, backing the car into a parking space so the rear license couldn't be seen and he could make a quick exit.

He had sent an innocuous e-mail two days earlier to a man he knew only as Sonny, an associate of the White People's Freedom Party. "Vacation screwed up. Low on cash. Pick a time and we can meet." It was signed "Al." His Yahoo account was based on false information and would be untraceable. He never used any account for more than a couple months. The responding e-mail just had a street corner and a time.

A half hour before the designated time, Beil sat by the corner of NE Davis and 22nd. He smoked a Marlboro that had been sprinkled with meth. Übermenschs, like Adolf Hitler and Timothy McVeigh, had been users as well. He sipped a beer to get the chemical taste out of his mouth while watching for signs of police activity.

He got out of the car after tucking the .32 Beretta in the small of his back. Holsters were a nuisance to get rid of if you were stopped by the *federales*. He strolled casually around the blocks looking for anything suspicious—from rooftop surveillance, to men sitting in vans watching the street. After so many years as a fugitive there was a vibe he could detect, a change in the rhythm of cars, movements, voices, like a white water rafter able to foresee the Class Vs by the sound of the river up ahead.

The contact stood on the corner, a gawky skinhead in an army jacket, camo pants, and Dr Martens. Beil glanced around to see if anyone was paying particular attention to the young man. The few pedestrians out on the drizzly evening seemed eager to avoid the skinhead.

"It's an honor to meet you, Mr. Beil," the youth said. "What can I do to help?"

"My car is a black Taurus, parked three blocks up and one block over," Beil whispered as he walked past, seemingly ignoring the skinhead. "Start walking toward it. I'll follow."

"Yes, sir."

The skinhead had a long, loping stride. Arnold let him get a block lead while he leaned against a parking meter as if waiting for someone. Beil watched, satisfied that no one had the youth under surveillance.

Beil followed the skinhead, who was standing by the Taurus, looking pleased that he had found it. They got in the car, with Beil behind the wheel.

"What's your name?" Beil asked.

"Jim Rogers."

"Why did they send you?"

"Uh, it was my turn to do a mission, and, uh, no one else was available."

Everyone else was probably too scared, and this kid was dumb enough to volunteer. "First off, you're supposed to blend in. It's great to let the world know you've got white pride. But on a mission like this, wear a fucking baseball cap. Don't dress like you're going out to kick ass. Blend in with the masses."

"Sorry."

"And don't tell anyone your real name. You have a code name?"

"Gunny. But they never told me why I need to use it."

"If I get arrested and roll over all I can tell them is 'Gunny.' Not your real, full name. It's part of the leaderless resistance principle. Understand?"

Beil saw Gunny mentally struggling with the complex words. "Yes, sir."

Beil pulled the car away from the curb and drove a block, eying the rearview mirror. He made a sharp U-turn. No cars followed. He repeated the move a few blocks farther and was convinced his countersurveillance moves were successful. "I have a mission to conduct."

"Anything I can do would be an honor," Gunny said stiffly.

"I'm looking for a meth dealer I can trust. Not with lots of potential snitches hanging around."

Gunny nibbled at his lip as he thought. "There's a guy named Chico I know."

"Will he sell to you?"

"I've known him since I was a kid."

"Okay."

"But I know guys with better stuff. Cheaper, too."

"That's fine. Let's visit Chico."

Hanson knew he was in for another long, sleepless night. He ruminated on Charlene King and Ron Harkins. He thought about how momentarily satisfying smashing Harkins had been. He thought of all the times he had talked with clients about behaviors that were short-term satisfying, but long-term destructive. Drugs, overeating, gambling, overspending. Just about anything there was a twelve-step group for. And violence. Rage-aholics. Did he have that in him? He had seen it in his father and absorbed the consequences as a child. What effect had it had on King, seeing Brian pummeling her boyfriend? Did it confirm that men were inherently violent?

And what about Louise? How much danger was she in? How bad was her own mental health? Could she adequately protect herself and if not, was she willing to accept help? She seemed at times agitated and other times blasé. Louie had said that the whole family was crazy. Had she mentally melted down after the botched raid? Was she making herself into a damsel in distress to get sympathy, attention, a stress pension, whatever? Like someone with Munchausen, only using the legal system instead of the medical system. But if she was fooling him, then he had to doubt his own instincts.

He drove to Louise's block. It was on a quiet street and in the drizzly night, there was no one out. No dog walkers, no cars passing. He shut the engine and leaned back in the seat. At least here, a couple houses up the block, but able to keep an eye on her house, his insomnia was constructive.

Chico's house was a little less shabby than the rest on the block in outer Southeast Portland. A few blocks off Powell Boulevard, it was where the city was petering out, with unpaved roads and pockets of undeveloped land. No one wanted the property because the neighborhood's main industries were meth and government assistance. Other thriving businesses included pawnshops, tattoo parlors, payday loan storefronts, and of course, bars. All with heavily gated windows. The convenience stores had earned the police nickname of "Shop & Robs." Now they were better fortified than many banks.

Sitting in front of the house, as Gunny was about to ask a question, Beil put his index finger to his lips and said, "Shhhh."

They watched as a twitchy man hurried away from the steel-reinforced door.

"Okay, let's go talk before he gets busy," Beil said, starting the car and driving off.

"What? I don't understand?"

Beil parked the car around the corner from Chico's house. His glare nailed Gunny back against the seat. "I don't want my car seen in front of a meth dealer's house. Got any other questions?'

"How much you going to buy?" Gunny asked, "Uh, I hope that's an okay question."

"Enough to keep me going for a week or so," Beil said, the gun tucked in the small of his back. "I've got a project in mind."

"Can I help?"

"Sure."

They sauntered around the block. Gunny gawkily walked up to the front door. The skinhead was jittery but Chico was used to that. It would allow him to charge more.

On the run-down front porch, Chico peered at them through the other side of the gate. He had a hog's leg .45 in a shoulder holster and looked like the corrupt Mexican cop he had once been. He'd taken his *mordida* and come north, investing his bribes wisely, and building a successful operation.

In response to Chico's caution, Beil said, "Maybe you don't care about making money." He turned as if ready to leave.

Chico turned to Gunny and said, "Jimmy, you vouch for this guy?"

Gunny nodded.

Chico turned suspicious eyes on Beil. "He looks like a cop."

"Cop!" Beil snorted. "You know a cop that's got a tattoo like this?" He rolled up his left sleeve, showing off a prison-made swastika tattoo.

Chico opened the steel door cautiously, his free hand loosely resting on his gun butt.

"C'mon, man, don't be wound so tight," Gunny said. "My man Beil's gonna make you a deal. Hey, that rhymes."

"Anyone else around?" Beil asked as they entered.

"Why?"

"People make me nervous." He peered down a hall and saw no one, then listened. Quiet.

Chico slid the gun down to his side, not pointing it, but not pleased. "You don't come into a man's house and go snooping around."

"Sorry, amigo," Beil said, putting his hands up in a placating gesture. There was a bottle of tequila on the table. "Hey, let me buy this off you and we split it. My treat."

Chico already had a slight liquor smell and the bottle was about one-quarter empty.

"You're sure no one's around to share a toast with us?" Beil asked.

"You calling me a liar?" Chico asked.

"No, no," Beil said, putting his left arm in a firm embrace across Chico's shoulder. With his right hand, he lifted the bottle, and smashed it down on Chico's temple.

Gunny yelped almost as loud as Chico. Beil grabbed Chico's gun and checked it was loaded.

Chico, dazed and bleeding from his forehead, folded his arms across his chest and shook his head. Beil shoved him in a chair, took a roll of duct tape from his pocket, and bound him tight.

Beil said slowly, "I want the drugs, the guns, the money."

"Please, don't do nothing. Chico's my friend," Gunny said.

"Chico, is Jimmy your friend?" Beil asked.

"Fucking *maricon* should die."

Beil nodded then said to Gunny, "I gotta tell you a secret." The wide-eyed skinhead, with beads of sweat lining his forehead, stepped in closer. "You should do a better job picking your friends," Beil whispered. He suddenly pressed Chico's gun into Gunny's head and fired. The contact wound muffled the explosion but some of the blood spatter got on Beil and he cursed. He returned his attention to Chico. "Okay, now you tell me what I want and I leave," Beil said.

"That's what you say. I don't trust you." He opened his mouth as if to scream and Beil punched him in the jaw, muffling the sound. He taped Chico's mouth shut.

The white supremacist fugitive made a quick tour of the house and found about one hundred dollars. He returned to the meth dealer and demanded, "Where's your safe?"

Chico shook his head.

"You don't have a safe or you won't tell me?"

Beil ripped off the tape.

"Fuck you."

"The sooner you give it up, the sooner I'm out of your life. And if you don't start talking, I'm gonna have to get rough." Beil pointed to Gunny's body lying on the floor. "And it won't be so quick for you."

For the first hour, Hanson was alert. The surveillance reminded him of ambushes he had been on. Giving the VC back what they were so good at. The classic L-shape deployment, careful the killing zone was clear, no chance of friendly fire hitting others in the squad. The silent stillness, not slapping bugs, noise discipline, peeing where you lay. Fighting the internal spurts of fear and rage to wait motionless.

The counselor knew about the trauma response, had educated hundreds of clients in it. But that didn't lessen the emotions he felt. Sweat beaded up on his brow, the car a claustrophobic box.

He watched Louise's house, trying to anchor himself in the here and now. Bungalow style, wide front porch with sturdy pillars, sloping roof, clapboard siding, painted blue gray, or so it looked in the low light. He should talk with her about getting more outdoor lights. The dark foliage surrounding her house encouraged his mind to drift back to the past.

Two young Asian men came slowly down the path. Telltale black outfits. Silk pajamas. They were smoking cigarettes, chattering, AK-47s held carelessly. Hanson sighted down the barrel of his weapon. Something wasn't right. What the guys in the squad laughingly called his "spidey sense." Hanson glanced around. The men were in place, the targets nearly into the L. Too easy. All eyes forward. Hanson turned away, behind them, nervously scanning the dense foliage.

Hanson's sergeant fired first, a solid chest shot, and one dropped. The other didn't even look surprised as a second shot exploded his head. Brian faced their vulnerable rear, and quickly emptied his clip, which momentarily slowed the VC counter ambush. Hanson's buddy next to him had seen him spinning and was only a fraction of a second slower. They managed to drop a half a dozen Vietnamese attackers.

Still, the ambushers were ambushed. A couple hundred shots fired in less than five minutes. American firepower versus VC cunning. By the time the battle was done, half of Hanson's squad was dead, three others wounded. His buddy had caught a stray shot through the throat and bled out over Hanson.

As he recalled the ill-fated ambush, Hanson wondered about the two decoy soldiers. Did they know they were staked goats? How could they not have? Yet they came down the path without apparent fear. The scene was one that Hanson replayed endlessly. And even early on, when he thought about it, he knew the U.S. could never win against that sort of dedication.

Hanson's armpit and groin were as damp with sweat as if he was back in the jungle. He breathed deeply, chest heaving. He rolled down the window and stuck his head out, gulping in the soothing night air.

"Got you, motherfucker!" a man shouted. A flashlight blinded him and a gun pressed against his head.

Beil got a steak knife from the kitchen. "I'm going to get the tape off your mouth but if you yell or do anything to piss me off, I will take your dick and balls with me as I go." He touched Chico's groin with the knife. "Got it?"

Chico nodded enthusiastically.

"Where do you keep your money?"

"I've got a safe in the floor in the bedroom closet. Money, drugs, guns. Combination is six right, ten left, twelve right," Chico gasped.

Beil put the tape back over his mouth. He found the safe where Chico said it would be. The white supremacist spun the combination and the safe opened smoothly. There was $5,300 in tens, twenties, and hundreds, a Mac-11, a few hundred .380ACP rounds in sixteen-shot clips, two large Baggies full of white crystal methamphetamine, and a couple of disposable cell phones. He left three hundred dollars and one bag of meth in the safe, and shut it.

Back in the living room, he told Chico, "I'm going to untie you. I'll take Gunny's body with me. You clean up the blood. This episode is part of the cost of doing business. A sales tax to support the underground." Beil used the steak knife to cut the duct tape. Chico stood, wobbly.

Beil plunged the dagger deep into his chest, the blade severing Chico's aorta. The meth dealer tried to scream, but the sounds were lost in the blood that bubbled up. Chico fell to the floor.

Beil spent the next few minutes wiping any surface that he could remember touching. Then he arranged the body, peeling off all the duct tape, put the .45 in Chico's hand and the knife by Gunny's hand. He left the rifle and shotgun in the closet. There were lots of details he couldn't fix—like arranging for powder residue on Chico's hands. But Chico's business would help him take care of that problem. He found a half-empty drum of acetone in the back room. He turned the five-gallon can over on its side, allowing the puddle to spill right near the bodies. He went into the kitchen and had another lucky break—Chico had a gas stove. Beil blew out the pilot light and lit the stove. Gas began to fill the room. He dipped a bath towel in the acetone puddle.

He found ether in another five-gallon can. He opened that up and made a trail toward the back of the house. He lit the acetone towel, took a step out the back, and tossed it inside on the ether trail. The flames began their rapid crawl.

No one else was out on the rainy night. As soon as he was on the street where his car was parked, he shifted to an ambling stroll. There was a loud "whump" and an explosion as he drove away. In the distance, he heard sirens.

When the fire department arrived and saw it was a meth lab, they would contain the fire from a distance, then call in a hazmat team. After the bodies were discovered, the police would be called. By then, everything should be either charred or washed clean. Considering the victims and the appearance of a drug deal gone sour, the cops would call it an NHI case—No Humans Involved. The police would keep the file open with a priority one notch above a hot jaywalking investigation.

The people he'd connected with to get Gunny might have been able to give police information but nothing helpful, even if they were willing to co-operate. For all anyone knew, Gunny and the dealer had had some sort of fatal falling out.

The Northwest had once been the Great White Hope of the white supremacy movement. But now Seattle was filled with latte-sucking poetry lovers with WiFi laptops, and Portland had been the site of major setbacks. The informant who led the FBI to Order founder Bob Matthews had done his Judas deed at a Portland motel. The White Aryan Resistance had been bankrupted by a Portland civil jury when followers had beaten a Mud person to death. And now the brutal raid on Jeb Heaven's farm had left more blood on *federale* hands.

Beil had money, meth, three more guns, ammunition, and a couple of disposable cell phones. A very successful shop. He was confident his actions over the next few days would go down in Northwest white supremacist history.

19

WITH THE GUN TO his head, Hanson kept his hands on the steering wheel. His assailant was professional, calm after the initial cursing. The counselor couldn't see much, only that the man was Caucasian, had dark hair, and was holding the flashlight and gun braced against each other in a classic police position.

"Slowly, move slowly," the gunman said.

"I can explain," Hanson said.

"I bet you can," the man snapped.

"You can put the weapon down," Louise's voice, approaching.

Hanson was still squinting into the flashlight's beam. The light went off. The gun and the light were lowered.

"You know him?" the gunman asked Louise.

"Yes. He's a friend."

"What's he doing sneaking around your block in the middle of the night?" the man asked.

"A reasonable question," Louise said. "Brian?"

"Couldn't sleep. I thought I could keep an eye out."

"Nice job," the man said sarcastically.

"Who're you?"

"Trent Gorman, if it's any of your business."

"He works with me," Louise said to Brian.

"FBI?" Hanson asked, knowing it was a dumb question as soon as it had left his mouth.

"Does she work anyplace else?" Gorman said snidely.

Hanson got out of the car, his vision returning. He was cramped from his surveillance time, sweaty from his flashback, and sullen from the encounter. "What's he doing here?"

"He was concerned, too," Louise said. "Trent got a tech to come out earlier and get molds of the footprints in the yard after my garden was destroyed. He convinced another computer tech to research that disgusting Web site."

"It wasn't hard to get help for you, Louise," Gorman said. "There are plenty of people who care about you at the office."

Hanson could see Gorman better now. He was movie star handsome, with jet black hair and eyes that shown as sky blue even on the dimly lit street. Strong jaw, cleft chin, slight smirk. Tall, in his early forties, with an athletic build. Brian was annoyed, and embarrassed.

"Nice to meet you," Gorman said, holstering his weapon and extending his hand for a shake.

Hanson accepted the gesture as briefly as was polite. His own hand was shaking. He hoped neither of the FBI agents noticed.

"One of the neighbors spotted you sitting in the car," Louise explained. "She called me."

"Well, I'm glad people are taking care of you," Hanson said. "I'll be going."

As he drove home, the craving for a drink was as strong as the pain in his heart. He had screwed up mightily with his clumsy surveillance. Louise probably thought he was her stalker, like a lovesick teen sitting outside a girl's house. And if she didn't, he was sure that Trent would convince her it was so.

The bars and liquor stores were closed but the convenience stores would have beer or wine. He didn't care if it was a Hamm's. A couple of six-packs would be the answer.

"There's no problem a drug can't make worse." He heard the voice of his old AA sponsor, McFarlane. He hadn't had a sponsor since McFarlane died in a boating accident. Hungry Angry Lonely Tired. Hanson was all of them. HALT. He could put off his drinking until tomorrow. One day at a time. Or one dark, bleary night at a time.

Trent Gorman sat on Louise's sofa. He had the knack of fitting in wherever he was. The son of a federal judge, he had earned a law degree then joined the bureau. Gorman, who had been labeled "eye candy" by some of the female office staff, was more than a pretty boy. His charm made him a skilled interrogator, able to get statements when others had failed.

Gorman focused his intense blue eyes on Louise and said sincerely, "I can stay the night if you'd like. Sleeping on the couch, of course. Or anywhere else you'd want me to." His disarming smile made it unclear whether he was trying to seduce or be obliging.

"Thanks. I think I'll be okay. What can you tell me about the investigation?"

"Well, technically, I probably shouldn't say anything." He paused. "But sometimes it's fun to break rules. Know what I mean?"

She nodded. "What can you tell me?"

He lowered his voice and leaned in closer. "The cyber geeks had a lead on a computer in Tacoma that hosted the porno Web site. But apparently it was some sort of dummy. They called it a slave. Sounds kinky, if you ask me."

"No suspect?"

"A World War Two vet, widowed, lives alone. No priors, no real computer expertise, no connection with you."

"You know his name?"

He shook his head. "I wonder about this guy Hanson."

"He's a friend."

"If you hadn't vouched for him, I would have run him through NCIC. He looked disturbed."

"He's a therapist."

"Oh, that makes sense," Gorman said.

"What do you mean?"

"Well, a lot of them go into the field because of their own issues. I got my bachelors in psych. Lots of weirdos, I can tell you."

Louise wanted to defend Brian, but didn't want to tell Trent about Brian's history.

"I'm sure he has the best of intentions," Trent said. "But he's not capable of doing a decent stakeout. And I don't know what he thinks he'd do if he actually saw a perp. I mean, how old is he?"

"He looks older than he is, but he's in good shape."

"I'm sure he eats his bran and checks his cholesterol."

"He's a Vietnam combat veteran. He's slower than he used to be but he can take care of himself."

"Sure, hey, I don't mean any offense. How well do you know him?"

"What do you mean?"

"The first DVD came from him, right? What if he liked that you got a little spooked by it, and then decided he could scare you more, then be a hero?"

"That's ridiculous."

"You know the first thing to do with a crime? Look at the people closest to the vic. He'd have access to your personal information."

"And his motive?"

"Heck, he's in the mental health field. Who knows what screws are loose upstairs."

"I don't believe it."

Gorman shrugged. "You know him better than I do. But if it was me, he'd definitely be at the top of the suspect list."

She took a few steps toward the door. He did, too.

"I do appreciate your stopping by and what you've done for me," she said.

"Shucks, ma'am, just doing my job."

They were a couple feet apart. Gorman's complexion was flawless, his expression a model of intent concern.

He said, "If there's anything I can do, please let me know."

She had the feeling she should kiss him goodbye. She stuck out her hand. He shook it and with a slight tug, pulled her in for a hug. It was professionally brief, chaste.

He gave her a farewell nod and walked out. She shut the door and sagged as she leaned backward. It had taken all her energy to maintain the conversation and a calm demeanor. She was emotionally exhausted.

She wanted to think more about the conversation, about Brian. Could the counselor be behind her harassment? If she could be deceived like that, could she trust anything? Would Brian be able to be so tender if he was disturbed? She thought about the wives of serial killers and rapists, who often seemed clueless about the horrendous deeds their husbands were perpetrating. The idea was too oppressive. She didn't bother to undress or brush her teeth before collapsing into bed.

It was past one A.M. and Duane couldn't sleep. He peered under Terry's door, saw the light was on, and knocked.

Terry was online, reading a Web site called SweetRevenge.com.

"What're you doing?" Duane asked timidly.

"Looking for ideas. To pay back that bitch."

"She seems like a nice enough lady."

"What do you know about her?"

"She works for the FBI. They go after criminals. She goes to church. And she's kind to her cat."

"Hmmh. Shows how little you know about people, Duane. Looks can be deceiving."

"What if God finds out I stole her wallet in church? He doesn't like people who steal in church."

"Ahhh, cut it out. I think we need to really teach her a lesson."

"Like how?" Duane asked. He glanced at the computer screen. "That looks dangerous."

"You can do it."

"She could get hurt. Even killed."

Terry clicked Print. "Don't worry, we'll follow the instructions." Terry mock sparred with Duane, who blocked the deliberately clumsy punches. Terry clinched and gave Duane a bear hug. Normally Duane was repulsed by physical contact, but it was different with Terry. "C'mon, you're the best at this."

"I don't know . . ." Duane said, nervously running his hand through his hair.

"C'mon, it'll be fun."

20

AFTER ANOTHER RESTLESS NIGHT'S sleep, Louise sat at her small home office desk, looking through the photo albums and documents that made up her life.

She was the second oldest of four girls, the one who had tried hardest to act more like a boy to please her father. He believed spare the rod and spoil the child but was never cruel. His four daughters were his possessions and, like his Oldsmobile, he treated them well. He had served in the earliest days of the Vietnam War, and it was only as she stared at pictures that she realized Hanson and her father had been in the same war, nearly a decade apart.

The pictures showed them as a stiff, happy family, on outings in Portland in the late sixties and early 1970s. Her parents now were retired, living in Utah. Two of her sisters lived there, the third in Texas. She had little contact with any of them. As a Mormon, the gap was particularly painful.

Her parents had wanted her to go to Brigham Young University but she had earned a UCLA scholarship based on her volleyball and academic ability. There were pictures of her on the beach in Southern California, tall, tanned, fit. She was always dressed the most conservatively, always the most prim, the designated driver, the one who would leave unruly parties. An honor student and athlete but an outsider.

She flipped through the wedding pictures. The marriage had been a brief fiasco, an attempt to appease her parents. She discovered her husband had been having affairs since a week after the honeymoon. She had insisted on a divorce after two years of being lied to. Her family and the community blamed Louise and wanted her to stick with him.

Clyde pushed under her hand, as if to disrupt the unpleasant memories. She turned the page. There was Uncle Louie, carrying the six-year-old Louise dressed in a pink princess costume. He had given her the best presents, like the Junior G-Man set she got for her tenth birthday. She could see in his eyes that he loved her just as she was. Louie had had a couple of marriages, but never any children, and Louise came to understand that she fulfilled that role

in his life. She had sweet dreams where he was her father, endlessly understanding, no matter what her mistakes.

Then there were pictures of her at Quantico, being sworn in. Even her father had seemed proud. She had finally done something right. Fidelity,
bravery, integrity.

One photo album, that was her life. And there were about a half dozen
pages in it yet to be filled. As her eyes filled with tears, she set down the
book and petted Clyde for a couple minutes. He licked her face, his raspy
tongue seeking out the salty liquid. She tried to smile but couldn't.

Louise opened up a thick manila folder filled with a lifetime of documents. Her birth certificate, a few elementary school report cards: "Quiet. A
pleasure to have in class." Her college diploma. Four commendations she
had earned in the bureau. Several yellowed clippings, stories on major arrests she had been in on. What were they worth? Scraps of paper with
meaningless words.

The phone rang, startling her. She dropped the papers and eased Clyde
to the floor. She hesitated, not wanting to talk to anyone. The phone rang
four times, then her voice mail kicked over.

"Hi, this is Louise. We're not in right now."

"Louise, this is Bishop Johnson. A couple of the congregants told me
what happened last week. It's a disgrace. Please decrease your tithing until
you've made up your loss.

"It had been a while since we've seen you. I hope this doesn't prolong
your absence. I would welcome you coming in and talking. I sense a great
sorrow. God bless," the bishop said.

"Amen," Louise said to the phone reflexively.

Why do bad things happen to good people? Are we pawns in a struggle
before Satan and the Archangel? The church didn't have the answers.
Maybe it was like Karl Marx had once said, religion was the opiate of the
people. The drug was wearing off and she was going cold turkey.

Arnold Beil stood in the downtown transit mall, talking on one of the disposable cell phones. He looked like a typical pedestrian squeezing in a
phone call before boarding a bus. If the phone was traced, it was impossible
to know where in the city he was heading to.

He called the voice mail of a private investigator in Fayetteville who was
also a *kledd* in the North Arkansas Klan. He knew the PI swept his phone

lines and followed the basic principle that every phone call was listened to, every e-mail was read, every new contact was a snitch until proven otherwise. And even a longtime associate could be turned by the treacherous feds.

"I need a home address for Louise Parker, around forty, Caucasian female. Fucking Bitch Idiot." He had heard that there were computer programs from the NSA that monitored phone lines, picking up key phrases like FBI. "I'll call tomorrow. Remember the Day of the Martyrs." The call had taken less than ten seconds. By a circuitous route, and reassured that he wasn't being followed, Beil returned to the Portland Underground.

It was a comfortable home, better than many safe houses he had stayed in. He had stocked up on nonperishable food, and set up tin can alarms and hoax bombs in several alternative passageways. There was a board over the entrance to his hidey hole, and debris carefully stacked so it looked like the area had not been disturbed. He had a regular radio, which he seldom played, and a police scanner he listened to constantly. The scanner not only would alert him if police became aware of his hideout, it allowed him to get a sense of the rhythm of criminal life in Portland. The ebb and flow as cops came on duty and went on break. The flurries of activity when kids got out of school or bars let out. The change in pace when it rained heavily, or the sun came out. He had his exercise routine, which now included three hundred pushups, five hundred crunches, and lifting of hundred-pound rocks. Going for a run was too high risk.

He had snorted a pinch of meth, enough to give him an edge and a warm energy surge. There was plenty left for when he did Louise. He could see the news stories, hear the arrogant ZOG bastards screaming for his capture. Running scared, the way his people had been for so long. Show them that, like armies of oppression, they couldn't escape the righteous force of the people.

He was fantasizing about doing Louise while holding a knife to her throat when he heard the tin can rattle. He grabbed a gun, blew out the kerosene lantern, and covered his belongings with a black wool blanket. He froze, silent as a hunter with a sixteen-point buck in his sights.

His eyes snapped back and forth nervously, trying to adjust to the near darkness. He felt a cool breeze in the tunnel and a sheen of chilled sweat on his skin. Ghosts? He crawled to a corner, back against the wall. Think logically, he told himself. Ghosts don't trip alarms. Probably just a stray homeless person, maybe even a big rat. What if it wasn't, what if there was truth in the spooky stories? His thoughts came quickly, stumbling over each other.

He slipped into the darkness with the .357, a six-inch-long dagger, and a flashlight covered with a red filter. He heard several voices, coming closer. About a dozen people. No effort to be quiet. They were coming down the main corridor, which he knew led to Hobo's Restaurant. Flashlight beams skittered around the tunnel.

"There are believed to be at least two levels down here," a man's voice said. "We've only excavated one layer. We've removed tons of debris by hand, but there's much, much more. If you're interested in volunteer opportunities, see me after the tour."

The man with the thick mop of dark hair and bushy mustache stopped and pointed to a brick wall with bars set in it. "This was one of the holding cells. Unscrupulous captains would place their order, and the unwilling crew would be delivered. Portland was notorious for the kidnappers, who were called crimps. We were worse than San Francisco, which was our nearest rival."

A couple of young men cheered, "Go Portland!" Their girlfriends looked at them with obvious disgust.

"We're going to dim the lights for a moment and you'll get a feeling for what it was like. Imagine being held down here, sometimes for days. No idea of the time, no idea when and if you'd be released. Sometimes people passed out or died around you."

Noise from the bar above filtered down. The Village People, ironically singing *In the Navy*. "Even if you screamed, the businesses above were paid not to hear. Many of them were in on the trade and the crimps would come down and savagely beat victims. This was a place without hope.

"By the way, the tunnels are in the top ten of haunted spots in the United States. Lots of death, lots of misery," the guide said cheerily. "I'll tell you more about some of the ghosts who are believed to haunt these catacombs later. But be aware that many people report strange touches."

He signaled his assistant and the faint light dimmed.

Beil watched the group from the darkness of a side tunnel. He had fixated on a pretty blonde standing near a frat boy, off to the edge of the group.

Arnie crept forward in the darkness. High risk, but he hadn't had any fun, and they'd interrupted his fantasy about Louise. He was next to the pretty blonde. His hand grabbed her buttocks, fingers wandering deep into her cleft.

"Joey! Stop!"

"I didn't do nothing," her boyfriend responded.

Seconds before the tour assistant turned up the lights, Beil slipped back into the side corridor. The blonde stood stiffly, shivering with terror.

Her boyfriend put his arm around her protectively.

"I want to go home," she whimpered.

"There's an exit about a hundred feet down the corridor," the guide said. "Anyone who needs to leave can."

The tour moved on, and the couple exited. Beil flexed his fingers, recalling her soft femininity and fearful jump. He bet her boyfriend would be getting some tonight. The fugitive leaned back against the corridor wall and stifled the urge to laugh.

21

L OUISE FLUCTUATED BETWEEN ANGER and sadness. At least when she was angry, she had energy. She'd use that time to get things done. She called her office and spoke briefly to her buddy Vic.

"What can you tell me about the lead in Tacoma?"

"The porno site was actually hosted out of Romania. The hosting company has hundreds of sites, mostly porno and some online gambling. No underage or snuff or anything that the Romanian feds would be interested in talking to them about. It's easy to get an anonymous hosting arrangement with these places. Site owners make arrangements through free public e-mail accounts, and send payments through ecash or e-gold or one of the other anonymous payment services. The owner uploads his content with FTP to the server library they specify, and bingo, he's a porn entrepreneur. We could try to hack in to their servers and set something up to trap him if he tries to upload more content, but I doubt he will do it again, at least through this host.

"We were able to backtrack the source to a home computer in Tacoma. There was some interest, since it is so close to Portland. With the Internet, after all, it could be in Mombasa or Kosovo as easily as Washington. But it wasn't. They did a little snooping, the old man who owned the computer uses it for e-mail and playing Freecell and Minesweeper when he's adventurous. They gave him a solid, brief checkup."

"Brief?"

"Well, it's not real life and death, Louise. Nonthreatening harassment. Could be any asswipe who saw your name in the paper and wants to give you a hard time."

"Can you get me a name and any relevant background info?"

"Listen, they did check. There's about twenty high-tech ways a hacker can access your computer and make it a robot slave. Just bounce communication out of yours, so it looks like you're the source of spam, porno, threats."

"I'd like to talk with him."

"I gather he wasn't real cooperative."

"Can you get me the info?"

"Technically, you're not supposed to be privy to this."

"I know."

"But it's a dead-end, why should they care? How can I say no to my cell-mate in prairie dog city?"

Duane and Terry sat in Duane's car, a 1994 Toyota Corolla with more than 150,000 miles on it. Duane's mechanical skills kept the car running as smoothly as a new Mercedes. They were parked on NE Columbia Boulevard near the airport, outside a one-story building that was a sprawling, gray concrete windowless box. The disproportionately small sign out front said "Modern Chemicals."

"Will you go in and buy it?" Terry asked.

"I don't want to." Duane had on his boyish pout, arms folded across his chest.

"Fine." Terry got out and slammed the door before walking into the store. Her hair was tucked up into a Mariners' baseball cap, a fisherman's knit sweater bulked her slender frame.

There was an acrid chemical smell in the air. Rotten egg sulfur, eye-watering vinegary acetic acid, goaty butyric acid. The fixtures were old, steel shelves thick with bottles and plastic containers. An elaborate spiderweb covered the emergency shower in the corner. There were brightly colored hazardous material signs on three walls.

The elderly man behind the counter looked pleased to have a customer. He was missing two fingers and had a nasty scar on his left hand. He had bottle-thick glasses and still was squinting to see.

"Quiet day?" Terry asked.

"We do most of our business mail order. My son got us into the Internet." He opened a door to the back room. It was like peering from the nineteenth century into the twenty-first century. A dozen men and women with headsets and computer terminals in front of them were busy processing orders.

"It's nice to see a person," the elderly man said. "How can I help you?"

"I'd like a couple pounds of saltpeter, maybe a half pound sulfur, and a third of a pound of sodium sulfate."

"Hmm."

"What does 'hmmm' mean?"

"I been in this business a long time. I know what you want it for."

"Really?" Terry didn't have a gun, but there was one in the car. Was it accessible? Could the old man know? Would they have to kill him?

"I bet you're a Civil War reenactor."

"Amazing. How could you tell?"

"Low intensity explosive black powder ingredients. Ever since 9/11 I've had to keep track. I did have some customers that I could tell were making high explosives. Trinitrotoluene. TNT. Mercury fulminate for blasting caps. Picric acid. That stuff is unstable and can do a lot of damage. I let the federal agents know about them right away."

Terry hesitated, unsure whether to bluff or run.

"Yours is either homemade fireworks or Civil War reenactment." He leaned in closer. "My secret, add a little sawdust for combustibility. It gives you more for the oxidizing agent to work with. And sugar will make your smoke clouds smokier."

"Thanks."

"Of course some teenage punks use them for pipe bombs. But you're more mature. And terrorists go with the C4 and the other high explosives." The shopkeeper waggled a finger. "But you can't be too careful."

"Definitely," Terry said.

"Too many laws nowadays. Too much paperwork. Too many lawsuits."

"Lawyers," Terry snorted sympathetically.

The old man wandered around the shelves, squinting as he read labels. He explained about explosive ratings, with TNT the baseline, dynamite about two-thirds as strong, ammonium nitrate less than half as strong, but Semtex or C4 about one-third more powerful. Assuming equal weight, of course. "Look how much damage they were able to do in Oklahoma City with C4. Of course it took a truckload of it."

"Of course."

He doled out several powders and shuffled slowly back to the worn counter.

"I remember a time when I could sell whatever I wanted over the counter without having to fill out paperwork or demand photo ID. My son doesn't mind, with his fancy computers. But for me, well, I'm a dinosaur."

"Too many people don't appreciate the wisdom of our elders."

The old man beamed. "What're your plans? Something to do with the Rose Festival?"

"They're not finalized." Terry made more innocuous chit chat about the Rose Festival—"Why does it always rain during Rose Festival?" "How come the Fun Center isn't fun anymore?" "Why do they have to have all those commercial sponsors on every event?"

After a few minutes, Terry took out a wad of cash and paid the merchant. He seemed genuinely sad to see Terry go.

"Are you sure you really want to do this?" Duane asked as he pulled away from the curb.

"Don't be such a nervous Nellie," Terry said, playfully slapping his arm. "Look, let's just build a couple. We can set them off in the hills for kicks if we change our mind."

"I guess."

"Hey, remember when we were teenagers? You made awesome ones back then. That abandoned car you blew up?"

Duane grinned at the memory. "It had been sitting there for days."

"Boom! I swear those flames went twenty feet high. And the cops never knew." Terry popped a cassette in the tape player. "They call this shit black powder. So this is righteous." AC/DC's "Back in Black" began blasting and Duane relaxed.

Duane lived in Terry's house, a large Old Portland style Georgian colonial in Northeast Portland. The house, built in the east side real estate boom after the 1905 Lewis and Clark Exposition, had belonged to Terry's great-grandmother, then her son, then Terry. In real estate agent–speak, it had "great bones" but a fair amount of "deferred maintenance."

The basement was largely Duane's workshop. The shelf-lined walls displayed electronic devices in various states of disrepair. Radios, a near antique oscilloscope, boxes of switches, microwave circuit boards, computer motherboards, disc drives, and gadgets that looked like tangled balls of wire.

At a clear spot on his workbench, he set down the three foot-long pieces of one inch pipe, plus six matching end caps. While he drilled a small hole in each pipe, Terry was by the sink in the small room with the washer and dryer, mixing up the chemicals. Duane created an electrical detonator by artfully twisting the wires so there'd be a tiny spark gap. He fed it into the pipe just as Terry was coming in, carrying a saucepan full of powder and a sheet of instructions downloaded off the Internet.

"Did you mix it in that?" Duane asked.

"This pot was the only thing clean."

"Be careful! You shouldn't use metal with the powder. It only takes one spark."

He took the pot back into the washroom and poured the powder into a plastic Rubbermaid container. He got a plastic ladle and returned to the work table where the pipes were. He used a funnel made out of newspaper, with more newspaper underneath to catch spillage.

Terry said, "You've got to leave space in there to allow the expanding gases to build up pressure."

"I know that," Duane said. "Does it say anything about sparks?"

"Okay, okay. I missed it, Mr. Science. Hey, you got nails lying around?"

"Why?"

"It says you get more cluck for your buck with them."

"The nails make it more of an antipersonnel device."

"Cool. Got any?"

"We don't need them," Duane insisted and Terry didn't push further. When Duane made up his mind, trying to force change could lead to a meltdown.

Terry read from the Internet instructions: " 'Apply wax, grease, Vaseline, or something similar to the threads on the uncapped end of the pipe. This will make it a bit harder to tighten that end—try a wrench—but will reduce the likelihood that any particles of powder that may be caught in the threads cause a premature blast. You may also want to use a fine brush to wipe away powder residue from those threads first. Wrap a cloth around the end of the wrench so as to make the distinctive trace marks from that particular kind of wrench harder to detect.' "

"I know that," Duane said. "I'm not some high school dweeb making his first bomb, y'know."

" 'Discard everything used and unused in the process, including the drill bit, any extra powder, any extra fuse material, etc. Get rid of excess powder, drill shavings, and so forth.' "

"Leave me alone and let me concentrate," Duane said.

Terry went to the kitchen and cleaned up, washing utensils used for making the black powder, as well as a bunch of dirty dishes.

Duane was focused on the mechanical task and soon they'd have a surprise for the lady FBI agent.

Vic had been terse on the phone, clearly having second thoughts about giving Louise the information. She'd taken down the basics: Kentaro Sukihiro,

AKA Ken, DOB 2/23/25, 2341 Oak Street, Fife, Washington. No hits in VI-CAP, NCIC, or the Washington State Criminal Data base. His worst, and only recorded offense, was driving over the speed limit twelve years earlier. A couple of calls to his home a few years back for domestic argument— unclear who was suspect, who was victim, no arrests made. Lived alone, widowed about three years earlier, wife died of a heart attack, in hospital, no sign of foul play. No known connections to hate groups or any of her other cases.

The report from the Seattle office was pretty clear. A dead-end. A quiet widower who volunteered at the Fort Lewis Military Museum for twenty hours a week.

She knew she had to see him face to face. The Seattle agents had already done a preliminary check—doubtful there was anything more she could get by phone. She dreaded the easy ride up there. How many times had she driven I-5 north? It would only take a few hours—she wouldn't even have to go into Tacoma if she could catch him at the base. Why was she overwhelmed by something she had done many times before?

If Brian would go with her, the trip seemed manageable. But why would he want to? She was hard to be around. And he could be so irritating. She called him anyway.

"I need to go up and question someone who lives in Seatac. Can you come?" she blurted after brief pleasantries. "I was hoping to do it tomorrow."

"Sure. I've got two out of the office appointments in the morning. I was planning on taking the day off."

"You'd be willing to?"

"How about I pick you up around eleven? We can grab a bite in Chehalis."

"Thanks."

"See you tomorrow."

She hung up and sagged back into her chair. He was so supportive. She tried to be happy.

22

H ANSON HAD AN EIGHT A.M. appointment to visit Kathy Wozniak at the VA. She had a tiny office in the washed-out blue-gray building. The papers on her desk were neatly aligned—a bulletin board above her desk was filled with snapshots of former patients.

Wozniak was well into her seventies but looked like she could climb Mount Hood. She had a bushy head of gray hair, gold-rimmed trifocals, and deep laugh lines around her eyes.

"I don't know why you came here to see me," she said. "As I told you on the phone, much as I'd like to help Morris, there's nothing we can do. His facial injury is not directly war related."

Hanson had brought pictures of Moose, as well as copies of the release he had signed. He pushed both forward. "I thought you might need the release so we can have a free exchange of information."

She picked up the photos and studied his mutilated face without a flinch. "If you think you'll shock me with these pictures you have no idea what I've seen. I was taking care of boys just back from Vietnam when you were in diapers."

"I served in Vietnam, ma'am. I remember you. I even had a crush on you."

"Hmmph. I've heard lots of sweet talkers in my time."

"You wore the nurse's hat back then. It went out to both sides and looked like a dog's ears. And a light blue sweater a lot of the time."

"They kept it cold in the wards," she said, her eyes shifting as she returned to memories. "Many broken bodies, broken minds." Then she snapped back, like she was afraid of appearing less sharp. "This war, I don't know whether people are more aware or what. It's gone from three thousand to close to five thousand vets per year being seen for PTSD. Of course we haven't had a proportionate increase in resources."

"Of course."

He commiserated with her for several minutes about the poor transition

from military to VA care, the red tape complications, the high risk of suicidality, and restrictive policies around substance abuse treatment.

"Not that we handled Vietnam so well," she said. "You probably know
the research, we kept you boys in battle too long. More than sixty days of
combat . . ."

"And about ninety-eight percent of us had two hundred days or more."

"Relentless stress," she said, gazing at him sympathetically. "More soldiers with psychological wounds than physical ones. It's nice to see someone
who was through it and came out the other side. I get a skewed view here."

"A lot of people would disagree how far out the other side I've gotten,"
Brian said. There was something powerfully maternal about Wozniak, even
with her clipped, no-nonsense air. Or maybe it was his memories of the earlier time in his life. "You used to come around with books for us to read.
Everything from the Bible to *Tropic of Capricorn*."

"Gosh, I hadn't thought about Henry Miller in years. You can guess
which was more popular." She leaned her chin in her hand and studied
Hanson. "Is that why you went into counseling? Because of your own
demons?"

"No. I did it for the excitement and glamour."

She squinted at him. "And the big bucks." She smiled, then looked at the
pictures of Moose. "First I heard of him was when he was a high school
football star. Dang, he had promise."

"He still does. But with his face the way it is, he's never going to be ready
to move on."

She peered over the edge of her trifocals. "You'd make a heck of a car
salesman. Let me try a few more options."

"You still loaning out *Tropic of Capricorn*?"

"I wasn't supposed to back then. Got in trouble for breaking the rules.
Nowadays, it's less risqué than prime time TV."

At nine A.M., Hanson had an appointment with Eric Jacoby. The attorney's
office was located on the fourth floor of a building at the edge of downtown. An area not quite as run-down as Old Town but not an address
that a Fortune 500 company, or a prestigious lawyer, would want to have
on a business card. The modest-sized waiting room office was sparingly
furnished with an Ikea look, the walls decorated with artwork by local
talent.

The secretary-receptionist sat behind a desk that looked like a slab of glass on ornately chromed metal legs. She was in her late twenties and had nice legs that were visible in a black silk skirt that was slit up the side.

She must have signaled Jacoby because he came out into the waiting room and shook Brian's hand.

"Thanks for seeing me on short notice," Hanson said.

"No problem. All I would be doing if you weren't here is making a pass at my secretary."

"Who has better things to do," the woman said.

"Brian, this is my wife, business manager, accountant, and general slave driver, Sima."

Hanson shook the woman's hand. She nodded. The phone rang and she picked it up. "Law office of Eric Jacoby," she said, switching from her light bantering tone to a serious voice.

The attorney waved for Hanson to come into his office. The large room was dominated by floor to ceiling bookcases filled with legal texts on two walls. A third wall held several photos from around the world, and diplomas, including an undergraduate degree from Columbia and a law degree from Harvard.

"You've got an impressive pedigree," Hanson said.

"My parents thought so. Pushed me since I took my first spelling test at PS 255 in Brooklyn to be a fancy lawyer on Wall Street. They got half their wish. I became a lawyer, but went pretty far from Wall Street."

"It seems to work for you."

"There are times when I've got a grateful, paying defendant or a pissed off, arrogant prosecutor, and I think, 'This is where I was meant to be.' Now, you told me a little on the phone. Let's hear the whole story."

Hanson detailed what had happened with Ron Harkins, and the charges he was facing. Jacoby took occasional notes on a yellow legal pad. When Hanson looked carefully, he saw that at least half the notes were doodling.

"What do you think?"

"Shouldn't be a problem. Self-defense exacerbated by severe emotional distress. PTSD, you thought he was a threat. Blah, blah, blah. Yada yada yada. We can plead it down so it's no worse than jaywalking."

"I'm not sure how it will affect my license or employment."

"With all due respect, it sounds straightforward. The guy's a scumbag and you beat the snot out of him. Correct?'

"Yes."

"Okay, so check with your licensing board and your company. I'm confident we can plead it down to a misdemeanor. Assault four. Small fine and a promise to stay out of trouble for six months."

"What if I contest the charge?"

"We go to a jury trial, I suspect I can get you off. It'll cost you about three times as much and it is a gamble. You're a sympathetic character. He's a creep. The key's going to be in the voir dire and the cross."

"Jury selection?"

"Get a vet or two on the jury. Weed out those who believe a man has the right to smack a woman around. It's always a crapshoot, and you might be better off taking a plea. But I'm certainly willing to go to court if you'd like. I can take a look at the paperwork the DA's got, see if the cops made any obvious mistakes or if there's procedural errors."

"I think I'm going to want to fight it."

"Okay, okay. I'll let the ADA know we plan on going forward. I'll see what they'll offer. On the way out, talk with Sima, and she'll work out the fee schedule."

23

L OUISE STRAIGHTENED UP AND seemed to regain spirit as they pulled off I-5 and entered Seatac, the painfully practically named city, bastard child of Seattle and Tacoma, dominated by the airport and the inevitable industrial parks that sprouted around such facilities. They drove past hotels, motels, industrial and commercial buildings that ducked low to avoid airplanes above.

Kentaro Sukihiro lived in a modest one-story wood frame cottage, well kept with a neat garden out front. The house was similar to other houses on his block, the only variation being in the colors. Sukihiro's was painted a muted brick red.

"Let me do the talking," Louise said.

Hanson nodded, pleased at the change in her demeanor.

Sukihiro was barely five feet tall, with close cut gray hair and a welcoming smile. He was dressed in a white shirt and blue slacks, with *tabi*-style sandals on his feet. He didn't have a left arm. He didn't seem surprised to see them, hear Louise introduce herself as an FBI agent, and ask to come in and talk. There was no request for credentials, nor for any further identification of Hanson after Louise introduced him as "my associate, Brian Hanson."

Sukihiro gestured for them to follow him in. "Please excuse my modest surroundings. I wasn't expecting guests." In truth, his place was as neat and tidy as he was. He had a couple of shoji screens and minimal furniture, and all the moldings had been scraped down to the wood, giving the home a traditional Japanese feel. He apologized for not having coffee, offered them tea, and indicated they should sit at a clean but well worn kitchen table. "I am a widower and don't have much," he said, setting out an array of Chips Ahoy! cookies on a plate.

"Mr. Sukihiro, I know my colleagues have already spoken with you about your computer being linked to a fraud involving an agent."

"Are you that agent?" he asked.

She nodded. "How did you know?"

"I looked at the site."

Hanson could see the blush rising from Louise's neck to her jaw and her cheeks. She gnawed her lip.

"Is there anyone other than you who might have had access to the computer?" Hanson interjected, to allow Louise to compose herself.

Sukihiro shook his head and said no forcefully.

"What do you ordinarily use the computer for?" Louise asked.

"I was part of the 442nd Regimental Combat Team during World War Two. Are you familiar with it?"

She shook her head.

"It was a segregated all-Japanese unit," the World War II veteran said. "I use the computer to stay in touch with others around the world. Those who are still alive."

"It was an amazing group," Hanson said. "The most highly decorated unit in U.S. history. Also the highest casualty rate."

Sukihiro looked pleased at Hanson's knowledge, then returned to his neutral smile. "More than eighteen thousand individual citations and eight Presidential Unit Citations. They called us the 'Purple Heart Battalion.' About seven hundred men killed and ninety-five hundred Purple Hearts. We were trying to prove something, since our families were being detained in camps."

"The internment was not an action my country can be proud of," Hanson said.

"Our country," Sukihiro said, waving dismissively with his small right hand. "E-mails, bulletin boards, blogs. We have a close knit group, from Hawaii to New York, Florida, Brazil, Canada. About twenty went back to Japan. I was born there, but this has been my homeland since I was a boy."

"Where did you learn how to do so much on computers?" Louise asked.

He cleared his throat then hesitated a fraction of a second before modestly saying, "I picked things up along the way. I only know the basics."

"May we take a look at the computer?" Louise asked.

"Your technicians have removed it. They promised to bring me back a loaner within a day. It amuses me how dependent I am upon it." He stood up. "I am sorry to not be able to talk any longer. I am due at my job in a few minutes. It would be irresponsible for me to be late."

"What do you do?" Hanson asked.

"I work in the museum at Fort Lewis." He stood and gestured toward the door. "I am sorry. Next time, please call ahead, and I will be pleased to talk to you for as long as you wish."

They said their goodbyes and returned to the car.

"He's covering up," Louise said.

Hanson nodded. "His responses became quicker when we started asking questions about the computer. He was eager to end the conversation."

"If I had any real authority, I'd press him."

"If we question him at his job, it could mean a loss of face," Hanson said.

Louise idly stroked her chin. "He'll be even more eager to get rid of us."

"I've always wanted to see that museum," Hanson said. He drove south to Fort Lewis. They were stopped at the gatehouse by uniformed security guards and directed to the visitors' center for a pass.

At the small visitors' center, a cinderblock, single-story building with the ambiance of a prison admission facility, the guard said they needed to get permission in advance to visit.

Louise handed over one of her FBI business cards.

"Anyone can get a card printed up," he said. "I'd need to see badge and ID."

"I want to speak to your commanding officer," Louise persisted.

He called over a thick-browed sergeant who had been standing in the background.

"You'll have to secure authorization and coordinate with the MPs or Army Intelligence," the sergeant said.

"Sarge, my girlfriend was just throwing her weight around," Hanson said, putting an affectionate arm over Louise. "I trained here back in 1971. We only want to go to the museum."

"What do you mean 'trained here'?"

"There was a fake village set up, complete with pigs running around, booby traps, seemingly friendly villagers who whipped out plastic AK-47s. I wound up in Vietnam. Some of the villes were like it, most weren't."

The sergeant said, "The village was gone when I got here, but I heard about it." He turned to Louise. "Listen, honey, I could demand to see badge and ID but that don't impress us much here." He tapped the guard on the shoulder. "Write them up a day pass."

Hanson gave the sergeant a casual salute.

The sergeant nodded. "It's open until four."

The guard took his driver's license, proof of car ownership, and insurance, and typed up a pass.

As Hanson and Louise drove toward the museum, she said, "I can't decide whether to be annoyed over that display of patronizing old boy sexism or pleased that you called me your girlfriend. Though it's the first I heard of it."

"Describing our relationship accurately would have taken too long," he said with a smile.

The museum was housed in a white, three-story western style building that looked like the lodge it had been during World War I. On the grounds surrounding the building sat tanks, armored personnel carriers, rocket launchers, Jeeps, and cannons. They were fifty-ton dinosaurs, looming with great weight and lethality, basking like cold-blooded carnivores waiting for prey.

Inside the slightly musty building, a howitzer dominated the entryway. A Jeep that had once belonged to camp commandant General Norman Schwarzkopf was the centerpiece in an adjoining room. Uniformed, weapons-carrying manikins depicted the roles soldiers had played in the Northwest since the Lewis and Clark expedition.

Sukihiro was at the front desk, where a sign by a donation jar noted that all staff were volunteers. He was talking attentively to a family of four. The preteen son wanted to buy a toy Stryker vehicle, and the mother insisted they could get it cheaper at the Tacoma Mall. Sukihiro was absorbed in explaining the differences in authenticity and didn't see Louise and Brian watching him.

They explored the galleries showing the fort's roles since the first World War. Hanson stood before the display with a few pictures of the training ville, and some captured homemade Vietnamese weapons.

Louise took his hand as he stared. "How're you doing?'

He forced himself back to the present. It was just a showcase full of old memories. "I'm okay."

"Anything you want to talk about?"

He shook his head and gave her a spontaneous light kiss on the lips.

They returned to the gift shop, where Sukihiro was talking to a couple of men who were indicating items inside the glass case. Sukihiro's perpetual smile disappeared briefly when he saw Brian and Louise. There was no other sign of acknowledgment.

"We'll let him finish this conversation," Louise said. "Let him wonder why we're here."

Hanson nodded as they casually walked across the lobby to the Soldiers of the Northwest Gallery, then to the Medical Corps exhibit. Hanson glanced out into the big courtyard in the middle and began walking away from Louise.

"Goddamn," he muttered as he moved forward like a driver who can't resist slowing for a car wreck. Louise, concerned by his tense posture, followed him.

Centered in the courtyard was a green army helicopter, its massive blades tethered down by wires.

"That's a Huey," Hanson said, so hushed that Louise could barely hear his words.

"The kind you had in Vietnam?" She stepped closer and read off the sign. "UH-1 Iroquois, 135 miles per hour with a range of 315 miles."

"UH-1 got transposed to HU and became Huey," Hanson said. "We always used kliks. Kilometers. About half mile."

"Transports fourteen," she continued reading. "Or six stretchers."

"Yeah, six stretchers. Blood and guts. Screaming you could hear even over the sound of the chopper."

She took his arm and tugged. "Brian, we've got to get inside."

"Hmmm. Oh, man, they saved so many lives. They'd fly into a hot LZ, our guys lying on the ground. That weird way the Hueys did, nose down, butt up. They didn't give a damn about the shots coming at them. Those guys flying them had balls."

"You were brave, too."

"I was just trying to survive."

She rested her hand lightly on his arm. "I need to talk to Mr. Sukihiro. I'd like you to be there, your perspective is helpful."

"Sure."

"I hope this was a good idea for you."

"Can't expect to go on a military base and not see military things." He patted her shoulder. "Let's go chat with Kentaro-san."

Back inside, Sukihiro stood behind the counter, and met their greetings with a neutral expression. "It is quite a coincidence your visiting the museum," he said.

"No coincidence," Louise said. "I don't think you told us everything you could."

"I'm not sure what you mean," Sukihiro said.

"We certainly don't want to embarrass you," Hanson said. There were about a half dozen people wandering around the museum. Sukihiro appeared to be the only staff.

"I might have to ask you to close early so we can talk in the office. Is there someone you can call to take over?"

"No."

Louise glanced at her watch. "We can wait until closing time, then drive up to the Tacoma satellite office for further discussion."

He was quiet, eyes slowly going back and forth between Louise and Brian.

"My nephew."

"He taught you about computers?' Hanson prompted.

Sukihiro nodded. "And convinced me to get such an expensive one. I told him I only needed it for e-mail and word processing. But the agents who took it away said it has great capacity."

"What's his name?" Louise asked.

"Steve Purdue. My sister married a Caucasian. That is part of his problem. I do not have any prejudices against whites. But even as a boy he was caught between two cultures." Having released his secret, Sukihiro now was eager to talk. "My sister and parents were held in a relocation camp. We Issei and Nisei did nothing to deserve such disrespect. Can you understand the humiliation of being held in the desert behind barbed wire, like common criminals? This was not done to Germans or Italians. Why not?"

Louise responded by asking, "Your nephew had access to your computer?"

"Yes. And he has had problems in the past. Minor charges to do with computers."

Louise took out a notepad. "What sort of charges?'

"Hacking, I believe it is called. Fraud. For a while he worked for a computer security company, since he was so skilled at finding ways to breach systems."

She asked, "Date of birth?"

"June 6, 1966. He's very smart. A good person."

"Did you tell the agents who spoke with you before about this?" Louise asked.

He shook his head. "And I have felt badly ever since."

"What else didn't you tell them?"

"Nothing."

Louise gave him a skeptical look, then asked, "Where can we find him?"

Sukihiro gave them an address in South Seattle. "It's a small apartment. Most of the time he spends at one of those Internet hangouts."

"Where?'

"Cosmic Internet. On Cherry Street."

"Where does he work?"

"From his house. Computer consulting."

Louise handed him her card. "Call me if anything else occurs to you."

He bowed his head. "I will."

"Protecting your nephew is a noble intention," Hanson said. "But if he's getting into trouble, it's better we reach him sooner rather than later."

"In other words, don't call him and warn him we're looking for him," Louise said.

Sukihiro looked both embarrassed and insulted. "I would never do that."

"We will handle this as diplomatically as possible," Hanson said.

"I appreciate that," Sukihiro responded, with a slight bow of his head.

24

I'D BE AMAZED AT white supremacists using a Japanese American, but I suppose it is possible," Louise said as they drove north on I-5 toward Seattle. "Particularly if Purdue passes as Caucasian."

"I agree."

She used her cell to call a friend. With name and date of birth, she was able to get his rap sheet read to her. "Sukihiro was telling us the truth. Nothing significant, but definitely not just a script kiddie."

"Huh?"

"Geek slang for a hacker with minimal skills. You can download things like do-it-yourself viruses or hacking kits off the Internet. I worked with our cyber squad."

They rode for a while in silence. "I know you've been thinking I'm depressed. You can see I function fine."

"For a diagnosis of depression it has to be mostly depressed most days for a couple weeks. Not bottomed out all the time."

"You think I'm depressed?"

"Probably."

"And what about you and the helicopter?"

"I don't deny my problems. That's what makes me so lovable," he said, trying to get her to smile. "Listen, Louise, I know that most people with depression don't get treatment. And I hate to see you suffer."

"So take a pill and it's happy time?"

"Or do some therapy. Or both. It mutes the pain and helps the process of moving on."

She harrumphed and they rode the rest of the way without talking.

They stopped at Purdue's address in South Seattle, a two-story clapboard-sided apartment complex. There was no answer when they rang the buzzer. His apartment was on the first floor and they peered in the window. Based on the level of empty Dorito bags, dirty clothes, and general chaos, it was clear Purdue was a bachelor.

"We'll try the Internet café?" Louise asked.

"Sure."

Pioneer Square's original wood frame structures were devastated by a fire in 1889, rebuilt, then deteriorated into the "Skid Road," where logs were slid down to waiting ships, and derelicts found a home. In the 1960s, preservationists got thirty acres designated a historic district to save the Victorian and Edwardian architecture.

The Yuppies and Gen Xers who had been taking over strolled the avenues in cell phone bliss, indifferent to the street types who lingered from "Skid Road" days. Each year there were fewer bars that catered to sailors and more trendy coffee shops that catered to those riding the ferries up to Alaska.

The club was located on the second floor in a brick, two-story building on Cherry Street. Entrance to the club was through the noisy bar on the first floor. The ground floor was dominated by a large tavern that couldn't decide whether it was a historical site or a sports bar. Large front-wheeled bicycles and turn of the century baseball uniforms adorned the walls. But the flat panel TV screens presented the latest games only a few feet away.

The stairway was narrow and smelled of cigarette smoke, the walls painted dark purple, worn wooden steps. The walls of the one large room on the second floor were glossy black with randomly placed posters from the latest video games, depicting overly muscled men swinging swords or blasting grotesque aliens while outlandishly buxom women looked on. A short counter, with a hand-lettered sign announcing prices for juice drinks, pop, and various unhealthy snacks, faced three rows with fifteen flat panel computer monitors each. Another hand-lettered sign announced rates for a half hour, an hour, half day, or full day.

Manning the counter was a gangly young woman with multiple piercings and hair dyed shoe polish black. Parker and Hanson were twice the age of most of the fifteen or so people who were at monitors. The one man in his late forties was at a monitor away from everyone else. The screen showed some combination of naked people.

Louise went to the woman behind the counter. "Steve Purdue?"

"I don't know who you're talking about," she lied. Her eyes betrayed her, flicking to a tall, slender man who looked more Asian than not.

Louise ignored the woman's words and moved to where Purdue sat. He was so lost in his screen—which had columns of indecipherable numbers and letters—that he didn't notice.

"Steve Purdue, I need to talk with you," Louise said.

He typed on the keyboard like Chopin at a piano, keys clicking so quickly that it sounded like one continuous sound.

"My name is Special Agent Parker. I'm with the FBI."

"Not now," Purdue said, continuing his typing without looking up. Brian noticed his posture had changed, and there had been a momentary blip in the rhythm.

Louise reached around Purdue and yanked the power cord out of the back of the computer.

"Hey! I've been working on that for hours," he protested.

Two of the young men at nearby computers had been watching the exchange. They were dressed all in black. They jumped up and went into martial arts poses, one facing Parker, the other glaring at Hanson.

The counselor stood calmly, adjusted his feet into a comfortable stance, and waited for the black-clad attackers to commit to the first move.

Louise casually pulled her blazer back, showing her holstered gun. "We're not playing Grand Theft Auto here. This is for real."

"You can't do this," the girl with piercings said.

"Yes, I can," Louise said loudly. "And I can have our cyber squad sweep every computer here for kiddie porn. Can you guarantee that no one has used these computers for that purpose?"

The man in his late forties, and half the patrons, had disappeared. A few continued to play games, others watched the confrontation with open-mouthed fascination.

The piercings girl walked back behind the counter. "I'm gonna call the manager. I bet you need a warrant."

"And I'm going to talk to Mr. Purdue for a few minutes. We can do it politely or with a squad of agents questioning everybody and going through your computers megabyte by megabyte. We'll have to shut you down for a few days, at the very least."

"I'll talk with them," Purdue said, starting to walk toward the door. Brian saw him tensing his body, as if getting ready for a sprint. He was no athlete and the move was clumsily evident. Hanson put his hand heavily on the man's shoulder.

"We can talk in a booth downstairs," Louise said. "Do you want to be led out in handcuffs or simply join us for a little conversation? You can be back at your terminal in ten minutes if I get the answers I need."

With Brian in front of him and Louise behind him, they walked down the stairs and into the restaurant. They found a booth toward the back. Parker and Hanson both got Cokes, Purdue ordered a scotch and soda.

"You use your uncle's computer as a relay for illegal operations," Louise stated.

"I can't believe he told you that," Purdue said indignantly.

"No, you just did. Who was the client for the job you did putting up that porno site with a faked picture of an FBI agent?"

"I knew you looked familiar," Purdue said with a smirk. He gave Louise a leisurely up and down look. "Not that it was your body or anything."

"Steve, you won't fit in real well with the other fellows in jail," Hanson said. "It's a collection of every high school bully you ever dreaded. Be as smart as I think you are and don't go pissing Agent Parker off."

The waiter brought the drink and Purdue finished most of it in one gulp. "What do you want to know?"

"Name, physical description, how you met him, where we can find him."

"White guy, around thirty," Purdue said, finishing the drink. "Called himself Angus Young."

Louise asked, "You said he called himself Angus Young. Do you have reason to believe that's not his name?"

He gave her a condescending look. "He was wearing an AC/DC cap."

Hanson and Parker waited. Purdue looked exasperated.

"Angus Young." He played air guitar for a moment. "Only the greatest lead guitarist in the history of the world. AC/DC."

"So you're saying the person who hired you used the name of AC/DC's lead guitarist and wore an AC/DC cap," Louise restated.

"No shit, Sherlock."

"What's your AC/DC fan look like?"

"Thin, kind've a wispy beard," he said.

"How'd he contact you?"

"By e-mail," Purdue said with a smirk. "I backtracked him once through Yahoo, a couple of bounces, a blind server. He hid his tracks."

"When did he contact you?"

Purdue scratched his head. "I'm not real good on keeping track of time. It took me a day to put up the Web site, and he contacted me a day before that."

"Where'd you meet?" Louise asked.

"Upstairs."

"When you say upstairs, do you mean he came here?"

"Online. We never met face to face."

"So your description is based on a picture?"

"Yeah, but I'm sure it's really him. I can tell when it's some fifteen-year-old nerd trying to act like a man."

"Do you have the picture?"

Purdue shook his head. "It was a while back. I scourge my hard drive once a week."

"Why'd he choose you?" Hanson asked.

"I'm good and I'm cheap."

"You know where your employer lives?"

Purdue looked smirky again. "He's my client, not my employer. I'm an independent contractor."

"I get the feeling you're holding something back," Louise said. "Let's go to the office and talk."

"Or should we advise him of his rights and book him now?" Hanson asked.

"Portland, Oregon," Purdue blurted. "One time I made a reference to rain, and we swapped a few e-mails about weather, and he mentioned where he lived."

"Address? Neighborhood?"

Purdue shook his head. "He was very guarded."

"What else did you do for him?' Hanson asked.

"Computer searches on a couple of names."

"Which were?" Louise asked. She had fallen into a natural rhythm with Brian. They were seated on either side of Purdue, firing questions, keeping his head ping-ponging.

"Louise Parker and Brian Hanson."

"What did you provide?" she demanded.

"Home addresses. License plate numbers and driver's license. Social security numbers, credit info. Even magazine subscriptions."

After a few more minutes questioning, they were convinced they had gotten what they could from Purdue. Louise gave him her card, told him not to leave the jurisdiction, and let him go.

"It was hard not to grab him and try to shake more out of him," Hanson said as he walked out with Parker. "Especially when he said what he had given the guy about us."

Louise nodded. "You did good. Now you know what it's like during questioning. I'm all for constitutional rights, but sometimes . . ." She sighed.

"In some ways it's a relief, confirmation that there is someone out there. And for the same reason . . ."

She sighed again, and he completed her sentence. "It also makes it more real. What happens now? Do you go to the bureau with it?"

She shook her head.

"Why not?"

"They might follow up, they might not. But they definitely would come after me for violating policy and procedure. They'd rather have a creep get away with harassment than an agent being a maverick."

"I can't believe that."

"Trust me," she said. "I'm feeling restless. Let's walk."

They reached Pike Place Market, which began in 1907 as a group of farmers who clustered at the corner of Pike and 1st to sell their wares. Now the market was four stories high, notched into the hillside overlooking Elliott Bay, with 240 stores, drawing hundreds of thousands of tourists to its tiered restaurants, craft shops, and various markets. Most famous were the fishmongers who shouted and tossed their catches from stall to stall. It was late in the day and workers were dumping out the ice and washing down the fish guts. On Elliott Bay, rain clouds were advancing, and boats bobbed on progressively choppier gray waters. Then the downpour began, and Brian and Louise sought shelter under an awning.

"I always knew you were tough but I hadn't seen you in action," he said. "If you had taken out handcuffs, I would've needed a cold shower."

She smiled.

"The description doesn't sound like Beil. Your harasser's probably a slender Caucasian male in his thirties who loves AC/DC."

"I have a vague impression of someone like that sitting near me when my purse was stolen. But I wouldn't be able to identify him."

As they hustled back to his car, the rain came down with such force it sounded like a strong creek. They were soaked by the time they reached the car. It was a little after seven, the sun was beginning to set, and Seattle traffic showed a hint of thinning out.

"I haven't been an easy person to be around," she said.

"You've been under extreme stress."

"I've been hard to be with at times."

"Yup."

She slapped his thigh. "A little too enthusiastic an answer." She left her hand on his leg.

"How do you feel?" Hanson asked.

"It's a cliché, and I don't want to cheapen the experience of being raped, but I feel violated. Exposed. But pleased that we made some real progress here. You?"

"Pissed off. And the creep hasn't done anything with my information." "Yet."

He nodded, wondering if Louise perhaps wasn't the target. Could one of his clients be wanting to get back at him, through Louise? Moose? Fred's partner, Tony? He mentally reviewed his past and present caseload, trying to think of anyone who looked like "Angus Young."

As Hanson drove, Louise's hand rested lightly on his knee. "This is our first out of town trip," she said. "I had ideas about what it might be, maybe a romantic trip to the coast."

"I had thought about it, too. Newport or Manzanita, or a quiet cabin near Mount Hood."

She squeezed his thigh and he hummed contentedly.

"You like that?"

"Your hand like that is going to be a distraction while I'm driving."

"Can you handle it?"

"I will take it as an exercise in mindfulness."

25

I N HIS OFFICE THE next day, Svetlana was his first client. At a Portland Community College English as a second language class, she had met a Mexican man and gone on a few dates.

"Do you like him?"

"He is gentleman and good with my son."

"Do you like him?" Hanson repeated.

Svetlana looked down. "I like. Not sure if there is more to it. I don't know if I have more than like in me."

"Is this something you want to talk about?" Hanson asked. For many trauma survivors, the concept of love and trust seemed impossible. Hanson sometimes wondered just how intimate a relationship he himself was capable of. He had to be wary to stay focused on Svetlana's feelings of numbness and questions about the future, and not to go too much into his own.

"Maybe," she said, continuing to avoid eye contact. "I'm not sure I want to talk to no one about my feelings for him. Let me show you homework from class. There is words I cannot understand."

Duane and Terry drove out I-84 in Terry's 2001 Ford Mustang. Inside the trunk, in a homemade wooden box, wrapped in bubble wrap, was one of the bombs.

They had disposed of debris from their bomb-making at different waste cans as they took the road to Larch Mountain, turning off on Forest Road 15, and driving slowly down a narrow unpaved road lined with tall Douglas firs.

"Remember when we first came here?" Terry asked.

Duane had been silent, brooding for most of the ride. He nodded.

"When I got that cool .32 in high school. You were quite a shot with it."

"You still have it?"

Terry took it out of a backpack lying on the seat between them. A flat, blue-black 1903 Colt, with a dime-sized silver Colt logo at the top of the textured handle.

"Why'd you bring that?" Duane asked, running his hand through his hair.

"We can practice some. I've got a box of shells in there."

"No way. We should get in, test the device, and get out."

"Test the device. Boy, how official sounding."

Duane said nothing.

"Weapons of mass destruction." Terry, with one hand still on the wheel, waved the pistol around. "God made men, Colonel Colt made them equal."

"Be careful with that thing," Duane snapped.

Terry slipped the gun back into the bag. "Fine. We set it off and get out. Okay, party pooper?"

Then they were at the quarry, an ugly fifty-foot-deep notch into the granite of the glacier-carved gorge. There was an abandoned pickup, riddled with bullet holes and rusted out of existence in several spots. Nearby was a bullet-riddled refrigerator, and an appliance that was so shot up and rusted it was impossible to identify. The ground sparkled with shards of broken glass and thousands of shell casings.

Terry took a bottle of Henry Weinhard's out of the backpack and offered it to Duane.

"Drinking and playing with bombs don't mix," Duane said.

"How about playing with devices?"

Duane didn't respond. He opened the car trunk and lifted the bomb, handling it like a mother with a newborn. Terry sipped the beer and watched silently as Duane placed it beneath the remains of the pickup, right where the transmission shaft met the rear axle.

Terry set the empty beer bottle on a rock and walked back to the car, where Duane was already digging the walkie-talkie out of the backpack. Duane adjusted the channel on the walkie-talkie while Terry reached into the bag and took out the gun.

"What're you doing?'

Terry fired two shots that kicked up dirt near the bottle, about twenty-five feet away. With the third shot, the bottle shattered into hundreds of pieces.

"Woooo! I still got it."

"Why don't you just call the Forest Service and tell them to come arrest us?" Duane said, hands fluttering through his hair like distressed birds.

"Yeah, like this is the first time anyone's been shooting here. Okay, Mr. Science, let's get it done."

"Start the car. I'm not sure how much spread the blast will have. The radio transmitter should work from at least two hundred yards."

Terry got behind the wheel and started the Mustang. Duane slid in the passenger side and Terry drove fifty yards. The pickup hulk was still clearly visible.

"Do it!" Terry commanded.

Duane pushed the transmit button. The bright flash came first, followed a fraction of a second later by the boom. The pickup disappeared in a cloud of flame and smoke. Terry stomped the accelerator and they raced down the deserted road.

By the time the Forest Service road became paved and connected with the highway leading to I-84, Terry had stopped whooping and cheering. "You the man," Terry said.

Even Duane was smiling, pleased at his achievement, and the praise Terry had been lavishing on him.

On the ride into town, Terry slid an AC/DC CD into the player and they blasted "Thunderstruck."

Media attention to the shootout at Jeb Heaven's farm had dwindled, but the in-house investigation continued. Special Agent in Charge Jerry Sullivan, steely eyed, with a lantern jaw and short cut gray hair, had been presumed by himself and everyone who knew him to be destined for FBI greatness. Now he was fighting to save his career.

He sat behind his blond oak desk, shuffling through the two-inch-thick stack of 302s the case had generated, knowing he wasn't even seeing all the paperwork. Since he had supervisory responsibility and culpability, the Office of Professional Responsibility was probably holding back information.

There had to be a scapegoat. When a mission went badly, there was no blaming it on fate. Headquarters needed to know who was responsible and that there had been consequences. Part of maintaining discipline. And Sullivan didn't personally care who it was.

Gibbons, the agent who had developed the informant, was extremely well connected. His cousin ranked high in the U.S. Justice Department. They could probably cover up his role saying anything revealed would disclose confidential sources and methods, jeopardize key informants, cripple ongoing investigations. Sullivan protecting him would earn bonus points.

Then there was Sanchez, who had been in tactical command of the HRT team at the scene. Sanchez had a fine record serving warrants and working with other federal agencies to arrest fugitives. But it seemed like he had screwed up that day on positioning. He had paid a heavy price. The fact that he was now brain injured and retiring on disability made him too sympathetic to be the fall guy.

Which left Louise Parker. She was a woman and Sullivan couldn't seem to be targeting her for that. She had been a competent agent, overzealous if anything, which could be stressed in the report on the incident. He had seen minutes of her somewhat inflammatory briefing. Of course most pre-raid briefings were. She had the dubious family history, with her uncle Louie a federal convict. That wouldn't be in the report, but might be leaked to a friendly reporter.

Plus she was unstable, not handling the incident very well. Maybe she could be convinced to fall on her sword for the sake of the bureau. Accept responsibility, and resign. He could probably arrange for the investigation to wrap up quickly and everyone could move on.

He'd have to have someone broach the subject to her. It would be unseemly if he did. And she had to know that rejecting the offer was bad for the bureau. And her. He'd see to that.

Arnold Beil was restless, running low on cash, food, and meth. He'd prowled the underground tunnels for days. He'd called the Tennessee PI a couple times and been told things were hot, that the PI was searching for Parker's home address, and Beil needed to be patient. What was so fucking hard about searching a few databases? If he had been a few thousand miles closer, Beil would have gone to the office and made sure the PI knew to make finding Louise his top priority.

Finally, in the nasal drawl that had come to annoy him, the PI read off Louise's southeast Portland address.

He paused as if he expected a big thanks from Beil. "Anything else?'

"I reckon that's all. Sieg heil!"

"Yeah, right."

26

ANSON WENT TO MOUNT Tabor after work not really sure who he'd find. He didn't expect to see Tidd there and was pleased to spot her practicing *wing chun*. With a fading sun streaking from the west, he admired her tight control, visualizing her sidestepping imaginary opponents while initiating crippling counterattacks.

When she finished with a powerful heel strike, he approached. "Nice moves."

"I bet you say that to all the girls."

"Want to push?"

She put her arms up and they began with the form, a dance where push faded to pull, moving backward and forward. After a few minutes, they naturally shifted to freeform, each trying to unbalance the other.

Within two minutes, she had swept his legs out and he was sitting on the cushy grass. She helped him up.

"You're stiff tonight," she said as they resumed. "Tough day at the office?"

"Some of that. More personal drama."

"Want to talk?"

"No."

"Okay." She came at him relentlessly, a blur of arms, an occasional kick or foot sweep. He parried and evaded with no time for counterattack.

She would tweak his ear or tap his groin with a light "got you" tag, just enough to let him know that she had him.

"If y'all don't relax, you're going to be getting hurt some."

His mind was no longer on Louise. He had to focus attention on the wolverine he'd chosen to play with. Finally he got into the flow and his parrying became smoother. When she advanced, going for a strike to his solar plexus, he slapped her hand aside, stepped behind her with his left leg, and kicked out her right leg with his right leg. She landed smoothly with a judo break fall and was up before he had a chance to comment.

"Don't you go gloating now, Brian Hanson. We're tied one to one. And now you've gone and made me mad."

"I didn't think martial artists of your stature ever got mad," he joked.

"I'm not mad about you throwing me, I'm mad that you were so awkward up until then."

He extended his arm and they restarted the form. Smooth, blending aggression and absorption like yin and yang.

"You're not thinking about drinking, are you?" she asked. Bonnie had had an alcoholic brother who had died in a drunk-driving accident when he was thirty-five.

"Stinkin' thinkin'. I've done a few meetings. I'm okay."

"If you're going to relapse, call me. Day or night."

"You're going to be my sponsor?"

"Nah. I'll come over and kick your sorry posterior so hard you'll need more than a drink to feel better."

And they continued until it was dusk.

Terry and Duane sat in the car, parked up the block from Louise's house. It was two A.M. and the quiet street was deserted.

"You sure you want to do this?" Duane asked.

"Is the bomb set?

"Yeah. I've got it wired to be motion sensitive. We can't sit around here all day with a radio transmitter and a timing device is unpredictable."

"Sweet. You don't sound happy."

"I don't think we should do it. It's mean."

"She's a bitch who deserves to be punished," Terry said. "You can tell she thinks she's hot by the way she walks. Doesn't she remind you of those girls in high school? Remember the one who acted like she wanted to go out on a date with you, then set it up to embarrass you? What did she call you?"

Duane flushed at the memory. "Stop! I don't want to talk about that."

"She's like those girls who didn't see how cool you are."

"Bitches," Duane muttered.

"Damn straight."

"Probably just scare her, right? Teach her a lesson," Duane said hesitantly, his hands alternating their glide through his hair.

"Sometime we can figure out where some of those bitches are nowadays," Terry said. "Punk them, too."

"That would be cool."

"I'll plant it," Terry said, slipping on latex gloves. Duane used the latch in the car to open the trunk. Terry walked behind the car and carefully lifted the bomb. The pipe had a cigarette-pack-sized mercury switch–operated motion detector on one side and a powerful magnet on the other.

"You activate it by flipping this," Duane said, pointing to a small black slide switch.

"I know, I know, you showed me a bunch of times already."

"Put it near the front, not by the gas tank."

"You've told me that already. Don't want to make too big a boom."

"You could kill her or cripple her," Duane stressed.

Terry sauntered to where Louise's car was parked, looked both ways, saw no one was around, and bent down. The magnet made a thunk as Terry attached the bomb to the gas tank. Terry felt around, then flicked the switch, activating it. She calmly walked back down the block. Duane started the car and pulled away rapidly.

Duane asked, "It go okay?"

"Beau-ti-ful," Terry said, dragging out each syllable and turning on the CD player. AC/DC sang about "Big Balls" and Terry bobbed in the seat. Duane drove without comment.

Louise Parker woke around lunchtime, but didn't have an appetite. The thought of chewing was exhausting. It wouldn't have mattered much; there was no food left in the house. She passed the hall mirror next to her front door and saw a glimpse of herself. Uglier than ever, her hair unwashed, wearing the clothes she had slept in. Putting on makeup was as ridiculous as the idea of showering. What was the point? She went back to bed and after a couple fitful hours sleep, awoke late afternoon when the phone rang.

"Hi, this is Brian."

"Hi."

"How are you?"

"Okay."

"You don't sound okay."

"I'm fine." Long silence. "Life sucks and then you die."

"You sound miserable."

"Don't worry. I'm not worth it."

"I want to come over," he said.

"Don't come."

"How about you do a few simple exercises? Go for a walk. Wash dishes. Fight back."

"Sure, sure," she said, with no believability.

"Promise me you'll go out? Even if just to a 7-Eleven. Pick up Ensure?"

"I'll try."

"I'd really like to come by."

"No."

"I'll call later."

"Okay." She hung up and went to bed. She couldn't sleep, brooding and wishing she could go back to the way her life was before the raid. Sullivan, Heaven, Trent, Brian. Even Uncle Louie was annoying. Clyde was the only positive male in her life, and his unemptied litter box was adding to her distress.

She forced herself to do a few moves she had once learned in a yoga class. Salutation to the sun; cobra, cat, camel, half lotus. She psyched herself up to walk to the grocery. To feel like she was actually accomplishing something.

But the thought of shopping was overwhelming. What would she choose? Could she carry it? She'd take the car. She could handle that. A short drive, not going on the freeway or a busy street. That would be safe.

She went out her door and stared at the car. Could she really drive? She sat on her front steps, unsure what to do.

As Brian hung up, wondering if he sounded too preachy with Louise, the phone rang. He thought it was her and picked it up immediately. The caller spoke briefly, and Brian quickly called 911.

Arnie Beil strolled down the street, carrying a red Armstrong gym bag. He heard sirens in the distance but they could be going anywhere in the corrupt metropolis. He was three houses away from Parker's home when he saw her outside. He hadn't expected it to be this easy.

She was sitting on her front steps like a dazed duck waiting to be slaughtered. She was looking at her car and he expected her to get in. Should he slip in next to her and have her drive them to a secluded spot, or force her back into the house for some private time together?

27

LOUISE STOOD SLOWLY. SHE could do it, she knew it. A short drive. She wouldn't let her world constrict down until she was a helpless recluse. As she reached her Camry, the first police car rounded the corner and parked across the driveway.

"Get away from the vehicle!" the burly black cop shouted.

Beil wondered whether they were on to him. His hand slipped into the gym bag, his finger on the trigger of the Mac-11. He'd go out shooting.

But the police paid no attention to him. After a stunned Louise was hustled to the street on the other side of the house, one sinewy cop knelt down on all fours and crawled toward her car, playing his Maglite across the bottom.

"Suspicious object!" the sinewy cop shouted. Two more cars arrived. The police began evacuating people from their houses, setting up sawhorse barriers and yellow crime scene tape. Beil lingered, hanging back, watching the distracted cops.

What the hell was that about? A bomb scare on her car, it seemed. The white supremacist was frustrated after getting so close. But he had confirmed it was her house, she was living there, and that she looked ill prepared. A cop had been leading her around like she was a zombie with Alzheimer's. No one looking at the pathetic cunt could guess she was a ruthless ZOG killer.

He'd have to write it off as a scouting mission. On that level, it had been a success.

Due to police cordoning off the area, Hanson had to park a couple blocks from the crime scene. He hurried toward Louise's home, relieved that he hadn't heard a blast. Even with all the tumult, as he passed the stocky man with the baseball cap pulled low on his head, and the red Armstrong gym bag in his hand, Hanson's internal alarm tingled. He turned quickly as the man walked away, but saw only his back. Brian soon was stopped at the police line until he identified himself as the one who had called 911.

They let him around the corner and he stood with Louise. Her face was frozen in a flat expression, her head tucked low in her shoulders like a frightened turtle. Several uniformed cops stayed within earshot of the couple, watching Hanson.

Brian held her and she didn't resist, but she didn't respond. As he embraced her, he recalled the man with the gym bag. He let his rational mind review what his spidey sense told him was wrong. The man was walking away from the police excitement; unusual but not unheard of. The gym bag had been heavy in his hand. Usually, those bags just held clothes. This looked like it held denser material. Metal? Not in itself a threat and maybe it was a large water bottle. The man, though clearly in good shape, didn't seem to have the groomed gym goer look. Though of course gym goers varied widely in shape, size, and presentation.

Hanson tried to recall the face, seen for a second. Scruffy beard, deep-set wary eyes under the shadow of a baseball cap, tight unsmiling lips. Alert, cold, predatory.

"Mr. Hanson?"

Brian turned, surprised. The cop had come up silently, or at least his advance was masked by the noise and confusion around them. His close-cropped black hair was streaked with gray. He had a gold detective's shield pinned to a blue blazer, which he was wearing over an orange and yellow floral Hawaiian shirt.

"I'm Detective Kohler. I'd like to talk with you."

"I saw Arnold Beil."

"Wow. Please come with me."

Brian turned to Louise and said, "I'll be right back."

The detective walked Hanson off to the side. "When and where did you see Beil?" Kohler seemed nonplussed by the information, as if Hanson had been commenting on a rainy day in May.

"He was walking that way." Hanson pointed. "Carrying a red gym bag. He's got a scruffy beard now, wearing a dark baseball cap."

"How good a look did you get?"

"He was walking past. It was quick."

"How sure are you?"

Hanson hesitated. "Pretty sure."

"Not positive?"

"Get him and I'll do a lineup," Hanson promised.

Kohler took a small walkie-talkie out of his jacket pocket. "All units in vicinity of Ladd's Addition, be on the lookout for Arnold Beil. Suspect is wanted in several shootings of law enforcement officers and is to be considered armed and extremely dangerous. Possibly heading west on Division. Caucasian male in his forties with a short cut beard wearing a dark baseball cap and carrying a red gym bag. Check your computers for full description and photo."

"Thank you," Hanson said.

"We still need to talk."

"I'd rather stay with Louise."

"You need to come with me." Kohler's tone remained pleasantly conversational, but clearly it was a command. "Can I see your driver's license?"

"Why?"

"Purely routine. You can wait in my car."

"Can I tell Louise?"

"It violated procedure to have you with her. I think the uniforms were showing her professional courtesy. Wave and I'll get you back to her as soon as possible."

"I don't have to go with you."

"But you do. If you push it, I can detain you as a material witness. Now please give me your license and go sit in my car," the cop said like a teacher who had never been disobeyed. Hanson waved to Louise, handed over his license to the cop, and sat in the back of a navy blue Crown Victoria. A police radio squawked in the front. The small computer screen displayed Beil's wanted poster. The counselor had an uncomfortable déjà vu feeling, seated in the back of the squad car, reminded of his arrest a few days earlier. At least he wasn't handcuffed.

The bomb techs pulled up in their truck with the blue spherical bomb disposal trailer. A cop activated the remote control and the bomb disposal robot rolled out the back of the van and advanced on Louise's car with a steady whiny hum. The cop worked the hydraulics and an arm with video camera extended under the car. Cops studied the monitor.

Houses had been evacuated three deep on both sides of Louise's home. The police line was several hundred yards back and congested with neighbors. There was lots of loud socializing, speculating, and complaining. People wore everything from flannel robes to formal attire, and the mood had as broad a range, from those anticipating an adventure, to those who feared it was yet another sign of the decline of civilization.

As Hanson sat waiting, he saw FBI Special Agent in Charge Jerry Sullivan pulling up with three well-dressed men. Did they wear suits all the time?

Kohler spoke on his radio for a few minutes, then to Louise for a bit longer, and then briefly to a couple of patrol officers.

He got in the car with Hanson as if they were old friends going for a ride in the country. He handed back the license.

"Can I go now?"

"Tell me about the phone call you got." He started the car and began driving.

"It sounded like a white male in his twenties or thirties. Called me about twenty minutes ago."

"Which phone?"

"What?"

The cop glanced up in the rearview mirror. "Home, work, cell?"

"Work."

"Direct line or through the switchboard?"

"I can't tell."

"Go on. The phone rang, you picked it up. There was a Caucasian male on the line. And he said?"

" 'If you care about Louise, you better let her know there's a bomb under her car.' Then he hung up."

"Are those his exact words?"

"Yes."

"Any accent? Southern? New York? Boston? Foreign?"

"No."

Kohler continued to question the counselor as he drove, dissecting exactly what Hanson had done from the moment he received the call. Brian debated whether to tell him what they had learned in Seattle, but he decided to let Louise lead on how much should be disclosed. Though shaded by depression, her judgment around law enforcement politics and procedures would be better than his.

Then they were at the East Bureau precinct. As they walked past the front desk, Kohler was thanking him for his cooperation.

"I'd like to go back to Louise," Hanson said.

"The most helpful thing you can do for her is assist fully with the investigation," Kohler said.

They sat facing each other in a windowless, cinderblock room with bolted down table and chairs. The room was more worn than the FBI's, but with the same oppressive ambiance. A small poster on the wall reviewed the Miranda rights. One wall was taken up by a large mirror.

"Is there someone watching?" Hanson asked, pointing to the mirror. He looked at his own face, surprised at how haggard he appeared.

"Probably not. Do you care?"

"Am I under arrest?" Hanson asked.

"Not at all. You're free to go if you'd like. But talking with me will help Louise. And can help you."

"How?"

"On your pending assault charge."

"You know about that?" Hanson asked. "Of course, you ran me when you took my license."

"Have to know who I'm getting in a car with. Brian Hanson. A few minor arrests when you were in your twenties. DUI, minor assault, open container. I understand you knew Bill McFarlane."

"He helped me get clean and sober. Was my sponsor."

"He was a good man. My partner for a couple years. This does seem like a small town sometimes. Then about six months ago, the incident with your ex-wife and the deputy mayor." His tone was as friendly as a buddy at a poker game, no matter what the subject.

"Nothing came of that."

"Nope. Just your name was in the files. Then that recent assault charge. And your girlfriend getting harassed. Convenient you got the call of a bomb?"

"Are you hinting at something?"

"No contact with criminal justice for more than twenty-five years, except for three parking violations. Then boom, life gets exciting. No pun intended."

"Do you have a specific question for me?"

"Would you like a cup of coffee?"

"How long will I be here?"

The cop glanced at his watch. "A few hours."

"Why?"

"We need to run through your statement for the record."

"What about all you asked in the car?"

"We need to go through it again. Slowly."

And they did.

28

T HE BEST PRICE SECONDHAND store was located on SE Foster Road deep in the Lents neighborhood. There were rusty bars on the window and a motley display of appliances behind them. Handwritten stickers showed deep discounted prices. A "Sale Today Only" sign was sun bleached and curled with age.

The FBI had already successfully conducted one major investigation of Portland's secondhand stores. The stores were less regulated than pawnshops and had become major fencing operations, using eBay and other online markets. The interstate, even international, nature of the business, and the Portland Police Bureau's lack of attention to the problem had led to wonderful PR after a slew of FBI arrests.

Trent Gorman had put pressure on informants gathered in that case to get a lead on Arnold Beil. When he walked inside the store, and loudly announced "FBI. I need to talk to the store's owner," it was like a dangerous gunfighter walking into a Wild West saloon. The few patrons were out the door faster than a stampeding herd.

"Why'd you go and do that?" the burly man behind the counter asked. He was in his forties, with short cut hair dyed blond and tattoos of snakes on his thick forearms.

"Not the smartest *nom de guerre*," Gorman said, pointing to the shopkeeper's forearms.

"Huh?"

"Your alias. Snake."

"I don't know what you're talking about."

Gorman leaned over the counter. "I don't give a damn if this place is packed with stolen property. I don't give a damn if your business is mainly cash, and IRS agents would wet their pants doing an audit. I don't care if you've got more building code violations than a Tijuana whorehouse." Gorman picked up a DVD from a foot-high stack on the counter. It was a recent film, not shrink wrapped, and the star's name was misspelled on the box. "Or bootleg DVDs. You know how at the beginning of movies they have that warning how the FBI is going to get copyright violators? Five years per crime. Two-hundred-fifty-thousand-dollar fine."

The shopkeeper nodded.

Gorman lowered his voice, as if confiding a secret. "It's not really a high priority." He leaned across the counter, his face inches from the shopkeeper. "But I can change that. You're going to tell me what you know. Then I'm going to leave. If not, I'm going to start counting DVDs. Each one is a count in the indictment."

"Maybe I need a lawyer?"

"Just listen, scumbag. Then decide if you want to lawyer up and make your calls from the jail downtown."

"Who'll run the store?"

"Not my problem. In fact, after I march you out of here in handcuffs, I think I'll announce that the door is open. How much of this delightful hot crap will be left by the time you get back?"

"You can't do that."

"Just watch me." Gorman grinned. "Your name is Snake. You're a white supremacist. You were a local contact for Arnold Beil. How am I doing so far?"

"I don't know what you're talking about."

"Okay," Gorman said. He moved quickly, handcuffs a blur, snapping one on Snake's wrist before the man even knew what was happening. Snake tugged back, and Gorman jerked hard on the other cuff, yanking Snake until he was bent forward over the counter.

Gorman took out his gun. "We can add resisting arrest to your charges."

"You didn't tell me I was under arrest."

"I did, you didn't hear it."

"What about my Miranda warning?"

"So remain silent."

"This ain't right."

"Listen, normally I'm the epitome of politeness, even with turds like yourself. But Beil has killed some brother officers. And he tried to kill a female agent here. A friend of mine. You know what that makes it?"

"Personal?"

"That's the smartest thing you've said. Do you want to tell me more or do you want a free ride downtown so your friends can pick this place cleaner than Martha Stewart's kitchen?"

"Okay, I know of him. And I was supposed to be a contact. I put him in touch with someone. Then that someone turned up dead."

"Names? Details?" Gorman asked, pulling on the cuffs. Snake was stretched across the counter.

"A skinhead named Gunny was supposed to help Beil out. Then Gunny wound up dead in a fire at a meth dealer named Chico. Looked like a robbery gone bad, I heard. Gunny wouldn't have the brains or the balls to pull something like that off."

"And so where is Beil?"

"I don't know, honest. No one's heard anything from him. No one wants anything to do with him. He's too hot. I heard a rumor he was heading to Canada."

"Where?"

"British Columbia. There's a Hell's Angels chapter up there, he's got some connections."

Gorman loosened his grip on the handcuffs and Snake slumped back over the counter. "Now, if you hear from Mr. Beil, what happens?" Gorman took out a business card and dropped it on the counter.

"I call you."

He unhooked Snake's wrist and slipped the cuffs back into his pocket. "You'll get yourself good karma in the future." Gorman held up a DVD box. "And by the way, the actress's name is not spelled Reece Weatherspon."

Snake bobbed his head appreciatively.

"If I find out you had any contact with Beil or his associates, or let him know I was here, or send him money or goods, I will be displeased. You understand what that means?"

"Yes, I swear."

"We have an understanding."

Gorman drove back to the office and wrote up his report as if Snake was a voluntary informant. In the 302, there was no mention of the force and the threats. Gorman had gone to the secondhand goods store alone to allow optimal denial interrogation. He doubted that Snake would be filing a complaint. It was old school but no one faulted an agent who got results. Particularly on a case with someone who had killed agents.

Louise Parker was one of the few women in the office, married or single, who hadn't given in to his charming persistence. He hoped that being a key player in the case would help him get in her tight drawers. Even if not, it would be a solid career move.

His report was filed and filtered up the chain of command.

Portland Special Agent in Charge Jerry Sullivan sat behind the desk in his corner office, fingers steepled in front of his face, waiting to get briefed by his assistant. The few papers on the desk were neatly stacked, the stacks parallel with each other and the edges of the desk. Like his idol, Ronald Reagan, he prided himself on being a skilled communicator who didn't have the time or inclination to bother with details. A one-page summary on a country, or better still, a video, was far more likely to be accessed than a cumbersome twenty-five-page report.

His assistant was thirty-nine-year-old Katie Naylor, a Brigham Young University graduate with an accounting degree and mind-boggling organizational abilities. He didn't trust her one hundred percent, since she was a woman and had been friendly with Louise Parker. But no one else could put together a complex operation with multiple sources of data so quickly, develop algorithms, effectively allocate investigative resources, and craft a coherent and politically sensitive report. Besides, it looked good to have a woman involved.

"What can you tell me?" he asked as she handed him a cup of coffee. It was one of the unstated rules that any woman going into Sullivan's office brought him coffee. Cookies, too, ideally, but Katie refused. He didn't know that most of the time she took an unwashed cup from the rack. And more than a few times, she had spit in it before giving it to the white-haired Special Agent in Charge.

"Your coffee is always so delicious," Sullivan said.

"My mother taught me how to make it." He also didn't know her mother had been artful at expressing passive-aggressive hostility.

"You have information for me?' he asked, sipping the coffee.

She sat before his desk in a seat that was deliberately softer and a few inches lower than his. The picture window behind him was festooned with the products of his hobby, stained glass panels. When the sunlight streamed, the homemade three-by-four-foot squares created a churchlike, medieval regal tone in the otherwise starkly modern office.

"First off, the call to Heaven's place apparently tipping him off that a raid was imminent. We dumped phone records and traced the booth it was made from. Downtown Portland. Canvassed for possible witnesses. Nothing. Dusted for fingerprints and found no known supremacist supporters."

"This cousin of his who was sleeping with him, she have any more information about the call?"

"Nothing. Though we understand her attorney is negotiating a book deal where she promises to reveal new information."

"Do you have any positive news?" Sullivan asked irritably.

"Promising information on the bomb. As you know, getting an undetonated device gives us a remarkable amount of information. The device was placed under the car by the fuel tank in a spot that would have done maximum damage. Most likely would have killed the occupant of the car and anyone within about twenty-five feet. The craftsmanship on the pipe bomb was slightly above average. No tamping or shaping of charge. Unfortunately, it doesn't have any fingerprints on it."

"That doesn't sound that helpful," Sullivan interjected.

"We have tracked down where the chemicals came from. The spectrographic analysis showed it was potassium nitrate, sulfur, sodium sulfate. A not uncommon amateur combination whose instruction patterns are widely available. The ingredients were purchased at Modern Chemicals on NE Columbia near the airport."

"Anyone able to describe the suspects?"

"Bad luck there. The man behind the counter is the owner, who is decidedly antigovernment. Apparently had a run-in with the IRS about five years ago and that confirmed his opinions. He's in his eighties, close to legally blind. Our suspect is female, medium build and height, wearing a baseball cap and sunglasses. Caucasian, somewhere between twenty and forty years old. Polite, intelligent, he thinks the person was quite nice. He was surprised but not shocked when he heard about the bomb. He said he thought the customer was a Civil War enthusiast."

"Security cameras?'

"They had a fake one. One of those big boxes with a blinking red light. They were robbed only once, about fifteen years ago."

"Is it worth bringing him in?"

"He looks like he could die of a coronary any minute."

Sullivan fiddled with his official FBI coffee cup while he thought. He wrinkled his nose and said, "Bring him in. Maybe he's got family working the business who will be more motivated to come forward when the old man is incommunicado. Let them know we'll leak the name to the paper that they supply bombers."

"That's actually liable to help their business."

"Hmmm. Okay, just pick him up. No physical roughness, obviously, but make it sound like he's going to be locked up as a material witness. Trent had mentioned this Brian Hanson as a possibility?"

"Hanson recently had a run-in with police and was arrested on an assault charge that seems unrelated to this case. He's a Vietnam veteran with a subsequent history of mental health and addictions problems, who became a mental health counselor."

"He's got demo skills?"

"His military record doesn't indicate that. Extensive combat experience. Skilled hand-to-hand and small arms. Our bomb people also say the device doesn't look like it was created by someone with military ordinance expertise. It's fairly simple, the kind of device you can get instructions for over the Internet."

"So it could very well be him. Is he Parker's boyfriend?"

"Doubtful." Naylor did not disclose that her information came from conversations she had had with Louise. While the women weren't friends, they were friendly. "He reports receiving a call from what he guesses was a youngish Caucasian male. He called 911 immediately then hurried over there. While standing at the scene, he spotted someone who he identified as Arnold Beil."

"Positive ID?"

"He's fairly confident."

"Credible?"

"I believe so."

"Even though he's a mental case with drug problems?"

"Louise spoke highly of his powers of observation."

"When was this?"

"Uh, before there was trouble. She mentioned him to me in passing."

"I see. You understand that anything we discuss today is confidential?"

"Of course, sir."

"No behind-my-back girl talk."

"No, sir."

"What do our BSU people say about Beil?"

"They're skeptical about the bomb being his. Never a past MO for him. And based on his past patterns of high mobility, they're also skeptical over whether he's in the area. There have been sightings in a half dozen field offices around the country. Reports also from Mexico and Canada. Nothing verified. Trent received information from a CI he describes as reliable that Beil has fled to British Columbia. Beil was born and reared in Portland, but BSU is confident that if he has come into the area, it would be for revenge."

"The office is at increased risk?"

"Yes."

"You should have told me that immediately."

"Yes, sir."

"Do they speculate how he might attack?"

"He does have expertise as a sniper." She glanced pointedly at the big window behind Sullivan. "But he's used handguns and knives primarily."

"I see. Well. I want daily briefings on this. And of course interrupt any meeting forthwith if there is urgent information. That's all."

"Yes, sir."

Even before Naylor was out of the office, Sullivan was moving to close the curtains behind him. She stifled her desire to smirk.

29

"WHAT THE FUCK HAPPENED?" Terry asked, holding up an *Oregonian* metro section where the story about a bomb found at Louise Parker's car was a brief item on page B-three. A law enforcement source said police were blaming white supremacist Arnold Beil, who had been spotted in the area. "How did she find the bomb under the car? That bitch has got nine lives," Terry fumed.

Duane said nothing, while his hands alternated through his hair, right, left, right, left.

"We could plant another one," Terry mused.

"I think it's too dangerous. They'll be watching her house."

"She doesn't go out of her damn house. How are we going to get her otherwise?"

"Maybe we should just stop?"

"That's fine for you to say. It's not your heart she broke."

"You don't even really . . ."

"Shut up. You don't understand. Stick to your wires and electronic gizmos."

Terry stormed out. Duane heard the door slam. He sat down in front of his Xbox and played Halo continuously for two hours. Several hundred aliens died before he felt better.

Beil punched the 125-year-old wooden wall until his knuckles were raw and bleeding. The meth and his fury muted the pain.

He had been so fucking close. A few seconds from taking her out. Even if he hadn't had a chance to have fun with her, seeing her face when she recognized him, watching the bullets chew up that federal pork, would have been so satisfying.

He had his exit strategy planned. Kill her, steal a fresh car, drive to Bonners Ferry, Idaho. Folks in the panhandle had a long history of minding their own business and helping fugitives. There were numerous ways to sneak into Canada.

He sat on the floor, picking splinters out of his hands. He could feel the influence of the meth waning in his system. The crash was coming. He had a few days' worth left. The local meth community probably had better information sharing than Interpol and word of Chico's demise had no doubt spread.

He grabbed a few beers and went to his sleeping bag. He'd get drunk and sleep off the crash. When he awoke, he'd be ready.

There was nothing dramatic about Louie Parker's presentation, just a weariness that made him seem more like the septugenarian he was. "Louise canceled our dinner," he told Hanson. "She hasn't done that more than twice in the past ten years. Both times she had reasons—once the flu, once a big case."

"Maybe she has a reason now."

"She's going downhill."

Hanson wanted to ask more about Louise but Louie was his client, and the counselor's job was to focus on Louie's feelings and coping, rather than the state of his niece.

"What are you doing to take care of yourself?'

"Can the bullshit, doc. I counted on you to help me get Beil. Once he's locked up or dead she'll start getting better."

"Louie, I'm sure the local police and the FBI are working as hard as they can on this."

"Look at that Olympic bomber Eric Rudolph. They made him one of the ten most wanted in 1998, and he got caught scavenging in a Dumpster in 2003 by a rookie cop. The Unabomber. He was sending out bombs for what, twenty years?"

"The point is, they did get caught."

"After how much damage?"

"What do you plan on doing?"

"Not me. Us."

Hanson leaned back in his seat. Whatever Louie asked was probably going to be an ethical concern, if not an outright violation. "What are you thinking of?"

"I know where Arnold Beil's mother lives," Parker said.

"Is she hiding him?" Hanson asked.

"Not likely."

"How can you be sure?"

"She's about eighty. Living in an assisted living home over in Southwest."

"Do you think she knows where Beil is?"

"About as likely as George Bush and Osama bin Laden playing croquet."

"I'm sure police would appreciate any information."

Parker snorted. "Cops. They've been out there already. Shirley won't tell them diddly. She used to be a stripper. That's how she met Pete Beil. She still don't like cops."

"She'll talk to us?"

"Could be. I was coming into my own when Pete's star was waning. You know about Portland organized crime history?"

"Not much."

"We had some characters back then. Not a Mafia thing, but guys with names like Big Jim Elkins, Swede Ferguson, Blubber Maloney. A police chief nicknamed Diamond Jim."

"Sounds like a *Guys and Dolls* cast."

"Damon Runyan and Times Square had nothing on us. We were the center for shanghaing sailors and prostitution around the turn of the century. Then for liquor during Prohibition. Before Vegas, there were more than two hundred fifty gambling joints or whorehouses here. Card rooms, after hours joints, strip clubs." Louie was silent for a moment, lost in a pleasant memory. "A great place for a guy to grow up. Though hard to hang on to your money."

"Not exactly the image the Chamber of Commerce promotes."

"We had enough going on to make a Chicago alderman blush," Parker said. "The party started coming to an end in the mid-1950s. Bobby Kennedy hauled a bunch of wiseguys to Washington, D.C., and made them perform at a Rackets Committee hearing. It forced officials to clean house at the police department, get an honest DA in. Elect a reform mayor. Pete Beil was one of the casualties. He died in the eighties. His wife, Shirley, was about twenty years younger than him. She was quite the dame in her time. I'm counting on your skill to get something helpful out of her."

"I'm not an interrogator."

"If you were, she would shut right down. Talk to her, maybe something will come out."

"I'm free after five."

"Then it's good I set the meet for five-thirty. Pick me up and we can drive out there."

After the session, as the counselor was walking down the hall, Betty Pearlman signaled him. "Got a second?"

He entered her office and she indicated for him to close the door. His first thought was that a client had attempted suicide. Svetlana? Moose? Freddy? Maybe he hadn't done enough outreach, maybe he hadn't worked hard enough to engage them.

"I'm worried about you, Brian," Betty began, ending his ruminating. "You continue to have an unhealthy edge."

"What do you mean?" Brian asked.

"The way you walk, your interactions with staff, even with clients. Beating up that DV perp."

"That was in part self-defense."

"I heard what his injuries were. You could have stopped after he hit the ground."

"I did stop. Sort of."

"I'm not going to debate the extent of assault with you. You recognize you probably retraumatized your own client by that display?" Betty paused. "The signs of burnout are in your eyes. They're angry and sad and alert and scary. The last time you were building up like this, you used paid time off. Things seemed to get better. You've got lots of PTO accumulated. Have you considered a vacation?"

"No place really comes to mind," he said. "I'll take time off. Maybe I'll get out of town. Maybe not. Are you ordering me to take leave?"

"Not quite yet. I'm strongly suggesting it. And I recommend you talk to a therapist. Consider the free counseling through the EAP, though I think you need more than six sessions. I know people in town, if you'd like a recommendation."

"I suspect I know them, too."

"Brian, you're one of the best I've ever worked with. But you're too close to the edge."

"I'll take some time off over the next week. Make my schedule a little less intense."

"That's a start. As much as I care about you as a person, and value you as a clinician, I cannot have you screwing things up. For the clients, for the staff who count on you, for myself and my responsibilities to the agency. However you exorcise your demons, it's time, Brian."

30

THE CEDAR-SIDED SILVER CLOUDS Assisted Living Center was located near the Beaverton-Hillsdale Highway, on a low ridge with a view of southwest Portland. The grounds were landscaped with rhododendrons, camellias, and azaleas. Residents sat outside on wooden benches, enjoying the sunny weather. For the more vigorous, there was a three-hole golf course, shuffleboard, and horseshoe pits.

As Hanson pulled into a parking space, Louie commented, "This is one of the fanciest geezer joints around. If I had skimmed half as much as the feds said I had, I'd be here."

Hanson had been in facilities for older adults that reeked of urine and decay. Silver Clouds was more like a hotel with nurse's aides instead of chambermaids. An activity board near the front door listed enough going on to exhaust a thirty-year-old. Residents moved down the hall with varying degrees of assistance, from those who relied on canes, to walkers, to wheelchairs, to being pushed in a wheelchair. One man advanced using a rolling IV pole as his supportive companion.

Shirley was waiting for Hanson and Parker when they reached her room. Her hair was dyed blond and rouge gave her cheeks an artificial glow. Her lipstick was a bright red, her eyes a pale brown. Hanson could easily see how she would've been the kind of woman a gangster would value as a prize.

"I believe a lady shouldn't entertain gentlemen in her bedroom," she said, and led them back down the hall to a social room with two couches, a gaggle of wingback chairs, and a large screen TV. There was a heavyset woman dozing in the chair.

"Gertie, would you mind?" Shirley asked.

Gertie gave Shirley a brief glare, but didn't say anything. Gertie took her walker and rolled away.

"She knows better than to take up public space when she can sleep in her room," Shirley said. "But she'll be up at the front desk complaining for the next half hour." Shirley sat slowly, wincing with an arthritic twinge. "Well, Louie, are you here to ask me out?" She lowered her chin, gazed at Parker with a seductive look, then turned to study Hanson. "And you brought a handsome chaperone."

"Shirley, you got too much pep for an old guy like me," Louie said. "I ought to fix you up with Brian here."

Their banter made Hanson wonder if they had ever been intimate. Shirley had a languid way of moving, engaging eye contact, and a husky tone that must have been siren-like seductive in her earlier years.

"Louie, you're a scoundrel. Of course I've always liked that in a man."

For a few minutes, they compared notes on mutual acquaintances. Several had passed away or were in the hospital dealing with hip replacements, prostate or breast cancer, osteoporosis, strokes, heart attacks.

"And Edie just got a face lift."

"Ah, Edie."

They gossiped about Edie who, Hanson gathered, was well into her eighties, passed for twenty years younger, and was still enjoying a life of sin.

"I've got to give her a call," Louie said with a wink.

Shirley slapped him playfully and Louie deliberately reacted like he'd be bruised for a week.

"Your young friend must be getting tired of our repartee," Shirley said. "But he's quite polite. And attentive. Not as judgmental looking as a police detective. And I wouldn't expect you to be keeping company like that." She turned to Hanson. "I suspect you're here about Arnie?"

Brian nodded.

Louise asked, "And what's your interest in him?"

Before Brian could respond, Louie said, "He's sort of dating my niece."

"Your niece. The FBI agent?"

"Yes."

"I have no sympathy for federal agents."

"Someone's been giving her a hard time. She's always played by the rules, Shirley. She deserves better."

"The police were by, asking questions. The FBI, too. I gave them my best doddering old lady impression. They probably think I'm senile." She smirked at the memory.

Louie gazed deeply into Shirley's eyes. "Shirley, she's all I've got."

"If Arnie had contacted me, I would tell you. He hasn't. I haven't spoke with him in fifteen years."

Hanson decided it was time to speak. "Shirley, I'm a therapist trying to get an understanding of Arnie. Hopefully we can find him and have him brought in peacefully."

"Fat chance. He won't be taken alive." A tear formed in the corner of her eye. Hanson spotted a tissue box and brought it over. Shirley dabbed at her eyes. "Arnie was a troubled child. Neither one of us were great parents. Pete had a mean streak and sometimes he took it out on Arnie. Pete tried his best. He didn't have such a good childhood himself.

"I never wanted to have children," she continued. "Deep down I knew. I didn't like anything about having a baby, getting fat, having someone so dependent on me, being called 'Mom.' I waited until I was in my forties to have him. Nowadays, women do that sort of thing. Back then, everyone had assumed Pete or I weren't biologically able." She paused. "Do you really want to hear an old woman ramble?"

"Shirley, you're not rambling," Hanson said in his soft therapeutic voice.

She turned to Louie. "A flatterer. I like that almost as much as a scoundrel." She turned back to Hanson. "Arnie was born, we were older, he was a colicky baby. Pete had his business, though things had turned sour after that ambitious little creep Bobby Kennedy. I was an okay mother, nothing special. It was Pete's stories that made Arnie what he is today. Talking about Jesse James, how Americans have to fight the government, going back to the Boston Tea Party. And telling Arnie he would have grown up a millionaire if the government hadn't stolen Pete's earnings."

"What was Arnie like as a boy?" Hanson asked. "Shy, outgoing? Did he have a lot of friends? Hobbies?"

"As a kid, well, he liked to play with fire. There were a couple of abandoned houses that burned down that I know he did. He wasn't kind, particularly with animals. A few cats, a few dogs." She shivered. "I don't like to think about what he did. I even tried to get him into therapy. Pete said it was a waste of money but let me take him. Arnie saw a shrink seven, eight times. The shrink told me he thought Arnie was a charming boy. Maybe he didn't want to tell a mother the truth."

"Hobbies?"

"Aside from setting fires? Well, there was one thing he and my husband liked to do. You know the Portland Underground?"

"The Shanghai Tunnels," Louie piped in.

"I've heard about them," Brian said. "Not sure how much was exaggerated."

"They were wicked, wicked places," Shirley said. "Men in the bars would be drugged and wake up out on the ocean. It was worse for the women. Women didn't patronize the bars, but would be lured from dances or even kidnapped from the streets by white slavers. They'd be taken to the Underground, taken advantage of repeatedly, locked in a dark room the size of a closet. After a few days, most were so terrified, their spirits broken, that they could be shipped to brothels in mining towns, San Francisco, or elsewhere on the West Coast. The shanghaied sailors often made it back to Portland, the women were never seen again.

"One woman tried to help reformers. She was thrown down an elevator shaft by corrupt cops. Her ghost is still seen on a regular basis." Shirley paused, took a deep breath. "I'm not one who generally believes in ghosts, but I wouldn't be surprised if that's what happened to Arnie. He got possessed by an evil spirit." Shirley was crying freely. "A fine way for a mother to talk about her son."

"When Pete and Arnie would go in the tunnels, did they talk about a particular part?" Hanson asked after what seemed like an appropriate wait.

"It was a long time ago."

"This is important," Louie said.

"You think he might be down there?" she asked.

Hanson shrugged. "I'm trying to understand him better."

"I remember one time him complaining about them closing off part of the tunnel near the Morrison Bridge. They were doing earthquake repair work. He talked about how when they tore down some of the old hotels, they sealed up passages, just filled them with rocks. Pete used to talk about the North End. That neighborhood's been known by so many names. Old Town. Chinatown. That was his favorite part. That's where most of the tunnels were. But they went over past where the courthouse is now. Pete tried to get me to go down there. I went once, down a flight of stairs, through a couple of basements. I got a chill right to my bones. I had to leave immediately."

"Do you recall where that was?"

She thought again, nibbled at her lip. "When I came out onto the street, I could barely breathe. I remember the corner. Third and Everett."

"Thank you. Is there anything else you'd like to tell me?" Hanson asked.

She shook her head. "I've read stories in the newspaper about what they say he's done. Sometimes people here will ask me if I am related to him. I tell them no." Silent tears started to flow again. "You know about these things; am I responsible for what he's done?"

The counselor patted her hand. "No, Shirley. I can tell you did your best. Sometimes things don't work out for people, no matter how hard their parents tried."

She closed her eyes, savoring his words. "Thank you, whether what you're saying is true or not. I hope he doesn't hurt anyone else." She turned to Louie. "Particularly your niece."

Louie gave her a tender kiss on the lips. "You're a good woman, Shirley."

She shook her head like Mae West, shifting back into character. "And when I'm bad, I'm very, very good."

Parker and Hanson were back in the car when Louie asked, "Do you think we can get the police to search the tunnels around Third and Everett?"

"We can try."

"If that place is anything like I've heard, it'll take an army to flush him out."

31

S ITTING IN THE SMALL windowless room in the Portland FBI field office, Hanson recalled this was where he had first met Louise Parker.
She had initially been skeptical, about six months earlier, when he'd reported his suspicions on a case. Now he was with Trent Gorman, the room
still unadorned and uncomfortable, and Gorman cynical, a veneer of stiff
professionalism over a core of hostility.

"Let me get this straight," Gorman was saying. "You think you saw
Arnold Beil for a fraction of a second. Then you interview his senile mother,
who talks about his childhood love for the underground tunnels, and you
want me to start a major manhunt."

"She's not senile."

"Are you an expert on dementia, too?"

"I've worked with people with Alzheimer's and other types of dementia.
She was as clear and lucid as you are."

"I read the agent's interview with her. The lights were on but no one's
home."

"She's also a good actress who doesn't like law enforcement."

"Mr. Hanson, are you in any way trying to get some sort of credit to mit-
igate your assault charges?'

"No."

"Maybe it's you want to look like a hero for Louise?"

Hanson was silent. "Special Agent Gorman," Hanson said, emphasizing
the word "special." "I'm telling you what I know. From my interview with
his mother, I'd say Arnold Beil is a psychopath, a mix of narcissism and sociopathy. I think he will be driven by a combination of feelings of safety in
the tunnels and rage over the narcissistic injury that occurred to him at
Heaven's farm, to seek revenge."

"Let me guess, the tunnel is a giant womb."

"Very nice, but I'm not that psychodynamic. It may be a remembrance of a more pleasant time in his life or a wanting the home turf advantage. Whatever the rationale, he's a serious danger."

"That's hardly news. And you're not exactly a poster child for mental health. When I found you skulking around outside her place that night, I checked your pedigree. You look normal. On the surface. But there's a lot of weirdo underneath."

"My history is no secret," Hanson said, trying not to sound defensive.

Gorman stood in a gesture of dismissal. "I'll note your suspicions. Thanks for being an upright citizen and coming in."

"Listen, Trent, we both want Louise to be safe."

"That's right, Mr. Hanson. So leave this to the professionals."

Clyde meowed loudly and Louise moved slowly to the kitchen. The pantry was empty. No more cat food. Louise had been living on peanut butter and jelly or cheese sandwiches, fruit juice, black coffee, Diet Coke, and chocolate ice cream. For how many days had she existed on a scavenged diet?

Clyde meowed again and her guilt grew. She had to get him food. Which meant going out. Which meant looking better than she did. A glance in the mirror confirmed what she knew—she looked like someone who could be living under a bridge. She had worn the same unwashed sweat pants and shirt for several days, hair matted, no makeup, dark bags under her eyes despite fourteen hours a day sleeping.

Louise peeled off her clothes and got in the shower. She struggled to find the right temperature and pressure, her skin sensitive to the water. She watched the water pool up in the tub, create a whirlpool, then disappear down the drain.

She remembered what Brian had told her about having to challenge depressive thinking, the four classic patterns: catastrophize, command, condemn, can't stand it.

Well, people had died because of her actions. And a bomb had been planted under her car. Wasn't that catastrophic? And she had to find the person who was after her to get her life back. Wasn't that a command? And her actions on the raid led in part to the deaths. Didn't that deserve condemnation? And would she be able to stand it if she was fired in shame from the FBI?

Okay, then Brian had told her to "Get busy to get better." With great effort, she cleaned up old laundry she'd left lying around, wrinkling her nose at the smell. Actually doing a wash was overwhelming, but at least there was no more clothing on the floor.

She sat at the kitchen table, making a short list of items to pick up. Other than cat food, it was hard to think of anything. What did she usually like? Nothing was tempting. She could get down fruit juice, and she knew from Brian that the brain needed glucose to function. Maybe crackers, apple sauce, and some Ensure to keep her strength up. The thought of anything chewy was too exhausting.

Dressed and ready to go, she peered out the curtains. The street looked quiet. She knew there had been a police car parked up the block much of the morning. She went out, forgot her keys, and went back in.

She returned to the car, bent down, and looked under it for bombs. She opened the hood and searched for anything that looked like it didn't belong. She flinched as she started the engine, then drove to New Seasons at five miles under the speed limit. It took her a long time to decide what she needed, but eventually she half filled her cart with essentials. She was relieved to get her groceries packed and carry her two bags to the car. They seemed much heavier than she was used to but held enough food to keep her going for a week.

The ride home went a little better. She was eager, focused on getting back into the safety of her house, though exhausted at the effort required to drive carefully, afraid she might hit someone.

She pulled into her driveway. Her neighbor across the street, Mrs. Halliburton, swooped down as Louise got out of the car. Louise didn't want to talk, but knew there was no way to escape without being rude.

"Louise, how are you?" Halliburton asked. She dressed like a sixties earth mother, but drove a Range Rover. She was a gossipy real estate agent whose partner did something with computers and was the head of the neighborhood association.

Louise responded, "Okay. Thanks for asking."

"You don't look so well."

"I've been sick. I'm getting over a nasty cold."

"That was a lot of excitement last night."

"Yes."

"I hope it doesn't happen again."

"Me, too. I better get my food into the fridge," Louise said.

"That sort of incident can harm property values," Halliburton said.

"Thank you for your concern."

"You never know what effect a bomb can have."

"Yes," Louise said, and hurried in. She closed the door, set the groceries down on her counter, and burst into tears.

"I can't believe you pulled that stunt on the bridge," Lieutenant Rosen kept repeating, tapping a pen on the edge of his beat-up desk.

"You know he would've jumped," Hanson responded.

The lieutenant stopped tapping the pen and threw it in a drawer. They were in Rosen's cramped Central Precinct office, crowded with papers, trophies, and plaques from Marv's police softball team, and backlogs of paperwork.

"The media played you up as a hero. Back here in the office, I got reamed. You know how it is with the new chief—better to go by the book and have a negative outcome than do some cowboy stunt that works."

"What do you think?"

"I think I don't want to jeopardize my assignment or my pension. Listen, Brian, you've been around the block a couple times. Lots of people know your history. This assault charge pending makes folks wonder what's going on."

"Like you never got in a little street justice?" Hanson asked.

Rosen looked up at the suspended tile ceiling, made a praying gesture, and said, "Why me, Lord?"

"C'mon, you know I'm probably right about him being in the tunnels."

"Probably isn't good enough. Your credibility isn't the greatest right now. And thanks to you, neither is mine. You've tried the FBI?"

"They took the report."

"Grandstanding bastards. They want us to do the work so they can come in afterward and take the credit without any risk."

"If you got Beil, it would show them."

"I'll see what I can do."

Hanson stood. "You're a prince."

"I'm an idiot."

32

I THINK WE SHOULD let it drop," Duane said.

"That's easy for you to say," Terry snapped.

"I've helped you with everything."

"Well, how come she didn't get blown up if you've been so helpful?"

"Maybe they were more alert because of that white supremacy guy. And that reminds me, they said on the news that it was planted by the gas tank, that it would have blown up the whole car. It would've killed her."

Terry shrugged. "Don't believe everything you hear on the news."

"I don't like this."

"Go play on your computer, okay?"

Terry shut the door to the room. For Duane, with such limited human contact, the rejection was as painful as a hot poker to the soul. He sat with his Xbox for hours, and reached several new levels.

But it was only when Terry came out and made them dinner that he actually calmed down.

Hanson got through to Ogelsby during a break between the professor's classes. "I hope you don't mind if I eat while we talk," Ogelsby said. "I'm working late, trying to polish up lecture notes before student meetings in fifteen minutes."

"I appreciate you taking the time," Hanson said.

"What's your clinical formulation?" Ogelsby asked.

Hanson ran through what he had told the FBI agent—narcissism plus sociopathy.

"A malignant narcissist or psychopath," the professor concurred. "I did an HCR-twenty on him. Are you familiar with the instrument?'

"Violence risk assessment?"

"Correct. Of course it's best face-to-face with the subject. Ten historical questions, five clinical, five risk. He was among the highest scores I've ever seen." There were loud eating noises as Ogelsby tore into a foot-long barbe-cued beef sandwich, brownie, and potato chips, in between sentences. "And I've done this with forensic populations for twenty years. He'd probably like to get revenge, certainly willing to perish in a blaze of glory. His fanaticism makes him the highest possible risk. The idea of being a martyr is probably as appealing to him as to a Hezbollah teen."

"Anything else?"

"Some things don't add up. He'd be a predatory stalker; the gift-giving is inconsistent. That is much more common with an attraction-repulsion schema. I also don't see him as a bomb-planting type. For revenge to be sat-isfying, he'd want to make it personal."

"A personal kill."

"Excuse me?"

"Military term. A grunt on the ground who eyeballs an enemy and shoots him. Infantry may kill a lot less than air force, but jet jockeys don't see the faces. A personal kill is more traumatic than spray and pray, where you empty a clip into the brush."

"I love the nomenclature. A fascinating argot." Hanson heard Ogelsby tapping on a computer keyboard. "It makes sense. The impact of killing varies with proximity and methodology. For example, a stab is more emo-tional than a slash, a knife more than a spear." He took a couple more bites. "Perhaps we could talk in the future. I'd like to check with a linguist col-league, there could be a paper in this."

"If you'd like."

"Definitely."

Portland Police Bureau Officers Jolson and Bauman had been partners for nine years, the last four working in Old Town. They had a reputation for not always following the rules, which had earned them the less than desirable patrol sector. They were competent, honest, and did enough work to get by. They were polite to business owners and patrons, treated street people fairly, and looked forward to pensions in a few more years. Both were in their late forties, fathers of three kids, divorced, and more out of shape than they'd admit.

They got the assignment to check the underground for Arnold Beil.

"Well, here's another fine mess you got us into," Jolson said in a Stan Laurel voice.

"Please, no bad impressions," Bauman said. "It sucks enough some rocket scientist thinks we should check the damn tunnels." Every few months they got a tunnel call, usually involving a homeless person sneaking into an Old Town hotel or restaurant basement. Bauman, with a mild case of claustrophobia, hated the task and tried to foist it off on the next shift. But they had come on at four P.M. and they couldn't delay it until the graveyard shift took over.

"C'mon, we're hunting for one of the FBI's most wanted. It's a win-win situation."

"How you figure that?"

"If they really thought this guy was down there, they'd send SWAT. We're supposed to do a little recon. If he does turn out to be there, we'll be the heroes who first found him."

"You're fucking amazing."

"That's what your ex tells me all the time. C'mon, let's get it done, then grab dinner at Fong Chong."

They had a key given to them by an appreciative merchant whose store was right by the Chinese Garden, which allowed them access to his basement. His basement connected, through a long dark passageway that always had damp puddles on the floor, to one of the wider underground corridors.

They walked down the stairs with flashlights and guns drawn. Once, they had been attacked by a knife-wielding drunk they surprised. Jolson had shot the man in the foot, earning a commendation for using restraint and less than lethal force. The knife-wielder had gotten into detox, maintained his sobriety, and now worked as a night clerk in one of the hotels. Although he had a limp, he was grateful to Jolson, and they could count on him for a nighttime cup of coffee and reliable street information.

"I hate this fucking place," Bauman muttered as they tried to move quietly through the puddles.

Arnold Beil heard the splashing echoing down the corridor. No need for a sophisticated alarm system—with his senses primed, it sounded like a couple of hippos enjoying a noisy bath. Beil saw flashlight beams play across the walls. He ducked low, gun in his belt, knife in his hand.

Two waddling cops. No SWAT. They weren't far apart—bad patrol practice. He could slit the throat of one and gut the other before the first body hit the ground. No need to take the chance of the noise of a gunshot. Even that wasn't much of a risk, between traffic noise and bar music, plus the pe-culiar acoustics of the tunnels, by the time people figured out where the sound came from, and backup arrived to find the bodies, Beil could be a half mile away.

Beil eased down a parallel corridor, slipping behind debris, never more than twenty feet away from the cops. He could sense that they were eager to do the bare minimum. No kicking over garbage piles, no venturing down side paths.

The white supremacist watched and waited. They were probably race traitors, the sort who would fraternize with colored officers or protect civil rights demonstrators. He saw them as ignorant and exploited. If only they understood the consequences of collaboration. Beil silently crept closer.

"You hear my stomach grumbling?' Bauman asked.

"I thought that was a truck overhead." Jolson kicked a pile of rock that had been moved recently. "Look over here. No cobwebs, the dust disturbed. He found a couple of empty tins of Spam, picked one up, and sniffed it from a distance. "Still some residue."

"Okay, Sherlock. What do you want to do?"

"Someone's been down here. Probably just lowlifes. Get it? Under-ground, lowlifes?"

"And you wonder why no one else will be your partner," Bauman said. "We've done a good enough job. Let's get out of here."

Jolson played his flashlight beam around dank walls. "Let's do another block or so." The ceiling had gotten lower, the corridor narrower, and both men, who were over six feet and 230 pounds, were scrunched.

"You want to roam around in the dark, fine. Come back tomorrow with someone else."

"You're really scared, aren't you?" Jolson asked.

"I'm smart enough to know there's nothing down here but rats and bugs."

"What about the Spam?"

"Remember the last homeless guy we had in our car? How long it took to clean the car out?" Bauman responded. "There's no one significant down here."

Jolson shined his flashlight up under his chin, creating an eerie face. "Maybe there's vampires."

"Cut the crap. I'm going to Fong Chong. You play explorer and stay in touch by radio."

Jolson clicked the button on his radio. All he got was static. "Dead zone."

Beil heard the exchange and edged closer. The cops were alone. Five seconds to have them both dead.

"Ah heck, I'm hungry, too," Jolson said.

"What if they want us to come back?" Bauman asked.

"We do it with more gear. Backup from SWAT. Tear gas grenades, night vision goggles, Kevlar underwear."

"We don't need that hi-tech gear. Dogs. We run a couple of them through the tunnel, they'll find anyone."

"We got a plan?" Jolson asked.

"Yeah, let's eat."

Beil watched the cops exit. As with the campers, he had tempered justice with mercy.

He was glad it had actually been humans. A few times, he had heard voices. Groans, hisses, soft screams. He had had nightmares of gaunt, bearded sailors in shabby uniforms begging for his help. A few times, he had heard his father. That had been the worst.

During calmer moments, he could blame the meth, the odd air currents in the tunnels, the strain of being alone in near darkness for so long. Calm moments were happening less often, and when they did come, they didn't last as long.

33

THE ROBERTSON TUNNEL FOR the west side MAX light rail line runs three miles under the West Hills of Portland. When officials were planning the massive project, although they mounted an international search for a lead engineer, the man they ultimately chose was a Portland resident. Kurt Schultz led the team that combined demolition with two monstrous twenty-five-foot-wide boring machines. Now the city boasted the deepest subway station in the world.

Schultz, as had all the men in his family going back to Ruhr coal miners in the 1700s, had a natural affinity for being below ground. During the Vietnam War, he had hunted down Vietcong who used the hundred-plus miles of tunnels, begun in the late 1940s near Cu Chi.

That was how Hanson knew him, and was able to get an appointment to see him on two hours' notice. Schultz's office was on the seventeenth floor of the downtown Wells Fargo building. Hanson was welcomed by a secretary, strode into the office, and admired the view.

"I bet you never expected to find a tunnel rat like me this high up in the air," Schultz said, as he gave a bone-crushing handshake, then pulled Hanson in for a hug. He was a bundle of sinews topped by a bush of white hair, with a droopy Western sheriff's mustache. "You look good."

"And you haven't changed a bit."

"Tell my urologist that. And my proctologist. Endocrinologist. Gastroenterologist. Internist. And a few orthopedic surgeons that put things back where they were supposed to be." He gestured for Hanson to have a seat in a high-backed maroon leather chair. Like the other furnishings, it was weighty, dark, with a well-worn look.

"What's so urgent that I had to cancel out my meeting on the Hong Kong project?"

"I didn't know you had to cancel something out. Thanks."

"Ah, they say I do too much micromanaging. My son-in-law is running it. I should let him have more authority. Worst comes to worst, he'll flood the tunnel and a few hundred thousand die. Life is cheap over there, ain't it?"

"Sure used to be."

After a moment, Schultz said, "I owe you for that group you were running for us vets. I did fine in Nam. Came back to the World and I could've killed someone. Or myself. Maybe become one of those characters living in a subway tunnel in New York."

"The group did the work."

"We felt safe with you running it. Some weeks it was the only thing that kept me sane. If anyone ever thought I was sane." He waved his hand in dismissal. "Now, let's can the love fest and tell me more about what you need to know."

Hanson briefed him on Arnold Beil and the theory that he was hiding in the Shanghai Tunnels. "You know much about them?"

Schultz grinned, hit a few keys on his computer, and a graphic model came up on the screen.

"Unbelievable," Hanson said. "How'd you do that?"

"I was consulted a few years ago. To see if it was possible to turn the Underground into a more developed attraction. Like Seattle has, you know, with a gift shop, snack bar, several tours a day. Right now there's a small part that's open to the public, on a restricted basis. Had to look at issues of retrofitting, earthquake hazard, property right of way, sewage, leakage from the Chinese Garden pond, historical preservation, geology. Dealing with the city council, the environmental groups, the landlords, it was about as much fun as poisonous centipedes, the black mambas, and the *pungee* sticks in Cu Chi."

"How accurate is this map?" Hanson asked.

"I can adjust it to show what is known, what is projected. Major landmarks are accurate, but details are a crapshoot."

"I can get a printout?"

"No problemo. It's confidential but I'm sure you won't show them to a rival firm."

"Of course," Hanson said. "Any chance you'd want to join me exploring?"

"You know, about five years ago, I went down in the basement of my old house. Broke out in sweats. It was around the time of my first grandkid, weirdest damn thing. Since then, I even avoid underground parking garages. In a word, no fucking way."

"I understand."

"Am I getting psycho in my old age?"

"PTSD is a strange beast. I knew one Ranger, lots of jumps, all of a sudden, couldn't tolerate anything higher than the second floor."

"Maybe you ought to get him to go underground with you. You're not thinking of going after this wacko alone?"

"I plan to go down and do a recon mission. No contact. I tried getting the authorities to do something. I heard from a lieutenant in the police bureau that a couple of cops went down and didn't see anything. But I suspect it was a half-assed sweep. And the FBI gave me the brush-off."

"I do have a suggestion," Schultz said. "Get those night vision goggles. Might help you level the playing field. They do depend on some ambient lighting. Or you got to have a light source for them not visible to the unaided human eye. Go with an infrared setup. And don't go alone."

Hanson could see Schultz slipping into his old mode, struggling with thoughts of joining the counselor on the underground quest.

Schultz sat at the terminal, staring at the screen. He played with the cursor, circling areas. "This is where you said his mother said he liked." He made a few right clicks and lines appeared. "These areas are closed off. He'd have to blast his way through." He studied the screen, tapped a few more keys. "This is where I'd concentrate the search. It's about a four-square-block area, goes from Old Town to under Tom McCall Park. He could raid restaurant basements for food, have high mobility, several exits. Of course, I could be wrong. There are still uncharted parts."

"Thanks, I owe you."

"I wish I could go down with you. But I know I can't do it," Schultz said, taking a jar of Maalox tablets out of his desk drawer and gulping a few. "Let me tell you something, don't rely only on the goggles. Remember in Vietnam we got bogged down with that hi-tech invulnerability. VC'd hang up a bag of pee and it would throw off our million-dollar sensors. When I was in the tunnels, it was my sense of smell that kept me alive. Forget sight, even with the goggles. Hearing can be tricky, echoes, muffled. Touch works, but you're already too close. And if you're tasting stuff, well, the bad guy won't be what kills you. Smell."

Schultz removed a thick Cuban cigar from a humidor. He offered it to Hanson, who declined. "Got a box of these as a thank-you after a job up in Canada." Schultz took a few puffs, then leaned back in his chair. "I could tell from fifty yards away when I was nearing a VC latrine or hospital. Even got to knowing gun oil, gunpowder, sweat. I recall, you had that spidey sense, right?"

Hanson nodded, feeling awkward.

"Don't lose that sense underground," Schultz said intensely. "You start to panic, lose that awareness, he'll be on you. If he's down there, he's established."

Bonnie Tidd's office was a short walk away and Hanson decided to stop by rather than call. The sign on the door read "Tidd Executive Services." The outer suite, where Cookie's desk was, was barely eight by ten feet, furnished with a small dark red love seat, matching hard-back chairs, and a low mahogany table covered with travel magazines. It could have been a temp agency, a CIA proprietary, or a deluxe call girl outfit, anything catering to beleaguered executives.

"Is Bonnie around?" Hanson asked.

Cookie, in her professional mode, looked at him frostily and acted like they had never met. "She expecting you?"

"No. I was in the neighborhood and thought I'd drop by. If it's inconvenient . . ."

"Let me check."

Cookie whispered into the intercom.

"She says go right in."

Bonnie's office was about twice as large. The artwork was Tidd's original watercolors. She painted as a hobby, saying that it sharpened her powers of observation. On the wall behind her desk, along with undergraduate diplomas from University of Oregon and a Masters in Criminal Justice from John Jay in New York, were certificates attesting to her ranking in various martial arts. Plus a second place award she had gotten in the International Association of Chiefs of Police close shooting competition. An Ashleigh Flynn CD played softly in the background.

Bonnie sat at a desk that was little more than a table with a clear glass slab. She had a Razr cell phone and a Palm Treo resting on top. The airy, clear top created a feeling of fluidity.

"I don't know as I've ever had the pleasure of your visiting my den of inequity," Tidd said. "I'm a might surprised at your dropping by."

Hanson stared at her. He was used to her without makeup, wearing sweats, in the zone between sloppy and casual.

"You look incredible," he said.

"You've never seen me in my lipstick lesbian mode."

"You look like . . ."

"I know, an older Cameron Diaz but without the nice ass."

"I was just going to say like Cameron Diaz."

"You are a silver-tongued devil. You must want something. Shouldn't you be at work, saving humanity from itself?"

"I'm taking a little time off."

"Suspended?"

"Not officially. My boss thinks I've got issues to work out."

"She right?"

"Probably."

"You interested in picking up some executive protection work? I meant it, I could use your help."

"Not really. I wanted to find out about getting some gear. Do you have resources for getting night vision goggles? And a handgun. Maybe a .45 Browning?"

"Well, now you've gone and piqued my interest. Would you care to share with me what you have in mind?"

Hanson did, then said, "No confrontation. Confirmation that he's there, then call the police."

"Sounds about as easy as those scientists who take the grizzly bears' temperatures while they're hibernating. Rectally. And you're contemplating doing this alone?"

Hanson shrugged.

"That's plain old dumb as a post. I'll make you a deal. I get the gear, I come along with you, you owe me a week's worth of your time."

"Your time is worth that much more than mine?"

"I'm cutting you a break, honeychile, 'cause things have been too quiet for me. I either got to get me an adrenaline jolt or triple up on my lattes."

"Done," Hanson said. "When can you have the gear by?"

"A few hours."

"Great."

"Now why am I thinking that you could've gotten the toys elsewhere but your plan was to hook me into this?"

Hanson tried to look innocent.

"You look like a fox sitting in a henhouse with a mouth full of feathers," Tidd said. "Next time we work out, I'm going to teach you a lesson about playing a naïve young thing like myself."

"I'll wear a cup," Hanson said.

"Best be made out of titanium."

They finalized plans for that night.

Hanson went for a run along the waterfront. There were more people than usual sprawled on the grass, more kids sprinting through the 137 jets of the Salmon Street fountain, fewer joggers, skateboarders, and Rollerbladers. It was an un-Portland like summer day, hot and humid, and he was dripping sweat after a few blocks.

He slowed to a walk and continued into Old Town. He imagined the catacombs below them, the ghosts of trapped seamen and kidnapped women hustled through the darkness until they were out past the Columbia River bar.

And Beil, plotting, skulking, waiting.

34

D RESSED IN BLACK, TIDD and Hanson met and parked their cars four blocks from the Burnside Bridge. Hanson had spent the late afternoon shopping, mainly at police supply stores, getting everything from steel-toed, rubber-soled civilian knockoff paratrooper boots, to black face paint, and a black Kevlar-weave tactical vest with many pockets. Wearing thick black leather gloves, both carried small, heavily-laden backpacks that Tidd had provided. They looked like an anarchist wannabe couple out for the night at an Old Town bar.

"I like the look," Tidd joked, pointing at Hanson. "Very avant garde."

"I had to accessorize. It looks like you already had all you need."

"Tax deductible clothing. I do physical security work."

As they walked toward the base of the bridge, Bonnie explained that she had brought Rigel night vision goggles and SureFire E2 Combat flashlights.

"The goggles have a built-in sensor system to protect the intensifier tubes from bright light. There's a built-in infrared illuminator. It has diopter adjustment, can run for twelve hours."

"Will I be cool wearing it?" Hanson asked, trying to mask the tension he felt.

"Like a science fiction superhero," she said. "The lights are twice as bright as a four cell flashlight, plus they've got a hardened bezel you can use to get someone's attention. Keep the filter over it to avoid flare and reduce spillover. Be sure you don't look directly at the light with the goggles. We want him blind, not you."

"Gotcha."

"You've got a Browning in the backpack. I've got my H & K 9 millimeter with a luminous sight. Both guns are easily traceable, so if we shoot anyone, you best be prepared to deal with the repercussions. Last chance to call this off."

"This is a scouting mission. We see he's here, where he's at, then let the authorities know."

"That's my plan, too. I reckon he's as reasonable as we are."

"I'm sure."

They easily found the manhole cover that Schultz had indicated, a few hundred yards from the Burnside Bridge's west side foundation. On weekends, the area was crowded with crafts people and customers as part of the Saturday Market. Now, a few intoxicated homeless people sprawled. Hanson thought he recognized one client, and quickly turned away. But the man looked too drunk to notice anyone.

Brian lifted the cover with a pry bar, rolled it aside, and he and Bonnie were down the rabbit hole within a few seconds. Standing on the mounted steel ladder beneath the ground, he pulled the cover into place as quietly as possible.

Tidd was already at the foot of the ladder, goggles activated, scanning. She held her gun extended in a Weaver grip, left hand supporting the right.

A car ran over the manhole cover, making a startling bump-chang noise. Hanson froze on the ladder and did relaxation breathing, a slow in and out, returning his heart rate to near normal. The echoes of city traffic traveled strangely underground, creating waves of sound and confusion. He climbed down and smeared on black face paint. He offered some to Tidd and she gave a few wipes. He breathed slowly in and out, adjusting to being a creature of darkness.

The oppressive darkness was pierced by shards of light leaking down from manholes and small gaps in the sidewalk. With the night vision goggles, it was like watching an old black and white TV with a dense green overlay—a flat depth of field, blurry images on moving shapes, and contours ill defined in the darkness. He took out the Browning, checked that there was a full clip and a round in the chamber. He had done it so many times in the service he could literally do it blindfolded. He made sure the safety was off.

"Don't trust me?" Tidd asked.

"Always pack your own parachute."

"Think he's here?" she asked.

Brian slowly surveyed the area, a forty-by-fifteen-foot-wide corridor that paralleled the street above and had electrical conduits and other unmarked thick tubes running along the wall. They were beneath the skin, viewing the arteries and veins of the city.

Though he carried the Underground map, he had worked hard to memorize it. Too many GIs had been shot while viewing a map and trying to determine coordinates. He fought the urge to take in deep gasps of air, seeking the balance between hypervigilant tension and effective alertness. He rolled his shoulder and neck muscles, feeling them knotting. His armpits were already soaked with sweat, despite the subterranean chill.

There was a slight rustling noise in a corridor to the left. Too small to be a human. Tidd stared warily at where it came from.

"Probably a rat," Hanson said.

"And that's supposed to be reassuring?" she whispered.

"Probably shouldn't talk," Hanson whispered back.

She handed him a Crosley headset with a five-inch wireless boom mike. "Don't rely too heavily on these. I reckon there's dead spots all over these tunnels." She showed him the transceiver, which he clipped on his belt. "If we're lucky and we find him, flick this switch, and we connect with a police frequency." She handed him an earplug and coiled cord, which he plugged in.

"Let's keep it to hand signals whenever possible." She lowered her voice to a whisper. "And you don't need to talk very loud to be heard through the mike."

He held the flashlight in his left hand, heavy Browning in his right, level with his waist. Neither had their flashlights on, relying on the otherworldly green luminescence of their night vision goggles. It was like they were exploring the ocean floor, with a man-eating shark just out of view.

Brian padded toward the door at the far end and Bonnie followed. He moved his head in an arcing pattern, side to side, slowly up and down. The first to search surroundings, the second to scan for trip wires and booby traps. He was well into his spidey sense, as alive as he'd been when walking the trails near Pleiku. But then he had heavy artillery he could call in if a ville seemed hot.

Beil heard the increase in rats scurrying. No sound of rain above, no signs of water coming. Something else. He was juiced on meth, Hammerskin, Bully Boys, Brawlers, Max Resist, Angry Aryans songs running through his head, an undistinguishable but arousing tumult of hate, drowning out the whispers of the Underground that had begun to haunt him.

Something was making the rats nervous. They were his friends, warning him, like rabbits scurrying when a cougar was on the prowl.

The white supremacist did a couple of snorts of the meth. He was losing track of how much was left, when he had last slept. In the tunnels, it was always night.

He could figure out where they were and take a narrow tunnel, not much more than a large air duct, that would let him look down on them, decide what to do. He tucked his .357 in his belt and his SOG Seal 2000 knife in a sheath on the other side. He got on all fours and began crawling into the cramped space.

35

H ANSON TRIED TO CONTROL the firing of his nerves. He thought of Greek mythology, Theseus entering the labyrinth in search of the Minotaur. Would the high-tech gear be of any more value than a ball of string?

The dank smell in the tunnels was similar to the perennial mildewy moisture of the tropics. The air here was cooler—even nighttime in Vietnam was a cloying sauna. And the foul organic odor over there was even stronger. The rice paddies smelled the worst. Fertilized with human waste. An infection waiting to happen. One of many reasons the CIA spookyspooks wouldn't go out on patrol. "I didn't graduate from Dartmouth with a degree in foreign affairs to go wading through dink shit."

"Brian where are you?" Tidd asked through the headset. "We shouldn't—if we—"

"You're breaking up," he said.

"That's what—" she said, fading out into static.

"I can see you up ahead, about twenty yards," he said. "Anything—"

"Some MRE wrappings. Look—"

"I'm coming—"

He smelled the cat-pee-like ammonia scent of meth. Or maybe it was a spot feral cats used as a litterbox? He had learned not to doubt his instincts.

"I think he's nearby," Hanson whispered into the mike.

Hanson was passing a low barrier of stonework, with Tidd a few yards in front of him. Suddenly his eyes were seared with the impression of the Incredible Hulk, a green, muscular, wildly strong creature coming at him, teeth bared, upper body clothing torn, bullet head on massive neck swinging his seven inch blade at Brian's neck. Hanson ducked and caught the brunt of the force on his goggles. The blow knocked him down and momentarily blinded him. The powerful swing sliced the top of the tac vest, and his shoulder. The attacker hit him twice across the temple with the .357 Magnum. The last word Hanson heard was Bonnie's "Brian?"

· · ·

Brian was down, injured or dead. No time to grieve, or blame herself for agreeing to this stupid idea. She double-checked the safety was off on her weapon, pointing back where she had heard the scuffle and thud.

She switched to the police frequency and got nothing but a static hiss. If communication between her and Brian had been so difficult, the signal wouldn't get far above ground.

Bonnie struggled to recall the map. Should she try and escape through an exit stairwell she estimated was another fifty yards down the corridor? Should she find a niche where her back was protected and wait Beil out? Should she go back to where Hanson had been?

Her mind raced over tactical options. There was a chance the stairwell would not be a viable escape route and movement would make her more vulnerable. Hunkering down was safer but she had never been very patient. And she couldn't forgive herself if she missed a chance to help Brian.

Tidd advanced with the sliding c-step familiar to fencers and other martial artists. Gun at the ready, weight evenly distributed, listening, scanning. She could see the counselor up ahead now, lying on the floor, bleeding.

Beil had left Hanson. Which meant he was stalking her.

Closer. She squinted through the goggles at Brian's chest, which seemed to be rising and falling. Or was that just her wish.

She passed a small hole in the wall, barely grapefruit sized. She was one step beyond it when she heard a slight scrape, and the two-by-four-inch stud launched through the hole toward her. The wood caught her solid in the temple and she fell to the fetid floor.

Hanson wondered whether he was dead. By the pain he felt in his head and the darkness around him, it wasn't heaven. He heard a faint groan. Female. He pulled himself upright. He was inside a closet-sized wooden holding cell, with a heavy door on one side and a window on the other. Thick, triangular-shaped metal bars set about a half inch apart impaired his view.

Bonnie Tidd was staked out naked on a crude wooden X cross on the floor, arms and legs bound with leather thong, a cloth gag stuffed in her mouth. Arnold Beil stood over her, lit by a few flickering candles, a huge grin on his face.

"There's nothing worse than a race traitor," Beil was saying.

Hanson leaned against the door, pressing all his weight against it. The cell was small enough that he could brace his legs against one wall and push against the door. It didn't budge. The counselor patted himself down. All his weapons, including the flashlight, were gone. He seemed to be bleeding from a cut on his head, and a small one on his shoulder. He tried the bars at the window. The bar on the far right worked loose easily, as if someone else had struggled with it before. The other bars were all solidly in place.

Beil was ramped up on meth, crackling with a twitchy energy, bobbing from side to side like an overstimulated troll in a fairy tale. He unzipped his fly and held his erect penis in his hand.

Hanson tried to use the freed rod to pry a gap in the door frame or loosen other bars. No luck.

Through the window, Brian could see Bonnie's eyes, glazed, helpless, but still defiant. The counselor shouted through the bars, "What's going on?"

Beil ignored him.

"We were just wandering around down here. Sorry to startle you. How about you cut us some slack?"

Beil gave a coughing laugh, like a lion with a fur ball in its throat. "With these guns and gear, you were hunting me."

"Not you. We're looking for a runaway girl. Heard she was being held captive down here," Hanson said. "You can let us go. No reason for us to tell anyone."

"You are funny."

As Hanson talked, Tidd, unwatched, wriggled against her bonds. She didn't seem to be making any progress.

"This isn't worth the murder charge," Hanson said to the twitchy Beil.

"One more murder charge don't make a difference to me." His words came out pressured, meth fast. "Cops've got no interest in taking me alive."

"Is this rape fantasy of yours brought on by homosexual panic?"

"What?"

"C'mon, you get your jollies seeing those cute boys with their shirts off and the SS tattoos. Pale bodies, can't even tell if they're male or female, all sweaty over the cause. Were you someone's girl in the prison shower?"

"Shut up."

"You know Eva Braun was a cover. Adolf liked to play hide the V2 with Goering."

Beil fired two shots into the cell. Both were chest high, right in the middle, and would have caught Hanson if he hadn't dropped to the floor as he'd seen the .357 Magnum rise.

"You discharged your big gun at me. Feel like you need a cigarette?"

Beil fired two more shots, near the floor, but Hanson had flattened against one wall. "You want to miss, playing hard to get."

"Fucking fruitcake, I'm gonna rip your nuts off."

"Castration fantasies?"

"I'm gonna spit in your face while you die."

"What do you think Freud would say about that?"

Enraged but still cautious, Beil stood back as he opened the door with the gun held waist high. Beil lifted the gun and pressed it against Hanson's chest.

"Now, motherfucker—"

The iron bar from the cell was concealed along Hanson's forearm. He held it loosely, as he'd done with the rattan *escrima* sticks. As he spun it, at the last second, he tightened his grip in a *redondo* whipping move. He slammed the bar down on Beil's wrist, the classic San Miguel strike.

He let it bounce off Beil's wrist on impact, using the momentum of the stick to drive up toward Beil's throat. The killer dropped the gun, but managed to twist and avoid the point of the bar. The rough metal scraped along his neck, not deep enough to hit jugular or carotid but causing heavy bleeding.

Beil staggered back and disappeared into the darkness.

Hanson quickly scooped up the gun and knelt by Tidd. He pulled the gag from her mouth and she gasped in air. "Did you hurt him enough to kill him?" she asked.

"I doubt it." Hanson tugged at the leather thong around her arms. "You see him, let me know." He had Beil's .357 within easy reach. He could see her pale skin by the candlelight, even paler where the thongs were cutting into the flesh. He kept fiddling with the straps, but they didn't give.

He bent over and gnawed at the one on her right arm. After about a minute of his teeth grinding across the leather, she pulled loose. He handed her the .357. "Watch for him, I'll get your legs."

"Go for it."

He moved to her muscular right calf and began gnawing at the thong.

"Brian!"

Beil charged out of the darkness, knife in one hand, Hanson's .45 in the other. His voice was somewhere between a growl and a roar.

Bonnie shot at Beil, bullet low, grazing his groin. He dropped his weapons, fell, then got up. Clutching at his bleeding genitals and screaming, he ran back into the tunnel, trailing blood.

Hanson grabbed Beil's fallen knife and quickly cut the leather. She handed him the gun while she rubbed her calves and arms to restore circulation.

"You okay?" he asked, keeping his eyes on the tunnel where they had last seen Beil. The candles around them were beginning to flicker, not much light left.

"Aside from my first root canal, I can't think of a time I had more fun." She stood quickly and grabbed her clothes. He stared down the corridor while she dressed.

"What now?"

Hanson found where Beil had piled their backpacks and belongings. Both sets of night vision goggles were broken. Hanson put the leather gloves back on, and handed the other pair to Bonnie. Their eyes locked and she knew what he intended. She nodded.

He checked both flashlights and they worked. "You stay here. Wipe any surface where we might have left fingerprints."

"I reckon I'd be better backing you up."

He shook his head. "I can follow a blood trail. He doesn't have much fight left in him."

"We can go above ground, radio for police."

"Too much to explain. And he's gotten away from authorities before."

"I don't know if I have the stomach to be part of an execution," she said. "Even for someone who did what he did."

"It's best you don't come with me." Again they locked eyes.

"We don't tell anyone about what happened here?" she asked.

"Yes."

"Not even your FBI ladyfriend?"

"Absolutely."

Hanson nodded, took the flashlight and the .357 Magnum, and moved quickly into the depths of the tunnel.

Tidd began wiping surfaces with a gloved hand, careful not to leave fabric. About ten minutes later, she heard a muffled shot.

She dug the H & K out of the backpack and held it at her side, waiting.

Five minutes later, she heard, "It's me." Hanson's voice. Calm. He stepped out into the area where two of the candles had already died.

Hanson noticed that she had broken up the wooden X she'd been strapped to. They retrieved the candles and stuffed them in the bag.

"What happened to the .357?"

"I wiped it and left it with him. His gun. Probably an interesting history."

She nodded. "Are we ready to go?"

"I've been ready for hours."

36

I T WAS TEN A.M. and Lieutenant Marv Rosen's stomach was protesting the three cups of police headquarters coffee he'd consumed. Rosen had been reassigned to oversee the police divisions that provided a number of community services—food boxes, women's self-defense classes, crime prevention specialists, and Police Athletic League. It was an administrative headache and something he had no interest in. His job also entailed going to meetings and pretending to listen to community complaints. He dreaded the distinct possibility that he'd be finishing out his career here, the kind of work that a social worker or a civilian could do.

The phone rang, he took another sip of the thick black brew, and gruffly answered, "Rosen."

"Lieutenant, this is Eric Jacoby. I'm an attorney here in town."

"I know your name. If this is a criminal matter, I'll give you the name of—"

"A client of mine wants to provide you some information."

"I'm not dealing with informants anymore. Not making deals."

"No deal. This is a gift."

"Who's your client?"

"That's covered by attorney-client privilege."

"Okay, why's he being generous to me?"

"Confidential. Do you want the information or should I just call someone else?"

"What is it?"

"The location of white supremacist fugitive Arnold Beil."

"What?" Rosen squeezed the phone while grabbing a pen and paper.

"Are you willing to keep my name out of it and not pursue my client?"

"Yes."

"Good. Then send detectives to the Shanghai Tunnels. Here's a touch of irony you might appreciate, his body is located near to the original police headquarters on Southwest Oak."

"Where?"

"You'll need to access the old tunnels. I understand there is a manhole about twenty-five yards east of SW Third and Oak that would be most convenient."

"You said his body?"

"Yes."

"Who killed him?"

"Don't know, to tell you the truth. Couldn't tell you if I did. Good luck, Lieutenant." The attorney hung up without waiting for a response.

"Please hold for the executive assistant director for administration," the crisp female voice said.

Quite a mouthful, Jerry Sullivan mused. The Washington, D.C., secretary had first connected with Sullivan's executive assistant. He wondered whether the woman in Washington was actually an executive assistant, which would make her the executive assistant to the executive assistant director for administration (EADFA). His fantasy of what she looked like swung between a pinched-face civil servant and a coy southern belle looking to land a ranking federal official. He had plenty of time to daydream—standard headquarters power play, he was kept waiting on the phone for more than ten minutes, even though he was returning an urgent call.

He knew Bill Slaughter, the EADFA. They had been at the academy at about the same time. Slaughter was right under the deputy director and in charge of the Office of Professional Responsibility. When he finally got on the line, Slaughter didn't waste time with "how are you?" or other pleasantries.

"I had called about Louise Parker and the fallout from the botched raid on Jebediah Heaven's compound," Slaughter said.

"My office has cooperated fully with OPR."

"I would expect nothing less. I have preliminary results on the investigation. We were able to get backchannel cooperation on Louise Parker's offshore account. Apparently it was opened with fifty dollars and that's all that has ever been in there."

"Why bother to do that?" Sullivan realized it was a stupid question even before he was done. "Unless she didn't really do it, and it was someone who wanted to make it look like she was hiding money."

"Very good," Slaughter said, and Sullivan couldn't tell whether he was being sarcastic or not.

"Parker could have done it, however?"

"If she did, she managed to wipe her electronic signature off everything, including the pornographic images. I don't have time to go over the details, but we tracked it from Romania to Tacoma, Washington. Complex, but nothing outside the skill set of a cyber punk. It was fairly easy for the lab to analyze the photos and see that her head was Photoshopped onto the naked body. The headshots were taken with a telephoto lens, an overhead light source that was most likely the sun. The investigators were able to say the probable location was a telephone pole a couple of backyards over from her house. The final report will have the details, but neighbors saw a lineman in the area, who the phone company has no record of."

"Parker did lose her identification," Sullivan said, knowing that he was sounding desperate.

"Yes, she did. And she should receive an admonishment for that."

"She exercised poor judgment by authorizing the operation," Sullivan persisted. "She should have insisted on better intelligence, had better tactical position, and a detailed exit strategy if they needed to abort. She was the responsible agent at the scene."

"True. And who chose her?"

"I've been trying to give female agents more responsibility as per the directive," Sullivan said, seeing the trap ahead of him.

"Well, are there any female agents in your office who might have more actual tactical experience? I understand Cindy Warne had a couple of years in Hostage Rescue."

"Uh, well, she was involved in another investigation. I didn't—"

"We're not looking to play the blame game. We want it cleared up and cleaned up. Recommendation will be for a letter of reprimand in her file. At her next eval, if you have problems, document them. A year or so from now, if she gets transferred to a quiet place in the Midwest where she can do no harm, that would be fine. Understood?"

"Yes, sir."

"I thought you might."

"If I may ask, what impact will this have on my career?"

"We'll see how Parker is handled before we reach any conclusions."

The line went dead. Sullivan knew his task. To get Louise to accept the mild sanction without contesting it. She could appeal, she could get a lawyer. She didn't need to know her upward rise in the bureau had reached its apogee. If she still had hope, she'd be more compliant. Best to broach the subject through a cutout. Plausible denial. Funny how the skills that had been important when he'd worked in counterespionage could be helpful in surviving in the bureaucracy.

Brian Hanson had called ahead—Louise sounded more animated. When he knocked at the door, and she answered, she still had rings under her eyes and no makeup, but was dressed in a clean sweats outfit and her hair looked freshly washed.

She waved for him to come in. "Trent is here," she said awkwardly.

"If it's a bad time . . ."

"No. Please. You said you had some news?"

Hanson glanced at his watch. It was a little after five P.M. Gorman must have gotten out early.

Gorman stood up and shook Hanson's hand, baring perfect white teeth with his smile.

Hanson smiled back, then turned to Louise. "You're looking better."

She nodded. "Trent tells me there's a rumor going around the office that I'm going to be welcomed back with only a slap on the wrist."

"Was anything truly your fault?"

"Ultimately, I had responsibility for the scene. Even if the intel was faulty, or wrong tactical decisions made, it's on my head. I can live with a reprimand. Would you like a cup of tea? I've got the green tea you like."

Brian stifled a smirk when he saw the petulant expression wash across Gorman's face. This is so high school, Hanson thought.

"Sure. That'd be nice. I do have great news. At this point, it might still be confidential."

Louise, who was already starting to heat water, looked quizzical. Gorman tried to look disinterested.

"They found that Arnold Beil guy," Brian said.

"Impossible," Gorman blurted. "I'd be one of the first to know."

"It was Portland Police Bureau. He was killed in the Shanghai Tunnels."

"By the police?" Gorman asked.

Hanson shrugged. "I don't know."

"Are you positive he's dead?" Louise asked.

Gorman was already on his cell phone, calling the office. He moved out of earshot.

"A friend in the Police Bureau said they're confident it's him," the counselor said. "I don't know much else."

Louise continued fiddling with the teapot. "You're sure?"

"My friend has always been reliable."

"Sonofabitch," they heard Gorman say. Then a few muttered words, and more cursing.

"I guess I'm very sure," Hanson said, moving into the kitchen.

"I've got to go," Gorman said. "Things are breaking on the Beil case."

"Is he dead?" Louise asked, her voice quivering.

"Yes. We're working closely with the Police Bureau."

"I bet," Hanson said.

Gorman shot him a nasty look and hurried out.

"I don't like that guy," Hanson said seconds after the door closed.

"You're jealous?"

Hanson scratched the back of his neck. "Tea's about ready."

"You are jealous! That's almost as good news as Beil being dead. I feel terrible saying that about him. I mean, more for what he did to other people than what he did to me. He was entitled to due process."

"Well, I can say it. I'm glad he's dead."

"Me, too," she said, sagging from the overload of emotion. "It's weird, my life seems divided up into before and after the raid. And the after the raid period seems longer." She pressed against him and let him support her. She squeezed hard, and he squeezed back, as if they could somehow blend into each other.

"Oh, God, I feel safe for the first time in weeks."

"Hmnnnnn," he murmured, his face resting in her hair.

"I was suspecting everyone. Doubting my own sanity. Ready to give up."

"You're too ornery to give up," he said tenderly.

She burrowed into him and sighed. "Mmmnnnnn. You know, when you were talking about depression, you mentioned lack of a sense of pleasure."

"Yes. Anhedonia."

"That's faded."

"You've got a craving for Ben & Jerry's?"

"No, that was there even when I was depressed. Are you deliberately being dense?"

"Yes." He kissed her, first gently, then harder as her hips ground against him. "My tea's going to get cold."

"You certainly don't want to waste a cup of tea."

"I can reheat it," he said.

"You're so romantic," she teased.

Then they were a swirling, whirling mass of hands and clothing and very quickly bare skin, moving from the kitchen to the bedroom to each other. Kissing and licking and squeezing and pressing together, the pent-up energy released.

As they lay in bed panting afterward, they sighed simultaneously. Hanson thought about *eros* and *thanatos*, love and death, the drive to create and the drive to destroy. He felt joyously primal, connected with every warrior who had ever made love before or after wallowing in an enemy's blood.

"You look lost in thought?" she said questioningly.

He kissed her lightly on the lips as a reply.

Time passed, they cuddled, bantered, snuggled, then made love again. Slower, a different rhythm, less desperation, more attuned to each other. For Louise, the great black dog of depression was no longer gnawing at her. But she could see his baleful eyes glowing at her from the dark corner he'd been pushed back to.

Hanson went out and picked up tandoori chicken, vegetable masala, and onion *naan*. There was little talk but lots of eye contact for most of the meal, as they savored each mouthful.

"I didn't think this was ever going to happen," she said.

"You mean sitting around eating Indian food?" Hanson asked.

"If I was a therapist, I'd comment about people who make jokes when someone is trying to talk seriously."

"Humor is a high order defense. But okay, you got me. I haven't dated as a clean and sober adult. I wasn't sure about reading the signs." He fed her a piece of naan bread. "I realize, of course, that faint heart never a fair maiden won."

"It's nice to be a fair maiden." She pulled her robe tighter. "I've never made love to anyone outside of my marriage. And I can tell you if everyone's experience with sex was similar to my marriage, the world would be depopulated." She blushed. "And if all people's experiences were like tonight's, there'd be a population explosion."

As they bantered and cleaned up, the domesticity of the scene was almost as pleasurable as the time in bed.

"Want to watch the ten o'clock news?" she asked.

Hanson didn't want a reminder of the outside world but he could tell

Louise was eager for more confirmation that Beil was indeed gone. Brian didn't need TV images, the memory of the white supremacist's snarling, sneering face lingered. "If you'd like."

"What were you thinking about?' Louise asked.

"Huh?"

"Your face, I don't know, it got kind of scary. Like you had with that sailor."

Hanson forced a smile. "TV news. All those sensationalist crime stories can be a mood wrecker."

She looked at him quizzically.

He kissed her. "It'll be fine to watch."

They lay in her bed and she switched on the TV just as the news began.

"Our top story, breaking news from the Shanghai Tunnels beneath Portland Old Town," said anchorman Dan Morain. "Police have found the body of a man believed to be connected to the deaths of at least six people, including an FBI agent, a couple of weeks ago."

Parker sat up stiffly, her own painful mental images replaying.

A police spokesman gave details about finding his body, based on a tip from a confidential informant. Hedged by a suitable number of "alleged" and "according to sources familiar with the case," the murder was attributed to a dispute among white supremacists. Police had released that shoe prints, consistent with the sort of combat boots worn by skinheads, had been found in the area.

Sidebar stories about local white supremacy groups showed shaved head tough guys denying any involvement with the death while posturing in front of large Nazi flags. Another TV reporter did a background story on the history of the Shanghai Tunnels, including archive photos from the Oregon Historical Society. The story and followups went for the first fifteen minutes of the newscast.

"He's really dead, I guess," Louise said, as the newscast shifted to a story about a high school lacrosse coach accused of molesting students. She clicked off the TV.

"Yeah. You okay?"

She sat quietly, gazing at him. "There's something about that story. A connection you're not telling me."

"What makes you say that?" Brian asked, trying to sound casual.

"Your eyes when you were watching. They were like a hawk watching a mouse."

"Sometimes violent stories are a trigger."

"Sorry," she said. She stretched out in the bed and lay back, looking up at the ceiling. Brian snuggled against her.

"Part of me feels like this huge weight has been taken off me. But another part can't believe it's over." She rolled over to hug him. "I feel guilty being so happy someone is dead."

"He got what he deserved."

She burrowed against him.

37

T RENT GORMAN STOOD IN the at-ease position in front of his boss's desk, letting Sullivan's angry words blow over him.

"I got four calls from Washington yesterday. Four calls. Did they call when we broke that big cyber terrorism case? No. Did they call when we broke that international kiddie porn case? No. Or when we busted up the secondhand store organized fencing operation? No. But this Beil case, they call when they first get into the office in D.C. Four fucking thirty A.M. I get woken."

He shifted his anger to hate groups, the Portland Police Bureau, and the media. Gorman had been nodding along and "yes sir-ing" at all the appropriate times—he sensed his turn was coming.

"What about the Beil case? Why are the locals getting headlines on what should be ours? Do you know anything that hasn't already been leaked to the press? Or do I have to check the damn *Oregonian* to see what's going on?"

"The weapon found by him can be traced to a meth dealer who died in a suspicious fire, along with a local member of a white power group. He may have accidentally shot himself in the groin with the weapon. Our theory is that Beil murdered those two for money and drugs and was himself murdered in retaliation."

"Is there any way to make it seem like the DEA fell down on the job on this?"

"I might be able to hint something like that to the reporter, but no guarantees."

"When you're not talking to those media jerks, I want you to find out why the Police Bureau knew before we did. If there's an informant we can identify, pick him up on federal charges and squeeze him for more info."

"Yes, sir."

"Is Parker going to take the reprimand?"

"She seemed receptive. I didn't present it as a firm offer, only a rumor."

Sullivan blasted Louise Parker, female FBI agents, female FBI executives, the media, civil rights attorneys, liberal judges, and juries "packed with numbnuts."

"I'll talk to Louise when I'm calmed down," Sullivan said.

"That's wise," Gorman said, and exited the room, stifling his own angry mutter.

Anchorman Dan Morain began the five o'clock news with "Our top story this evening, in breaking news you'll only see on News Channel 7, is that federal sources say the Underground murder of white supremacist Arnold Beil may be the start of a bloody drug war. Tiffany?"

Cut to Tiffany Chang, standing by old police headquarters on Southwest Oak in Old Town. "Dan, the FBI refuses to comment but my sources say the death of the alleged white supremacist killer Arnold Beil can be tied to a couple of murders at a local meth lab. Beil's body was found yesterday by local police right under where I am standing." Cut to day-old footage of the SWAT team emerging from a manhole. Chang rehashed the case with lots of references to "federal sources familiar with the investigation" and ended with "Although the DEA is supposed to be the lead agency as far as federal drug investigations, my sources say they were caught unawares on this case. The FBI refuses to comment, but my sources say they have a number of promising leads on this case."

"Thanks, Tiffany," Morain said.

"Yeah, thanks, Tiffany," Gorman said to the screen. He had met her a month earlier at Murphy's Law, a popular downtown bar favored by hard-drinking cops and reporters. She was gorgeous and every guy in the place had tried to get her attention. Gorman remembered a story she had done a week earlier on a lockdown at an elementary school. While others were offering to buy her a drink, he praised her for her intelligence and sensitivity. Truth was, she had neither. Without a skilled cameraman or woman field producer, she wouldn't have been able to capture the concrete setting. And she was far more callous than her twenty-five years would indicate.

In bed she was imaginative and ambitious. The leak he'd provided to her was better than a floral bouquet the next morning. And had the added advantage of being an appeasement to SAC Jerry Sullivan for the Police Bureau running ahead of them.

His cell phone rang and it was Tiffany. "What'd you think?"

"I look at your lips and want to shove my tongue between them."

"What about the story?"

"As perfect as your body."

"Do you have any new information?"

"I can find something," he said confidently.

"Then come by my place later. You and I can find something together."

He watched the TV, which had a followup backgrounder on the Shanghai Tunnels, then a few minutes on the Northwest white supremacy movement.

He could probably give her a tip on Chico, the dead meth dealer, and Beil. Let the Portland police find out information by watching TV. He knew they'd hate it as much as he'd hated them jumping ahead on discovering the body.

He thought about Louise and the effort he had put into wooing her. There were few women he had targeted who he had not bedded. If it wasn't for that damn Hanson, he would have nailed her.

Gorman wondered about the counselor and the timing on how he had known about Beil's body. Based on what he knew about when the SWAT team had actually found the body and positively identified Beil, it meant that a cop must have called Hanson immediately. The FBI agent would have to check into that.

It was a drizzly Saturday, enough to keep away all but the more serious martial artists. Bonnie Tidd was working out with a stout dreadlocked Brazilian woman with the lower body of a professional ice skater. The woman used the sweeping leg kicks and graceful circular movements of *capoeira*. The slaves who developed it had to disguise it from their masters and made the martial art look like a dance. *Capoeira* was among the most beautiful martial arts to watch.

Bonnie was holding her own, though the woman had a couple of inches and about twenty pounds more muscle. Bonnie got in close, with tight blocks and punches reducing the effectiveness of the sweeping leg action. Hanson could tell that Tidd was hitting harder than usual. After a few minutes the dreadlocked woman held up her hands in surrender, bobbed her head in a bow, and headed off. Bonnie spotted Hanson where he was doing a slow yang *tai chi* set. She pointed to a park bench at the end of the open area, sheltered by a few leafy maples. He nodded and after ten minutes completed his set.

When Hanson walked to the bench, Bonnie was sipping tea from a thermos. She had set a second cup out, and poured as he sat down. He swished it around his mouth. "Impertinent, not fruity. A fine bouquet. Grown on the slopes of a mountain where an albino Sagittarian lives."

"It's Lipton."

"Really?" he asked skeptically.

"No. It's an oolong."

"How are you doing?" Hanson asked, shifting to a serious tone.

"I've been jumpier than a tree frog on a gallon of lattes."

"I'm sorry. Listen, I don't play counselor with my friends, but I can tell you that's normal. In the first few weeks after a trauma, most people experience PTSD-like symptoms. The mind working through the upsetting event. It should go away. If not, I can recommend a few counselors in town."

"And it will help me telling someone I was tied up in a tunnel by a hateful maniac and could have been killed?"

"A good trauma counselor will help you process what you did to survive."

"Not much. You saved me. I can't say I like that."

"The alternative is less appealing to me." He smiled but she didn't respond. He could sense her anger, her uncertainty with the universe, her pain. He had sat with hundreds of people who had been through traumas. For him, being at the edge with someone was as familiar as a traffic jam to a cab driver. "Remember, you saved me by coming back. If you hadn't come back, I'd be dead."

She sipped the tea and they were silent, watching a couple doing chen style *tai chi,* and farther down the hill, a lone man practicing a *tae kwon do kata.*

"So thanks," he said after a few minutes of silence.

"There's a part of me that wishes I had run away. And I feel guilty about that. Mostly, I feel bad that I missed."

"You nearly shot his balls off."

"I wasn't truly aiming for them. I was aiming for the center of his body mass. I flinched. I don't much like that, either."

"You took a shot with an unfamiliar weapon in low light, in a rotten position, and managed to hit him."

"Maybe." She poured herself more tea, offered him some, and he took a half cup.

"I wanted to check in with you about the boots and gloves," Hanson said, deliberately switching to an area where he knew she had taken action.

"I cut them up, put some pieces in my garbage, which was picked up the next day. Other pieces I dropped at a half dozen different garbage cans around town."

He nodded. Probably unnecessary, but trauma survivors often responded in an excessive way.

"I've been thinking a lot about church in the past few days."

Hanson nodded.

"I was raised Southern Baptist. Pretty strong in my faith until I got caught at summer camp with Mary Lou."

"There's gay friendly congregations."

"I don't know if it can give me what I need. Faith. Like when I thought my momma or daddy could protect me from all that is evil."

"Faith. Belief in a just universe," he said, as much a question as a response.

"I didn't lose my faith, my faith lost me," she said. "I miss it."

They sipped tea in silence, together.

"What about you?" she asked after a few minutes.

"I think about it. More than I used to. My sacred moments are when I connect with someone in treatment. I'm out of my own problems, part of a bigger universe. It's why I do what I do. I did things I'm ashamed of in Vietnam. Now, most of the time, I'm proud of what I do."

"I know what you're saying. But what about what happened in the tunnel?"

"What do you mean?"

She lowered her voice, though there was no one within listening range. "You know you were nearly killed. And then, well, you executed him."

He looked intently at her. "You don't know that. You don't want to know that, if it ever comes to it."

"It doesn't bother you?"

"I wouldn't say it doesn't bother me. That's the other part of sacred, I guess, being scared for your life, and coming out alive." He took a few, slow deep relaxation breaths. "Did you ever shoot someone before that night?"

She shook her head. "I hope I never have to again."

"I hope so, too."

38

T HE TUNNEL WAS DARK, candlelight flickering. Hanson felt Beil was
like a tiger just outside range of the campfire. Bonnie was tied to the
wood cross and he bent to gnaw at the leather strap. He got through
one, then suddenly her hands were on his head. Startled, he looked up.
Mariah Flynn was dragging him to her body. He tried to warn her about
Beil but she laughed and kept pulling him to her nakedness with a surprising strength. He was trapped, her laughter getting louder.

The counselor bolted upright in bed, soaked with sweat. More nightmares,
easily startled around sudden noise, irritable, the craving for a drink. Several
times he'd smelled marijuana, even though he knew it wasn't in the air.

He glanced at the clock. Five A.M. For most, it was the time when the
body was in its deepest slumber. Brian's pulse throbbed at his neck. He
knew how to relieve the fear, just how many blocks to the 7-Eleven, and exactly where the beer was.

He thought of his conversation with Bonnie and how therapeutic the
talk had been. Too long a time since he'd gone to a counselor. Brian gazed
out the window. The sun was beginning to come up, a few lights were on in
the buildings. He wondered whether they were from cleaning crews or the
overly ambitious.

He spent the next hour practicing his forms, doing pushups, situps, and
stretches. It was past six-thirty when he finally calmed down. He set his
alarm for eight and managed to get another hour's sleep.

At eight A.M., Louise Parker passed her ID card through the lock and was
buzzed into Portland FBI headquarters.

Female support staff and a few of the women agents gave her hugs. Male
agents swatted her on the shoulder. A sign was draped across her cubicle
saying "We Missed You." She fought back tears, distracted herself by turning
on her computer and responding to e-mails.

She was disappointed that Trent didn't give her a personal welcome. Special Agent in Charge Sullivan offered a terse hello and told her, "Come by my office when you've settled in and we can discuss your new assignments."

"Not much of a welcome," muttered Vic, who was in the next cubicle over. "But I'm sure you didn't expect a brass band from him."

"No. I guess not."

"Put up with the crap and request a transfer as soon as you can." Vic was talking so low she could barely hear him, like an inmate, communicating with someone in the next cell.

"What do you mean?" she asked, rolling her chair closer.

"Whatever he says or does, he's not going to like the way the office was embarrassed. Word is he's had to field a few calls from hindquarters. He needs someone to hold responsible for the shootout and Beil adventure."

"I've heard I'm only going to get a slap on the wrist."

"Maybe. But don't expect anything other than a lump of coal in your stocking at Christmas."

Vic rolled back to his computer.

Trent had made it sound like all would be forgiven after the mild sanction. She trusted Vic's advice more.

Sullivan was cordial when she went to his office but didn't invite her to sit.

"I'd like you to get back up to speed slowly. I have a couple of paperwork intensive cases that you can devote your time to." He handed her thick files. She recognized them as cold UFAP cases, Unlawful Flight to Avoid Prosecution. Fugitives where the trail was nonexistent, but the bureau still needed to pretend to be looking.

"I trust these cases will be resolved less spectacularly than your last one?" he said with a flat sarcasm.

"I'll do my best, sir."

Hanson's first full day back and like Louise, he got a big welcome. But instead of federal politeness, it was tempered by the gallows humor that pervades emergency rooms, morgues, police stations, and community behavioral health care. There was a pair of boxing gloves on his desk along with a coupon for a *Soldier of Fortune* magazine subscription. A couple of colleagues questioned him, with excited gleams in their eyes, about what it was like to pound a domestic violence perpetrator.

He waded into his voice mail. Several were from parole and probation workers wanting to check on how their clients were doing. The counselor had mixed feelings about the calls. The pressure of imprisonment was a great motivator—mandated treatment had been researched and shown to work. At the same time, clients would be less forthright when they knew that the results of their UAs, and potentially their disclosures, would be reported back. It was part of the job, but when clients angrily accused him of "working for the man," he had to acknowledge the truth.

He caught up on paperwork until his first client, Mariah Finn, arrived. "Where'd you go?" she demanded.

"I stayed in town, just took a few half days."

"What've you been up to?"

"Relaxing. What about you? Do you have your emotions diary card from the past week?"

"I was too upset. I missed our session. Did you think about me?"

"What did you feel when you thought about our canceled appointment?"

"Sad. Like you might be gone forever." She patted her hair and stretched, pushing her breasts forward. "I wondered if I did something wrong."

"Did you remember us discussing the possibility that I might take a little time off?" he asked gently.

"Yes. But it was so sudden."

"It was short notice, I agree. What leads you to feel my vacation was about something you had done and not simply my need to take time off?"

"You didn't answer my question whether you thought about me or not?"

"What makes that important to you?"

"You're doing that therapist thing of answering a question with a question."

"Because we're here to talk about you and your thoughts and feelings, not mine."

"But I care what you think. And feel." She giggled. "I called your voice mail a few times just to hear the sound of your voice."

Object constancy was an issue for people with severe personality disorders as much as for babies. A teddy bear out of sight was gone and never coming back. He knew of other clinicians who had had clients commit suicide because their therapist went on vacation.

With a great deal of effort, he guided her back to talking about her emotional diary card, trying to get her to apply rational thought to her emotions by observing and quantifying them.

His next client was Freddy, who seemed to have lost ten pounds since Hanson last saw him.

"How are you?" Hanson began.

"My T-cells have gone down. I'm taking my medications, eating as we all should, getting exercise whenever physically possible. Treating this mortal coil with the respect it is due. You know what's amusingly ironic, I don't feel suicidal."

"That's a positive change."

"Knowing my life is truly limited, whether I like it or not, has been an epiphany. I'm more content than I've been in a while. Maybe it's because I know I am going to die. Most everyone goes through life in a state of denial about it. But my time is within view. Your time is further down the road, the time of that newborn baby emerging from its mother's womb is further still. But eventually, we all recycle."

"And how does that feel?"

"Good and bad. I've had some episodes recently that redefined hurt. Shingles is such a silly name for such a hurtful ailment. I won't miss that pain. And I don't know about heaven and hell. My uncle was a minister who told me I'm going to hell because of my unnatural fornication." Freddy used his fingers to put aerial quote marks around "unnatural fornication." "He beats his wife and gambles excessively, so I question his wisdom."

"Do you have a spiritual practice?"

"I've found solace in Buddhist books. I read an image of reincarnation once that resonated. It's as if we are candles and we light the next candle, the flame lives on, but the original candle goes out."

"Nice image."

Freddy continued to talk about books he had read, meditation and acceptance. Hanson nodded, saying little, listening intently. Freddy set as a goal that he would visit a Buddhist temple before their next appointment.

Writing a progress note was banal after the intense appointment. It was the sort of session that was Hanson's real payment. The deep connectedness with another, the willingness to be with them in their pain, and to know that being there allowed them to feel less suffering.

He ended the day with Morris Brown, who seemed to be doing well. "I got a call from the VA. There's an experimental surgery, take skin from my butt and graft it to my face. Can you believe it? They're going to make me butt ugly."

"How do you feel about it?"

"Can't make me worse than I am," he said with a shrug. "There's something I've been meaning to tell you. I got a girl I been talking to. Karen. I never thought she'd have anything to do with me. And she's like a thirty-six double-D."

"How'd you meet?"

Moose looked boyishly shy. "She actually started talking to me. Said we been neighbors for more than a year and I ain't said a word to her. She said most guys ain't like that."

"How is it for you?"

"She said she could tell I was a decent guy, being too hard on myself. I didn't tell her about what I've done."

"She's seeing you the way you are now, not who you were. Can you see the difference?"

"She helped me to."

The session continued with Brown switching between talking about Karen and his anticipation of the surgery. Moose's surgery was a week away, and they set an appointment for three weeks out. But Moose promised to call Hanson as soon as he felt up to it.

It was a little after five P.M. when Hanson was done with clients, paperwork, and phone calls. He kibitzed for a few minutes with a couple of the alcohol and drug clinicians who would be starting evening groups at six P.M. He momentarily considered discussing his increased cravings with them. Brian knew he'd find compassionate listeners, but he didn't want to allow his vulnerability to be seen at work.

Strolling down the hall, he saw the office he had been unconsciously drawn to. Conversations with his supervisor had been brief since he beat up Ron Harkins. The easy camaraderie was gone.

Betty was hunched over paperwork, intently making pencil marks on an Excel spreadsheet.

"Got a minute?" he asked.

She looked up and he tried to read the emotions that flashed across her face. Annoyance. Concern. Curiosity.

She waved him to a chair. He shut the door behind himself, his signal that he needed her attention. She responded by setting her pencil down and pushing away the papers.

"Thanks for saving me from that," she said, pointing to the papers. "Billing reports and who I have to nag to get their service activity sheets in."

"I'm almost up to date. Working less might solve my paperwork problems. Most of my clients seem to be doing better with less contact. I might try doing a journal article. Leave your clients alone and they'll get better."

He smiled and she smiled back but said nothing. The old therapeutic silence, Hanson thought. But there was nothing for her to say, it was Hanson's move.

"I'm sorry about anything I did that could embarrass the clinic."

"You mean like playing Superman on the bridge? Or beating up the domestic violence perp?" She leaned forward. "Brian, I'm still worried about you."

"I'm okay."

"What is it they say, denial is also a river? You often look like a bomb about to go off. Like when we had that incident at the clinic a few weeks ago. That accused sex offender. You were crisis clinician of the day. Remember? Every inch of your body language was screaming out you wanted to kill him. I didn't know someone could clench their fists so tight without breaking bones. Look at your hands now."

Hanson's fists were clenched tight.

"You've been an exceptional counselor for more years than just about anyone. You've seen your share of misery, at the clinic, and before you ever came here."

"What are you saying?"

"I know burnout when I see it. Your assaulting that domestic violence perp was a symptom. As your supervisor, and someone who cares about you, I don't want to see you melt down."

"You think I should quit?"

"I'd hate to see that," she said sincerely. "Any effective healer has to really understand suffering. But balance empathy with sympathy. You know what happens if you give up rational detachment?"

Hanson sagged into his seat. He wished he could talk openly with Betty about what he had been through with Beil. He felt the pressure to talk welling up within. "Can we do a few minutes supervision?"

"Any time."

"I said that my clients are getting better. There's one who's stuck. We've talked about her in the past. Mariah Theresa Finn. Caucasian female, thirty-two. Presented with PTSD, depression, and definite Cluster B."

"I remember. She comes from that banking family, traces her roots back to pioneer days. She's been flirtatious with you."

"Yes."

"What's your concern?"

"She's bright, verbal, and it takes a lot of effort to keep her on track. If we explore emotions, she's all but sticking her tongue in my ear."

"You've done treatment with provocative clients before. Is it at the point where you need to work with her with the door open or transfer her to another clinician?"

"No. It's more about a nightmare I had."

Pearlman had started out as a Jungian, and though the pragmatics of modern counseling didn't allow the philosophically oriented treatment, he knew she enjoyed dream work. The question was how to describe it without letting her know the reality base.

"There was a nude female figure tied to wooden beams with leather thongs. I thought it was someone else that I knew. Candlelit, there was a menacing figure outside the lit area. I had to gnaw through her bonds to help her escape. As I did, I realized it was Mariah. And she grabbed me and kept dragging me in, like a lion pulling down a struggling wildebeest. Then I woke up."

"Hmmm. Interesting. Any idea who the menacing figure was?"

"Someone from my past." He hated being evasive and regretted going as far as he had. "Maybe I shouldn't have eaten a heavy meal before going to sleep."

"But why did your mind choose those particular images?"

"Random firing of wayward neurons?"

"You're backing away from the disclosure. What about it is anxiety provoking?"

"Disclosing sexual thoughts about a client."

"Everyone has had erotic countertransference. The therapy relationship itself is oddly intimate. There's no shame in it. The problem comes if you act on it or aren't honest about it with yourself."

"That's what seems ego dystonic. I don't honestly feel any erotic urges toward her."

"Hmmmph. An attractive young woman who thinks you're wonderful and keeps making suggestive remarks?"

"Well, to the extent I can ever really know how I'm feeling."

"You're better at it than most. But everyone has blind spots. Answer quickly, what emotion do you feel when you think of her?"

"Fear."

"Fear of what you'll do or she'll do?"

"What she'll do. She's unpredictable. Intense."

"How?"

"Axis II anger and general lability."

"Plus sexuality."

"Yes."

"Does sexuality scare you?"

"Not in general. Hers does."

"Why?"

"It's her way of controlling. Predatory."

"Not unusual for an abuse survivor. A sexually abused child can't say no and learns the power they have when they give in. They rationalize that they want it, control it. I'm sure this isn't news to you, you've worked with hundreds of survivors. What is it about her?"

"I don't know."

Betty leaned back in her chair. "Interesting dream. Has elements of religiosity, with the tied to the cross and candles imagery. I get the feeling you have a good idea who the menacing figure is but don't want to discuss it. That's fine. If you don't, do you remember that technique I taught you a while back?"

"Substitute different faces for the person."

She nodded. We could try some word associations and see what comes up."

Hanson stood. He'd said more than he wanted. "I better let you get back to billing."

"I should finish. My son is filling out college applications and he wants my help. It's not often he asks me for anything. I promised him I'd be home at a reasonable hour. Which will be a remarkable event in itself."

"Thanks again."

"I don't have any answers, but remember Milton Erickson."

"We've got the answers to our problems inside of us."

She nodded again. "And trust your subconscious."

39

A S SHE PULLED INTO her driveway, Louise Parker was surprised at how tired she was. It had been a ten-hour day but that was not exceptional. Her weeks of depression, and she was reluctantly willing to admit to herself that that's what she had been through, had weakened her. Powerful emotions roiled just below the surface. Recalling her welcome at work, her eyes moistened. At least now there was no one around to see her get weepy.

It was a night for TV and cuddling with Clyde. She had stopped at Safeway on the way home for a limited grocery shop. The most important item was the Little Friskies chicken liver. Clyde's favorite, so he could celebrate her return to functioning.

"Clyde, I've got a treat for you," she said, opening the door.

Normally he would sit by the entrance, indifferent, and then with the calm of a *tai chi* master, come over and rub against her, as if he was doing her the favor. Which of course he was. He had been greeting her like that for years. In three different cities, five different apartments. His wise cat eyes had watched, accepting her for the flawed human servant that she was.

"Clyde?"

She felt a slight breeze. She had left neither door nor window open. Louise drew her gun and released the safety.

"Clyde?" she whispered, crouching low, scanning behind furniture while keeping an eye on the door. The back door was open. She peeked out, saw no one, no cat, and shut and locked it.

She clutched her cell phone, ready to call 911 or the FBI's 24/7 duty officer. She hesitated. No more attention. All the bureau needed to hear was that she had called in the cavalry because her cat was missing. She'd get a nickname like "No Pussy," and be stigmatized for overreacting and wasting federal resources on personal issues.

Clyde had wandered off twice in all his years, both times after a move, and he had returned after a few hours, a weary adventurer with an ear nipped once, and fleas another time. There was no excuse for an odyssey this time. The only other time he hadn't greeted her was when he'd been sick. She checked his sanctuary, under the bed, but didn't find him.

Continuing to explore the house, looking everywhere from inside the refrigerator, to the washing machine, to behind the TV, she dialed Brian on her cell. Trying to sound more casual than she felt, she asked, "Were you planning on coming over?"

"I was thinking about it. Is everything okay?"

She was upstairs, looking behind the toilet, in the hamper, in the closet, under her bed. "Clyde is missing," she said.

"Has he run away before?"

"Not like this. My back door was open—I'm almost positive I had left it locked."

"Are you safe? Get out."

"I've searched the house. There's no one here."

"I'm on my way. Hopefully he'll be back before I get there."

She hung up and continued the search, pausing only to check the back door. There were no obvious signs of forced entry, but peering closely, with a flashlight shining at a forty-five-degree angle, it seemed like there were scratch marks on the snap lock other than those she'd expect from a door's normal rubbing. She cursed herself for her carelessness, her negligence, her overconfidence, as she prowled the house. With all her time sitting home, why hadn't she done something constructive like put in dead bolts?

"Clyde! Clyde!"

Hanson found her sitting on the couch, makeup streaked from tears.

"He's gone and it's my fault," she said as Hanson embraced her.

"What do you mean?"

She told him about the back door.

He sighed and held her closer. "I was praying the abuse ended with Beil," he said.

"It didn't." As much a statement as a question.

"The harassment you went through, that's not Beil's style," Brian said. "It's more of a sick dance than he's capable of. His idea of subtle would be a sniper attack."

"I thought so, too, but dismissed it as depressed pessimism. I can't take this uncertainty, not knowing what rotten thing is going to happen next. Not knowing who is behind it. Not knowing what to do." She was breathing rapidly, hyperventilating, fighting the urge to cry.

"Let's look for Clyde in the neighborhood. Maybe he just chose a really bad time to get wanderlust. You have a picture of him?"

"Of course." She dug out a photo album with a tight head shot of Clyde, staring smugly at the camera.

"Handwrite a poster. It's more emotional than something done on a computer. We'll stop at the photocopying store on Hawthorne, then put these up all over as we walk."

"Would you mind if I called for someone else to help us?"

"Go ahead."

"It's Trent."

"Oh. That's fine."

"I know you don't like him. But he has been nice to me."

"I said that's fine."

She punched in his number on her cell. Hanson noticed that it was an easy redial, meaning she had called him not that long ago.

"Hi, Trent. Clyde is missing." Pause. "Yeah, I'm upset. Brian and I are going to walk around the neighborhood looking for him, putting up flyers. I was wondering if you were free?" Long pause. "I see." Pause. "No, it's not that simple." Pause. "Yeah, sure. Goodbye."

She tucked the phone in her pocket, her sorrow momentarily replaced by anger.

"What happened?" Hanson asked, trying not to sound too eager.

"He said he was busy. And if the cat ran away, I could get another one."

"Hmmm. I guess he's not a cat person."

"Jerk," she repeated, and Hanson didn't say anything to contradict her. "Do you have a staple gun?"

She nodded, sat down at her little desk, and did up a quick flyer with descriptors, the date, and her phone number. Then they drove to the photocopying store and made up fifty posters on bright yellow stock.

"Do you have any idea who is behind all this grief?" Hanson asked as they walked the streets around her home.

"I've thought about my cases and can't imagine who." She stapled a flyer to a telephone pole. "Any suggestions?"

"No. Have you notified the police? Or the bureau?"

"Yes to both, and no to both. I'm sure a missing pet report won't get much attention from the locals. And Sullivan will pigeonhole me as a cat lady gone berserk." She reached over and squeezed his hand. "Thanks for being with me on this."

Could Louise have been forgetful and the cat slipped out on its own? Was it possible Louise was overdramatizing to remain as the center of the show? He also knew of cases where the stalker had targeted the partner of their love object. Was it narcissistic on his part to imagine that he was the one who the stalker was fixated on? What if someone had fixated on Brian and saw Louise as a rival?

When he thought about possibilities, only one name came to mind.

Mariah Finn glared at the cat, tied to a leg of the couch with clothesline looped through his collar. The cat glared back.

Although Duane had worn heavy leather work gloves, Clyde had managed to scratch his forearms. Duane was in the bathroom, washing the cuts.

"Did you put the bug in?" Finn yelled to her brother.

"I did," he said, coming out of the bathroom.

"Where?"

"In the living room and in the bedroom."

"You couldn't get them to broadcast here?"

"They'd have to be bigger, more expensive, more easily detected. They're sound activated. I hid the recorder in a bush a few houses away. I'll pick it up when I bring the cat back."

"I'm not sure you're bringing the cat back."

"But that was the plan," Duane insisted.

"Plans change. We can keep the cat longer."

"It scratched me bad before I got it in the box. You should've left it in the box."

"I wanted to look at it."

"The joke has gone on long enough. We ought to give it back. Stop everything. We should go away. To the coast, like we used to do."

"After."

"After what?"

"Pick up the tape tomorrow morning," Mariah ordered. "We'll see then."

It was close to ten P.M. when Louise and Brian returned to her house. They had put up all the signs, wandered through the mazelike alleyways, spoken to more than thirty-five people, called Clyde's name a few hundred times, waved little bits of kitty treats. They had drawn several other cats but no Clyde.

Hanson stood in her living room. "I can stay if you'd like. Or go home."

"I'm not feeling romantic, but I'd like you to stay."

It was six A.M. when Duane returned with the paperback-book-sized Panasonic tape recorder. A bleary-eyed Mariah sat with the recorder on the kitchen table, leaning close to hear the faint voices.

"Couldn't you get any better quality than this?" she snapped at Duane.

"For a few thousand dollars, sure."

Turning the volume up increased the hiss, but she heard Louise inviting Brian to stay, and her saying she was "not feeling romantic." She knew that meant they were sleeping together. The image of the two in bed flooded her brain, linked with the sight of her father screwing the maid. His swearing her to silence. Her compliance. Then his bringing women into the house when her mother was away and not caring whether the door was open to the bedroom. It had started when she was seven, continued until she went to college. The one therapist she had disclosed his behavior to had described it as symbolic incest, sleeping with her vicariously. The therapist had wanted to report him. She had accused the therapist of molesting her and convinced him that if he reported her father, she would turn him in. She told her father how she had covered for him, and while he denied ever sleeping with any women other than her mother, he bought Mariah a new Audi the next day. Her father had been the only one in the family to call her Mariah, named after a folk song he liked. Her mother called her Theresa, her brother called her Terry.

"Terry, I don't think . . ."

"Shut up!" She stopped the tape and rewound it, listening intently. The bitch did much of the talking, how much she missed Clyde, this cutesy shit about the stupid cat. Terry glanced over at the cat, which had curled up but kept a wary eye on her. Duane had shut the door to his room. She could hear him blasting "Thunderstruck."

Then Louise was babbling about her Uncle Louie, and how he had given her the cat, and how wonderful the two of them were. Blah, blah, blah. She knew who Louie Parker was from around the clinic. He was another client of Brian's, a friendly old man, sometimes annoying, acting like he owned the place.

"Want to go to bed?" Louise was asking on the tape. A click and hum, slight change in background noise, as the voice activated mike in the living room shut off and the one in the bedroom turned on.

Sounds of faint bathroom noise, the couple settling in.

It should be me snuggling into bed with him, not her, Mariah thought, feeling her gut tighten.

Rustling sounds, barely audible talk. The mike clicked on and off, picking up the sounds of movement. Not sexual, no sounds of passion, just bodies moving against sheets. The mike clicked off, then on again to a muffled shout. Then her name. His voice, saying her name.

"It's okay, sweetie," Louise said. "You had a bad dream."

Brian mumbled something.

"It sounded like a woman's name," Louise said on the tape. "Mariah? Like Mariah Carey."

Mariah sat with her ear pressed against the tape recorder. Brian was dreaming of her.

"Just a nightmare," Louise said. "C'mon, let me hold you, let's go back to sleep."

The mike clicked off.

Mariah smashed the tape recorder, sending it flying through the air. "Fucking cunt! A nightmare! He's dreaming about me! Fuck, fuck, fuck!"

She moved slowly toward Clyde. He sensed the danger and strained to get under the couch. But she pulled him out using the rope. Desperately, he clawed at her, getting one swipe across her forearm before she lifted him into the air by the rope.

The collar cut into his neck and he hissed and yowled. She jerked up harder, watching him struggle.

She threw the body down to the floor.

"Just a nightmare," she said, coarsely imitating Louise's voice. "A fucking nightmare is right."

Duane picked up Clyde. "You shouldn'ta done this, you shouldn'ta done this." He walked outside, carrying the limp body, not waiting to hear what his sister had to say.

40

HANSON WAS SITTING ON the small porch to Louise Parker's house when she came home after work.

"How was your day?" he asked.

"All I can think about is Clyde. Fortunately I've got mindless work to do." Her voice was tense and brittle. "Responses to habeus motions filed by jailhouse lawyers. Scut work. I'm not good for much else right now."

"I spoke with my friend who has a security firm," Brian said. "She thinks we were nuts to stay there last night. Possibly some hostile breached your perimeter and took Clyde. There could be another bomb, there could be a bug. My friend said we should go to my place, or better still, someplace the perp doesn't know."

"I will not be intimidated out of my own home," Louise insisted.

She took out her key and was about to put it in the lock when Hanson patted her hand. "Hold on. My friend Bonnie is due here any minute to do a sweep. Have you been contacted by a cop named Dave Kohler?"

She shook her head.

"He's pretending to be my friend but manages to ask potentially incriminating questions every time we chat."

"He thinks you're behind my trouble?'

Hanson nodded.

"That's ridiculous," she said, but Hanson sensed that she'd entertained the thought.

"I'm not, in case you wondered," Hanson said, smiling.

"Believe me, I know. I'm the other likely suspect, like those firefighters who turn out to be arsonists."

"When not accusing me, Kohler's asking questions about whether you were the attention-seeking type."

"What'd you tell him?"

"That if he was insinuating what I thought he was insinuating, he was a horse's ass."

Louise hugged him with a fierce intensity. "I love you."

"I love you, too."

Before he could say anything else, Bonnie Tidd pulled up and got out of her Mazda 626 with a large vacuum and a suitcase-sized zero Halliburton aluminum case. A magnetic sticker attached to Tidd's door said "Maids of Honor" and Bonnie was wearing scruffy work clothes.

Brian and Louise exchanged an intimate look. Bonnie noticed and shook her head. All three stepped into the small foyer. Louise began to speak and Bonnie held her finger to her lips.

She turned on the loud vacuum and set it in the center of the room. She opened the aluminum case and removed one of several short wands capped by chemically sensitive pads. It had a small fan that pulled in air, with swatches responsive to the organic chemicals found in the more common explosives. She went around the house, waving the wand like a lethargic fairy princess. The swatches did not change color and she set the wand back in the case.

Every few minutes, Bonnie moved the vacuum to make the cleaning sound authentic. In between, she opened the telephone, looking for a bug feeding off the phone's power. Nothing.

She moved the noisy vacuum into another room, then took out a brick-sized device that resembled an old walkie-talkie with a large meter on its face. As Bonnie rotated the Marlin eavesdropping detection analyzer's antenna, LEDs began to glow on the faceplate and the meter jumped about halfway. She turned slowly around the room. The signal was strongest in the couch area. She moved forward and slowly waggled the antenna until the meter peaked.

A circle that looked like a quarter was attached to the back of the couch with a dab of adhesive. Bonnie pointed to it, held her index finger to her lips in a "shhh" gesture, then continued her search. She uncovered nothing in the kitchen or bathroom, then another metal cylinder right next to the bed, attached to the box spring. Louise's eyes grew wide as Bonnie took it off and held it up.

Bonnie wrote on a sheet of paper, "Don't let them know we know."

Leaving the vacuum running, she crooked her index finger for Brian and Louise to follow her into the bathroom. Once inside, she turned on the sink and as the water ran loudly, said, "I'm going to take the bedroom mike and bring it to someone whose got a knack for identifying bugs. It looks custom made," Bonnie said. "You shouldn't stay here. The explosive screening I did will only pick up a half dozen different chemicals. Nitro, C4, Semtek. That's no guarantee."

"I can't leave," Louise insisted. "What if Clyde comes back?"

"I'll stay here with you," Brian volunteered.

"You don't have to."

"I want to."

Bonnie rolled her eyes when only Brian could see her face. "It's too late to get him tonight but I'll talk to my friend first thing tomorrow morning. You lovebirds can stay right where some psycho hostile wants you." She turned to Louise. "You got a gun?"

Louise nodded.

"You want one, Brian?" Bonnie reached in to take out her Sig Sauer.

"We'll be okay," Hanson said. "Thanks for the help."

Bonnie muttered something, gave a deep sigh, and headed off taking the vacuum and the listening device with her.

Charlie was in his store, located in a nondescript strip mall, less than a half mile from Tektronix headquarters in Beaverton. He had once worked there and been a casualty of layoffs. The one-time electrical engineer liked familiarity. His interest in electronic listening devices was a hobby that he tackled with the same obsession and precision as everything in his life. He served as a consultant for a number of police departments.

He glanced up from his workbench and finished a solder on the computer motherboard before saying hi to Tidd.

"How you doing?"

"Busy."

"Are you willing to take a look at a bug I found?"

"For you, of course."

He set the soldering iron in a stand and she handed him the bug. He had a magnifying lens and studied the device. "Basic RadioShack grade," he said with more than a hint of condescension. "Power source, mike, antenna. Far from government specs, the kind of thing a clever high school kid could do."

"You have anyone in your group who might be a white supremacist?"

"Half the members are from India or Asia. If you don't like people of color, it's not a place to hang out," Charlie said. "I don't know white supremacists. From what I hear, their idea of high-tech is the deep-fryer at McDonald's."

Bonnie smiled. "Can you tell who made it?"

Charlie got a set of jeweler's screwdrivers and opened the bug. He hummed as he studied it further. He waved a radio frequency detector that looked like an electric toothbrush over the listening device, pressing buttons. Then he opened the bug with a screwdriver and stuck the probes from a tiny voltmeter in it. "Interesting."

"Care to share?"

He gestured for her to step in close to his workbench. She did, and was aware that he smelled like he had basted himself with Axe. "Looks like about two gigahertz. I'd say the battery will only last another eight hours. The range would be a hundred yards, tops. I betcha there's a more powerful receiver near wherever you found this. Either someone sitting in a car listening, or it's connected to a recording device and the tapes are picked up.

"You see this wiring here?" He pointed with the jeweler's screwdriver. "The way it's looped. We call it a pigtail. Kind of quirky. Effective, in a simple way."

"Is it distinctive enough that you can guess who did it?"

"In my circles unusual and quirky is not unusual." He had an ingratiating smile. She gave him a peck on the cheek and he blushed.

"You see this coiling here, connecting with the antenna leads," he said, pointing again with the screwdriver to a wire as thin as a human hair. "It's not necessary. A flourish. I remember a guy who liked to do this, an odd duck. He was at a few of our meetings a year or so ago. The Rose City Electrical Hobbyists. He seemed very uncomfortable. Said his sister wanted him to get out, make new friends. He had this annoying habit of running his hands through his hair."

"You remember his name?"

"Something with a D. David. Or maybe Derek. No, maybe it was a W. Wayne?" He rubbed his fingers on his furrowed forehead as he tried to recall. "No, it was Duane."

"You're sure."

"Pretty sure."

"Last name?"

"We weren't big on last names. If I did hear it, it's long gone."

"What did he look like?'

"White guy, probably about thirty now. No beard, long dark hair, average build. He told me he liked the band AC/DC."

"Any idea where he lived?"

Charlie shook his head. "I'm surprised I remember as much as I do."

. . .

Louise, still struggling with unpredictable emotions, had arranged to take the day off. "I'm staying here in case Clyde comes back," she told Brian in the morning.

"You won't go walking around looking for him without me, right?"

"I can take care of myself," she said.

"I know you can. But don't the toughest cops work with backup in a potentially dangerous situation?"

She frowned.

Before he left for work, Hanson told her, "I'll be back in a couple hours and we can go out looking then."

He had a ten A.M. appointment with Louie and wanted to see how Louise's uncle was doing. How much did Louie know about the harassment, and how was he handling it?

Brian's cell phone rang and he recognized Bonnie's number. She quickly reviewed what she had learned about the listening device, including the name Duane. He thanked her before hanging up.

Brian had another reason for going into the office. He retrieved Mariah Finn's records from the chart room and took it to his desk. She was moving from nuisance to threat and using the file for investigative purposes was less of an ethical dilemma. Though still something he'd have a hard time explaining to his company's HIPAA privacy officer.

Hanson pondered how to best handle Mariah as he thumbed through the papers. Of most interest was her emergency contact—Duane Finn, brother, who shared the same home phone number.

Hanson knew he should talk with Betty about Mariah Finn. Just the way an attorney who represents himself has a fool for a client, clinicians making major ethical decisions who don't seek supervision are setting themselves up.

It was ten A.M., time for Louie's appointment. The counselor walked to the lobby, since the front desk sometimes got too busy and forgot to summon staff to meet their clients. Louie wasn't there. The old man liked to stroll from his single room occupancy hotel room to the clinic. Sometimes he'd meet cronies and begin talking, then come in a few minutes late.

Hanson went back to his office, tidied up an overdue treatment plan, and filled in paperwork to schedule a client evaluation for medications with one of the nurse practitioners.

He checked the clock. Ten-fifteen. He called the front desk.

"Is Louie Parker there?"

"No. I'm getting worried," said the receptionist who had a motherly demeanor for clients, even if they were twice her age. "You want me to give him a reminder call?"

"I'll do it, thanks." Hanson disconnected, then dialed in Louie's number. After five rings, he got the answering machine. "Hi, Louie, this is Brian. We had a ten A.M. today and you're not here. Please call."

Louie Parker lived in a Rose Community Mental Health and Addictions Agency–owned property. Hanson telephoned the property manager and got another answering machine.

The counselor looked at his watch. Ten-thirty. He decided to walk to Louie's hotel.

Louise sat at her small desk, sorting through bills. A few were now overdue and she paid them first. She couldn't believe how much she had left things unattended.

The depression was still there, lurking in her brain like a small tumor. She had never understood people who were suicidal. Now she could. Not that she ever would. But she was more sympathetic to those who felt they had no other options. The depression tinted the world gray. If only Clyde were back, and whoever was harassing her would stop, she'd be fine. But could she really get back to the way she had been?

The idea of a talking cure seemed weird even though she knew that Brian had helped hundreds of people. She had grown up in a culture of "pull yourself up by your bootstraps." Hanson had given her a list of therapists. She had the list somewhere. Maybe she'd give one of them a call. She rummaged in her desk and found the list.

Hanson had insisted that it took courage to go to a counselor and face inner demons. She looked at the list of therapists, a mix of men and women, with little notations in his sloppy handwriting. "Active, will push you," "In his sixties, very smart," "New grad, up on the latest research," "Strong spiritual advocate."

She wished she could talk to Brian more. He kept telling her she needed a neutral counselor, that he had his own feelings toward her, his own self-interests.

The mailman knocked and waved cheerily as he walked off. There was a manila envelope set near her door. With her gloomy mood, her first thought was that it was a bomb. It couldn't be motion sensitive, since the mail carrier had handled the parcel without it detonating. The device could be on a timer or there could be someone waiting to throw a switch. There was no return address. Too small to hold much of a threat. No ticking or unusual chemical smells.

This was no way to live, she thought. She gave the envelope a little shake, then set it down on her desk and cautiously slit it open. Louise knew how if it really was a bomb, she should call professionals. But she didn't want to be embarrassed and have the bomb squad come only to find it was a Bible from her sister.

She gasped as she pulled out Clyde's collar. Parker turned it in her hand, as if she had never seen it before. Then she sagged into her chair, too overwhelmed to cry.

41

THE "HOUSING FIRST" MOVEMENT in mental health and addictions treatment stressed that unless people had a safe place to live, they had a slim chance of avoiding further trauma, showing up for appointments, taking their meds, or going into recovery. And since finding housing for poor people, particularly those who might have an eviction or two in their history due to mental health symptoms, was difficult if not impossible, more and more behavioral health care companies had become property owners or managers. Hanson's agency controlled forty-five houses, apartment complexes, or single room occupancy hotels, with a total capacity of more than five hundred units. There was always a waiting list.

Louie Parker lived in the Belvedere Arms, a four-story, twenty-unit hotel on the edge of downtown. Louise had tried for years to help him get into better housing, but he refused, saying he didn't want her help. He had his friends and his routines and ultimately was as stubborn and independent as she was.

The Belvedere Arms site manager was a tough Latina named Conchita who had personally thrown out dozens of troublemakers. She had been with the agency nearly as long as Hanson, but since she worked in a different program in the large agency, they had had minimal contact. Still, they knew each other from interdepartmental meetings and as fellow long-time service providers.

She was behind the battered wooden desk in the lobby where industrial strength cleaners fought a failing battle to overcome the smells of body odor and bad plumbing. After a minute or so of greetings and quick catchup, Hanson asked, "I'm here because Louie Parker didn't show up for an appointment. Can you please check his room?"

"I'm sure he ain't there," she said.

"You've seen him?"

"Girl picked him up about an hour ago."

"What did she look like?" Hanson asked, hoping for a description of Louise.

"Early thirties, white, flashy dresser. Nice red hair," Conchita said, her hands waving down to touch her shoulders. Hanson pictured Mariah's mane.

Hanson nodded. "What time was this?"

"Maybe nine-thirty this morning. Louie didn't look too happy. The girl was standing close to him, like she was worried he might fall."

Brian suspected it was to keep a gun or knife on Parker. "Which way did they go?"

"She had a car parked by the hydrant. I noticed because I knew if she left it there long enough the cops would ticket her."

"What kind of car?"

"Red car. Like her hair. I didn't pay much attention. Toyota. Honda. One of those typical-looking ones, what do you call it?"

"A sedan?"

"Yeah, that's right. A sedan."

"Anything else you can think of?" Brian asked.

She scratched her ear for a few seconds, then shook her head. "Louie's not like a lot of the others. He's a nice guy. Is he all right, you think?"

Hanson made the gesture of crossing his fingers as he hurried off.

Brian returned to Louise's home and found her sitting at her small desk, staring at the collar. "Clyde didn't disappear. He was taken." She showed him the collar.

"I'm sorry." He embraced her but she sagged in his arms. "Did the collar come with anything else?"

She shook her head.

"Fingerprints?"

"I can see about getting someone to do it," she said flatly. "If they wore gloves, the only prints on it will be mine. The envelope, too. I wasn't thinking. It's too late anyway."

Brian's cell phone rang before he could answer. From the trill, he knew it was the crisis line that handled clinic calls after hours and emergency calls during the day. "This is Brian."

"Hi, Brian, Robin here."

"Don't you ever take off?"

"You know the city would fall apart. I got a call from one of your clients. Louie Parker. Said it was urgent that you call him. He denied suicidality or homicidality, but he was adamant. The computer shows you're off duty and I hate to bother you, but he said he's been a client for years and never called in a crisis."

"No bother. He leave a call back number?"

Hanson took down the information and said goodbye. He quickly briefed Louise and dialed the number.

Louie picked up on the first ring. "Hello?"

"Are you okay?"

"Fine, fine." Despite his reassurance, Louie sounded tense. "I'm with another one of your clients. Mariah Finn."

"Oh?"

"She invited me over. I couldn't say no." There was a sound like Louie was getting poked. "Couldn't say no to such a determined pretty woman. She'd like to see you."

"She could've contacted me directly. What's going on?"

"She wants to see you right away. She knew you'd be reluctant to come to her house alone, that you'd want a chaperone."

"Do I need to come right away?"

"She's upset. I think she'd take it out on the people around her. Meaning me."

"Does she have a weapon?"

Another rapid inhale from Louie, as if he'd been poked. "I've got to go."

"What's the address?"

He gave the counselor an address in Northeast Portland.

"I'll be there," Hanson said.

The line went dead.

Hanson turned to Louise, who had been listening intently. "It sounds like a client named Mariah kidnapped Louie. She wants me to come to her house." Hanson saw surprise, fear, and then anger play across Louise's face.

Hanson hesitated, reluctant to ask Bonnie for another large favor after what they had been through, but he couldn't think of anyone he would trust more in the situation.

"Who're you calling?" Louise asked in a monotone, her expression settled into a stoic glare.

"Bonnie Tidd. She'd be great backup."

Tidd, however, was out of town, doing a bodyguarding stint in Seattle that would last four days, Cookie told him.

After hanging up, Brian said, "I'll call 911."

"Calling them's a waste of time," Louise said flatly. She got up and walked to her closet. "It won't be a high priority. A mentally ill old man went off willingly with a woman. There is the possibility they know each other from your clinic, isn't there?"

"They never mentioned each other, but it is possible."

"At best they'll send a uniformed officer to her house to ring the doorbell. Which if the situation is innocuous, won't do any harm, and will make us look silly. At worst, it will escalate the situation." She took out her gun.

"What about Clyde's kidnapping?'

"What about him? He'll be just a damn cat to them. Like Trent said. Theft of a pet counts as little more than property damage. And we don't have enough evidence to link Louie and Clyde's kidnapping. I need to handle it."

"Could we get the FBI interested?" he asked.

"No indication of interstate lines being crossed. They'd say it is a local matter, especially since I'm perceived as a problem child." She worked the action on her gun, checked that it was loaded, safety on. "If this kidnapping leaks, Louie's criminal history, his being my uncle, my recent problems, all become news. The bureau would probably prefer that my uncle disappear," she said flatly, pocketing a spare clip. "Either that or they're liable to overreact. Police, too. Send a SWAT team. I don't trust them. I know only too well how a raid can go wrong."

She slid the black .40 mm automatic into a well-oiled holster that she clipped to the inside of her waistband, holding the gun angled for a quicker draw in the FBI style. She put on a loose-fitting blazer that covered the weapon but allowed easy access.

"If you don't want to get involved, I can handle it without you," she said. "I need her address."

"Of course you're not going alone. I can talk to her. Promise you'll let me try?"

She nodded.

"And if there's proof of kidnapping, like we see Louie tied up, we call 911." She nodded again.

They got in his car and Brian drove.

"What can you tell me about the woman?" Louise asked flatly.

"Mariah has a severe personality disorder. A mix of narcissistic, antisocial, borderline, and histrionic traits. It's called Cluster B. She doesn't see consequences of her actions, externalizes responsibility, emotionally volatile, can be self-destructive. The effects in people's lives are as severe as schizophrenia or bipolar disorder. There's constant crises, sometimes dangerous behaviors."

"Hmmmh," Louise said.

"It's harder for people to understand personality disorders as a mental illness. If someone is having hallucinations, mental illness is clear. But clients with personality disorders present as more 'normal,' and others are surprised when they act so irrationally."

"I'm short on sympathy right now," Louise said. "I don't care as much about her diagnosis as her physical description. In case there are other females in the house, what does she look like?"

"Caucasian female. Thirty-five. Redhead. About five foot, five inches." Hanson thought of her body. "Uhh, average build. Dresses provocatively."

"Does she own any weapons?"

"I asked during assessment. She said no but I can't be sure."

"Park about a block away. You'll walk up to the front. I'll go around and check the back for an easy way in. Do you know if she lives with anyone?"

"A brother. A couple years younger. He's probably got his own mental health problems."

"Violent?"

"I don't know. I suspect he's the one who loves AC/DC and used the name Angus Young. He's probably an electronics whiz who probably made the bugs Bonnie found. Could be mildly autistic. Unpredictable if pressed into a social anxiety–provoking situation."

"His name?"

"Duane."

"Mariah and Duane," she repeated.

Hanson eased into a parking space on Northeast Alberta. "I'm going to go through a neighbor's yard and into the back," she said. "You try the front door and keep her attention."

She walked quickly, about ten paces ahead of him, pretending to talk on her cell phone, strolling down the street, seemingly not paying attention to her surroundings. The block was typical of the Alberta Street area, a mix of run-down houses with overgrown yards and beater cars and remodeled fixer uppers, gentrified with well-groomed yards and late model Subarus.

The house next door to Mariah's had huge overgrown hedges, unpruned trees, and a broken fence. Louise slipped into the neighbor's yard easily, after checking to see that there were no signs of a dog.

Hanson reached the door to Finn's house. Thick clumps of moss seemed to be holding together the worn-out roof, which was edged by a sagging gutter. The gray paint was peeling in spots and the three wooden steps going up to the wrap-around porch showed signs of rot. While pieces of the elaborate detail work had fallen off and were rotting on the ground, it clearly had once been a near mansion.

Through the picture window to his right, he saw no activity in the high-ceilinged living room, just a large couch and a matched pair of wingback chairs facing the fireplace. The furniture looked old, expensive, and worn out. He peered in the big, dirty window on the other side of the door, noticing peeling caulking around the edges.

The counselor was momentarily startled when a figure appeared, then realized it was his own image in the mirror that lined one wall of the foyer. Four elegant Chippendale chairs were positioned around an antique table in the small room. A cloisonné tray on the table lay waiting for visitors to set their calling cards. The room looked like it hadn't been used in years.

Hanson knocked at the front door. The knob opened as he tried it.

"Hello?" he shouted as he stepped inside.

42

H ANSON STOOD IN THE threshold, senses alert. AC/DC's "Bad Boy Boogie" played in the background. Separating the foyer to his right was a ten-pane, glass-paneled French door. One of the panels was missing. There was a poster of Mariah Carey in the hallway, and two from AC/DC.

He moved toward the music. The door to the room was shut, another AC/DC poster on it. "Mariah?"

"In here," she said.

Her voice came from the room behind the living room. He stepped into the high, double-wide doorway.

Mariah was at the head of a dining room table that could seat ten. Wearing truckstop hooker-level makeup and a formal black dress with a plunging neckline, she eyed him like a seductive forties movie star. Behind her, there was a small baby monitor on top of a glass-doored china cabinet. The glowing red LED showed the monitor was on. There was another door, which probably connected to the kitchen. On the wall were a couple of old portrait oil paintings.

"So glad you could make it," she said. She took a puff on a cigarette and set it down in a plate-sized ashtray on the lace tablecloth. Next to the plate was a long-barreled .38 revolver, dark blued steel against the pure white, as ominous as a landmine in a playground.

"Mariah, where's Louie Parker?"

"He's in the basement." She took another puff, then a slow exhale. "He didn't behave."

"I need to get Louie and leave. We can talk about this at our next session."

She pouted. "I've been thinking about this scene for weeks. Don't ruin it." The anger under the surface bubbled up like methane in a tar pit. "I know what's been going on, how she's tried to entice you."

"Who's she?"

"His niece, Louise. The slut." She took another puff on the cigarette, then ground it out.

"We can talk about this later. Please give me the gun and show me where Louie is."

She picked up the gun and ran her hand down the barrel. "You boys and your guns. Don't you know there are other fun things to play with?" Her desperate vamp fantasy was more sad and scary than seductive. "We're soul mates. When I saw you with that slut at the Starlight Parade, I knew she wasn't right for you. I'll forgive you."

Hanson moved from the doorway, the full length of the table between them. She would interpret the gesture as him being lured to her. "Let me have the gun, please."

"Suppose we wrestle for it," she said as she stood, holding the weapon loosely.

Hanson took another step forward. "Give it to me and we can continue talking."

"Talk, talk, talk, you silly boy." Was that a line from an old movie? How absorbed in a film noir sex scene was she? "You look all hot and bothered."

"Please give me the gun, Mariah." Hanson's voice quivered, his hand trembled from the adrenaline. "Give me the gun, then we can talk."

The intercom squawked, the sound of AC/DC suddenly much louder. "That woman is outside," a man's voice said.

Mariah suddenly had a tight grip on the gun, and pointed it at Hanson. "You were supposed to come alone."

"Louise needs to see her uncle."

"She's got you wrapped around her little finger, doesn't she?"

"Mariah, put the gun down. Let Louie go. This can be worked out."

"She just opened the front door," the male voice said through the intercom. The house, and the grounds around it, were probably wired, with Duane at the center of the electronic spider's web.

"Here, pussy, pussy, pussy," Finn said nastily. "Did she like the gift I sent her?"

"What gift?"

"It's true, I sent her lots of gifts, but she didn't get the message."

"Louise, I'm in here with her," Hanson shouted. "She's got a gun."

Mariah glared at Hanson. "She does have you pussy whipped, doesn't she?"

"You better come in," Mariah said loudly. "I've got a gun on our boyfriend. We need to settle this." The counselor was about four feet away from Finn, just out of arm's length.

Then Louise was in the doorway, gun pointed at Mariah. Mariah lifted her weapon, aiming at Louise and away from Brian. He dove forward, knocking the gun down with his left hand, and slamming his open palm under her jaw. The palm heel strike rocked her head back and she couldn't aim. Hanson grabbed Mariah's gun hand with his left and twisted her wrist, simultaneously locking up her shoulder and elbow with his right. She dropped the gun on the table as he bent her forward in an arm bar.

Louise moved in quickly, scooping up the gun. "Where's my uncle?"

"The basement."

"Who's blasting the music?" Louise demanded. "Duane?"

"Give me her gun," Hanson said. He pointed toward Duane's room. "I'll keep an eye on the door."

"I called 911," Louise said. "Police should be here any minute." She handed Hanson Mariah's revolver and ran downstairs. Brian kept Mariah bent forward, leaning on the table, with the gun in his right hand, aimed at the door.

"You could do me right now on this table," she said, grinding her hips against him. "Wouldn't that be a turn-on?"

"Mariah, take it easy," he said calmly. He was not surprised that she reverted to primitive sexuality as a way to regain control.

She shook her head. "Her uncle's not in the basement."

"Where is he?"

She nodded her head toward the door behind them. Brian adjusted his grip, keeping her arm locked up behind her in a modified half nelson. He tugged her and they moved to the door. With the hand holding the gun, he clumsily twisted the knob open.

The room was a narrow passageway, shelves on each side, a butler's pantry going into the kitchen. Louie was in a chair, his mouth duct-taped shut, his hands and legs taped to the chair. His eyes were shut, his skin a deathly grayish hue.

"Louie wasn't down . . ." Louise began as she strode into the dining room.

She saw her uncle's body and gasped. She bit her hand to keep from screaming.

Hanson was momentarily distracted and Mariah broke free. She raced past Louie into the kitchen and grabbed a foot-long steak knife off the butcher block counter.

She held the knife in front of her as Brian and Louise stepped into the room. "Stay back," Mariah said.

"Put the knife down," Louise commanded.

"Don't tell me what to do," Mariah hissed.

"Put it down, Mariah," Brian said.

"Are you going to make me? Who're you going to choose?"

There were the faint sounds of sirens in the distance.

Mariah advanced on Louise. "You think you won? Brian and I are soul mates. It doesn't matter what you do to me in this lifetime, I'll be with him forever."

"Put the weapon down," Louise said. Hanson saw the coldness coming over her. He knew the feeling. She was going into the zone where the person on the other side of the sights was no longer a human. She had acquired a target. Hanson sidled forward. The two women didn't even seem to be aware he was in the room. He was about five feet from Louise, twice that from Mariah.

"You should've seen your cat die. I wished it was you. He was wiggling so hard, the collar so tight."

Louise and Mariah were about a dozen feet apart, Finn advancing. Louise stood with feet planted, arms braced in her well-practiced shooting stance. The gun was aimed at the center of Mariah's body mass, an inch or so above her solar plexus.

"And your Uncle Louie. I had to put tape on his mouth. He just kept talking. Trying to get me to let him go. Too bad, so sad," she said in a mocking singsong.

Mariah charged and Hanson stepped in front of Louise, blocking her shot. Finn was trying for a downward slash, which Hanson blocked with his left. His right hand snaked behind Mariah's, then grabbed the back of his own forearm. As he moved forward fast and hard, he felt Mariah's shoulder separate. She screamed and fell, dropping the knife. He twisted her around, facedown on the floor, then Louise was over them, knee on Finn's back, cuffing her hands behind her.

Duane raced into the room. "Leave her alone." He pushed Louise, who kept the gun trained on him. He curled up on the dirty floor, next to his moaning sister, face inches from her. Hanson took the knife and put it on the counter. Louise kept her gun aimed loosely at the brother and sister, while sidling over to her uncle. She pulled the tape off his mouth and felt at his neck for a pulse.

Brian moved quickly, getting Louie out of the chair, setting him on the ground, and beginning CPR.

"He's dead," Louise said. "And you saved his killer." A question and a statement.

Thirty compressions, two breaths. Thirty compressions, two breaths.

"No, I saved you," Brian said, while pressing down on the old man's chest.

"I could've killed her. A righteous shooting. She was attacking and I had her cold. You saved her," Louise repeated flatly.

"And you," he responded.

Then the front door smashed open and police charged in.

43

THE SWAT COPS HAD everyone down and immobile on the floor until they verified that Louise was FBI and had been the caller. She vouched for Hanson and he also was allowed to stand without being handcuffed. The paramedics found a weak pulse on Louie. They had defibrillator paddles charging and an IV running within seconds.

Mariah Finn demanded a lawyer even as her Miranda rights were being read. She tried to spit on Louise as she was escorted away. Duane kept muttering, "What's going to happen, what's going to happen?"

Another paramedic came over to Hanson and cautiously lifted Hanson's arm with his blue latex gloves. There was blood running from a six-inch gash.

"Doesn't look like anything serious," the EMT said as he wiped it down with antiseptic and taped on sterile gauze. "But get your doctor to take a look at it. He'll probably tell you to get a tetanus shot. Be alert for infection and keep putting clean dressings with antibiotic cream on it for the next few days."

Detectives secured the crime scene and technicians began cataloguing evidence. Louise had watched Hanson's treatment dispassionately. When the medic moved off, she said, "I could've killed you."

"I knew you wouldn't."

"She could've killed you."

"I took my chances."

"Why?"

"Have you ever killed anyone?"

"No."

"I could tell you were ready to and that you'd regret it."

"How do you know that?"

"Only psychos don't regret it. No matter what the provocation, a part of you dies, too."

"You've killed lots of people. Is it really that bad?"

Hanson let her look deeply into his eyes. She turned away after a few seconds.

At nine A.M., a call came through on a back line. "Hey, I hear you saved my life, though you busted a couple of ribs in the process," said a raspy voice Hanson could barely understand.

"Louie?"

"I just got out of ICU. They had a tube down my throat, I can barely talk." He had a dry hack for several minutes. Hanson could hear a woman's voice in the background scolding him, telling him to get back into bed.

"If this nurse wasn't so cute, I'd ignore her completely. They want me to stay here a few more days. I swear they wanna see how many tubes they can stick in one banged up geezer."

Hanson couldn't make out what the nurse was saying, but it had a nagging tone.

"Okay, okay." Louie coughed. "They tell me I had a mild heart attack when I heard the ruckus you were making. You saved my life. You know in Chinese custom, that means you're responsible for me now." He tried to laugh, but it became a painful cough. "Louise-y says I'm gonna stay at her place after I get out. You can kick me out when you want some quiet time together."

"Don't worry about it. I'm just glad you're doing okay."

"I better get back to bed before Nurse Ratched ups my drugs and checks my prostate with a broom handle."

"I'm so glad you made it," Hanson said sincerely.

"Don't get all mushy on me, doc." Louie coughed, then said goodbye.

Hanson smiled as he imagined Louie's survivor grin. The counselor was settling in at his desk when the receptionist buzzed him. "There's a Detective Kohler here to see you."

The counselor went up to the front and escorted the amiable cop back to his office. He sat in the chair facing Hanson's desk like an old friend.

"Can I help you?" Hanson asked guardedly.

"Did you ever piss off a Feebie named Trent Gorman?"

"I might have."

"He's been asking around about you and how you knew about Beil's death so quickly."

"Hmmh."

"That's what I say. I've done more checking on you. It doesn't seem like you're the kind who would try and blow up his girlfriend, but you might be the kind who would take things into his own hands to protect her."

"Hmmh."

"You ever been in the tunnels?'

"Much as I'd like to chat, I've got a busy day."

"I didn't come here about that anyway," Kohler said. "I've got sad news. Charlene King was found dead. Harkins is the prime suspect."

Hanson was silent. He had expected it to happen, but hoped it wouldn't.

"The ME said she died quickly. Apparently he threw her out a fifth-story window. He's a fugitive but we've had a tip he's still in the city. We'll find him. With his priors, he's more than a three-time loser. The DA wants you to testify about his past abuse of her. They'll drop assault charges against you and make sure your licensing board doesn't bust your chops."

"You know I'd testify even without a deal."

Kohler nodded. "They also know it would sound better if they didn't offer a deal. But if you went to trial for assault, Jacoby would bring up why she couldn't be in court, and the case would go kaflooie. You'll be getting an official call soon with the offer."

"Let me know when the hearing is. I'll be there."

As Kohler was leaving, he shook Hanson's hand.

The counselor was eager to see his first client, Moose Brown. The former football player's upper face was swathed in bandages, but he was smiling. With him was a buxom, well-dressed Scandinavian-looking woman.

"This is Karen," Moose said, pointing to the woman.

"Moose respects you," she said bluntly. "There's not many people he feels that way about."

Hanson nodded. "Nice to meet you."

"I'll let you two talk," she said. Morris watched her backside as she sauntered out. Hanson suspected that she knew Moose was looking.

"Does she have a hot bod or what?" Moose asked.

"I'm glad you're enjoying the relationship. How are you feeling?"

"Sore, but better." He hesitated. "Karen wants me to talk about something."

"What's that?"

"While I was in the hospital, she read me a book about the Civil War. *The Red Badge of Courage.* You ever hear of it?"

"I read it in high school. Stephen Crane. The soldier marked by the wound."

"Yeah. That was me. Everyone thought I was a hero, but all I did was get injured in an ambush. No bad guys shot. No good guys saved."

"You served. You were ready."

"Whoop-de-do."

"You sure are hard on yourself," Hanson said. He sensed that Moose was ready for a breakthrough. "You willing to try something?"

Moose shrugged.

"Let's try a role play. You know I'm a vet. I want you to be a counselor. Talk to me."

Moose shrugged again.

Hanson sagged down into his seat, letting some of the devastating emotions he fought wash through him. He had to allow the depression to flavor the exchange but not overwhelm. This wasn't about getting his needs met.

"You know, I served in Vietnam, but that don't mean nothing," Hanson said.

"What do you mean?" Moose asked, getting caught up in the complete change in his counselor.

"I seen people killed, I got wounded, and for what? Who really gives a rat's ass?"

"You did the right thing."

"Says who?"

"Me," Moose said.

"Why's it the right thing?'

"You got called up. You did what you had to do."

"Lots of people didn't go. Some did brave stuff, and some did diddly."

"You did what you did, did what you had to do. It's like you were playing football. Maybe you didn't throw a touchdown or intercept a pass, but you were on the field. You can't judge yourself by someone else's bull."

"I got this pain inside me all the time," Brian said. "It's like I never left the war."

"Some people get wounded on the outside. Some get wounded on the inside. Some get double fucked."

Hanson sat quietly, letting the words hang in the air. Slowly, he adjusted his posture, shifted back into counselor mode.

Moose was crying. "I can't let Karen see me like this."

Hanson handed him some tissues. Moose wiped his face.

They talked about life and death, war, and its aftermath. They sneered at politicians who never served but were quick to send young men and women off to risk life, limb, and sanity. Hanson for the first time was optimistic about Moose's recovery.

"See you in a week," Moose said. As they stood, they hugged. Not something Hanson did often. The big bear of a man nearly squeezed the breath out of him. Hanson recalled what psychologist James Bugental said about tears—they're not the goal of therapy, just the way blood isn't the goal in surgery, but they can be cleansing.

As he finished off his progress note, he took out Charlene King's chart and began the paperwork to close it, checking off the "deceased" box as the reason for closure. He looked over his progress notes. One mentioned Harkins's favorite strip club, the Shaky Thong. Harkins had coerced her into dancing during an amateur night. She had talked about her shame at the experience and being unable to say no.

The counselor had agreed to meet Louise after work, near her office by River Place. The mile-long esplanade, in front of high-priced condos above trendy stores, was a crowded spot for couples and families on sunny days. But there was a slight drizzle, thinning the crowd to a few hard-core joggers, a few couples, and some lone men who gazed at the river as they walked alone.

Hanson watched the Willamette, the murky brown aorta of the city, one reason Portland was where it was. So often he'd used river metaphors with clients: the always changing but constant flowing to the sea; following the currents and eddies, the harnessed power, the dangerous rapids. From Heraclitis, to Pete Seeger's "Waist Deep in the Big Muddy."

"Lost in thought?" Louise asked as she approached.

"Still water runs deep," he said with a weary smile.

She looked at him quizzically, but didn't persist. They walked side by side, lightly holding hands.

"I heard you spoke with Louie."

"He's quite the guy. Speaking of tough guys, how's Clyde doing?"

"His purr is huskier, but other than that, he's fine."

"That's so great."

"Your client is facing kidnapping and attempted murder charges," Louise said somewhat abruptly. "Plus a slew of lesser felonies. I've heard she's going to be using a psychiatric defense."

"No surprise."

"You'll probably be a key witness," she said.

"For the prosecution or defense?"

She shrugged. "Finn is already claiming that you wanted her to harass me. Part of an elaborate romantic plot you had."

Brian sighed. "And Duane?"

"He confessed to eavesdropping on cell phone calls around the FBI office," she began. "You'll never guess who was blabbing over an unsecure line?"

"Trent?"

"No. Jerry Sullivan. He was talking with his wife about the raid on Heaven's farm. Apparently something to do with dinner plans they had. They're talking about transferring him somewhere, a step down in rank as well. Duane confessed that he was the one who alerted Jebediah Heaven. Mariah hoped that I'd get killed in the raid," Louise said. "On the plus side, Duane was the one who called you about the bomb under my car. He had told his sister not to put it near the gas tank. And he also saved Clyde, despite Mariah. He took Clyde to the emergency vet service. Duane'll probably get time served and intensive probation. Mariah was in charge and there's a legitimate diminished capacity question with him."

After a moment's silence, she inhaled deeply and said, "I'm taking a leave from the bureau. I never considered anything else, but now I'm not sure what I want."

He nodded.

"I'm planning on traveling once Louie is better. By myself."

Hanson was silent for a long time. "I understand."

"Do you really?"

"Yes."

"Is this part of your therapist neutrality?"

"I don't do therapy with people I love. I'm going to miss you, but I do understand." He held her tenderly. "I'm sad and angry and scared we'll drift apart. But I also know being clingy would be the worst thing for us."

"Louie wants us to be together," she said.

"We're not done."

They had a long passionate kiss before she walked away.

Alone in the drizzle, he savored the relative quiet, the only sound freeway traffic passing on the towering Marquam Bridge a quarter mile south. Hanson felt a deep inner ache, as much emotional as physical.

Saturday morning and it was still drizzling as the counselor headed to Mount Tabor with his *escrima* sticks. The thin fog softening the landscape made it look like a Chinese painting. On a level spot overlooking the reservoir he began his yang *tai chi* set. With each movement he flowed through transitions, imagining the applications of the blocks and strikes.

The light fog had burned off by the time he spotted Bonnie watching him.

"Hey, how you doing?" she asked.

"Fine."

"You didn't look rooted in the form."

"I'm that obvious?"

"Only to the skilled eye," she said with a wink.

"How you doing?" he asked.

"Better."

"You think about the tunnel much?"

"Reckon it's going to be a while before it doesn't bother me. I've made peace with whatever happened with you and Beil. I remember going hunting with a couple of my uncles and my daddy when I was about ten. They gut shot a deer. One of my uncles didn't want to bother hunting it down, said to let it die on its own. My daddy said the right thing to do was put it out of its misery. I figure Beil might not deserve as much courtesy as a deer but it was the right thing to do. I got myself a therapist I'm talking to. One of the ones you recommended."

"Excellent."

"Reckon I'll see if this talk-talk-talk really does any good," Tidd said with a challenging smile. "Want to push?"

He put his arms up and they began the pattern, one hand on elbow, the other on forearm, shifting lead, alternating sides.

"I saw the article in the paper about that Finn woman," Bonnie said. "Sorry to hear about your girlfriend's uncle."

He updated her on what had gone on with Louise. "She needs her space to work out her issues."

"Space? Issues? You sound like such a girl. Have you been watching too much *Oprah*?"

"I'm a Dr. Phil fan."

"I'm losing what little respect I had for you." She switched to free style. "At least he's from the right part of the country."

Hanson said, "I was thinking, there's this strip bar I need to go to. The Shaky Thong. You interested?"

"You *need* to go to? You don't seem like that sort."

"There's someone who may be there. Or maybe they can help me find him." He gave her the background on Charlene King and Harkins.

"Is this going to be like our underground adventure?" she asked.

"I doubt it. But you never know." She pushed suddenly, but he countered, and kept his balance.

"Last time I went to a strip bar, I wound up dating a dancer," Bonnie said. "More excitement than my poor little heart could bear."

"You prefer not?"

"I didn't say that. What time do they open?"